Tokyo Suckerpunch

TOKYO SUCKER-PUNCH

A NOVEL

Isaac Adamson

HarperPerennial

A Division of HarperCollins*Publishers*

HarperCollins books may be purchased for educational, business, or sales promotional use. For information please write: Special Markets Department, HarperCollins Publishers, Inc., 10 East 53rd Street, New York, NY 10022.

FIRST EDITION

Designed by Lindgren/Fuller Design

Library of Congress Cataloging-in-Publication Data

ISBN 0-380-81291-6

00 01 02 03 04   10 9 8 7 6 5 4 3 2 1

For David and Cynda.

Thanks to...

Caroline Bouffard	for making it possible.
Serapio "Mike" Baca	for making it digital.
Dan Hooker	for making it happen.
Bret Witter	for making it readable.

And thanks to Chee-Soo Kim for making it all worthwhile.

Editor's Note

This is a work of fiction.

Sato Migusho never existed. And even if he did, his movies were mostly bad, so don't bother tracking them down.

Kwaidan, Brando Nabiko, and possibly the Man in the Hat are completely made up.

Orange Blossom may or may not be real—only time will tell.

Cleveland, despite its fantastical depiction herein, is a real place.

As for Japan, perhaps Oscar Wilde said it best: *"In fact the whole of Japan is pure invention. There is no such country, there are no such people."*

Tokyo Suckerpunch

I'm hardwired for geisha. I don't know how it started or what it says about me psychologically and all that jazz—I just know I'm obsessed and have been for as long as I can remember. Over the years, geisha have been my motivation for acts heroic, embarassing, and often criminal. This time, I'd been in Japan less than three hours when trouble started.

I was in Tokyo covering the Nineteen and Under Handicapped International Martial Arts Championship for *Youth in Asia*, Cleveland's hottest-selling and most respected Asian teen rag. I was feeling a little blue without the company of Sarah, my young assistant. She was back in the States getting another tooth pulled, which is what she always does when she doesn't want to accompany me to Japan.

On top of that, it looked like Sato Migusho wasn't going to show. Sato was an old friend of mine, and one of the most famous directors in the history of Japanese cinema. He'd made over forty films in his life, almost one a year since he began his career at the age of twenty. When I'd made this lunch date with him, he told me he had just gotten back from scouting locations for his next film, but he wouldn't tell me what it was about. All he'd say was that he was very excited about it, but then he was always excited about his next film. Unfortunately, audiences didn't always share his enthusiasm.

You couldn't blame them given the bombs he'd turned out lately.

He was supposed to meet me at a fisherman's bar on Dogenzaka-dori called the Purple Dragnet. No actual fishermen hung out there, as it was nowhere near water. But the walls were adorned with starfish and stuffed marlins and even a dead dolphin—so I guess that made it a fisherman's bar. I passed the time drinking a very rare sake that made even most high-grade *tokkyu* sakes taste like dishwater. I forget the name of it, but it translated as something like "fortieth heavy sheep," which meant roughly the same thing as "the last straw" in English. It used to be served to kamikaze pilots on the eve of their suicidal missions, and there were said to be fewer than seventeen bottles remaining in the whole world. Actually, there were probably only fifteen now. I had polished off two bottles in the last hour. After drinking the stuff, I felt ready to smash a plane into the side of a boat, too.

"Sorry, Chaka-sama. That is the last of the special reserve," said Hiro Bhuto sheepishly. Hiro Bhuto was the bartender. He felt eternally indebted to me because I had saved his brother from a probable prison term by writing a brilliant—if wordy by Japanese standards—plea to the state to drop the charges when the guy got mixed up in an exercise video pirating ring. I argued that his only crime was making it possible for the poor to have leaner thighs and tighter abs. He got a full pardon and often used my defense of his character as a letter of introduction.

"That's okay, Hiro," I said with a smile. "Looks like my lunchmate isn't gonna show."

I felt a little guilty about taking advantage of Hiro's hospitality and sense of gratitude. He'd been saving that wine since 1945, and selling just one of those bottles could have put all three of his kids through cram school.

"Say, Hiro, how's the missus?" I inquired. Perhaps it was a little rude, but you can get away with being rude if you're American. It's expected. In fact, sometimes it's deemed impolite for an American not to treat his Japanese host with the proper degree of disrespect.

"Things could be better," Hiro said while he studied the ground. From the many years I'd spent carefully observing Japanese body language and colloquial euphemisms, this could only mean one thing. Hiro Bhuto's wife had kicked him out of their bed.

"Say no more, Bhuto old buddy. Give me a beer, a brush, and some scrolls."

He beamed gratitude as he ambled toward the back office behind the bar. By the time he returned with my supplies, I'd already composed a deeply moving, somewhat lyrical love poem—exultant, but with a hint of sadness at the ephemeral nature of the world.

I took a sip of beer, then quickly wrote the poem in expert strokes. When I finished, I handed the scroll to Bhuto.

Bhuto unrolled the scroll and began to read. I carefully studied his face. At first he was skeptical, but the words didn't take long to work their magic. As he read, I could see the emotions rise to the surface. His initial placidity blossomed into a look of near-religious fervor. Toward the end of the poem, the part where I got a little corny, his eyes seemed to burn right into themselves for a moment as he let out a tiny, almost inaudible gasp.

Then his face went cold. He looked up at me, puzzled. Then back down at the scroll, and up at me again.

"You called my wife a donkey?"

I yanked the scroll away from him. There it was—donkey. I had no idea what character I'd been trying to write, but I suspected the sake had taken over. Come to think of it, Bhuto's wife did look a little donkeyesque, though. But this was no time for that kind of honesty.

I grabbed the brush and amended the poem with a quick series of wild strokes. After the flurry, I handed the scroll back to Bhuto.

"'Seraph,'" he read aloud. "Much better."

While Bhuto went on reading, I downed my beer. When he finally finished, his look was one of deep quietude—such a look as is only seen on monks with decades of no-mind or on regular readers of my column in *Youth in Asia*.

"What's the verdict?" I asked.

"Chaka-sama," he replied, trying to choke back his tears. "It is so perfect, so beautiful. My wife...she will never believe I am capable of such...such sentiments."

"Nonsense." I handed him the brush. "Just give it your seal." I nodded encouragingly, so he put his signature on it, then quickly rolled the scrolls and whisked them away to the office, as if afraid I would change my mind. He came back to the bar and bowed very deeply, the type of bow usually reserved for great-great-grandfathers.

"I am forever indebted to you," Hiro Bhuto told me. "If there's anything I can ever do—"

"Forget it, Bhuto." I cut him off in the manner proper for Japanese/American relations. "Your friendship in this strange land is reward enough." It was kind of a stupid thing for me to say, since I had hundreds of Japanese friends in all levels of society and the country was no more strange to me than a pair of tennis shoes. But I liked Hiro Bhuto, and it sounded nice. Bhuto poured me another Kirin lager then scurried off to help a customer who'd just walked into the bar.

And that's when I saw her.

I don't know how long she'd been standing in the doorway, swaying and trying to hold herself up. She saw me staring at her and tried to fix her eyes in a gaze back at me, but it was no use. Her hair clung to her face in sweaty strands and her lipstick was smeared all around her mouth. She looked like a circus clown who'd emerged from some primordial swamp. But beneath the guise, I could tell.

She was geisha.

Hiro Bhuto caught me staring at her. "Don't mess with her," he said to me as he pulled the customer a beer. "She's trouble."

I ignored him, picked up my drink, and made my way toward her.

She saw me coming and managed to focus her eyes somewhere in my general vicinity. She tried to regain her balance, but ended up reaching out for the support of the door frame. Her head lurched backward in what looked like a prelude to vomit. Then she steadied herself and even managed what I interpreted as a smile. She had only five teeth; two above and three below. It reminded me of Sarah. I felt myself going into soft focus.

"Where's your pole?" she gurgled.

"My pole?"

"You ain't fisherman?" She spoke a dialect you usually only hear from steelworkers in Osaka.

"No shit I ain't," I mimicked. "And you ain't really gutter trash the wind blowed in."

She slapped me.

She swung a second time, but the movement of her arm disrupted her precarious balance and she fell toward the floor. I caught her and instantly felt like a fool. I hadn't been slapped for a long time. It felt as good as I remembered.

Leaning over her, I whispering in my soberest Japanese. "Save it for a matinee, *kokeshi* doll. You're not drunk. You are performing the part of Mikura Sansuto from Nakashito's

eighteenth-century drama *The Wayward Butterfly*. The slap
you just gave me occurs in the third act, when Mikura finds
out her husband is having an affair with a puppeteer. You're
not a lush—you are a geisha with a full mouth of teeth."

Her face pulled together into an expression of surprise.
Years of training in the theatrical arts couldn't hide the fact
that she was impressed. She winked at me, and then slipped
back into the role of Mikura Sansuto, the alcoholic middle-
aged wife of an unfaithful, aging homosexual tile merchant.

"Uuuullllll," she wailed for all to hear. "*Tasukete*, I'm
going to be sick." She lurched inside the door and stumbled
toward the bar.

"*Chikusho!*" Bhuto cursed. "Get her to the bathroom before
she makes a mess."

I supported her as we moved toward the bathroom like a
set of Siamese twins shot with a tranquilizer dart. I don't
know why I was playing along. I'm a sucker for geisha.

We got inside the bathroom and she instantly straightened
up and shoved me away. Then she marched toward the window and stopped. She folded her arms and looked at me
impatiently.

"Well?" she said.

I just looked at her dumbly.

"You're supposed to open the window now."

Rather than waste my breath, I walked over to the window and yanked it open. Then she leapt up, grabbed the
ledge, and swung herself through the opening in a single,
fluid motion.

She was gone. Completely out of sight as if she'd never
even been there. Just like that.

Her sudden transition from stumbling drunk to powerful
acrobat left even a geisha veteran like me a little dazed. I

stood there in the ladies' room for a moment, looking down at my feet and wondering about my shoes.

She was good all right.

I walked back out to the bar, readying explanations for Hiro Bhuto. Before I could open my mouth, Hiro shot me a glance, warning me to keep it shut. I looked over to the entrance of the bar.

There were four men coming through, their bulky silhouettes blocking nearly all the light from the street outside. They looked like sumo wrestlers after a few months on Slim-Fast—large and powerful without all the excess fat. They wore showy suits and pitbull buzz cuts. They definitely weren't fishermen.

"We're looking for a girl," the shorter one in front said.

"Aren't we all," I quipped.

The shorter one made his way over to me. The rest followed suit. "Ah, a *gaijin* comedian. Why don't you tell me a joke, butter-stinker? I could use a good laugh." There was a menace in his voice usually reserved for death threats and obscene phone calls.

"Okay. Here's one," I said, catching the panicked look of Hiro Bhuto from the corner of my eye. "Four overdressed thugs walk into a fisherman's bar looking for a girl. Instead, they meet an American journalist who tells them, 'Sorry, no girl. Guess you'll have go fuck each other.' Get it?"

No laughs, just a lot of puzzled faces. They seemed unsure whether they were just dealing with a drunken, crazy American whose jokes didn't translate, or something more dangerous.

I didn't give them time to decide.

Doubled over, I suddenly sprang up and forward, catching the apparent leader with a swift right uppercut to the groin. With my left hand, I reached over and grabbed one of the empty bottles of kamikaze wine and bashed it against the side of the larger thug's head.

The other two finally reacted. The one in the cataract-blue suit reached into his jacket. Before he could retrieve what he was after, the second bottle of "fortieth heavy sheep" caught him squarely in the mouth. The blood that issued forth as he fell over backward reminded me of the smeared lipstick of the geisha girl. My mind formulated obscure feminist metaphors involving makeup, violence, and the image of women as victims in film and television.

But there was no time to dwell on it. The fourth thug was coming at me with a large dagger in his right hand. Not a very subtle form of attack, so I had a chance to really show off some of the moves I learned while covering the Junior Ms. Taipei Kickboxing Competition back in '86. I ducked beneath the knife and swung a hard spinning heel kick right into the back of his knee. He gave out a yelp and buckled over sideways. Still in the crouching position, I swung around and delivered a brutal blow with my forearm to the back of his other knee. It collapsed, too. He let out another yelp. With my right hand I snatched the knife from him, and with my left—just for fun—poked him in the eyes as he crumpled to the ground.

I went over to the shorter one. He was still clutching his nuts, the ones I'd punched 2.5 seconds ago. I grabbed the back of his collar and stuck the knife inside, deconstructing his Armani suit and the silk shirt beneath it. His entire back was covered with a huge red dragon. It was just as I feared. He was yakuza—a member of the Japanese crime organization famous for their unparalleled ruthlessness and colorful tattoos.

I walked calmly but quickly out of the bar. Goddamn geisha, I thought.

. . .

I hadn't walked more than twenty feet outside the bar when I heard my name being called.

"Mr. Chaka! Mr. Billy Chaka!"

I turned around to see a thin guy in sunglasses wearing a mustache that looked borrowed. He was screeching breathlessly and waving his white-gloved hands over his head. At first I thought it was just another crazed fan of mine, seeking an autograph or worse. But this guy was a uniformed chauffeur, not the usual teenage hipster wanting to rub shoulders with the best and brightest beat journalist for Asian young adults.

"You are Billy Chaka?" he said as he jogged up to me and stopped. He bent over with his hands on his knees, gasping for air. You'd think he'd just ran the Tokyo Marathon.

"How many times have you read *Catcher in the Rye*?"

"Zero. I'm the chauffeur. Mr. Migusho's chauffeur. My name is Shinto Hirohito. Chauffeur." Still panting, he produced a cigarette and lit it. The smoke restored his breathing to a rate approaching human.

Shinto Hirohito was one of the screwier names I'd ever heard. It went well with the mustache.

"Good to meet you, Hirohito. No relation to the late emperor, I suppose?"

"No. I'm Mr. Migusho's—"

"Chauffeur. Right. Where is the old man?"

"He sent me. Change of plans."

"No lunch?"

"Not here. His house. Change of plans."

Hirohito's conversational style was stripped of the pleasantries normally used by chauffeurs. It was missing a lot of the ones used by everyday people, too. He was so odd he had to be Sato's driver. I remembered Sato once had a beautiful maid with Tourette's who would shout the names of soap opera stars as she cleaned the tatami mats. Sato had a great compassion for those outside the mainstream, whether they had Tourette's or just a bad name and a worse mustache.

"All right," I said. "Let's go."

The automatic door of the taxi swung open, and I settled down into the seat. The taxi was indistinguishable from any other cab in the city, right down to the requisite lace seat coverings. The only thing it lacked was a meter.

"Why doesn't Sato use a limo?" I asked.

"Mr. Migusho sometimes travels in secret," Hirohito whispered as the doors closed behind me. It was kind of a cryptic answer, but the best I was likely to get from him.

The fact that Sato Migusho hadn't shown up for our lunch engagement worried me. Sato was notoriously punctual, almost to a fault. One of his producers told me confidentially that, though he appreciated the fact that Sato always completed his films on schedule and under budget, he felt Sato's work sometimes suffered from it. Sato often refused to reshoot, and rushed through postproduction to the point of allowing errors to survive into the final print. I remember when I interviewed him about the oft-cited jump cuts in *Yellow Mustard Scabbard* (noteworthy for preceding the famous "groundbreaking" jump cuts in Godard's *Breathless* by more than five years), he confessed that the revolutionary editing technique was actually an error, the result of hurried, sloppy editing. But then innovation, as he was fond of saying, is largely the result of mistakes.

I still didn't like the change of plans. Sato had never been late for an interview, never missed a train, and in fact was said to have been born exactly nine months following the hour of his conception. Not the kinda guy likely to change plans on a whim.

"Japan has become a nation of weaklings in blue jeans!"

It wasn't Hirohito shouting. I looked out the window.

"We have traded our national spirit for Dunkin' Donuts and Barbie dolls!"

In front of us, a giant speaker atop a truck boomed loud enough to rattle the taxi's windows. Several young men on the truck cheered and waved pictures of their leader, some fat wrinkled guy.

"The Tsuguri Society pledges to bring true Japanese values back to Japan!"

Several cars blasted their horns, but it was impossible to tell whether their responses were in agreement, dissension, or related to the Tsuguri sentiments at all. The Sword Society ultranationalist ideology truck was bringing traffic to a standstill.

"We Japanese, the people of the sun, were once feared and respected as the mightiest nation in Asia. Now countries laugh at us. We have no defenses, no warriors, only an army of greedy slaves bowing to the West! We have traded our swords for cell phones, our pride for microwave pizza!"

Tokyo, the city of noise. I sat back and tried to block out the antipizza propaganda, my thoughts turning to the strange geisha who'd stumbled through the doors of the Purple Dragnet and into the swirling cauldron of adventure called my life. What the hell was she doing at a fisherman's bar acting like a ragdoll drunk? Why were the yakuza after her? Or were they just looking for another girl? Or had they in fact come looking for me?

Like the seven hundred or so Zen koans I'd learned, I didn't know the answer, but I thought it would be somehow helpful to ponder the question.

I thought Sato lived in Mishuku," I said to Hirohito after about forty minutes of driving in the other direction.

"Mostly. But now, three weeks in the Garden."

"The Garden?" I said, not believing my ears. "Not just *a* garden, or *some* garden or some other garden—but the one...and only...Garden?"

"Sato is at the Garden of Earthly Delights," Hirohito said, unimpressed.

"Wow. Is it really like they say?"

"Never been inside. I'm a chauffeur. I wait outside. Pick him up in the garage, drop him off in the garage. I don't know what they say." Hirohito didn't care one way or another about it. He obviously didn't know what I knew.

Just after Sato Migusho finished writing a film and got all the preproduction chores out of the way—location scouting, casting, budgetary quibbling, lining up a film crew, etc.—he secluded himself for three weeks in a converted urban luxury suite to hide out from the Tokyo film world and relax before shooting began.

Only a few people knew the location of his baroque pleasure dome. From the outside, it looked like any other boxy, overcrowded Tokyo apartment building. But Hiro's cinematic success had enabled him to secure that most precious of

Japanese commodities—space. Since the early sixties the entire four-story building had served as his private pleasure dome.

Legend had it that the inner structures had been gutted, providing Sato with his own gigantic screening theater and a tacky waterfall cascading into a huge *onsen* style bath which Sato liked to fill with Mr. Bubbles to create a foaming, pinkish froth that would've sent Liberace into paroxysms of jealousy.

"Yes, I'm very decadent," Sato would say with a schoolboy's grin. "But only for three weeks of the year."

This was true. The rest of the year he lived in cramped spartan quarters like most of his countrymen. He never even took extravagant golfing vacations in Australia or sex vacations in Thailand. But for those three weeks in his secret getaway, the otherwise ascetic lifestyle of Sato Migusho exploded with the spirit of a hermetic Caligula.

Sato indulged himself mostly by himself. Often he would allow only one woman to accompany him, with the stipulation that she be blindfolded when coming or going so she could never figure out the location of his compound. More psychodrama than actual sex, according to my sources. Sato was interested in what made people frightened, what made them passionate, what made them tick much more than he was interested in the act itself. In a way, he was just doing research for his films. The guy could never fully quit working.

But as he got on in years, Sato was more likely to spend his three weeks totally alone. He once admitted wistfully that he hadn't had female companionship in the building for nearly eight years. "Now," he'd said, "I mostly just get sloshed and watch old silent movies. At my age, Buster Keaton is more interesting than busty women."

For myself, I just wanted to see the place where Sato spent his free time—the secret retreat of a famously reclusive director that was rumored to make the places on *Lifestyles of the Rich and Famous* look like Philippine flophouses.

But we never got inside Sato's retreat.

There were too many fire trucks and police vans blocking the way. We only got close enough to see a few resilient flames still licking the charred remains of the crumbling facade.

I vaulted out of the car and ran toward the building, nearly tripping over a line of fire hose. An angry fireman shouted at me to get back into the car. I ignored him and rushed up the sidewalk, pushing my way toward what was left of Sato Migusho's blackened retreat.

I was restrained only when a policeman tackled me from behind just as I was entering the building.

The fall helped restore my senses. "It's too late," the cop admonished, softening it with a look of sympathy.

And it was. For as I lay on the ground, the wheels of a stretcher nearly ran over my head. I craned my neck up and saw a thin, charcoal-black arm drop over the side of the stretcher from under the blanket. At the end of the arm were five twisted, charred fingers. Fused onto one of them was the warped band of gold putty that used to be Sato's ring, the one he'd received as third runner-up in the Mekong Delta Documentary Film Festival so many years ago.

As I watched the black column of smoke disappear into the darkened sky, I was reminded of a scene in Sato Migusho's last, and it seemed final, movie. It was called *Silt* and was about two children in Hiroshima who'd been orphaned when the bomb was dropped. While wandering among the smoldering remnants of the city, they come upon a gutted building and the little boy suddenly stops. "I think this was my house," he says. He stands there for a moment. A single tear rolls down his face, in close-up. Then he turns and slowly walks away. Actually, it was a pretty bad movie.

Some pal I was. A friend dies and all I could think of was a scene in one of his cheesiest flicks. I guess grief manifests itself in many forms, if grief was really what I was feeling. It was hard to tell.

Shinto the chauffeur just kept shaking his head, averting his eyes from the blackened skeleton of the building. Oddly, he didn't seem terribly surprised. Perhaps he was just being stoic, or maybe he was in shock. It's difficult to guess what someone with a mustache like that could be thinking.

"Let's go," I said to Shinto, who was sitting on the hood of the car, a limp cigarette dangling from one of his white-gloved hands. He looked at me, confused.

"Sato is dead," I said. "You need a new job, you can start by driving me back to the Purple Dragnet."

"But—"

"Whatever Sato paid, I'll give you thirty percent more. Think quick—there are plenty of people in this city with driver's licenses."

Shinto Hirohito hopped off the car and got in on the driver's side. My door popped open and he fired up the engine, the cigarette still burning between his lips.

"You better put that thing out," I said. "You're working for Billy Chaka—journalist."

He tossed the cigarette out the window. As we pulled away, I watched it land and smolder near a pile of discarded newspapers.

I guess it didn't matter if they caught fire now.

I half expected to find Hiro Bhuto lying bloodied on the floor, curled in pain amid shards of broken bottles and splintered chairs, yakuza threats still ringing in his ears. Instead, the

Purple Dragnet looked much like I had left it—minus the four thugs who'd gone off to lick their wounds.

"We're closed," Hiro said when saw me stroll in. I'd left Shinto to wait in the car.

"You're okay?" I said, looking around the place in amazement.

"Why shouldn't I be? I didn't do anything to those guys."

"Did they grill you?"

"They asked about you."

"And?"

"I told them."

"You told them?"

"I have my business to look out for. My family. You come into my place, start beating up on guys best left alone. What am I supposed to do? Take a beating for you? They'd find out who you were, anyway. And then they'd come in here every day and harass the customers until I had to close business, as a punishment for protecting you. So I told them."

I shook my head in disbelief. I wasn't sure what to do now. But I knew Bhuto was right for doing what he did, even if it meant my stay in Tokyo would be more eventful than I'd planned.

"I told them you said your name was Pee-Wee Melville. You represented a wealthy American whale breeder and were in Tokyo on business."

"Whale breeder?"

"Those guys don't read anything that doesn't have pictures of *zo chichi* girls." Bhuto smirked. "They don't know."

I hadn't heard the expression "elephant boobs" from anyone this side of junior high. Hiro Bhuto was full of surprises today.

"Why did you have to beat those guys up, anyway? They weren't going to do anything but put on a show and then run off after the girl."

"You don't understand. She was geisha."

"Geisha! How many geisha do you know who sleep under the blue ceiling?" Bhuto chuckled.

"You are wrong about her."

He just shrugged. "She looked like a bum to me."

"Looking like a bum was the idea."

Bhuto said nothing. He knew debating me on matters of geisha was useless. Instead, he walked behind the bar and picked up a card. He handed it to me.

"Whoever she was, she left this for you."

I looked at the card.

"I found it in the ladies' room when I was cleaning."

I suppose she could have dropped it without my noticing before she vaulted out the window. My reporter's eye for detail was compromised when there was geisha in the room. I couldn't even remember what color the Purple Dragnet's bathroom was, though my guess was purple.

"She's the only woman we've had in here today. I don't know why I bother cleaning the ladies' room. I haven't had to put out a new roll of toilet paper for twenty-six days. Either we don't get many women in here, or the ones we do get..."

I held my hand up for silence while I studied the memento from the geisha. The card was frustratingly innocuous. It was simply the Yotayo Motors logo printed in plain black on plain white. No phone number, fax number, URL, e-mail address, or name. It could have belonged to anybody, but that didn't really make sense. Why carry a business card with a corporate logo and no other information?

And then I got an idea.

"Hiro, bring me a glass of water," I said, striking a match in order to see better in the dark surroundings.

Hiro returned with the water, and placed it on the bar.

"Watch and learn, Bhuto," I said. "Watch and learn."

I dropped the card into the water. I waited. Bhuto looked on with a mild disinterest. I took the card out of the water, and held the match up to it. The card was wet.

Bhuto didn't say anything. He let his face ask all the questions.

"I'd say the test was negative," I said.

"Did you think there was invisible writing?" Bhuto chuckled.

"No. I only wanted to make sure the ink was real. That this card was not a fake."

"Well?"

"This card is not a fake."

I would never find the geisha like this. At least it wasn't too late to go home. I could forget about the geisha, try to make sense of what happened to Sato. Send someone else, Sarah would know who, to cover the tournament while I wrote a biographical piece on one of Japan's greatest directors.

As I stared at the soppy piece of paper, it occurred to me that this might be my last chance to go back, to get away. Because something told me that if I went on from here, I was going to have to see this thing out to the end. And I had no idea what this thing even was, much less where it ended.

I gave myself the space of seven breaths to decide what to do next, and if I couldn't come up with a plan, then it was the next jet back to Cleveland, Ohio. Back to my desk at *Youth in Asia* and the piles of fan mail awaiting my return.

I was exhaling the eighth breath when it hit me.

I held the dripping card up to Bhuto, my eyebrows dancing in a lascivious pantomime. He didn't get it, so I flicked out my tongue and wiggled it around.

"Bullshit," he said.

"Come see for yourself," I responded. I flicked my tongue some more to speed his decision.

As darkness settled over outer Tokyo, I directed Shinto Hirohito through a maze of twisting streets, desperately trying to remember just where I'd last seen the billboard. We crept closer to Ginza, with Bhuto muttering "bullshit" about every fifteen minutes and Shinto not talking at all, just playing nervously with his mustache. I couldn't remember if we were going the right way or not, and several times made Shinto double back. With each moment Bhuto was upping his "bullshit" count and I was starting to lose faith. Maybe the place didn't exist after all.

And then I saw Sean Penn.

He was fifty feet in the air, squinting down with puffy eyes from a giant billboard with that edgy, hungover scowl of his. His hair looked like he'd been sleeping under the bar in a puddle of stale beer ever since last call. A bent cigarette drooped from the corner of his mouth, burned down to the butt. There was another one waiting behind his ear.

And next to him stood a big, brightly colored box of Eat Me! breakfast cereal. Sean Penn was looking sideways, glowering at it like it was paparazzi. He looked ready to kick the cereal box's ass.

EAT ME! the sign said. BREAKFAST OF STARS.

It wasn't the worst movie-star product endorsement I'd seen. All kinds of Hollywood big shots were shilling for Japanese products—it paid well and they figured no one important would see it, anyway. Francis Ford Coppola used to endorse an instant food product called Applesauce Now. A couple years ago, De Niro did TV spots for a hearing aid company which featured him in his Travis Bickle outfit. He'd cup his ear and ask, "You talkin' to me? You talking to me?"

In the ad, a helpful GoodEar salesman comes along to solve his problem.

My all-time favorite, however, had to be the Barbra Streisand nasal decongestant billboard. In the photo, she's using one of those little squirt bottles, struggling to maintain the poised, dignified look of the true *artiste* as she jams the thing up into her honker.

Now, *that's* advertising.

"That's it," I said, pointing up to the sign with Sean Penn.

"Bullshit," Bhuto grunted.

I made Shinto pull over and hopped out the car. Ginza wasn't exactly bustling tonight, but then it had lost some of its luster over the years. The hipsters had all moved west and left the place to daytime shoppers, corporate showcase buildings, snobbish art galleries, and overpriced craft boutiques.

I was directly beneath Sean and his cereal now, standing outside some fashion store and looking for the black phone that was supposed to be there. It wasn't. I looked down the street, and glanced up at the billboard again to make sure I was directly beneath it. I was under it all right, just where I was supposed to be. The giant ash from Sean Penn's cigarette looked like it could fall off and land on me any second.

I walked up and down the street, but still couldn't find the black phone that was supposed to be on the wall. There was nothing else to do but walk back to the car.

Bhuto started in on me right away.

"Like I said—"

"I know. Bullshit."

I sat in the back and thought a moment. Maybe it wasn't Sean Penn I was looking for. Maybe the secret entrance was beneath the Dennis Hopper toothpaste billboard over in Aoyama, or that Al Pacino ad for hair dye in Akasaka. I get my method actors mixed up sometimes.

"You know," Bhuto said, "this Eat Me! billboard is every-where."

"There are more of these?"

"All over. There are at least two or three I can think of right off the top of my head. There's one on Tomachi-dori, another one over by Akihabara—"

"Hit it, Shinto," I said. Shinto pulled into traffic, and we headed west, chasing after another Sean Penn. Bhuto was starting to get critically annoyed, not even bothering to say bullshit anymore. He was careful not to protest too much, though, because if I turned out to be right, he knew he was in for a real treat.

That's what kept him on the journey as he stopped under at least five more Eat Me! billboards. Each time I got out of the car to look for the legendary black phone, each time I came up empty. After about the seventh miss, Bhuto had fallen asleep. Shinto just kept wordlessly taking directions. As Sato's driver, he'd probably been subject to all kinds of endless location scouting, so driving around aimlessly was nothing new.

Finally, I gave up and told him to turn around and head back to the Purple Dragnet. Maybe Bhuto was right, maybe the place didn't exist after all.

As we rounded a corner about a mile from Bhuto's bar, I spotted Sean Penn again, up in the sky, mocking me. I was sick of looking at the guy. Why some ad exec thought that his mugshot looks would appeal to the most hygiene-conscious people on the planet, I'll never know. Then again, if Eat Me! cereal could get Sean Penn moving the morning after, just imagine what it could do for the average hungover salaryman.

The billboard was atop another mid-size high-rise, wholly indistinguishable from fifteen hundred or so of its counterparts around the city. Shrines to the god of monotony. When I looked closely, though, there was one standout feature.

The building had no windows.

Either some committee had achieved the ultimate in productivity-enhancing architecture, or I'd stumbled upon a contender.

I made Shinto pull over. He was getting pretty good, almost anticipating the request before I made it. I hopped out and dashed to the front of the building. There wasn't even a front door. It could have been a giant block of solid concrete for all I could tell.

But there was a black phone mounted on the wall. Just a plain black receiver without any numbers. I picked it up and listened.

"*Moshi moshi*..." said a voice on the other end.

The Japanese are famous for their discretion when it comes to sexual matters. As such, there are many love hotels scattered throughout the city where one can go without making any contact with hotel clerks, bellhops, or other customers. High bushes and large fences usually guard the entrance to the sometimes garish, sometimes undistinguished buildings, and some even use tarps and fake construction scaffolding to help customers disguise their coming and going.

Inside, you never knew what you'd get. They ran the gamut from four-walls-and-a-futon flea traps to expensive fantasy suites tailored to satisfy even the most obscure fantasies. I'd been in a room designed to look like Cleopatra's love nest and one done up to look like a dentist's waiting room. I stayed in an exact replica of the Marquis de Sade's La Coste Château and once spent a horrible night in the Lucasfilm Love Planet's Ewok Suite.

But the Yotayo Love Hotel was rumored to be in a league all its own.

I cleared my throat, and sang into the phone.

> "Yotayo rises like Fuji in the white mist,
> Resplendent technology and hopefulness are united
> In the labor our sweat mingles with the grease,

> *Our hearts pound with the happiness*
> *And pride of Yotayo.*
> *Yotayo! Yotayo! Yotayo!*
> *The Emperor of the Nippon Automobiles,*
> *Great, Mighty, and Economical!"*

There was a sudden electric hum. I looked up to see a row of bushes sinking into the ground. Behind it was an entrance to an underground parking garage. I hung up the phone, motioned to Shinto Hirohito to drive through, and hopped into the car as he passed.

"I can't believe this bullshit," whispered Hiro Bhuto in awe.

The Yotayo Love Hotel was one of those entities that everyone knew about, but most people thought was just a cultural myth—like the hidden bigwig lounge located in Disneyland's Magic Castle, or the sealed vault that houses the secret formula for Coca-Cola. Really more of an entertainment complex than a love hotel in the usual sense, it was created as a place where Yotayo's higher-ups could indulge in their fantasies without being exposed by an overanxious, uninitiated member of the weeklies press. It was a sovereign zone in which the most decadent of vices was permissible and provided for, where the only sin was violating the strict code of secrecy.

We parked the taxi—ours was the only non-Yotayo car in the lot—and walked over to the elevator at the far side of the garage. The doors opened automatically and we stepped inside. As they closed behind us, a large video monitor above them came to life.

"Welcome," our video hostess addressed us in English, "to the Palace of Many Fantastic Encounters." She was standing in front of a ripe blue waterfall, wearing a tight silver body suit. Her spiky, yellow hair made her look like a dandelion wrapped in tinfoil.

"We have settings for pleasure at the Palace," she continued in English with Japanese subtitles, "to which you may select the most desired in your heart." I caught Hiro Bhuto and Shinto Hirohito smirking to each other. The madame continued, "On floor number five, you return to feudal times of old, where you can test out your samurai sword on some of the courtly ladies of utmost friendship."

I wondered who was responsible for writing this speech. Reading the subtitles revealed it was equally bad in Japanese.

"On the fourth floor you visit the Old West, where you will have many opportunities for saddle-up horse girls with many-galloned hats and sex-hot six-shooting pistol guns."

On the screen, a peroxide Thai woman clad in nothing but a cheap red cowboy hat strutted around a mock saloon and suggestively licked the barrel of a plastic gun. Old West themes were big in Tokyo this week, I guess.

"On the third floor we take you to Le Grand Castle of French Decadency. Opulent ladies of wigs and powder titillate you with the multitude layers beneath her frilly courtesan chic."

The opulent ladies writhed around on a giant circular bed with a glittering gold bedspread. I had to admit it was a pretty good imitation of the inner Palace of Versailles—except for the seven Hitachi video cameras and monitors, "smart-located for much angles of viewing pleasure."

"On floor number two take a blast up on the moon for the Lunar Sexcapade. Our cosmic gravity simulation technology provides you launch to the stars with sexy astrowomen of lunar hunger. Shoot off orbit!"

This sounded pretty interesting, until they revealed that the zero gravity simulator was really just some awkward-looking harnesses and bungee rope connected to the ceiling. The woman onscreen was nude except for a huge bubble space helmet. She looked like a pornographic gumball machine.

"And on floor number one, together with me and other Cyberfoxes in the Land Ultra Future where you may experience the pleasures of tomorrow, right here now."

The Cyberfoxes did robo-erotic dances around a foggy stage lit by multicolored lasers and strobe lights. The pleasures of tommorrow looked a lot like the eighties.

That's when it hit me; I'd bumbled my way into an X-rated, miniature EPCOT Center. Still, I had to admit it was a lot more fun and imaginative than some run-down trailer park outside of Vegas. I turned to Hiro Bhuto and Shinto Hirohito.

"What will it be?" They looked at each other and then turned to me. Hirohito spoke.

"Whatever looks most appealing to you, Chaka-san."

"Your deference is touching, but my decision skills seem to be on the blink. It's your call." They glanced at each other again. Hirohito seemed to have been elected spokesman.

"We would like to see the Old West."

They seemed anxious that I approve, for the attempt to express an interest in my homeland culture was a compliment. Telling them that naked platinum blondes from Southeast Asia wearing cowboy hats had about as much to do with my culture as *The Karate Kid* did with theirs would have been insulting. Instead, I smiled graciously and pushed the button for the fourth floor.

The doors opened to the theme from *The Beverly Hillbillies*. Not exactly "Home on the Range" but at least it featured a banjo. Banjos were considered a very mysterious and exotic

Instrument by some people here. I never tried to explain that many Americans equated banjos with toothless backwater inbreds.

"Howdy, all of you all," our video hostess purred on the screen. She was wearing a goofy-looking ten-gallon hat and big smile. "Please select the number of members in your pleasure posse this evening. Howdy!"

I pushed number three on the touch-activated screen. A key slid out of the slot at the bottom of the video console, along with nine condoms packaged with the Yotayo corporate logo.

"You will find your Western dubs in Room twenty-three. Have a wonder-filled stay, partners. Giddy-up!" She cracked a whip and the screen went blank.

We walked down the hall until we found Room 23. It was your typical hotel room, but Wild-Westernized. A horseshoe hung over the door, and there were a few depressing paintings of cowboys on the walls. An antique spittoon squatted in the corner, and the wallpaper was supposed to look like the inside of some clapboard shack. There was even a fake window painted in, looking out over a sweeping vista right out of a John Ford movie.

The Western "dubs" were hanging neatly in the closet. Chaps, cowboy boots, bandannas, hats. Even Lone Ranger–style eye masks were provided to help conceal one's identity. There were props such as horsewhips, branding irons, lassos, and spurs with rubber safety tips. I started thinking cowboys must had been a bunch of perverts.

Even with all the toys, I was having a hard time mustering up much enthusiasm. For me, the most interesting thing in the room was the bed, because I hadn't seen one in over twenty-six hours. The jet lag was starting to hit me, hard. Everything was taking on a surreal edge, which might not have been a bad thing. It protected me from the harsh reality lurking underneath.

The utter finality of Sato's death was something that probably wouldn't sink in for days. Then out of the blue it would blindside me as I walked down the street or shaved in the mirror. And then it would hurt.

Though I couldn't yet see the link, the timing made me suspect it had something to do with me. After all, I had spoken to him only hours before his house burst into flames. Then the geisha came in the bar, then the gangsters. It was a lot of coincidences to swallow in one afternoon.

I looked at the bed again. I was growing more weary by the moment, but I couldn't afford to waste any hours in sleep. The seventeenth-century samurai strategist Miyamoto Musashi once wrote, "Do not let your mind influence your body, nor your body influence your mind." Good advice, but I wondered sometimes how he could tell the difference.

I slipped on my cowboy gear, donning both the bandanna and the Lone Ranger mask, and pulling the big cowboy hat low over my eyes. Billy Chaka, paranoid cowboy.

Hiro Bhuto, on the other hand, looked right at home in his getup. I wish I could have taken a picture, but the only cameras allowed were the closed-circuit type.

"Jeez, Hiro," I said. "You look like John Wayne. I wish your wife could see you now." He smiled broadly. Apparently mentioning his wife in this glitzy bordello didn't bother him.

Shinto Hirohito was having a more difficult time. He couldn't figure out how the bolo tie worked, and his holster was on backward. I didn't know how to correct him without offending him, but I also didn't want him to be embarrassed when he found out he had done it wrong.

"Hey, Shinto." I motioned him over. "Give me a hand with this holster, will ya?"

He tried, but he didn't exactly have the world's greatest motor skills. I ended up pretty much doing it myself. But as I'd hoped, he then realized his own holster was on wrong and turned it around. I fixed his bolo tie for him. He still hadn't bothered to take off his white chauffeur gloves, but they looked oddly fitting with the getup.

I looked at the two of them for a moment, a strangely touching study in cultural exchange, and it struck me that this wasn't exactly how I pictured spending my first evening back in Tokyo. I don't know what I expected to learn, or how I was so sure the geisha would be here. If I thought about all the ways I could be wrong, I'd be standing in the room all night.

"All right, greenhorns," I said. "Let's hit the trail."

The saloon was hopping. The top executives of Yotayo and their guests were doing their best to create a real Wild West atmosphere, complete with mah-jongg gamblers in fancy Western outfits, outlaw types with black hats, and a huge ex–sumo wrestler with a tin star. His white-fringed jacket strained to keep his impressive mass from spilling out in all directions, and the ten-gallon cowboy hat looked like a yarmulke on his oversized cranium. He was Texas-size, all right.

The main attraction were the Western gals dancing on the stage and draped around every table. Some dressed in plumed hats and flouncy dresses, like fancy whores in the movies. Others were outfitted Daisy Duke style—cowboy boots, short cutoff jeans, and checkered plaid shirts with the ends tied in neat little knots underneath their ample bosoms. As advertised, they all had blond hair. Some were Asian, some Scandinavian, but no real cowgirls.

I surveyed the crowd, scanning the room for familiar faces. I recognized Yoshiya Shimazu, head of domestic mar-

keting for Yotayo Motors. He'd spearheaded Yotayo's massive
television product placement campaign. Every time you
turned on the TV, someone was driving a Yotayo. Whether
the character was a cop, a robber, a single mother, or a struggling *manga* artist, they drove a shiny new Yotayo. Even six-
teenth-century shogun Nobunaga Oda had a horse named
Yotayo in the TV miniseries.

I spotted Haruki Yoshida, the man responsible for introducing global positioning systems into Yotayo cars. Legend
had it that his wife was always getting lost and calling him
up at work to ask for directions, so he helped develop a navi-
gation system to put in her car. It worked so well that she left
him. The joke was that she had been trying to leave him for
years, but couldn't find her way out of Tokyo. With two
painted ladies on either side of him tonight, he looked like
he was taking it in stride.

Kakuei Moriyaka, head of Yotayo's massive domestic
sales force, was getting smashed at a table in the corner.
According to my sources, Moriyaka was one hell of a motiva-
tor. If a dealership wasn't meeting its quotas, he'd would
show up with a baseball bat and smash a new-model Yotayo
on the lot. If the dealership was unable to sell the battered
car at full price within a month, Moriyaka would close
them down. I'd seen so many beat-up Yotayos on the street, I
doubted he ever had to make good on the threat.

And there, off in the far corner beneath a giant stuffed
buffalo head, was my mysterious and dangerous geisha.

The transformation she had undergone since our last hurried
encounter was astounding. But then she was geisha, well
versed in the theatrical arts of disguise. Gone was the rat's-
nest hair and smeared eye makeup. Instead, she wore a
sparkling silver cowboy hat and a lacy eye mask. Her blouse

was a silken purple with the word LASSO embroidered in gold thread like neon across the chest.

But what caught my eye was the corner of her mouth. Her lipstick was smeared ever so slightly, like her mouth was being pulled down to one side. It was her all right.

She was standing next to a slight young man in an Indian costume wearing a strangely serene expression. He leaned over and whispered something in her ear. She looked toward me, though it was hard to tell if she was actually looking right at me since the lace mask obscured her eyes. Then she flashed a cursory smile and made for the exit.

I bolted across the saloon, tearing through the crowds of drunken square dancers and yelling, "*Geri o shiteimasu!* I'm going to be sick." But the music was blaring too loud for many of them to hear me. I saw the geisha and her faithful Indian companion nearing the swinging doors of the saloon exit and doubled my pace, hell-bent on cutting my way through the mob.

It was like a nightmare. The faster I tried to move, the more people stood in my way. By this time, my panicked flight had drawn the attention of the oversized sumo sheriff, and the geisha had an insurmountable lead. She gave me one last vicious wink as she slipped through the swinging doors.

I should have just stopped right there. And I would have stopped, had I not crashed headlong into a mah-jongg table. The tiles went flying skyward in slow motion, while the glasses of beer and whiskey arched high into the smoky air. For a moment, everything seemed suspended in time and space. I was reminded of the zero-G lunar fantasy room, and wished I was there instead. And then everything came down again, much of it on me.

I looked up. The saloon doors were swaying gently in the vacant doorway. She was gone.

• • •

In most Japanese bars, mere drunkenness is absolution for antisocial behavior. And being a *gaijin* usually insured forgiveness for all sorts of transgressions. But from the looks on the players' faces, I had ruined a game of pretty high stakes. And this was a rough-and-tumble frontier watering hole, after all.

Hiro and Shinto started to rush to my aid with half-formed explanations, then seemed to think better of it. They were practicing the ancient custom of *jicho*—avoiding trouble as a way of self-preservation. I picked myself off the floor and confronted several angry faces that wished to put me back on it. I started to offer apologies, but abruptly stopped. Years of barroom training had taught me the limited power of words.

There was going to be a brawl.

The first chair came high, and with only a slight movement I was able to duck it. Instead of hitting me, it connected with the forehead of the dude behind me. I swung a low back-heel kick into the knee of the man to my left, my spurs halting his attack and causing him to lose hold of the whiskey bottle he was swinging toward my head. The bottle sailed across the room before shattering against the back of Tetsuo Iguichi, coinventor of the shatterproof windshield.

The third assailant tried the old kick to the solar plexus. I caught his foot and used his own momentum to bring his other one high off the ground, sending him onto his back. Chaos was breaking out all over the saloon. Using a method I'd acquired while covering the Nagasaki Myopic Judo Tournament, I managed to fix my eyes in the "attitude nonattitude" style, the effect of which can be described as looking through both ends of a telescope at once. It allowed me to concentrate on both immediate close-range attacks and impending threats from across the room.

The first attack came from the outlaw cowboy just in front of me. His spinning back fist was no match for my spinning leg sweep. I caught him just as his back was fully turned, so that he launched into the air, still rotating uselessly when he crashed to the ground. The next attack came from afar, in the form of a twirling horseshoe that had been taken from the wall and hurled. I caught the horseshoe in my left hand, and planted it in the groin of a Yotayo VIP who was about to lunge at me from behind.

There was a shrill, high-pitched noise.

I shifted my focus to its source. It was the bartender blowing a tin whistle. The sound had the riot-quelling effect of the barkeep in Western movies discharging a single blast from his shotgun. Everyone suddenly stopped. Those not already sprawled out on the ground turned their faces to it in obvious shame. The bar was totally silent, save for "Rowdy Yates," still pumping through the speakers.

After the initial silence, people began resuming their usual activities and helped each other off the floor. The Scandinavian cowgirls, previously huddled together in all corners of the room, now began to rejoin their men, no doubt commending them on their bravery.

Only I was unable to go back to pleasure as usual. The giant hand I felt on my shoulder forced me toward the exit. The sumo sheriff was surprisingly graceful, guiding me through the crowd much more skillfully than I had done myself. Soon we were through the swinging doors and into the hall.

My cover was thoroughly blown.

"Sir, I would like permission to ask you a few questions, if it is not to much trouble," he said, as if I had a choice. His voice was a high wheeze, disconcerting on such a giant man.

If you heard him on the phone, you'd think he was some frail emphysema patient.

"It would be my pleasure to speak with you," I lied. After all, I'd never been beaten up for being too polite.

He guided me into what I assumed was his office, and motioned me to take a seat. I acknowledged the offer, but made sure I waited until he'd settled himself into a massive chair behind his tiny desk.

I sat down in my chair and felt a sharp pain in my butt. I leapt up, suppressing a yelp. I glanced down at the seat cushion, but couldn't see what had caused the sting. Nothing irregular when I ran my hand over it, either.

"Is the furniture unsuitable?" the sumo asked. He looked at me like I'd just called him fatboy.

I shook my head and sat down. No sting this time.

Like the other room the office was cluttered with Old West bric-a-brac. As it was supposed to be the sheriff's place, there were a few humorous wanted posters with faded photos of some of Yotayo's Most Wanted Criminals, including Lee Iacocca and several yesteryear Detroit auto-world figures.

"*Thar's gold in them thar hills! Hic! Gold, I tell ye!*"

"Excuse me for a moment," the sumo wheezed uncomfortably.

"*Thar's gold in them thar hills! Hic! Gold, I tell ye!*" the voice said again from behind me.

I turned around. The rear third of the room was taken up by a phony jail cell with big black rubber bars. Inside, an Animatronic drunk ol' raggedy coot sat on a wine barrel. He had a raspy beard and only one eye, and held a jug labeled "XXX" in his hand. His head lurched forward mechanically and his arm jerked upright and shook.

"*Thar's gold in them thar hills! Hic! Gold, I tell ye!*"

Then his head tilted back and he hoisted the jug for a long swig. Two seconds later, he was talking about gold again.

The sumo walked into the cell and started flipping switches, but the old drunk robot wouldn't shut up. The sumo tapped it on the side of the head. The head went flying off and shattered against the wall with a metallic crash. It refused to shut up, though. The sumo sheriff grabbed it with one hand and slammed it against the wall.

"*Thhhhaaaarzzz goooollld . . .*" it slurred, and then fell silent in a heap on the floor. Justice served.

"That's police brutality," I said.

The sheriff wasn't amused. He walked out of the cell, settled back into his chair, and tried to regain his composure.

"We got it from Tokyo Disney," he said. "The ministry of education had him taken out of the Gold Mine ride. They decided it was irresponsible to teach children that drinking is funny. Damn thing got on my nerves. I hope you don't."

"I'll drink to that."

He sized me up for a moment then handed me his business card. It was printed in English and read *Aryoshi . . . Man with Badge.* I found myself in the embarrassing position of not having my own *meishi* handy, so I snagged a Post-it note from the desk and wrote *Billy Chaka—Journalist.*

He looked at the note with deserved suspicion, and then tucked it neatly into his hat band.

"As you know, Yotayo prides itself on the anonymity granted to its patrons of the Love Hotel," he began in a slow, deliberate tone.

"I find the informal atmosphere very gratifying," I blurted. I felt it was a good time to interrupt, in order to feign naïveté of protocol.

"I'm sure you do." He wrinkled his forehead in a pained expression. Much conversation here is based on the pretext that certain things are left unsaid, which means gestures and inferential tones become the true medium of communication. Right now he was implying that I was getting on his nerves. I went on anyway.

"Although I've never had an opportunity to enjoy its pleasures prior to tonight, I am certain that it must be a highly desirable privilege for the deserving members of the wonderful Yotayo Corporation."

The intricate series of physical subtleties which accompanied my response served two purposes. The first was to show that I understood that the Yotayo complex was a closely guarded secret, even in a land of secrets. The second was to let him know that my visit here was not by some fluke, and that despite my behavior, I understood the rules that went with such exclusive membership.

"We get worried when it appears as if one of our guests isn't enjoying himself," he said.

I thought this a little blunt. Basically, he was accusing me of not coming for leisure, but because of some ulterior motive. The sumo sheriff obviously had good horse sense. Still, I thought he was tilting his hand. Not that horses have hands, or play cards, or whatever. Before my thoughts got any fuzzier, I responded.

"Surely, there are many ways to enjoy oneself in such a unique place as this."

Translation—back off, I have my reasons.

"At times it is best to relax using more traditional methods."

He meant I'd acted out of line. And even though I was really only trying to defend myself, I could see where it might have appeared as if I had deliberately smashed into the table and then assaulted several of the surrounding people for no apparent reason. As the Hindus might say, it was a problem of *maya*—subjective isolation. Rather than try to explain my point of view, I decided to seek the path of least resistance.

"I'll be honest with you. I had no intention of causing such an unruly disturbance, and I take full responsibility."

"I'm sure your intentions were honorable," the sheriff said in his peculiar high voice. "Nevertheless, when such disturbances occur it sometimes has a negative effect on the atmosphere we work so hard to create. When this happens, it is my duty to find out the cause of such unpleasantness and work toward a suitable solution."

"I respect your position. You must be a man of high honor to be granted such an important role."

"I am happy you understand my feelings in this matter. Still, I fear I will have to breech the customary code of *na-katta koto ni suru.*"

That was bad news. I always liked the code of pretending it never happened. It was a great code, one of my long-standing favorites. I nodded to the sheriff.

"You are not employed by the Yotayo Corporation," he said. "I am curious to know how you gained an invitation here."

"Several years ago I did a piece on the Yotayo Driver's Education Program."

"You are a reporter?" I could see the alarm gong going off in his head. Apparently, he hadn't connected the word "journalist" from my improvised business card with the word "reporter."

"I only write articles of interest to teenagers. I can assure you that the nocturnal habits of the Yotayo executives do not fall into that category."

"Who is your employer, may I inquire?"

"I write for *Youth in Asia.*"

"The magazine out of Cleveland, Oregon?"

"Cleveland, Ohio. It's the most popular magazine of its sort in my country," I said matter-of-factly. "You are familiar with it?"

"I have come across it. Please continue."

I got the feeling that he wasn't a big fan of the magazine. Most sumo types weren't, due to an exposé I'd written years ago about the cruel rigors a teenage sumo hopeful must undergo to reach the top. I faithfully chronicled the pounds of fattening *chanko-nabe* stew they had to eat and the hours spent mindlessly slapping wooden telephone poles in the rain. I shared the unpleasant fact that young sumos' duties included washing their superiors' loincloths by hand, and— worse yet—unclogging the sumo-sized toilets in the training facilities after inevitable stop-ups. Many complained that my article was a little heavy-handed, but the facts were indisputable. Of all my writings, this was one of the top twenty in the controversy category.

"As I was saying, I wrote a piece on Yotayo's Driver's Ed. Program. I called it the most advanced in the world, what with the hundreds of free cars donated to the school, the expert driving instructors who undergo a three-year course on all aspects of the automobile—from history of gasoline to advanced defensive-driving techniques. I even mentioned the elite kindergarten. Very progressive, indeed. And great for public relations."

I was vaguely aware that I was babbling, and switching back and forth from Japanese to English. Now that the adrenaline rush from the bar fight had worn off, my weariness must have been taking over.

"It is a wonderful school. I learned to drive there myself. Go on." The sumo smiled brightly, and his high scratchy voice sounded as soothing as rustling sheets in a warm bed.

"After the piece was published, I was contacted by an executive in the Yotayo PR division. He told me my article was very flattering, and that enrollment had increased thirteen percent since the article appeared. He said the next time I was in Tokyo, I should visit an 'exclusive' Yotayo getaway. Then he gave me directional hints in the form of a riddle. Something about Madonna. I actually thought he was putting me on, but here I am, and happy to be here."

I was, at that moment, very happy to be there. The white-fringe jacket of the sumo seemed to virtually glow, making him look like some glistening snow-covered mountain. Even the empty spaces around the room were filled with a swimming benevolence.

"And we are pleased to have you. You brought two guests with you tonight. Are they also journalists?"

"Who, those guys? The greenhorns?" It seemed like a really funny question, so I laughed. "Oh, no. They are just some friends of mine. Great guys."

I saw myself in a mirror on the wall over Aryoshi's shoulder. My face was contorted in a wild, cartoonish grin.

And that's when I realized what had happened.

For when I thought of the word "grin" I always thought about Sarah and her wicked, nearly toothless smile. And when I thought of Sarah, I thought about her back in Cleveland, floating on drug-induced endorphins. And when I thought about drugs, I remembered the sharp pain in my butt when I sat in the chair. My foggy euphoria had been induced by a hidden injection needle. Probably MDMA, or perhaps a particularly hallucinogenic form of sodium pentathol. The realization only made me laugh. Some corner of my mind tried to remind me I was in trouble, and that this four-hundred-pound sumo was not my friend.

Of course, that just made me laugh harder.

But this second laugh was only to mask the fact that I was regaining control. As a young, immature reporter suddenly unleashed unto cities like Gao, Phnom Penh, and Bangkok, I had experimented a great deal with drugs of every kind. During this time, I'd mastered The Way of the Poppy-Eater, a philosophy to help the mind neutralize the effect of narcotics. Using this technique, one can identify the sensations and impulses that would not otherwise occur, then usher them toward a safe part of the mental labyrinth before they are acted upon. Of course, this requires an extremely intimate understanding of the inner processes of one's own mind. Most people lack this self-knowledge. That's why some jump out of buildings thinking they can fly and others just act like assholes.

"What are the occupations of these friends of yours?" Aryoshi kindly inquired. But now I could see through him. I identified the impulse to tell the truth, and then shuffled it down a dead-end corridor in my brain.

"One is a racecar driver. In my language, the word 'racecar' is a palindrome. He's not a very good one, but he still hopes to one day be sponsored by Yotayo. And the other guy, the one with the mustache, he's an entertainer. A mime actually. That's why he doesn't talk much. He wears white gloves all the time, just like Mickey Mouse." It was important that I let some drug babble through, in order to give the sumo sheriff the idea that I was still in a mildly psychedelic euphoria.

"I see," he said with a nod. "Mr. Chaka, why were you rushing toward the exit in such a hurry?" He asked the question as if congratulating me on my flight. The rational part of my mind was angry at his manipulative tactics, the druggie part gracious about his curiosity.

"The man who told me about the Yotayo Love Hotel was slipping through the doors. I only wanted to thank him for introducing me to this wondrous facility. It really is a wondrous facility. I wanted to tell him what a wondrous facility it was."

"This fellow . . . he was leaving with a girl, correct?"

"I didn't notice," I said with a dismissive wave of the hand. "But I'll tell you something interesting, Sheriff. When I was a child, about three years old, I thought that small animals lived inside my stomach during winter. Hibernating. How fucked up is that?"

The sumo smirked but otherwise ignored the comment.

"I tell you what else," I blurted. "You've got a great gig here. Surrounded by all those beautiful women, listening to great shitkickin' tunes all day. Beats the hell out of stomping around a little circle and grabbing guys by the diaper, eh?"

Aryoshi thought I was doped to the gills, that he had me right where he wanted me. I let him keep thinking it.

"There are many beautiful girls here at the Yotayo Love Hotel, Mr. Chaka," Aryoshi said, relaxing a little. "Perhaps in the future you may be able to enjoy their company. But in light of tonight's unfortunate events, I think it would be better if you and your guests came back another time."

"I couldn't agree more, Mr. Aryoshi. Thank you very, very much for your generous offer and for your hospitality. You are a very kind man, and very handsome in that fringed jacket. Any town in the real Old West would be proud to have you as their sheriff."

Aryoshi the four-hundred-pound ex–sumo wrestler blushed.

"Can I ask you something, Sheriff?" I said.

He nodded.

"Is your voice kind of high, or is it just me?"

Aryoshi gave me a sideways look. Maybe I was pushing it too far. He stared at me, hard. Even his eyes were sumo-sized. I let my eyelids sag, trying to look dopey and drugged out. Sean Penn as Jeff Spicoli.

"I got hit in the throat during a match when I was fifteen," Aryoshi said at length. "Crushed my larynx."

"Sorry to hear that," I said.

"I broke the guy's neck," Aryoshi wheezed. "So it all worked out okay."

I wasn't sure how to respond, so I just smiled uneasily.

All four hundred pounds of Aryoshi got up and led me toward the door.

As we drove out of the parking garage, I mused upon the whole episode. At bars in the real American West, you were forcibly manhandled and thrown out into the street by a surly bouncer with overdeveloped machismo. According to the movies, anyway. At the Yotayo Secret Love Hotel's Old West Saloon, you were quietly guided into a room, plied with trippy truth serum, and interrogated by a giant soprano, then escorted out the door with an invitation to return under more favorable circumstances.

And Sarah didn't think Japan was exotic.

Thankfully, neither Bhuto nor Shinto asked what the hell had gotten into me. They were fairly casual about the whole thing, but behind their reserve I sensed resentment. Spending an evening in Japan's most legendary secret love hotel was not something that was likely to occur again in the life of a barkeep or a chauffeur.

At least the hotel let them keep their Western getups. I don't know what use a bunch of cowboy clothes would be to them in their everyday Tokyo lives, but it was a nice gesture just the same.

As I sat in the gym waiting for the handicapped teen competitors to arrive, I read through the morning papers. They were filled with accounts of Sato Migusho's death. Investigators believed that the fire started in Migusho's private screening room while he was watching an old print of the groundbreaking Japanese expressionist masterpiece *A Page Out of Order,* a title from Sato's private film library. Since it was an original print from 1927, it was made on nitrate-based film stock instead of the modern plastic-based type. The newspaper called nitrate a "relatively flammable" material, which was like calling my sheriff friend from last night a "relatively large man." I found it odd that a person who had spent his entire life in the film business would not use a newer print (according to the paper, the film was rereleased in 1973 on the more benign acetate), or at least take the necessary precautions in dealing with such a volatile substance. But the police had ruled it an accident, and as the press granted them a status of virtual infallibility, there would likely be no further investigation.

Among the accompanying articles was a retrospective of the films Migusho had either directed or produced. It also said that just before he died he had been scouting locations in Hokkaidō for his next film, as well as trying to secure the rights for a bio-pic about an unnamed American reporter.

Maybe that explained why Sato had been so anxious to do lunch with me.

As I read through the papers, I found myself looking for a hint of some greater meaning behind it all, something beyond the dry recitation of a few facts that made up his outer life. But it was just another second-tier-celebrity death, the kind the press in its limited vocabulary always refers to as "tragic"—as if that says anything at all. Words which more readily sprang to mind included ridiculous, absurd, suspicious, and awful—which really didn't say much, either.

I tossed the paper in the garbage can where it belonged and thought for a moment about the uselessness of so-called objective journalism when confronted with an event of this magnitude. Sure, it was just an aging film director who had died and the world could go on with its business without so much as a hiccup. One personal tragedy in a tragically impersonal world wasn't going to derail a stock market, crash a corporation, or affect a sports team's shot at the title. Maybe all it would do is make some *gaijin* reporter sing the existential blues.

Hiro Bhuto said he didn't expect any trouble from the yaks, even though his little Pee-Wee Melville joke was bound to be found out sooner or later. Crediting the yakuza with a sense of humor was like believing monkeys could play chess, but it was his call. Hirohito was now officially my driver. I told him he'd be on duty twenty-four hours a day, but that it would be worth his while. I called Chuck, the head accountant at the magazine, just to make sure it would and got the usual grumbling mathematical threats. Chuck hadn't learn to say no yet, but he was making progress.

The competition wasn't scheduled to begin for another three hours and only a few of the competitors had arrived at the gymnasium. The facility was one of the largest martial-arts centers on the crowded main island. It used to serve as a secret storage hangar for kamikaze planes before they were shipped out to the Philippine bases, and had since been converted into a state-of-the-art sports facility. Despite the painstaking efforts to disguise the building's previous purpose, there was still an eerie feeling about it. As I watched the young handicapped martial artists stretching their muscles and fine-tuning their wheelchairs, I couldn't help but think of the "divine wind" pilots nervously checking their instruments before an attack.

I always liked the atmosphere of a large, empty auditorium just before a big youth competition. The room would soon be filled with anxious teenagers, hormones and adrenaline coursing through their sweaty, agile bodies. The sound of crutches clanging against each other in fierce combat. Wheelchairs squeaking as they spun and twirled in graceful evasive maneuvers, the auditorium echoing a dense melody of overanxious parents cheering to the *ki-aies* from their adolescent warriors. But at this moment, everything was silent save for the electric hum of the lights and soft whistle of the ceiling fans. I'm sure the residual drugs in my system helped add to my reverent feelings, but at times like this I knew being a writer for *Youth in Asia* was the best job in the world.

I was happy to be alone. It was the first substantial time I had spent by myself since I walked into the Purple Dragnet and the geisha walked into my life. I remembered how she draped herself in the door frame as the light blasted into the dark barroom, her bloodred lipstick smeared about her mouth as if she'd applied it on a roller coaster.

Maybe the yakuza weren't really after her. Maybe she wasn't a geisha, but just some crazy kid with a weird idea of fun. Maybe Sato's house burning down had even been an accident, just like the papers said. Maybe I was just paranoid.

Without tangible provocation, I had started two fights and managed to get thrown out of the Yotayo Love Hotel. All because I'd gotten it into my head that the mysterious woman was a geisha.

I was reminded of a Zen parable in which a student confides to his master that he is having nightmares about a terrible and powerful enemy. The master tells him that the next time he confronts the enemy in his dream, he is to mark the enemy with a giant *X* across the stomach. That night the enemy comes to the pupil's dream and the pupil does as instructed. Suddenly the enemy vanishes into thin air. The next day the student wakes to discover a giant *X* scrawled on his own belly.

I figured I'd probably have played tic-tac-toe on myself by now. But that was just the yin of the situation. The yang was that I had a hunch the forces against me weren't wholly imaginary. Hunches had propelled me through situations where cold logic would have left me dead.

I was measuring the possibilities when I noticed the three sinister looking characters standing on the far side of the gymnasium.

They were staring right at me. It wouldn't have been unusual in rural Japan, where white skin was as rare as a friendly native in New York. But this was Tokyo, and these stares didn't seem to be the type you chalk up to curiosity.

There are basically two modes of dress for yakuza—the swanky fashion-plate gangster costume and the bathhouse thug getup. The swanky ones were like those I'd encountered at the Purple Dragnet—flashy Italian suits, sunglasses, and hair gel, inferiority-complex jewelry. The second type preferred more traditional garb—black hopi-coats opened to the waist so you could see their tattoos, *hachimaki* headbands with the nationalist stuff like the Rising Sun, and *geta* sandals on their feet. Of course, every outfit is a uniform, a way of proclaiming to the world audience what role you play, and this is especially true with gangsters. They hate misunderstandings. That's what made these three guys across the gym so hard to figure.

They didn't fall into either of the above categories. In fact, they didn't look like any societal clique I could name. They wore identical black suits, none of which seemed to fit especially well. Even across the gymnasium, I could see that their black wing tips were scuffed and beaten. One of the men wore glasses and a fedora, while the other three all had short, unremarkable hair. They reminded me of Secret Service types after some severe budget cuts.

With their arms at their sides like soldiers, they stood anchored shoulder to shoulder, not speaking and hardly glancing around. Suddenly, as if they were a single organism, they simultaneously began making their way across the gym with short, pensive strides, heads bowed to the ground.

They were so weird I figured they had to be there for me.

It seemed to take them forever to cross the gym, but then all of a sudden they were at the bottom of the bleachers. The one with the glasses and the fedora stood directly in front of me, flanked on both sides by his comrades, who stood a half step behind him. I nodded respectfully and waited for him to make the first move.

"May I sit down?" he asked. He spoke slowly, his voice matter-of-fact.

"Sure," I said. "Plenty of empty seats."

He bobbed his head and made his way up the bleachers, choosing a seat directly to my left. His buddies waited until he was seated, and then walked up the bleachers and sat down shoulder to shoulder, directly behind us.

"Mr. Billy Chaka, you look remarkably well for a man who has had such an eventful evening." He spoke like he had a black belt in manners.

I replied with a dumb grin. I was a master at it.

"I don't want to waste your time, Mr. Chaka, and under the present circumstances I hope you will forgive me for being so forthright."

"*Burei ko de hanashimasho,*" I said. Let us speak without formality.

"Very well. Her name is Orange Blossom. She must be found."

I was a little disappointed that the alluring and deceptive geisha had such a dull, trite moniker. It sounded right out of a comic book. I was expecting something more exotic like ... well, not Orange Blossom.

"In the spirit of mutual cooperation, I think it would be best if we combined our efforts, in order that we may work more productively toward our common goal. We think you have something to gain from this pursuit. As for us, the very livelihood of our organization depends upon finding this woman."

The spirit of teamwork was truly a force on all levels of Japanese society, it seemed. I thought about playing dumb some more, but sooner or later I was going to have to start getting some answers.

"I wonder, Mister ..."

"My name is not important."

"I wonder just what organization you represent."

By way of an answer, the man produced a metal cigarette case with a curious insignia etched in black on the cover. It wasn't any gangster crest I recognized, and I was fairly certain I hadn't seen it anywhere before. He let me study it a moment, then slipped the case back into his pocket in a smooth, soundless motion.

"Am I supposed to guess what you do?"

"What our organization does is not really important," he said. "What is important is that we reach some sort of agreement."

"I appreciate your concerns," I said respectfully, "but not having the wisdom you no doubt possess, I fail to see how I could be of much help to your organization."

The guy nodded reassuringly, showing off his manners again. I glanced at the other two sitting behind us. Their lids were sagging heavily over their dull eyes, like they were meditating on the nature of boredom.

"Like any organization, we have limited resources. Unforeseen emergencies can be very draining. And there are legal and ethical complications, political and religious issues to be considered. We have done the considering, and we have chosen you."

Legal and ethical complications weren't the kind of things that kept yakuza types awake at night. I was too confused to say anything.

"We have been very selective about where we choose to make our presence known. This is where you could help us. We have made many inquiries about you, and have found that you have a very broad face in Japan, especially for a *gaijin*."

"I know a few people. Lately, I've been meeting all the wrong kind."

"That is unlikely to improve in the immediate future. Orange Blossom is involved in a world you can't possibly imagine—"

"Don't fret over my imagination. I've seen enough to keep it well fed."

My interviewer didn't even raise his eyebrows, which would have been a spectacular display of agility compared with the other two. They looked as radiant as wax dummies.

"Very well. So it is agreed. You find her, and you bring her to us."

"Slow down. I don't recall agreeing to anything. Maybe I'm not interested," I said.

"We already know you are interested. She is a geisha. She's many other things, too—but this feature alone is enough to ensure your interest. We know you, Mr. Chaka."

"If you know me, you know I don't like to be pushed around. Sure, I like geisha—but I like lots of things. One of them is making my own decisions."

The man in the hat smiled and shook his head.

"I must speak frankly, Mr. Chaka. Your admiration of geisha is like an alcoholic's appetite for liquor. Your reason is severely constricted by your craving. Autonomy for you in this matter is limited to deciding which method you'll choose in seeking out Orange Blossom. The choice to ignore her is one you are incapable of making. All of this we know. We represent the best option and will enhance your own chances of success in this pursuit."

I was insulted, but he was probably right—I would go after Orange Blossom regardless. It was the guy's tone that upset me, treating my lifelong obsession as a simple, passionless fact. Still, there would be no harm in finding out just how badly they needed her.

"Your observations don't impress me," I said. "Even if I had some terminal geishaphilia, you haven't presented me with a single advantage of joining your little club."

"You may know many people, Mr. Chaka. I assure you that we know a great many more. You may think of yourself as a naturalized Japanese, but you will always be a foreigner. Life is hard enough when you belong here. We can make yours infinitely harder."

"Now you're hurting my feelings."

"It's just a fact. Xenophobia can be a useful tool. But let us not focus on the negative. Let's shift emphasis to the compensatory aspects of our proposal."

It was amazing the way the guy spoke. He went from thinly veiled threats to pitchman jargon without changing his inflection or letting even the smallest ripple of emotion break the utter placidity of his expression. It was like playing poker with a robot.

"What's the carrot?" I said.

"Two hundred and seventy-three thousand four hundred and four dollars and a two-year membership to the Joon Park Golf Club," he said. Matter-of-fact, just like everything he said.

"Two hundred and seventy-three thousand four hundred and four dollars? That's a nice round number. You take up a collection or something?"

"We run on a budget, just like any organization."

"I don't golf."

"The membership is transferable. It's worth over a hundred thousand dollars. You should have no trouble selling it."

That's what was on their side of the table. A payoff of over a quarter of a million and the privilege of walking around abusing a little white ball on a few acres of grass. What exactly was she worth, I wondered, in terms of the "stick"? A broken leg? My life? Or something more exotic, more painful...

It didn't matter, because my side of the table was completely empty. No stick, no carrot. Nothing. There was really no choice. Ever since Orange Blossom walked into the bar and into my life, there never had been.

"All right," I said with a shrug. I figured I'd play along for now, and when the time came I'd give them the slip. The path of least resistance.

"Very well," the man in the hat said. "We'll be in touch."

The guy stood up. His companions did likewise. Then all three of them bowed very deeply, going lower than reasonably expected. I felt honored, and then reminded myself that these guys, whoever they were, were using me to get to a beautiful geisha. Still, it was a nice gesture, and in this world, you take what you can get.

I bowed back to them, then they turned around and walked away in unison. I watched them stroll out of the gym and wondered where on earth three guys like that could possibly be headed.

The first day of competition was fairly slow. There were some very promising young hopefuls, but there were also a number of children who clearly didn't belong at this high level of competition. For the more elite, the day was spent quietly eliminating the untalented without making them look inept. In the traditional effort to conserve the opponent's "face," all of the matches were superficially close. Scores that could easily have been skunks were often settled by a mere point. This tradition forced the better combatants to become amateur actors, feigning rudimentary mistakes in order to give their opponents openings.

One particularly absurd match took over half an hour. A fighter named Hitaki was one of the favored two-crutch open sparring contenders. Getting a little carried away, he quickly got within one point of victory. But then his responsibility dawned on him. He became clumsy and slow, his attacks obvious and ill-timed. Still, his opponent took no initiative. Hitaki began to stumble around, almost swaying directly into his opponent. He took two penalty points by deliberately stepping out of bounds.

That helped even out the score. The problem was, if Hitaki took any more penalties, he would be disqualified from the match. So he grew even more desperate, trying to force his opponent to get just one more point to make the score 4–3 before striking the winning blow. But his opponent seemed content to just slowly move about the ring, never taking advantage of the openings Hitaki presented. Hitaki tried hurling his shoulder into the opponent's crutch, but the opponent dodged him. They circled each other like this for some time, Hitaki trying to somehow get himself hit, and his opponent steadfastly refusing to let him lose a point.

It became a very interesting match, an odd illustration of the way pacifism can frustrate the aggressor. Of course, such a tactic might not directly translate outside the ring. And in the end, Hitaki got close to his opponent and then flung himself to the ground in a grotesque pantomime of having been swept at the feet. A sympathetic and no doubt equally frustrated referee awarded the point, ensuring that Hitaki could now finish off his opponent without making him lose face.

After that, the match was over in mere seconds. The loser came off the mat with a cheeky grin, while Hitaki looked a little shaken. I made a mental note to think more about how this battle could later apply to my own situation.

Covering the tournament had been refreshing, even better than sleep. It made me remember that underneath it all, I was a still a writer—a writer for the most well-respected Asian teenage publication in the English language. I had my weaknesses—my love for geisha, my need of Sarah, my inopportune sense of humor, and my ability to get myself and those around me into life-threatening situations. But as I looked over my notes from the tournament, I was reminded that despite these failings, I was perhaps the best writer ever to cover the Asian adolescent martial-arts scene. That fact filled me with a renewed sense of confidence. I would find the geisha. And I knew that somehow I would be able to shake whoever the Man in the Hat represented.

If these men were somehow affiliated with the yakuza, I wouldn't have to worry about the safety of Hiro Bhuto or my driver Hirohito anymore. I wouldn't have to hide, but could return to my usual plush hotel. But first I needed to visit the less comfortable confines of the Tokyo Metropolitan Prison, where I hoped to learn certain things about a certain fire.

Hideaki Kawabata was serving a life sentence in the Tokyo Metropolitan Prison's "Dormitory of Atonement" because he had gotten a little too involved in student activism during college. A precocious student of both chemistry and electrical engineering, he was spending his college years like many Japanese—letting his hair down (literally and figuratively) and exploring radical politics. Unfortunately, his final year in college coincided with the building of the Narita Airport in 1979.

Narita Airport was a cause célèbre among Japanese radicals. They objected to the seizure of "peasant" farmland in order to build an airport whose function would be primarily to serve the international bourgeoisie. Japan had become affluent and worldly enough to make its children question affluence and worldliness. America had its '68 Democratic National Convention, France its May '68; and now, ten years later, a decade of Japanese student revolt would culminate in the violent clash over Narita Airport.

The numbers were easy enough to recall—during the Narita Airport Resistance of '79, a total of twenty-six bombings occurred. Thirty-two people were injured. Eight people were killed.

Hideaki Kawabata was found guilty of two of those murders. As he only manufactured the bombs, he could have escaped with a lesser charge. But evidence was lacking for the other suspects, and he became something of a scapegoat. It didn't help that he saw himself as a political hero and refused to renounce his beliefs and atone in the usual manner.

In the end, most of Kawabata's radical cohorts left their various causes, cut their hair, and joined the mainstream Japanese society they had railed against during their college years. The Narita Airport was built, and Kawabata began serving his life sentence as a historical footnote.

His conviction turned him into a rather humorless left-wing fanatic. It is hard to live out a life sentence as the result of youthful idealism, and it proved more comforting to Kawabata to make Marxism a lifelong pursuit to match his lifelong prison term.

When I was guided into the visitors' room and saw him sitting at the wooden table, my first impression was of how little he had changed since I'd last seen him. He was the same thin, bespectacled man whose expression remained serious without seeming introspective. He looked more like he was doing calculus in his head than dreaming of world revolution.

"Chaka, they didn't tell me you were my visitor. I would have brought some of my writings," he said in the closest tone to friendly he could find. Kawabata was always giving me obscure ranting tracts on "Youth's Role in Instigating Worldwide Revolution" and such things in hope that I would have them published in *Youth in Asia.* They were the rambling, didactic diatribes you'd expect. As a writer, Kawabata was a pretty good terrorist.

"Good to see you, Kawabata. You look like you've taken the dissolution of the Soviet Union and the entire eastern bloc pretty well." I liked goading Kawabata. He never knew whether I was kidding or trying to engage him in a debate.

"It was the natural end for an evil government that warped the ideas of Marx. Now that the Soviet Union no longer has its nose in everyone's affairs, true homegrown revolutions can prosper."

I wondered where he thought that was gonna happen, but I didn't want to upset him before I got what I came for. "Perhaps you are right. You should write something about it."

"I did. I sent it to you several months ago. Have you not read it?"

"I haven't been in the States for a while. Maybe I'll have my editor send it here. I'm very anxious to see your take on the current world situation."

I consider myself a decent liar when called for, but this was unusually hard. Thankfully, Kawabata didn't seem to notice my deception. He was too busy looking around to see if anyone was listening.

"I have discovered a secret communications system," he whispered. "An underground, worldwide computer network devoted to bringing down the system. Criminals, pedophiles, and all manner of revolutionaries can now share information. Best of all, it is completely unknown. The multinational corporate despots have no inkling of its existence."

"Is it called the Internet?"

"Quiet!" he said, looking over his shoulder again. "You're familiar with it?"

"Kawabata-san," I began, not wishing to bust his bubble, "I wish we could talk politics and technology all day, but I'm afraid I've come seeking your esteemed opinion on another matter. You've heard about Sato Migusho's death?"

"Sure. We get all the reactionary propaganda here," he answered woodenly. I took it he was referring to the big-three newspapers.

"What do you think about it?"

For the first time, his face lost a little of its rigidity. His eyes grew wider behind his glasses. It was apparent that despite all his political pretensions, his first love and true genius was for fire. He knew virtually everything about pyrotechnics and demolition, a hobby he'd also taken with him to prison. The last time I saw him, he was staying in a new cell as the result of a failed escape attempt using a bomb made out of common cleaning products.

The homemade device had blown a large hole in the wall just as Kawabata had planned, and he would have escaped were it not for one detail; Kawabata was restricted to a solitary, windowless cell, and he had no idea he was on the twelfth floor. Seeing he had miscalculated, he merely shrugged and lay down on his cot, enjoying the view for the first time in seventeen years.

"Well," Kawabata began. "I only know what was printed in the papers, but there seemed to be a few logistical problems. The paper said that the fire was caused by an explosive nitrate film print. I know for a fact that the National Archives will not loan films made of such a volatile substance. I tried it once. Wanted to light up some reactionaries with a print of *Intolerance.* No dice. And that was years ago. By now, they've converted almost all the nitrate to acetate, anyway."

"What if it was from his own private collection?"

"Was it?" Kawabata said. "There is no reason to have it. The newer prints look better, won't turn to soup as fast, and are far less dangerous. The only reason you'd want an old one would be if you were planning an 'accident.'"

"Interesting. Anything else?"

"That fire must have started at least an hour earlier than reported for it to be raging out of control by the time the firemen arrived. Nothing burns that fast, unless it had already been doused. Even then, the fire would have had to start earlier than they said."

This was something I hadn't thought about. If what Kawabata said was true, the fire would have to have started around the time my phone conversation with Migusho ended. Now I realized how silly it was to think that someone had gotten to Sato because of me. This was much bigger than me, probably even bigger than Sato.

"Whatever happened," Kawabata continued, "that wasn't any freak exploding movie. Whoever torched that place wasn't just playing with matches. No evidence left behind, no witnesses—at least living ones. I would have been proud of that one myself." Kawabata leaned back and almost smiled.

"Kawabata, you've been a greater help to me than you know. I'll do everything I can to get your work published when I return to the States." I tried to sound as insincere as I could. It's hard to lie to convicts because they are often such expert liars themselves, but I'd learned the trick of fooling them by acting as unbelievable as possible. If you deliberately act insincere, a good liar won't notice because they are too busy looking for dozens of subtler telltale signs. Zen and the art of lying.

Kawabata thanked me and I got up to leave. As the guard escorted him back to his cell in the Dormitory of Atonement, I called after him.

"Thanks again for taking time out of your day. I know you must be busy, what with planning the revolution and conspiring on the Internet and everything."

He winced at the very sound of the word, glancing at the guard to see if it had registered.

"When the revolution comes, Chaka," he said in all earnestness, "you will be remembered as a great hero for publishing my writings."

He showed just a hint of a smile as the guards led him back to his cell to plot the downfall of capitalism. The smile made me wonder if he'd meant his parting comments ironically, but I decided against it. It was too late in the game for Kawabata to discover the healing power of self-deprecation.

I was always a little depressed after talking with Kawabata. He was a guy who didn't recognize his own gift. His genius for fire was so innate it must have been genetic. But because this talent came so easy, he didn't value it. So instead of doing any number of things, like becoming an arson investigator, an explosives man for a mining company, a pyrotech for the movies—or even just a better terrorist—he had devoted his life to a political cause that didn't really suit him. By historical accident, his explosive talent had merged with a dying dogma and that was pretty much the end of the story for Kawabata.

As Shinto drove toward the hotel, I wondered how many stunted geniuses there were in the world, slaving away at pursuits they considered worthwhile, ignoring their latent talents.

I thought of the late Emperor Hirohito lying on his deathbed, correctly identifying a new strain of cherry tree by a blossom brought to him from the imperial court outside. In almost his final moment he revealed that, though born a supreme leader and godhead, in his heart of hearts he yearned to be a simple botanist, passing the days studying the beautiful specimens offered from nature's bounty. Of course, it was too late, both for Emperor Hirohito and Kawabata.

As the evening fell and the car meandered through the streets, I was reminded of a poem written by Ryoshuan, the seventeenth-century Buddhist monk.

I think of the people in this floating world
My face in my sleeve
Wet with tears

I wasn't crying or anything like that, but you get the idea.

Most of the real action of the tournament wouldn't take place until the quarterfinals. A lazier journalist would have just waited until then to get his scoop, but I've learned that the big stories are usually the little stories that happen off the mat, away from the fanfare surrounding the combat.

There were two potential blockbusters in the making this year. Yoko Torikata, flamboyant nineteen-year-old actress and one-armed wunderkind, was competing for the last time. She was a gifted and controversial young woman, and in my opinion, a superficial, pretentious brat. But she could fight, and I had to admit her body spoke for itself. It spoke loudly. It wouldn't shut up. She would get plenty of ink no matter how she fared in the competition.

The other promising headline grabber was the rumored return of Master Yado, easily the most revered living figure in handicapped martial arts. During WWII, Yado amputated his own right leg to avoid serving in the military and spent the next fifteen years secretly developing his own lethal fighting style. The result was *magari-yari-do*—Way of the Three-Pronged Spear. Inspired by the ancient weapon rather than teaching its use, *magari-yari-do* was the most innovative, deadly martial-arts discipline ever developed by a pacifist. Master Yado soon became the most highly sought after martial-arts instructor in the world, but he insisted on taking only handicapped students. When he discovered that prospective pupils were amputating their own legs to qualify for his school, he abandoned the world of martial arts altogether.

Now he lived a secluded life near Mount Yariga, and almost every year there was a rumor that he was to return. Every other year I held a cautious hope that the rumor was true.

Sato Migusho and I had a standing bet about Master Yado's return. If he returned on an even year, Sato had to show me outtakes he'd saved of actress Suzi Murimo in the nude, cut from his 1979 film *Sex Up the Hotrod, Baby!*—a second-rate rip-off of the third-rate *Cannonball Run.* It was the only nude footage ever shot of Murimo, and Sato told me she'd made the most of it.

On the other hand, if Master Yado returned on an odd year, I had to violate a lifelong abstinence by playing a full eighteen holes of golf with Sato. This year was an odd one, but Sato would never see me tee off.

As the car neared the gym, I reread a letter I'd brought from a young filmmaker named Brando Nabiko who had written to me back in Cleveland. After gushing over how he'd read everything I'd ever written and all the usual fan stuff, he'd let it drop that he was a friend of Sato's and would be working on a documentary for NHK covering the tournament. He knew I would be there and said it would be an honor to meet me, etc. I didn't think much of it at the time, but now that Sato was dead, any person associated with him suddenly became interesting. Perhaps this Nabiko would have some clues as to what really happened. I had nothing to lose in trying to find out.

It also occurred to me that I'd never really asked Shinto, perhaps the last person to see him alive, about Sato. I decided to start with general, conversational questions.

"Say, Shinto, how was it working for Sato, anyway?"

"Well," he began, "I liked it all right."

That was it.

"I bet you've met a lot of movie stars."

"Some," he said, never taking his eyes off the road.

"I bet some pretty powerful people have been in this very car."

"I guess so."

I slumped back into my seat, defeated, and decided to let it rest for now. Some people have no sense of celebrity. Maybe immunity to fame is an occupational hazard for chauffeurs.

Still, his reticence was odd given his vocation. I'd been in all kinds of conversations with Japanese chauffeurs. I had one try to convince me of the moral superiority of dogs over cats. Another told me a funny story about driving Arthur Miller to the Japanese opening of *Death of a Salesman*. Some drunken American GI had him confused with Henry Miller and kept asking if he "really did all that shit in *Tropic of Cancer.*"

I'd met all sorts of drivers, and although some were quiet, none were as conversationally challenged as Shinto Hirohito. Of course, none had mustaches that looked as stupid as his, either, so maybe his silence meant no more than silence means.

Contemplating the meaning of silence, however, would have to wait. The renovated hangar loomed ahead, as did hordes of nervous teens.

When I arrived at the gym, I spotted the camera crew right away. They were in a corner setting up lights, and two of them seemed to be arguing. I made my way over, maneuvering through a group of wheelchair athletes waiting for their match times to be posted. As I drew closer, I could hear what all the fuss was about. A paunchy little man with a face like an overinflated red balloon was listening to the gaunt fellow on his left trying to explain something. It looked like a

Japanese version of Abbott and Costello discussing their next scene.

"You want the banner in the shot? Fine. But we'll need more lights if you want it in focus, and we'll have to use different gels, we'll have to get another light reading and retape the marks. It will take more time," the thin man said.

"The match starts in two hours. I need the interview in thirty minutes. And I need the banner in the shot. Make it happen."

I gathered from his overbearing manner that he was either the King of Siam or the director, and Siam didn't exist anymore.

"Sir, I don't think that is very realistic," the tall one said. I pegged him as the cinematographer.

"What does moviemaking have to do with 'realistic'?" the director snorted. "Besides, you're a documentary crew. People make movies in the middle of wars and in goddamn jungles crawling with poisonous friggin' snakes and shit and you can't even shoot in a gym?"

Now it was the tall one's turn to lose his patience.

"Nobody demands a deep-focus dolly shot in the middle of the jungle. It's unwise to piss off the crew with all the hungry lions hanging around."

I was enjoying their little spat. This sort of open disagreement was all but unseen in Japanese professional society. Movie types.

Looking around to see if anyone else was as amused as I was, I spotted a guy a short distance away loading film into the camera. I strolled over to him, certain it was Brando Nabiko. A good journalist knows his fans on sight.

"So," I said, surprising him a little, "which one is right?" He hardly glanced up at me as he expertly snapped the film cartridge into place.

"The director is right. It would be a more impressive mise-en-scène with the banner. But the cinematographer is also right. We could never pull it off with our time constraints. Besides, this is a documentary for NHK, not a samurai epic." He shook his head as he looked over at the debate.

"What happens if they're both right?" I asked.

"Nakato, the cinematographer, will give in to the director, Tonda. He'll finally say something like, 'I think I know a way we can pull it off.' Then he won't change a thing. He'll just shoot it the way we've planned all along."

"And Tonda won't be upset?"

"The important thing is that Tonda appears to be in charge in front of the rest of the crew. Nakato will always appear to agree with Tonda in the end, no matter how unrealistic his demands. There are more cinematographers than there are films to work on, so it is very important not to be difficult. In fact, sometimes the cinematographer will instigate a minor disagreement with the sole purpose of backing down just to demonstrate his flexibility."

No sooner had the young man said this than I looked over my shoulder to check in on the conversation.

"Now I understand," said Nakato, nodding. "I'm sorry, perhaps I wasn't listening closely."

"Then the shot can be done?" Tonda said imperiously.

"It will require only a few minor adjustments. I'll get right on it." Tonda merely nodded and waddled off triumphantly. Nakato turned around and shrugged. Nabiko started screwing a lens onto the camera.

"You trying to get in the film business or something?" Nabiko asked.

"No. I'm a writer."

"A screenwriter?"

"A real writer. A journalist."

He stopped messing with the lens, and gave me the twice over.

"You are Billy Chaka?"

I nodded.

"Wow, I love your stuff. I've been a subscriber to *Youth in Asia* since I was a thirteen. You really are Billy Chaka?"

"Did you think I'd look different?"

"You don't look much like Freddy Taechiba..." He laughed.

"Freddy who?"

"He was going to play you in *Tokyo Suckerpunch*. Of course, that was before the accident..." He trailed off, losing himself for a moment. "Forgive me, Mr. Chaka. I have not properly introduced myself. My name is Brando Nabiko." He bowed deeply and extended his hand in an international mixed greeting. I returned the gesture, wondering what the hell the *Tokyo Suckerpunch* was all about.

"I know who you are. I got your letter. In fact, Sato Migusho spoke very highly of you, and insisted that I make an effort to meet you while I was covering this tournament," I lied. And smiled.

He winced visibly at the mention of Sato's name. Maybe mentioning dead people on a shoot violated some cinematic superstition, or maybe it was just that Sato had only died yesterday. I decided to change the subject.

"How did you end up with a name like Brando?" I asked.

"I dunno exactly. The story is that Brando was supposed to be one of my father's favorite actors."

"Good thing Pops wasn't a Fatty Arbuckle fan."

He chuckled and took a peek through the viewfinder of the camera. "You know," he said, growing more somber, "Sato was very excited about doing the film about you. He told me he thought it would be the crowning achievement of his career. I was excited, too. It was to be my first big feature as a cinematographer. I was probably gonna even do some second-unit directing. Now I guess we'll never know."

Just then, Tonda came waddling angrily back toward the crew.

"All right everybody. Your laziness has paid off. Li-Ang's sensei says there is no time for an interview now, you've taken too long setting up. She must prepare herself for the match, so I've lost my moment with the favorite for the advanced freestyle open wheelchair kata competition. Everyone take lunch. Maybe you can do that right." Tonda's eyes burned inside his fat little head. I wondered if there was some sort of film-school course that taught directors how to throw temperamental fits. "Everyone back in an hour to set up on the third sparring stage."

He turned around to storm away, but the effect was ruined when he smacked his head on an extended gobo arm.

"Goddamn!" he shouted, clutching his head with one hand and sending the lighting stand to the ground with the other. Tonda the angry bundle raced off the set while his crew respectfully stifled their laughter.

"So, Brando, "I asked, "have I just witnessed a real-life frustrated genius?"

"No"—Nabiko laughed—"a great director would never have run into the gobo arm. It is said that Ozu never once bumped into any lighting apparatus, so vast was his knowledge of the filmmaking process." Nabiko grinned conspiratorially at me.

So far, I liked this assistant cameraman just fine.

"You wanna grab a bite to eat or somethin'?" I said in my inept impression of Marlon Brando mumbling Japanese. Nabiko looked confused, confirming my own suspicions of my talent as an impressionist.

"That'd be great. We must hurry, though," Nabiko replied.

As we made our way out of the auditorium, I spied the three weird men in black perched at the top of the stands like rigid vultures. The Man in the Hat sat in the middle, his motionless pals on either side of him. As I passed, he nodded down at me, his head moving slowly. The subtle gesture was unnerving, even ominous.

I didn't let it bother me too much, though. Omens were for old women and peasants.

We walked to a nearby restaurant called Nice Catch. It was a combination American-style sports tavern and traditional sushi bar—perhaps the very embodiment of modern Japan, if you're a fan of convenient platitudes.

We took off our shoes and our hostess approached. She was wearing a silk white Yuzen kimono worth barrels of yen and a Yomiuri Giants cap worth maybe twenty bucks. She led us to our table, and bade us take a seat on our mats, which were actually Denver Bronco bleacher cushions. I looked around at the *suiboku* paintings and closed-circuit televisions showing WWF pro wrestling.

"Quite an ambience."

"Yes." Brando sighed. "Some older Japanese find it almost blasphemous. Most younger Japanese find it too unhip."

"What do you think?"

"Well, the food is good enough," he said.

I appreciated Nabiko's sense of the bizarre. It would take one to fathom the situation I was in. Of course, I wasn't going to get into that with him now. But the kid seemed all right and it put me at ease.

"How well did you know Sato?" I asked, trying to sound casual.

Nabiko stopped looking at the menu and locked eyes with mine.

"I've seen every movie he's ever made, many of them dozens of times. I've read every scrap of paper ever written about him. I've talked to dozens of people he's worked with, and people who knew him in a...*nonprofessional capacity,* shall we say. I spent three years writing to him, and even tried to sneak onto a set while he was shooting near Kobe when I was a teenager. I guess you could say I was obsessed."

"Well, I know how teenagers are about their idols. It's natural," I said—although I wasn't sure it was. "Your persistence must have finally paid off."

"Not really. Meeting him was dumb luck more than anything else. Dumb luck and a lot of hard work," he said, taking a sip of his water. "Forgive me, I am being obtuse. Do you really want the whole story?"

"Stories are my business," I said.

Brando took another sip of his water, paused briefly, and then plunged headlong into the story.

"Like I said, I was obsessed. With movies in general, but with his films in particular. For a time, all I did was watch movies. Nothing else was worth the effort. I was a failure in school and a social zero, and all of a sudden I was nineteen and didn't have a thing going for me. I left my house, or I was kicked out—I honestly can't remember and it doesn't really matter. I was just a kid in Tokyo, like millions of others. Looking back, it was probably only my cowardice that kept me out of any serious trouble."

"How did you get by?"

"I got a job at a movie theater. The owner was a friend of a friend of my uncle. My uncle was a nice guy and felt sorry for me. He got me a job, and helped me get a cheap place to take off my shoes."

"Movie theater, huh? Must have been heaven."

He frowned gloomily. "It was hell. Two years I worked there, and all we ever showed were second-run, third-rate American films. No offense. Big explosions, big tits, and cops who said smart-ass things while they killed ugly criminals. It was almost enough to cure me of my fixation with the movies forever. I was ready to quit the job, I didn't care what happened. Then one day—Wednesday, April fourteenth—my life changed forever.

"I was working alone that afternoon. It was during *hanami,* the cherry blossom festival. The kind of day that respectable people spent at picnics looking at the cherry trees and getting drunk. We had a real stinker, so I was in for another slow day. The boss took off for a while to hit the *pachinko* machines—he wasn't the type to look at cherry trees—and left me to sell the tickets, sell the popcorn, and run the projector. At the rate we were doing business, it wasn't even enough to keep me distracted. It was about five minutes until show time and no one had shown. Then, right as I'm about to lock the door and go into the back to grab a smoke—this guy walks in by himself."

"Sato?"

"In the flesh. Of course, I knew he caught a matinee every Wednesday no matter what part of the world he was in, but I never thought he'd walk into this particular dive on this particular day."

"You must have flipped." I chuckled.

"I was totally calm. It was like I had been half expecting this all my life. My feeling was more like, 'Well, it's about time, old man.' I addressed him as Mr. Migusho and bowed, which I never did back then. But I was also cool, treating him like just another guy. Respectful but not obsequious. I warned him the picture was a real stinker, and said maybe his money could be better spent on cigarettes or goldfish—"

"The line from his movie *Shadow of a Woman*."

"Right. Funny thing was, he didn't recognize it. He just kind of looked at me and then told me he'd seen this movie twice already. I said, 'This piece of junk?' He laughed and nodded. He invited me to come down and watch it with him once I got the projector rolling. You better believe I got the projector running in a hurry.

"So I sat down next to him, just as casual as could be. We split a popcorn and watched the flick. The whole time he just kept saying, this guy, this actor, is gonna be a star. He's going to be huge, he'd say, and shake his head. He seemed to think it was troubling and amusing at the same time, but of course I can only say that now. Then I didn't know what to think of it. Do you know what the movie was?"

"Haven't a clue."

"*Bio-Dome*."

Stephen Baldwin or Pauly Shore? I wondered. Scary either way. Brando kept laughing. The waitress looked at us suspiciously as she brought our food.

"I closed down the theater for the second matinee, and we just talked movies. He told me how he got certain shots, certain performances from his actors. I asked more questions than I had any right to, but I was trying to impress him with my scant knowledge. I think it was my enthusiasm more than anything else that made an impression. At any rate, he offered me an entry-level position at the studio as a gofer of sorts. He said he could get my foot in the door, but after that it was up to me to make something of myself.

"I busted my hump for the next eight years, doing every-thing imaginable. From set painting, to Xeroxing scripts, to taking care of Anna Wong's pet monkey. I learned about screenwriting, pyrotechnics, light rigging, and even did some kendo for a crummy *jidai-geki* sword scene in *Flashing Steel in Spring.* I came into contact with Sato only sporadically. You can be assured that he made things no easier for me than for anybody else. I asked everybody I met about the details of Sato's life and his work, to the point that I was the butt of a few jokes. I didn't care. I was following in the footsteps of the master.

"Finally, about two years ago, he calls me into his office. He says everyone is pleased with my work and my dauntless enthusiasm for even the most modest of tasks. Then he said, I'll never forget it, 'But if you and I are ever going to make a movie, you have got to learn the art of the camera.' A movie with Sato Migusho!

"From then on, I was a cameraman. I won't bore you with my credits, but I helped make a lot of bad films at least look good to the eye."

I nodded distractedly. The whole time Brando was speaking, Pauly Shore's goofy face kept popping into the picture. I couldn't shake him. Maybe Pauly was trying to tell me something.

Then I got it. Brando said he first met Sato over eight years ago—but *Bio-Dome* was a fairly recent movie. It didn't make sense. Could he have been thinking of *Encino Man*? Possibly *Jury Duty*? In the end, it didn't matter and I wasn't gonna make a big deal out of it. I told Pauly to beat it and focused on Brando.

"About eight months ago, Migusho called me to his office again. He didn't say anything at first, only pushed a script across the desk and said, 'Read it. This is going to be my comeback film.' And then he smiled at me and added, 'I'd like you to be the second-unit director.' My life's ambition was within reach."

"And that script was *Tokyo Suckerpunch*?"

"You got it."

"That's a remarkable story," I said, dipping my sushi in the *wasabi*. Nabiko hadn't touched his food.

"I guess you know how it ends." He sighed.

I nodded. Sato always did have trouble with endings.

"You knew Sato pretty well. Did he have any enemies?"

"I knew him well enough to know he would never do something as stupid as burning down his house with an old film, if that's what you mean," he said.

"Did he have problems with the yakuza?"

"Well," Nabiko mused, "I don't think anyone could be in the business and not have problems with the yakuza once in a while."

"The film business that rife with organized crime?" I knew the answer but wanted to hear it from Nabiko.

"Not as bad as Hong Kong. And not the actual business itself. But certain... *support industries*," Nabiko said, and gave me a knowing wink. I got it, but the best way to get info from people is to play respectfully stupid. Journalism 101.

"Support industries?" I asked, making a slight pronunciation error just for effect.

"Prostitution. Drugs. Gambling. Showbiz vices."

"And Sato was involved in this?"

"Everyone is involved. If it means turning a blind eye, this is still involvement. And there is always the question of finances."

"How do you mean?"

"Sato hadn't produced a moneymaker in years," said Nabiko slowly. "Yet he kept coming up with the funding for more pictures. No studio is loyal enough to keep throwing money at a guy who makes unpopular films."

"You think the yakuza were financing his films?"

"It's a popular theory. I can't say one way or the other."

"Why would the yaks deal with him if the films didn't get returns? What's in it for them?"

"I'm not the one to ask," he said. He seemed to be growing uncomfortable with the yakuza questions, so I let it drop for now.

I paid the bill, which was printed on a baseball scorecard. Brando had done so much talking his plate was pretty much untouched. I caught him nervously glancing at the scoreboard clock next to an old autographed picture of pro wrestler Giant Baba.

"Let's get back to the tournament. I wouldn't want that squatty little director to begin without you." I smiled at him, hoping I hadn't insulted him by ridiculing his boss. I wasn't too worried, though. One thing my travels had taught me—worldwide, everyone enjoys ridiculing the boss. It's always a safe subject.

As we left, I thanked Brando Nabiko for sharing his knowledge. I also requested a favor.

"I'm dying of curiosity on many levels," I said. "You can help me on at least one."

"You name it," he said. "I'll do anything I can for the guy who wrote 'The Artist and the Detective.'"

He really was a fan. I'd written that piece on Japan's most famous death-row inmate and his charismatic nemesis so long ago I'd all but forgotten it. I smiled in recognition.

"I need a copy of that script he was working on."

"I'll see what I can do." Nabiko frowned. "It was a pretty secretive piece of work. He had it printed on red paper so it couldn't be photocopied. He never let the thing out of his sight. I even had to read it in front of him, in his office."

"Just do what you can," I said.

"Fair enough," he said with a smile. This Brando kid was all right.

I decided to skip the rest of the day's tournament. Normally, I wouldn't want to miss a single kata—but right now there was just too much on my mind.

Sato Migusho had been writing a script about me, without my knowledge or collaboration—even though I'd turned him down three times previously when he tried to secure the rights. So he must have known something I didn't. Or perhaps he had something to offer me which he knew I couldn't refuse—which could be where Orange Blossom came in.

I hoped to ease my mind with a visit to Ihara—the private dick who'd set me up years ago in Yokohama, nearly getting me killed by a gang of angry marines. It's a long story. Suffice it to say that Ihara's preference for what he called "proactive" surveillance techniques involved setting me up with military wives and getting the results on film. I was younger and stupider then, and I couldn't really blame Ihara for taking advantage.

I'd settled the score long ago, but I could never really trust the guy since. Still, he was my best source of information about the seedy world of organized crime. If he didn't know what this weird band of yakuza types were up to, I could rest assured things weren't as dangerous as they seemed.

. . .

Ihara's office was near the intersection of Roppongi-dori and Chichukai-dori, right across the street from Tokyo's first photography museum. Appropriately enough, it was called "The Photography Museum." I'd visited the place before, and remembered its collection of pen-and-matchbox espionage cameras. Ihara had chosen an ideal place to situate his office. If he required inspiration, he need only walk across the street.

Shinto dropped me off without a word, as was his style. The guy was starting to give me the creeps.

I walked up the stairs to the seventh floor, where Ihara's office was located. I'd made it a habit never to ride elevators, no matter how high the climb. Anyone can get cornered in an elevator, no matter how clever they imagine themselves. And once you're stuck in an elevator, there's no escape. Even when you're in an elevator alone, it is no guarantee of safety. Someone could be a couple floors up in the shaft, eyeing the cables with a devilish grin and powerful scissors. These scenarios were probably a little paranoid, but I had a more practical reason as well—earthquakes. I was, in fact, in a stairwell the exact moment the devastating Kobe earthquake first registered on the Richter. Of course, I was thousands of miles away, in Cleveland, but it still seemed like some sort of warning.

I was breathing pretty hard by the time I reached the seventh floor, which reminded me of another advantage of the stairwell—exercise. I walked down the hallway toward Ihara's office. He'd renamed his firm since the days in Yokohama, perhaps to appeal to the more sophisticated Aoyoma-Roppongi clientele. No longer was it simply Ihara Investigations. Now it was called SpyLens.

When I walked in the door, the secretary jumped. She tossed the comic book she'd been reading into the top desk drawer and glanced at an electronic panel on her desk.

"You didn't take the elevator," she said.

"Nope. Don't trust 'em."

She was a mildly attractive type, but not a real headturner. Pretty much every business had one. *Jimusho no hana,* they were called—office flowers. This one was the type of girl you'd want your friend to marry—cute enough but nothing to make you jealous.

"There is nothing wrong with our elevators. They are in complete working order."

I couldn't tell if she was just being funny, or if she really thought that I distrusted the mechanics of the device. Either way, she was by far the rudest office flower I'd encountered in Japan. I felt like I was back in Cleveland.

"Let's just say I have a thing about elevators," I said, hoping the discussion could now move forward.

"You shouldn't have a *thing* about this elevator," she said, dashing my hopes. "I have worked here for three years and I take the elevator every day, four times a day. Up for morning, down for lunch. Up for the afternoon, down to go home. That means I have ridden this elevator at least"—she rolled her eyes back—"three thousand five hundred times—without a single problem."

"It's like that old saying," I offered. " 'The man who has never erred is dangerous.' Same goes for elevators."

"Hmmph!" she snorted. "Okay, fine. I suppose you don't drive cars either, you hate the subway and won't use a microwave oven. You probably don't live in a house because it could collapse at any moment, having never erred!"

The only woman who talked to me like this was Sarah. My heart jumped with a little pain.

"How did you get over to Japan anyway? You couldn't have taken a plane—it could go down at any moment. And a boat could have sunk the second you left the harbor! You must have swum all the way from America, or England. You look like you're from England . . . but I don't think an Englishmen would swim all the way. He might catch a cold."

I turned around to make sure that I had walked into the right office, fearing perhaps I'd stumbled into some dominatrix den for abusing corporate kingpins. But the sign on the door read SPYLENS in plain old English.

"I'm here to see Mr. Ihara," I said.

"Really? And all along I thought you were the elevator inspector."

"You ever want to live in America, I could get you a good job with the postal service."

"Are you a cop?" she blurted, lowering her tone.

"How many American cops do you know in Tokyo?"

"I don't know any cops in Tokyo," she replied coolly. "Nor anywhere else. They're bad for business."

"I'm a journalist. We've been very good for your business," I said, though she probably had no way of knowing the Yokohama episode I was referring to. It didn't matter. She was preoccupied with the little electronic panel next to the phone.

"How come you didn't take the elevator?" she whined in a high, chirpy voice. If the Tokyo police hired her for interrogations, the conviction rate might reach 100 percent. Maybe even 120 percent.

I was stuttering something or other when Ihara popped his head out from behind a door.

"Is there a problem out here?" he asked, looking at his secretary and not noticing me.

"Yeah, there's a problem," I answered. "Your secretary seems to think there is a law against walking up stairs."

Ihara adjusted his focus to me, and only now did I notice the thick spectacles he wore. He'd probably gone blind from so many years of staring through telephoto lenses aimed through faraway windows in the dead of night. It took him a moment to recognize me.

"Billy Chaka," he said, obviously amused. "It's been a long time. Please, come in."

He turned and walked back into his inner office, leaving the door open for me to follow. As I passed his secretary, I met her scowl head-on. I resisted the urge to stick my tongue out at her, but just barely.

Keiji Ihara's office was a dreary, windowless cavern that looked more like the office of your average junior-high-school principal than the inner sanctum of a cutting-edge detective. There was a faded, airy photo of Prince Akihito taken back in his bachelor days framed in a high corner above an ancient metal file cabinet. Perfect to conceal a wide-angle camera. I settled into one of the cheap wooden chairs, if you could call it settling. Ihara's seat looked much cozier. It was one of those expansive leather reclining numbers right out of a catalog. To Ihara, it was just a prop. He preferred to stand imposingly behind his cluttered desk.

"So, Mr. Chaka," he began. "What brings you to Tokyo? Never mind. What brings you to SpyLens?" Ihara made a big deal out of the name.

"I've come to ask for your secretary's hand in marriage."

"Yes." He chuckled. "Well, I'm sorry about that. Ms. Yukio was just doing her job. You see, we have yet to install video cameras in the stairwells. She makes the logical assumption that anyone who would walk up seven flights of stairs must be trying to avoid the cameras in the elevators. She is just being cautious." There was a note of pride in his voice. Whether it was over his secretary or his elevator video systems, I didn't know. Then he switched courses.

"You really should ask for a raise," he said.

"You lost me, Ihara."

"Or some wardrobe guidance. In clothes like yours, it is always going to be a struggle to be taken seriously."

I glanced over myself quickly. Black wing tips, black pants, a thin black leather belt, and a decent white button-down shirt. Not exactly a clown suit.

Noting my confusion, Ihara cleared his throat and said, "They've done some remarkable things with color in the fashion industry."

"I'm sure," I said woodenly. Sarah used to call me the human yin-yang symbol. She tried buying me colored shirts—reds, blues, greens—but it never took. They made me feel like a flag.

"Besides," he said, sensing colored clothing was a touchy topic, "it's foolhardy to use the stairwells higher than the fourth floor. Everyone knows that." I had no idea what he meant, and said as much with my expression.

"Tsk, tsk...Billy '*Baka.*'" It was the term for "idiot" that rhymed with my name. "With your tendencies, I'd imagine you've made your fair share of enemies. Yet you would do something as foolish as using the stairs. Don't you see why stairs are much more dangerous than elevators?"

My opinion was unshakable, and Ihara's probably was, too. He enjoyed talking more than I did, so I just sat back and let him do it.

"Nobody takes the stairs past the fourth floor. The only people that do, do so only because they assume no one else will. Why? They don't want to be seen. Why? Because they are criminals, about to enact or having just enacted a crime."

Ihara paused to let his logic settle in. I thought about how guys who answer their own questions are usually the same guys who laugh at their own jokes. Guys who enjoy the hell out of themselves.

"Now, let us assume that you are lucky enough not to be the poor bastard that the crime was to be enacted upon. You just happen to be walking up the stairs, past the fourth floor, minding your own business as much as any nonelevator user can. Even then, you run the risk of passing the criminal on the stairs. And obviously, the perp doesn't want to leave any witnesses who may give a physical description, or attest to the suspicious fact that said party was seen in a stairwell. Of course, the defense would attempt to discredit the character of the witness during the trial by the very fact that he, too, was in the stairwell past the fourth floor, and doesn't that in and of itself bespeak of criminal tendencies, etc., etc....But this is a legal risk that few criminals would have either the guts or the foresight to consider. Why? No witness is still better than a discredited one. For who knows, there might be a sympathetic stairwalker among the jury.

"So most likely, the criminal would try to kill you there in the stairwell. Even if, in his haste, he did not succeed in perishing you outright, there is a good chance that even a minor scuffle could leave you in fairly serious condition, especially if the bandit was able to push you over. Falling down stairs is a lot more hazardous than being pushed to the ground in an elevator car.

"What's more, if you were injured in the stairwell, chances are that you wouldn't receive help for a long time. Why? Nobody takes the stairs above the fourth floor. And even if your injuries left you strong enough to cry out, most stairwells are virtually soundproof. On the other hand, my secretary is only one of the one hundred and twenty employees in this building who take the elevator at least four times a day. How many daily trips is that?"

"Four hundred and eighty trips," I said, stealing his thunder.

"Exactly," he grumbled. "Of course, that's assuming they always travel separately, which they don't. But close enough to prove the point that if you were injured in the elevator, you would receive almost immediate medical attention, particularly if you were lucky enough to be attacked over lunch break. In the stairwell, who knows how long it might take you to be found. Your best bet would be the night janitor, but as it is an accepted fact that no one takes the stairs, he may neglect to clean them for a number of days. If he is a particularly cautious janitor, he may not venture into the stairwell for weeks, mindful that it functions primarily as a criminal thoroughfare."

As mind-numbing as it was, I was fascinated that someone had actually thought about it in such great detail. Paranoia-wise, I was out of my depth. He continued, seemingly oblivious to my presence.

"The second person you're most likely to meet as you lie dying in the stairwell is a second criminal! And you'd be lucky, in your weakened condition, if they didn't finish you off for good."

He chuckled with a flourish. Then he drew a breath and sobered himself, lowering his tone. "So you see, the elevator is actually much safer than the stairs, if one is trying to avoid being murdered." Ihara crossed his arms and swayed back on his heels like Mussolini.

I was impressed with his lecture, but perhaps not for the reasons he intended. In a country with one of the lowest murder rates in the entire world, what could possibly make a person dwell on such paranoid trivia as whether stairs or elevators are the safer vertical transportation apparatus? (Ihara's logic notwithstanding, I still had to stick with stairs. You'd have a better chance of not getting attacked at all, since you could run away, an impossibility when confined in an eleva-tor.) I decided that Keiji Ihara must have gotten himself in some sticky situations lately for his mind to be turning toward murder avoidance techniques. And as for myself...

"You've convinced me," I lied. "From now on, I'm an ele-vator man."

"You'll live longer for it," he said. "Now, what brings you to SpyLens?"

"I need some information on an organization."

"What is the name of this organization?"

"I don't know. This is all I have to go on." I reached into my pocket and produced a crude sketch I'd done of the crest that appeared on the cigarette case shown to me by the Man in the Hat. It was no work of art, but all the key elements were there.

Ihara glanced at it, and then looked up at me. His face did a funny little dance. He looked at the paper one more time, then he reached one hand under his desk.

Suddenly the wall on my left swung open. Before I knew what was going on, my head was slammed into the desk. Then it was jerked up by the hair, and I focused my eyes just in time to see a thickset, angry little guy put his fist through my face. My head snapped back, was caught from behind, and slammed back into the desk.

Everything was a blurry red. The taste in my mouth told me I was bleeding, but my face was too numb to tell if it was my lips or nose—besides, what was the difference? I was being held by the arms on both sides by two medium-sized, stocky guys. The smaller one who'd punched me just a moment ago was now behind me. He shoved the chair hard into the back of my knees and I was forced down into the seat.

"You still sore about Yokohama?" I blubbered. "I thought we were all square." As I spoke, my hands were cuffed to the chair.

"Who sent you?" Ihara demanded.

"Strong wind," I replied. "Blew me right in the door."

Ihara nodded toward the little guy again. The little guy punched me in the face, sending me and the chair reeling on our backs. The two other guys picked me and the chair up again. Blood was gushing from somewhere and someone would have a lot of cleaning up to do when I left.

"Billy, you don't want to do this all day, believe me." Ihara sounded sincerely concerned. I glanced to my left, and spotted the concealed door through which his goons had sprung. I wondered if this was punishment for taking the stairs.

"I'll ask again—who sent you?" Ihara glared across the desk at me. I thought about slipping into unconsciousness, but decided this wasn't the time.

"I sent me," I said, and turned my head to spit some blood out. The little pugilist looked over to Ihara, anxious for permission to punch me again. Ihara signaled for him to wait.

"Why?" Ihara said. I waited for him to answer it all by himself, but he didn't. It struck me that I'd asked the wrong guy for help.

"I need information. It's personal."

"These people aren't the personal sort," Ihara said, softening a bit.

I spit again to buy time. Going into the whole geisha quest story at this point was a bad idea. It sounded too farfetched and would probably only earn me another amateurish blow to the face.

"I think they have a contract out on me," I said.

"If these guys wanted you dead, you'd already be ashes in an urn." He smirked.

"Who are they?"

"Billy, I don't want to have this conversation."

"You owe me, Ihara," I said, hoping to appeal to his sense of *giri*. It was like trying to appeal to a shark's sense of compassion.

Ihara sighed, and motioned to his helpers. They shuffled back to their hiding place behind the false wall. I wondered if they just stood in a closet all day or if there was actually a room in there, but I couldn't turn my head far enough to get an answer.

"I may owe you something, I may not," Ihara leaned over and whispered to me. "But if you're up against these guys, all obligations are canceled."

"You better give me something to go on because I'm not leaving until you do. You're gonna have to work those closet goons overtime. It takes me a long time to shut up when I don't feel like it, and I can bleed with the best of them. I'm kind of a pain in the ass that way."

It was about as threatening as I could be, my hands cuffed behind my back and a few punches behind.

"Where did you see this insignia?"

I came halfway clean and told him about the tournament. Ihara glanced around nervously and shook his head, hissing short breaths between his teeth.

"These yakuza from Tokyo?" I asked.

"Don't be an ass, Billy. They're not yakuza."

"They're politicians?"

"No, they're something much worse," he said. "They are a religious order."

"Scientologists," I said. My head ached and nothing was making sense. Being strapped to a chair, beaten and bewildered, was not how I'd planned to spend the afternoon.

"It's not funny, Chaka. I don't know where you saw that insignia, but I wouldn't show it to anyone. I say this to you as a friend and lover of humanity."

I needed a new kind of friend or humanity didn't stand a chance. I thought it over, and decided Ihara wasn't just blowing smoke and pummeling me for kicks. He was not a cruel man, just a businessman. In his business, the difference was subtle.

"At least tell me what these guys are called," I said.

"Not a chance. It wouldn't mean a thing to nine hundred and ninety-nine people out of a thousand, but you mention it to that one guy and you're liable to be beaten to death with your own severed head."

"They came to me—"

"That's your funeral, pal, not mine. I don't want to hear another word about it."

"All right," I said. "Can't help being curious."

"If there is one thing this business has taught me, it is that curiosity is overrated," Ihara said.

That and the thing about elevators.

"What's with those guys anyway?" I asked, indicating the punks behind the door. "Do they just stand back there all day waiting for one of your clients to mention the wrong clan?"

"They live in there," he said nonchalantly, as if they were merely his neighbors.

"In the closet?"

"It is more than a closet. There is a bunkbed, a cot, a toilet. It's free and space is limited in this city. I give them plenty of spending money, a place to stay. They watch out for me."

"Business must be booming if you need an in-house security force," I ventured. Ihara emerged from behind the desk and undid my handcuffs.

"They help me say things I can't always put into words."

I knew the feeling. Despite my fluency in several languages, there were a few things I'd like to communicate to Ihara in a nonverbal fashion. But it would have to wait.

He handed me a towel from his desk and I began wiping the blood from my face. Still a healthy red.

"I don't believe your story, Billy. At the same time, I can't figure out your angle, but it's none of my business. If it involves these people, you're on your own."

"I'm used to it." I reached into my pockets to make sure those thugs hadn't taken anything while they were working me over.

"I can't take your money because we never met," Ihara said. Did he think I was gonna pay him for being punched in the face?

"Take the stairs so no one sees you," he continued. I guess he wasn't so concerned with my safety anymore.

"Nice seeing you, Ihara." I shrugged and turned to walk out. I paused by the concealed door in the wall and gave it a quick rap with my knuckles. I heard a shuffling noise inside as someone made their way to the door. It opened slightly, and I could just see a crop of black hair sticking out.

"Yeah?" the guy behind the door started to say. I gave it a powerful side kick, sending the door smashing into the side of his head. There was a loud cry and I heard the body on the other side fall to the ground. I closed the concealed door, and walked out of Ihara's office.

I hoped it was the little guy.

I walked down the stairs as Ihara instructed and didn't run into any criminals or anybody else. Outside the building, Shinto was waiting. I had to admire his ability to always be curbside in this crowded city, and frankly I wondered how he managed it.

I got in the car, and he gave me the double glance in the rearview mirror. But of course he said nothing.

"I just got hit in the face," I told him.

"That so?"

I nodded. Then it was back to the hotel.

Ihara had definitely acquired an acute case of cult paranoia. It had spread through Japan after the subway gas attacks of 1995, making every religious organization that asked its members for any commitment greater than a check now and then seem fanatical and probably homicidal. Even so, Ihara's fear of being beaten to death with a severed head seemed a fairly severe reaction to some lurid headlines. It was strange, because Ihara was a pretty levelheaded guy. Yeah, he was paranoid—but his job consisted primarily of sticking his nose in other people's business and revealing unpleasant facts. A little caution was not unwarranted.

Whoever this strange insignia represented, they weren't yakuza. I believed Ihara on that one. They didn't look like yakuza and they didn't act like any yakuza I'd ever encountered. I wasn't sure about the secret, deadly religious cult part, but they were definitely not just citizens.

However, those thugs I'd pummeled at Bhuto's bar were undoubtedly 100 percent card-carrying, finger-chopping, Takakura Ken–watching yakuza to the core. Either coincidence had been working overtime, or they were also after Orange Blossom. Popular girl.

It was only just beginning to sink in what I'd gotten myself into. A dead friend, a beautiful woman, secret organizations, and well-known thugs. All I'd wanted to do was watch some martial arts and maybe take in a few *bunraku* puppet shows. Now this. Maybe Sarah was right to avoid Japan. Or maybe she was just avoiding me. Smart kid, either way.

I thought about all the more pleasant things I could be doing on my trip, then made myself stop. It was fruitless thinking. Instead, I just rode along, forgetting Sato and Orange Blossom and Ihara and damn near everything else—just letting my mind drift while outside the car, Tokyo did what cities do on an early evening in late autumn.

Back at the hotel, there were two messages waiting for me on the answering machine and two messengers waiting for me in the lobby.

There is something about yakuza that makes them stand out in any crowd. Even when dressed to the nines and trying to look respectable, it didn't work. They just had too much swagger, and the sort of outer confidence that told you they didn't care if they belonged in polite Japanese society or not, because they were lifetime members of the only club that mattered. Smart suits and nice watches didn't fool anyone. It was like putting a party hat on a crocodile.

The thinner one with the crew cut had his feet draped lazily over the coffee table as he reclined in a sofa chair and blew smoke slowly out his nose. The other one was leering over a *manga* called *Machine-Gun Virgin* and leaning against a column. He was older and had one of those ridiculous punch perms that were so popular with yakuza in the eighties.

I could have walked right on by without their noticing, but the nervous glances from the hotel desk clerk told me that these guys were here for me. So I just walked over without a word and stood right in front of them until they noticed me.

Finally, the one in the chair did. He leapt up and snubbed out his cigarette, snapping to like a sentry guard caught napping. The guy with the comic book was more relaxed.

"Mr. Chaka!" the younger one said.

"Yeah?"

He didn't seem to know what else to say, so I started to turn around to leave. The punch perm guy shot him a dirty look.

"Forgive his rudeness, Mr. Chaka. He just fell off the potato truck." The younger one seethed but said nothing. I turned back around.

"What do you guys want?"

"You weren't at the tournament this afternoon."

"No."

"We looked for you there."

"Yes?"

"And you were nowhere around—"

"You weren't there!" the young guy interjected.

Punchperm glared at him, and then turned back around to me. "We have something to discuss with you. Something urgent."

"Who the hell are you?"

"I'm just a guy. And he's a nobody," he said, pointing to his partner. "But we're here on behalf of someone very important."

"What does Mr. Important want with me?"

"I'm sure he'll tell you exactly what he wants from you," Punchperm said with a smirk. Then he handed me a card with a single word printed on it.

KWAIDAN

I knew all about Kwaidan. Everybody did. He was the aging leader of the Yamagama-gumi, one of Japan's most notorious crime syndicates. He had also been somewhat of a minor celebrity before he started pulling a Howard Hughes. Rumors ran the gamut. Some said he weighed four hundred pounds, while others said he was rail thin. It was said that he lived in constant fear of volcanoes, or earthquakes, or AIDS, or all three, depending on what tabloid you read.

"I thought Kwaidan was dead," I said to Punchperm.

"That's crap," he spat. Well, there was one rumor laid to rest.

"It's only asshole writers like you who spread such lies," Crewcut huffed.

It had been a long day, and I was in no mood to have my journalistic integrity insulted by some semiliterate goon. That's what made me say what I did.

"I didn't know you Matsuda-gumis could read," I deadpanned.

Matsuda were the Yamagama's hated rivals, their sworn enemies of the Japanese underbelly. Mistaking them for their counterparts was the best insult I could think of.

The older guy's eyes burned, threatening to catch his bushy hair on fire. The younger guy stepped forward, veins throbbing like tunneling worms in his skinny neck. His fists were clenched at his sides.

"What did you say?"

There are all sorts of silences, and this wasn't the kind you wrote haikus about. Nobody knew what would happen next, but I wasn't about to get suckerpunched twice in one day. On the other hand, I didn't want to lay out these creeps in the hotel lobby. It was a nice hotel, and there was a lot of tournament left to cover.

So I played the old standby—the *gaijin* card.

"Well, I thought yakuza you Matsuda clan? Mafia, yes?"

Crewcut glanced at Punchperm. Confusion was already dissipating their anger.

"I think," Punchperm began, his face cooling to a normal hue, "there has been some kind of misunderstanding."

"We're no fuckin' Matsuda-gumi!" Crewcut spat. Punchperm put up a hand to silence him.

"Only a fool or a *gaijin* would mistake us for those scumbags. I guess you are both. But I wouldn't make the same mistake again. You are liable to get another bump on your nose."

So they'd noticed.

"Or a fuckin' bump on your, um . . ." Crewcut sputtered.

"Go get the car," Punchperm said.

"It's right out front."

"Go sit in it, then."

"But . . ." He had nothing to say. Punchperm had rank, so Crewcut skulked off out of the lobby.

"I'm sorry about that guy." Punchperm shook his head. "He's just joined us, some new recruit from Kyushu. You know those southerners—they don't know the difference between friendly business and shakedowns."

"Which is this?"

"Come visit us tomorrow at our headquarters in Ikebukuro. Ask anyone who doesn't look respectable, they'll tell you where to find us. Don't make us come looking for you."

"What if I'm busy?" I asked.

"You'll be typing your future columns with just one hand," he said, and turned around to leave.

Yakuza say the cutest things.

The first message on my machine was from Brando Nabiko. He said he'd gotten hold of "the document in question" and to show up at the west exit of Shinjuku station at nine A.M. He said he'd find me. It was all hush hush like a spy film.

The second was from Sarah. It was hard to understand what she was saying, not because of any bad connection but because she was on so many drugs. Her speech was jumbled and slurred. She would babble out little machine gun bursts of nonsense and then remain silent for several seconds. I listened to the message five or six times, and I think at one point she said, "I wish I could hate you." But it might also have been, "A fish in a lake grew." After hearing it over and over, I still couldn't be sure. It was like listening to a record backward to find hidden messages.

I missed Sarah terribly. She had been with me ever since she'd walked into the *Youth in Asia* home office as an ambitious nineteen-year-old with a bad punk hairdo and an attitude to match.

Years had passed since then, but despite the many ways in which she'd changed, I still thought of her as the nineteen-year-old intern, the young beauty with a quick mind and quicker temper.

And that was part of the problem, part of the reason she refused to accompany me to Japan. She said she was sick of being the Tonto in my Lone Ranger lifestyle, and I couldn't really blame her. At the same time, I wasn't going to be trading in my mask and silver bullets—not as long as readers of *Youth in Asia* were still hungry for top-notch, shoot-from-the-hip stories about the fascinating microcosm of the Asian teen.

And not as long as there were mysterious geisha like Orange Blossom appearing, coaxing me to follow them into the black mist.

I had chosen a rather unfortunate place outside the Shinjuku train station to wait for Nabiko. I was seated just to the left of a series of vending machines that functioned like a coin-operated mini 7-Eleven. They were stocked with soft drinks, hard drinks, shaving cream, toothpaste, newspapers, comic books, and the latest OK!Heartache CD. I'd even seen machines that sold used underpants supposedly worn by Japanese schoolgirls. I bought enough to fill a whole suitcase once, just so when customs asked me if I had anything to declare, I could say, "Panties!" The payoff wasn't so great. The customs guy didn't even smile. Neither did Chuck the accountant.

The annoying thing about the machines was their insistence on imitating the overbearing politeness of Tokyo shopgirls. Every time someone purchased so much as a cup of coffee, a machine whined "*arigato gozaimashita*" in a computer-generated nasal tone. Every machine seemed designed to appear more polite than the last. The Coke machine said, "Thank you kind patron. Enjoy your cola," whereas the Pocari Sweat machine said, "Thank you kindest of patrons. Enjoy your beverage to the utmost satisfaction." There was even one machine that showed its appreciation coin by coin. "You are most generous. Please insert three hundred more yen. You are most generous. Please insert two hundred more yen."

The customer could be praised for his generosity up to ten times before receiving his portion of preheated rice and being dismissed with, "Thank you very much. It has been a pleasure to serve you Gendeki Fried Rice."

Lots of people ate up the praise. I'd heard more than a few people tell the vociferous machines, "You're quite welcome," or caught them unconsciously bowing ever so slightly. One sociologist I knew theorized that the Japanese love of talking machines had deep roots in the animistic beliefs of Shintoism and the fact that some Buddhist beliefs granted even rocks the status of sentient beings.

Maybe. Most Americans I knew disliked the machines, seeing them as frightening harbingers of a world dominated by robots. Personally, I found the mannerly vending devices not all that bad. If the world is going to be run by machines, at least let them be polite ones.

The only one I found truly unbearable was the one I happened to be sitting next to, a machine that sold little paper shot cups of whiskey. It told a joke, invariably a bad one, as the whiskey was being served. Perhaps it was part of a government program to gradually wean the customer off alcohol by making him negatively associate liquor with painful humor.

I was considering these possibilities when someone came strolling up to the comedic machine and inserted some coins. The man would have looked out of place anywhere. He had on a long overcoat, a wide-brimmed hat that cast a shadow over his bushy eyebrows, dark glasses, and a long mustache. He looked like Fu Manchu dressed as Philip Marlowe. As the guy put in his coins, he kept looking around, as if fearful that someone would see him buying whiskey from a vending machine at eight forty-five in the morning.

"What's the difference between Gojira and a member of the Liberal Democratic Party?" the machine asked the poor slob.

"Mr. Chaka!" the man whispered to me. "I've got what you asked for."

It was Nabiko.

"Thanks," I said. "But I never drink before nine A.M. Call me a square."

"Not the whiskey. The script," he whispered loudly, taking a look around. I pretended not to understand.

"These things sell scripts? On second thought, I'll take that whiskey," I said, getting up.

Nabiko tore off his sunglasses. "Chaka! It's me, Brando Nabiko. I've got the script."

"Nabiko?" I said. "I didn't recognize you in the overcoat."

"It's not mine," he said, grinning behind the dangling strands off his fake mustache. I wondered how my driver, Shinto Hirohito, would look with this kind of mustache. Probably just as ridiculous.

"Do you know what you look like?" I asked.

"Yes," Nabiko said, so I guess there was no need to tell him. "You may think this is a little overboard, but I have the only copy of *Tokyo Suckerpunch* left. The rest were burned in the fire."

Tokyo Suckerpunch. I still wasn't used to the name. It sounded like a garage band that did bad covers of the Ramones. I asked him how he got the script.

"I know a script girl at the studio. She got me the script, all right. But now I have to take her bowling twice a week for a month. I hate bowling."

"I owe you one," I said as he handed me the script.

"You owe me one big time. When we make this thing, I want to bring you to the set. Introduce you as my friend."

"You promise to dress like that, I'll be there every day. You can introduce me as your dad if you want."

Brando looked around nervously. Probably thinking of all the bowling he'd have to do.

"Seriously, Nabiko, thanks. You've been a great help," I said, bowing fairly low to him considering the discrepancy between our ages. He seemed genuinely touched by my gratitude.

"It was my duty. I'm sure Sato Migusho would have wanted you to see it," he said, putting his sunglasses back on. "Well, back to the set of *The Manchu Falcon*." Nabiko did a pretty fair imitation of Bogart doing Peter Sellers doing Fu Manchu as Sam Spade. Better than I would have done, which isn't saying much.

He ducked inside the station, leaving me holding the shot of whiskey. I took another look at his costume and couldn't help but laugh.

"That's odd," I overheard a salaryman say as he passed by. "I never thought those whiskey machine jokes were that funny."

Ba-dum-bum.

TOKYO SUCKERPUNCH

Original screenplay by Sato Migusho and Brando Nabiko based on the adventures of journalist Billy Chaka.

Fade-in . . .

INT. The Pistolwhip Club—NIGHT

Billy Chaka sits at a table in the corner, writing furiously and pausing only to down shots of whiskey lined up on the table in front of him like little soldiers. He is a rugged-looking man with dark hair and a face that suggests wisdom beyond his years, gained from a life of rigorous adventurism and perpetual introspection. He pauses in his writing, and then, as if struck *by a revelation, resumes with redoubled fury. Suddenly two men approach from the other side of the bar. They stop at CHAKA's table, eyeing him dangerously. CHAKA can tell by their unfriendly bravado that his years of martial-arts exposure may soon be paying off.*

CHAKA Sorry. I prefer to drink alone.

The two GANGSTERS exchange mocking glances.

GANGSTER #1 You should be more social, Chaka. That kind of attitude will only get you into trouble.

The two GANGSTERS laugh maliciously. CHAKA remains calm, though inwardly he is a fuming tough guy.

CHAKA I'm not feeling very social at the moment. Beating up four ninjas before breakfast can do that to a guy.

GANGSTER #2 Those were four of our finest ninjas. Now what good are they to us? You should be more respectful of people's ninjas, Mr. Chaka!

CHAKA shrugs and snatches up a straw from the table, inserts it into a glass of bourbon, and sucks down the entire drink. He licks his lips, savoring the taste, savoring the moment.

CHAKA The next time you send some two-bit ninja after me, you might want to choose guys who know the difference between throwing stars and seeing them.

GANGSTER #1 There won't be a next time, Mr. Chaka.

The GANGSTERs draw guns from inside their jackets.

GANGSTER #1 (cont.) Hand over your memoirs, Billy Chaka!

CHAKA Right. And reveal to you the names of the infiltrators
who discovered your insidious plot to smuggle Colom-
bian cocaine aboard the prime minister's private hover-
craft? That may work on tourists at Yomiuri Land, but not
on a literary-supernova-type guy like me—Billy Chaka.

GANGSTER #2 Can't you see we have guns pointed at your
head?

CHAKA I do my best work with guns pointed at my head.
My editor is literal about deadlines.

*CHAKA reaches for a pen and resumes writing. The two
insulted GANGSTERS can see no choice but to fire on
CHAKA. Just as their fingers begin to squeeze the triggers,
CHAKA, with speed that would impress the fastest cobra in
the desert, grabs a pen in each hand and jams them into the
barrels of the GANGSTER'S pistols. When the GANGSTERS
fire, the guns explode in their hands. They shriek in agony.
CHAKA bends over and picks up three of their freshly severed fingers, and then holds them up to the GANGSTERS.*

CHAKA Go home and tell your boss he has about this many
days left! He's messed with the wrong journalist this time.

*CHAKA storms out of the bar, scribbling on a notepad as he
walks away.*

FADE-OUT...

I stopped reading, carefully closed the script, and laid it beside me on the car seat. I closed my eyes and inhaled deeply, holding the air for a count of five before slowly exhaling.

I really had to hand it to Sato. In all my years as a journalist, rarely had I come across a piece of writing so unabashedly terrible.

Fuming tough guy?

It made me sad that a respected man, my friend Sato Migusho, had spent the final days of his life working on such misguided tripe. I even felt a little guilty for inspiring it. But above all, I felt relieved that Sato's death had ensured this particular ineptitude would never be projected on the big screen. Relieved not just for my own sake, but for what was left of the reputation of the late director.

Sato's funeral was slated for the afternoon and it was sure to be a gala event, attended by all those sudden admirers that death creates in its wake. The type of people who might have had their picture taken with the director for credibility, but who wouldn't pay to see his films, much less finance them. The funeral would serve as just another photo op for all the hollow celebrities and bean-counting moneymen of the Tokyo film world.

I'd given Shinto the rest of the day off to attend the funeral of his late employer after he dropped me at the tournament. He seemed reluctant, but I'd insisted.

I wondered just what sort of relationship Sato had with Shinto. I knew that Sato had been fairly picky about the hired help, preferring stray humans, nubile young women, or starry-eyed, would-be filmmakers anxious for bits of cinematic wisdom.

Shinto was none of these, not even a stray. And for all the time I'd spent locked in Tokyo traffic with him, I'd learned only a few things. He smoked Mild Sevens. He always wore his white gloves. He had a stupid mustache and he never talked.

He dropped me off at the tournament and I made my way toward the giant structure, too late to get good seats, so in no hurry. Just before entering the building, I looked back over my shoulder.

I don't know why such an innocent sight should give me the creepy crawlies, but it did. It was just Shinto—a chauffeur, standing outside the car enjoying a cigarette while the boss went about business.

But there was something unmistakably sinister about the way he stood there, watching me. I'd seen that same look on other faces, and the faces didn't belong to bored chauffeurs.

I decided there was more to this guy than a funny mustache.

Most of the day's hot action was gonna be in the wheelchair kata competition. Nearly every different style was represented. There were the hard, traditional Okinawan styles that focus more on effective punches and low footrest kicks. There were the Chinese Wing Chun styles, more dancelike with their intricate hand motions and animal poses. Then there were the Brazilian capoeira offshoots, noticeable for their insane samba spin maneuvers. In between were a thousand hybrids with enough esoteric distinctions to fill a lifetime of research.

The kata competition is best suited to bring out these differences. The kata is a solitary exercise in which competitors battle a barrage of invisible opponents with a series of choreographed moves. Like in gymnastics or ice dancing, competitors are judged on a combination of technical mastery and originality. As the combatant is unimpeded by any real opponent, she is able to display her particular style in its purest form, free from real threat. The kata competition isn't about practicalities of self-defense, but aesthetic appeal.

Some people preferred the jarring, almost robotically efficient movements of traditional karate, while others went for the slower, more meditative ballet of tai chi. Some got off on the insane animal styles, like the lurching comedy of the Drunken Monkey or the erratic attacks in the Way of the Petulant Butterfly. In the kata competition, anything went. This was why it was mercifully free from the perennial squabbles that plagued the sparring competition.

Sparring participants were forever complaining that certain rules favored one style over another. The kung fu crowd complained when eye gouges were outlawed, the bujitsu guys bellyached when kicks to the knee were banned, the tae kwon do types got bent out of shape when throat kicks were barred, and so on. The essential dilemma was that tournaments were designed as a way to test martial-arts skills without hurting others—but martial arts are inherently designed to inflict pain.

The new, tournament-oriented styles were a reaction to this problem. Most traditionalists looked down their noses at such mutations as somehow blasphemous. But, as a young competitor once told me in an interview during the Pan-Asian Christian Judo Competition a few years ago, "All societies must have rules, the martial-arts society included. If our style functions best, it is because we have better adapted to the society." These adaptations were often referred to as the Darwinian styles, both by their detractors and their practitioners.

The kata competition was mostly free from this kind of name-calling and controversy, probably because it was a less testosterone-fueled event. No one got punched or kicked, they just went on the floor and did their thing. As such, the

macho brickbreaker types dismissed it as show-offy—as if
busting bricks wasn't—and some hard-core martial-arts magazines didn't even cover it.

That was fine with me. Their negligence had helped
Youth in Asia corner the kata market over the years. This
year, the fourteen-and-under open wheelchair division
looked ripe for a cover story.

Miyuki Nishimura was a thirteen-year-old from the north-
ern island of Sado. She had been paralyzed from the waist
down in a car accident when she was only seven years old.
It was then that she began her martial-arts training. In the
years since, she'd developed an almost superhumanly strong
upper body and abdominal muscles. And, as her coach con-
fided in me, "She has not even had her period yet. When
those hormones kick in, she will become a real terror."
Miyuki was a pretty real terror already, using her stomach
strength to send her limp legs whirling into the air with star-
tling speed as she did handstands on the arms of her wheelchair.

The wheelchair was one of the Kitaka style—a wider
wheelbase and larger wheels, strong, high armrests, and no
backrests. Functioning like a set of gymnasts' parallel bars on
wheels, it allowed the user to move rather freely about its
confines. The vehicle's weakness was that it was too large
and unwieldy for quick feints and dodges.

Miyuki's main opponent, Li-Ang Wang, took a different
approach entirely. She was Taiwanese and had suffered a
bizarre stroke in her infancy that paralyzed the left side of
her body. The right side had since developed breathtaking
speed and control, enabling her to hide the reality that she
was functionally split down the middle. Using her right body
strength, she could propel the limbs of her left side like
whips ripping through the air at her target. Her wheelchair

was Wang-shu all the way. Designed with the intricacy of a Swiss clock, it allowed the expert user to send it into a series of tight whirls, good for quick attacks and subtle evasive maneuvers. Its weakness was mechanical frailty; it could be disabled with a strong blow to the exposed axle of its small wheels—a weakness of little consequence in the kata competition.

Two different handicaps. Two different styles and two very different machines. A pair of precocious teenage girls from separate parts of the world. It was going to be a doozy.

I took out my pen and paper and jotted down a quick sentence capturing the excitement I felt preparing to witness this spectacle in the auditorium that once housed the weapons of the kamikaze, a fighting force that had secured its mythical position in history as the recent embodiment of the timeless Japanese warrior spirit.

At such moments, I was no longer Billy Chaka—hopeless geisha chaser, unwilling dupe of Japanese crime lords, quick-tempered, two-fisted student of antiquity, bumbling detective in search of the truth in the death of a famous friend. I wasn't even Billy Chaka the ace journalist and friend to Asian teenagers worldwide, humble egomaniac and inspiration for bad movie scripts.

I was simply a guy awed by a world forever strange and new.

I half expected Shinto to be waiting outside the tournament, sucking on a Mild Seven in his oddly sinister way. I doubted he had actually gone to the funeral, but at least he wasn't waiting for me. Neither were any yakuza errand boys, or creepy guys in cheap black suits. I felt like throwing a party.

I had a few hours to kill, so I decided to hop on the train to Shibuya to pay my respects to Sato Migusho in my own, more personal way—by watching a print of one of his biggest flops, *Double Longing*. It was about a guy who falls in love with a woman, or maybe two women, or maybe he just goes crazy, or she does. The film was never distributed internationally due to its supposed similarities to some Luis Buñuel flick. I guess that was in the days before directors took pride in ripping each other off. Anyway, I was anxious to see it and judge for myself.

On the trains, I was reminded why I preferred driving, or rather being driven. Trains depress me. They make me feel like some guy in a bad French movie about ennui.

American trains made me think of old blues songs. Somebody was always breaking somebody's heart by leaving on a train, lured by the promise of a better life. Southerners migrated north, Easterners fled to the West, all of them on trains, all of them chasing something. Now that there was nothing in America left to chase, the trains felt like a vestigial organ, a network of ancient iron-and-steel ruins.

In Japan, it was different. The trains were surgically clean, built with cutting-edge technology. To preserve their famous efficiency, they were crammed too tight for sentimentality. When you rode them, you didn't even feel like you were traveling, but being transmitted from one place to another like ones and zeros being sent over the Internet. Japanese trains were just as depressing, only in a different way.

Maybe trains bugged me so much because they're a closed system—there's no thrill of the open road, no sense of trajectory, of possibility, of interruption. No sense of freedom. No chauffeurs with funny mustaches. Everything seems as rigid and humorless as the steel tracks beneath the wheels.

Maybe that's why the salarymen buried their heads in the latest issues of *LoveBlonde* or *Rapeman,* where ink drawings had heroic sexual adventures and lived epic, two-dimensional lives. In the *manga,* nobody had to take trains to their boring jobs, their box homes, and statistically average families.

I didn't read *manga,* but I had my own escapsist fantasies. I spent the ride thinking about Orange Blossom, wondering what she was doing at this moment. I was certain she wasn't riding a crowded commuter rail.

The funny thing was that I couldn't picture her in any physical sense. I could see parts of her—her supernaturally white face, her dark hair limp like a dead thing damp around her shoulders. And of course, her bloodred geisha mouth, smeared at the corner, evoking the signature, deliberate imperfections admired in Japanese pottery.

But beyond that, she was featureless. I couldn't remember if she was tall, or short, how she talked,or what she'd said. Her movements came to me in fragments, like a film in slow motion where someone had cut out most of the frames. The more I tried to cement her image in my mind, the less tangible she became. As the proverb goes, it was like trying to grasp mist by closing a fist around it.

In the end, I was left with nothing but words. Jumbled adjectives, vague descriptors. Exotic...dangerous...elusive... beautiful. Not a damn one that would help me find her.

For this—a loose collection of weak adjectives and half-formed images—I'd punched and kicked and been punched and kicked and embarrassed myself and been thrown out of a swank corporate sex hideout? For this I'd involved myself with the dregs of society, perhaps compromised my sense of journalistic duty during the most important teenage handicapped tournament in Asia, and created yet another potential source of friction with Sarah—far away and one tooth shorter, growing older and losing patience?

Yes.

And it was only going to get worse. Because in perhaps the only part of my brain forever unknowable, I was hard-wired for geisha. No amount of common sense could stop me once a geisha was involved—nor could gangsters, the death of a friend, or any of the rest.

My obsession was just that bad.

Sato's movie was intriguing, but there weren't many people around to notice. It was shown in one of those *meigaza* that were sprouting up all over Shibuya, the kind of place that only held about a hundred and fifty people. Today, it was just me and a couple of students out on a date, probably their first. Throughout the film the guy kept making hesitant, arty little comments to the girl and she would agree in hurried automatic whispers.

HE: That cut...reminds me...of that scene in Zubriskiev's
    The Bitter Tea of Petra Von Braun. You, uh, you know
    the one?

SHE: Yes yes yes.

HE: Um...the uh...that color red evokes James Dean in
    Rebel Without a Cause...

SHE: Yes, oh yes...

HE: The jacket he wore...

SHE: Yes. Yes...

And so on, for over two hours. I felt sorry for the couple. He was trying so hard to impress and she was trying so very hard to be impressed and neither of them seemed to enjoy it much. I found myself longing for days of arranged marriages. In those days, the poor guy wouldn't be in some mad scramble to seem charming and intelligent and the girl wouldn't have to constantly reassure him with knee-jerk encouragement. And most importantly, I wouldn't have to listen to it while I was trying to watch a film that was dense and difficult enough to follow without a real-time comedy of adolescent sexual angst playing out behind me.

But—I reminded myself—these kids and kids like them were my audience. It was up to me to understand young Asians the world over, in order that I might better serve their needs and desires through my columns and features.

The film itself was a masterpiece of ambiguity, a tale that explored issues of sanity, identity, love, and desire. Part love story, part ghost story, part diary of a madman. It was utterly unlike anything Sato had ever made—containing hallucinatory sequences where characters may or may not have been dreaming while they uttered elliptical soliloquies and ate pickled plums.

The film was shot in black-and-white on a budget of pocket change and utilized nonprofessional actors and location sets. It was a trick Sato had learned from the Italian neorealists, but that's about as far as the realism went.

I recalled an interview where Sato claimed *Double Longing* as the most personal of his films then refused to answer any further questions pertaining to it. If this was Sato's muddled personal statement from the sixties, there were a lot of things about Sato that I didn't know.

The plot concerned a married man in his late twenties who falls in love with a woman he believes had lived in his village when he was a child. The woman disappeared after some scandal, but the man can't recall the details. Years later, the man meets the same woman in Tokyo. She appears not to have aged a day. He never asks her about the incident years ago, for it is impossible that she can be the same woman—yet somehow he fears she is. His marriage and career begin to fall apart as he becomes obsessed with learning the secret of this beautiful strange woman, who in the movie is played at first by one, then two, and finally seven different actresses as the protagonist slips deeper into what may be madness.

On the verge of collapse, he decides to confront her, to find out who she really is and what happened all those years ago in the village. But of course, she is gone—vanished without a trace. When he asks her neighbors and landlord about what has happened to her, they seem to have no idea who he is talking about. When asked to describe her, he can't—because at different times she had the features of seven different women. Absolutely at a loss, he realizes the pointlessness of trying to solve her.

The film ends with the man staring out the window of a train, wondering if he can patch things up with his wife and his boss, and yet hoping, fearing, that the strange, ghostly woman will one day return to wreak havoc with his life.

It was not the typical *mono-no-aware* ending, that uniquely Japanese coda of wistful acceptance, but with something disturbing and foreboding. One got the sense that the real, more terrifying story was yet to come.

What'd I tell you about trains?

The sparring quarterfinals were scheduled for ten, and if yesterday's kata competition was any indication, the day could feature some of the most excellent fighting in the history of the tournament. The amazing new wheelchair technology allowed the competitors to really flaunt the grace and beauty of the ancient forms. Happily, the competition this year was mostly free of the flamboyant, pseudo-martial-arts "posing" and uselessly flashy acrobatics of the previous years. The trend was toward basic, traditional minimalism.

The refreshing return of substance over style may have been due to the fact that in the last competition, Yoko Torikata had finished a disappointing third because the judges found her kata resembled (according to one) "a temper tantrum thrown by an unruly, extremely curvaceous, and underdressed acrobatic child" rather than a display of precision technique acquired through years of discipline. Reacting in a fashion typical of the overpaid, petulant sex kitten she was, the teenage controversialist questioned the judges' sexuality and vowed to give up the kata competition as long as it was judged by "white-haired old patriarchs with petrified balls." She later apologized while denying the exact wording of the statement, even though it had been publicly televised.

That she was allowed to compete at all this year was a testament not so much to her immense talent as to the number of people who depended on her to make a living. Coaches, agents, advertisers, and television stations—not to mention the tournament brass with the "petrified balls"—were aware that Yoko meant serious yen.

Unfortunately, so was she. Maybe this year someone would bring her down a notch and restore the same sanity to the sparring competition that the kata contest had enjoyed. But if it happened on this particular Saturday, I wouldn't be there to see it.

It was time to pay the Yamagamas a visit before they got proactive on me. I'd already put off seeing them the day before and was sure their patience was wearing thinner than a supermodel.

That morning Shinto was as punctual and reticent as ever. During the drive I asked him about the funeral. He told me there were a lot of people there, many of them celebrities (including Yoko Torikata). I already knew that from reading the papers, who called it the fourth-biggest funeral since that of Kaota, leader of the Yamagama-gumi in 1981. But that was all that Shinto was willing to tell me.

My suspicions were heightened by his curiosity about how I spent my afternoon. His questions were awkward and probing, and he seemed dissatisfied with my answers, fingering his mustache with his white gloves. I got the feeling he wasn't just trying to chat with me. Chatting wasn't Shinto's style. He did it about as naturally as a hippopotamus does ballet. So why was he trying?

He was somebody's puppet. I didn't know who was pulling the strings, but I had a feeling that whoever it was had something to do with Sato's fiery death. After all, Shinto had been perhaps the last person to see Sato alive—and he didn't seem to be particularly broken up about it.

I wanted to figure out some way to break Shinto's shell and get him to talk, even if it meant directly confronting him. That meant keeping him around. But not now. I was going to meet Kwaidan, the head of one of the most powerful gangs in Japan. The thought of Shinto tagging along and monitoring my actions for some unknown third party was one I didn't relish.

As we passed through Harajuku, near Yoyogi Park, I decided it was time to ditch Shinto. I figured I'd call him later, make up some story. He'd get over it.

He dropped me off near a McDonald's, after I said I was in dire need of some American fast food. I asked him if he wanted anything, but he just shook his head and played with his mustache some more.

I leapt from the car and headed toward the Golden Arches. Just the sight of them made me feel relieved.

Every time I went to McDonald's in Japan, I couldn't help but think of an old sailor named Captain Jukichi. Captain Jukichi was shipwrecked in 1815 and rescued by sailors he believed to be Dutch. He praised his luck, thinking he was just off the coast of Nagasaki and would soon be home, alive and well. But when his boat landed, he was shocked to find there wasn't a single villager who was Japanese. A devout vegetarian, he was moved to tears at the unholy sight of cattle being slaughtered for beef in this strange land. The horrifying event prompted him to write: "This cannot be Nagasaki. I must have come to animal hell."

In reality, he was at the present-day sight of Santa Barbara, California, which has since evolved into an entirely different kind of hell. And now, nearly two hundred years later, a piece of animal hell had come to Japan.

As usual, the place was packed with teenagers. It was Saturday, the day when the various cliques would gather in the closed streets nearby and rebel together. They'd dance to rap music, smoke cigarettes, admire each other's leather jackets and cool hairdos, and just generally hang out and revel in the group spirit of nonconformity. This phenomenon prompted one writer to quip, "If these kids ever got serious, Japan would have the most highly organized anarchy movement the world has ever seen." Looking at the kids chomping on Big Macs and goofing around with their cell phones, the possibility seemed pretty remote.

Outside the restaurant, the square was crowded with young hipsters passing the time between rounds of burgers and fries. They were neatly divided into their respective subgroups. There were the break-dancers with their cardboard over in one corner, the metalheads doing air-guitar solos in front of Snoopy Town, the punks drawing anarchy symbols on their faces with erasable Magic Marker to show they didn't care. The bridge to the Meiji shrine was dominated by the goths, who were busy looking miserable and admiring each other's pale faces, black nails, and elaborate burial dresses.

And then there were the *bosozuku*. The speed tribes were Japan's teenage motorcycle gangs, and they were everywhere. Some of them were pretty benign, little more than glee-clubs-on-wheels. Others were made up of hardened juvenile delinquents and vicious young yakuza-in-waiting. I surveyed this particular group for a moment, trying to size them up as they stood around ogling each other's bikes and revving up their engines intermittently. They looked like bad eggs. To borrow a bike, I was going to have to crack some shells.

I strolled over to the lead biker of the group and began looking over his machine. I knew he was the leader not only because he had the most expensive-looking bike, but because his girlfriend had the biggest breasts. I have found this to be the best indicator of teenage hierarchies.

"Get this dickhead. Old fuck never seen a motorcycle," the lead biker said to the delight of his biker buddies, unaware of course that I spoke Japanese. I smiled at him like I didn't understand the joke but thought it must be funny if everyone was laughing. Then I continued going over his vehicle, inspecting. The busty girlfriend sneered at me. I bet she was a big fan of Yoko Torikata.

"You lose a contact or something?" the owner of the vehicle said menacingly. I just smiled at him and gave the front tire of the Harley a swift kick. A chorus of gasps emanated from the group, followed by mutters and whispers.

A greasy pimple king approached me from the left. Years of studying the social phenomena of the Asian teen gang had taught me that this was the strongman, the Enforcer. It helped that the word ENFORCER was written in English down the sleeve of his jacket.

"You crazy or somethin', round-eye? Nobody touches the *Velvet Fuck*." Sure enough, the motorcycle had the *Velvet Fuck* airbrushed neatly on the gas tank. Bilingual punks. I just shrugged at the acne enforcer.

Then I gave the *Velvet Fuck* a quick jab to the headlamp, scattering glass across the pavement.

No one was smiling now.

The Enforcer was the first to come at me, but I stopped him with a whiplike backfist across the bridge of his nose. Next I was attacked by the dumb guy—every gang had one, the guy who was actually tougher than the Enforcer, but was too dumb to enforce much of anything. He earned his title this time, practically walking right into a spinning sidekick that sent him toppling to the pavement.

Next, it was the Jester, the wise guy of the gang. He was usually smarter than the others, but his big mouth and delicate sensitivity often made him an outcast. I buried my forearm in the bigmouth's mouth, pushing a few teeth into his sensitive throat. I was probably being too hard on the Jester, but I hated seeing intelligent kids turn to gangs. Maybe this would be a lesson to him.

Besides a few bit players, that left only the leader of the gang. He came at me halfheartedly with a bike chain. I taught him how hard it was to breathe with a bike chain wrapped around his throat. I let him gasp and choke for a while, and then threw him to the ground with the other three. It was all over before anyone saw it happening.

"What's your name?" I asked the leader.

"Fuck you," he wheezed in tough Japanese, still gasping for breath.

"All right, Fuck You," I said playing along, "do you know why I punched out your bike lamp?"

"'Cause you're an asshole?" the Jester said, and spit a mouthful of blood.

"I didn't ask you, snaggletooth. Don't make me put you on the bullet train to enlightenment."

He wiped his mouth with the back of his hand and narrowed his eyes.

"Now I'm gonna ask you again," I said to the leader of the pack. "Do you know why I busted your headlight?"

"No," he said, showing me a little more respect.

"No? Let me ask you this. Do you know where that headlamp was manufactured?"

The kid just shrugged as if he were thinking, *Like, adults are so weird*.

"I'll tell ya one thing. It sure as hell wasn't made in Sturgis, North Dakota! Get it?"

He didn't get it.

"All right, here's my problem," I said, trying to sound a little friendlier. "You are riding a top-of-the-line 1978 Harley Chopper. Born and raised in the U.S. of America to be enjoyed in Japan. Fine. I'm all for cultural exchange. But then, misguided as you are, you go and put a Suzuki headlamp on it. Why?"

Again, the kid merely shrugged, more baffled than ever.

"Don't get me wrong. Suzuki makes excellent motorcycles, as does Honda and Kawasaki. I once owned a Kawasaki myself. Don't remember much about it. It was green. Maybe a 750? But the point is this—you don't wear cowboy boots with a kimono, you don't eat a cheeseburger with chopsticks, and you sure as hell don't put a Suzuki lamp on no goddamn Harley!"

I waited for the tirade to settle in on them. I took a couple of paces, and tried to look as if I was struggling to solve this dilemma.

"You're one lucky ratchethead. I can fix your little faux pas. So, I'll ask you again: What's your name?" I took out a pocket notebook.

"Aki," he said "Aki Rokahara."

"Address?"

"Four-three-fifty-five Komaba, Meguro-ku."

"Okay," I said, nodding in approval. "I know a guy in Ikebukuro who specializes in this sort of thing. It'll take seventy-two hours, max. Now give me the keys." Before he even realized what he was doing, he had already handed them to me.

"Don't give him your keys, man!" the Enforcer pleaded.

"Shut up, Taiji," Aki Rokahara told the Enforcer. Aki had proven to be a wise leader, provoking guilty feelings on my part for making him look stupid in front of his gang. The only way I could ease my conscience was with a sponta- neous show of yen. I ripped out a wad of bills and tossed them to the ground.

"No hard feelings. Go get yourselves some Band-Aids. And a cheeseburger or something," I said, hopping on the *Velvet Fuck.*

I left the bewildered teens in a cloud of blue exhaust.

Traveling by stolen motorcycle is one of those simple, time- less pleasures. As I tore through Shinjuku-ku on the pilfered chopper, I vowed that I would never get too old to enjoy the smaller things in life. True, I felt a little bad about smacking around the *bosozuku*—maybe they weren't the thugs I'd pegged them for, but simply kids trying to look cool. On the other hand, I hadn't really hurt them and I fully intended to return the *Velvet Fuck,* repaired headlamp and all.

It would give them something to talk about, maybe get them some sympathy from their girlfriends. And the encounter had put me in the right mind-set to deal with the Yamagama- gumi. I wasn't sure what Kwaidan was after, but I had a feel- ing he wasn't going to ask me to write his biography. On the off chance he did, I knew enough to get a good start.

Kwaidan had ruled the Yamagamas since the big gang wars of the eighties with a ruthlessness matched only by his keen business acumen. He had increased the gang's holdings in legitimate ventures like bars, Laundromats, and bowling alleys, and all but cornered the condom vending-machine business. Kwaidan supposedly worked with the head of Ronin Condoms to develop the famous talking machines that dispensed fortune-cookie sex predictions along with rubbers. Stuff like "A stranger will soon ask you to perform cunnilin- gus" or "Your erection will be strongest when the tide is weak." His gang could almost be considered a respectable outfit—were it not for occasional strong-arm tactics that permanently placed people on the missing-persons list. The often unreported violence with which the Yamagama-gumi ran their "legitimate" affairs paled in comparison with their actions in the more traditional yakuza fields of prostitution, gambling, drugs, gun smuggling, pornography, and other staples of the *mizu-shobai.* In the "water business" they were a known quantity to be feared and respected.

Kwaidan was a real public figure for a time, often getting his picture in the papers, smiling and shaking hands with nervous looking local politicians. A national weekly magazine had even invited him to do a piece about his favorite golf courses in Asia and in another he had shared the recipe for his signature drink, something he called "Ogosho Punch."

But this was before the loan scandals of the nineties and the antigang legislation that followed forced Kwaidan to become a less public, but no less powerful figure. Rumors of his retirement were greatly exaggerated. They were just a ploy to get him out of the spotlight for a while.

Despite his carefully crafted media image as a modern, forward-thinking businessman and fun-loving playboy, Kwaidan was at his core a traditional, even conservative yakuza. He still believed that the yakuza were akin to the masterless samurai of yesteryear, the Robin Hoods of modern Japan. In public, he dressed like middle management, but I had it on authority that in private he often donned ridiculous samurai garb and liked to strut around with his sword and scabbard talking about *bushido*—the way of the warrior. It was said that his behavior was becoming more erratic with age. Stories ran the gamut. One said he refused to have his picture taken, and had a pesky paparazzi dropped into an active volcano. Another was that his fear of earthquakes would cause panic attacks, during which he'd spend days, even weeks at a time in helicopters, circling the islands and waiting for the Big One.

What such a person could want with Orange Blossom or myself was beyond me. Here was a man who had all the money and power that money and power could buy and yet he sought a lone *gaijin* and some disappearing woman for reasons unknown. Maybe she saw something she shouldn't, or maybe she knew something he didn't. Maybe he had simply lost his mind. Or maybe it was just that Kwaidan was like me when it came to geisha.

I cruised through the pink district near the Ikebukuro station. The daylight stole whatever neon charm the place had at night. All the porn emporiums and strip clubs looked gray and washed-out in the sunlight. The touts that would line the sidewalks this evening would now be sleeping off hangovers in shabby little apartments.

Just as Punchperm had told me, the first sketchy-looking guy I ran into pointed me right to the Yamagama headquarters. Then he asked me if I wouldn't like to meet a nice schoolgirl.

"She's thirteen, almost totally bald down there. Good at math, too."

Why did I waste time fighting teen gangs when there were so many people like this who deserved it so much more? Sure, you've gotta choose your battles, but maybe I'd been choosing the wrong ones.

"She sounds like a nerd," I said, and drove on before I got upset and had to do something about it.

The building was a squat three-story box just like its neighbors. It didn't really stand out except for the big American luxury cars parked in front and the gold-lettered sign on the door which had the gang insignia and the words YAM-AGAMA GANG HEADQUARTERS LOCAL 312. Such bold flaunting of their gang status was a direct affront to the rules set out in the 1992 Act for Prevention of Unlawful Activities by Organized Crime Members. It was a testament to their power. Though they had been one of twenty-four organizations fingered as criminal, they'd made no effort to hide the fact by fronting as a business or a charity. So far there had been some minor jailings, but no real repercussions. The gangs were too big for a mere government to push around.

I parked the motorcycle and walked up to the building. I rang the buzzer.

"Who's there?"

"Chaka. Billy Chaka."

"So what?" the gruff voice wondered.

"I have to meet..." I realized that I had no idea what Punchperm's name was, much less any title he may have had. But I knew haircuts, so I played the odds.

"Yeah, yeah. Who?"

"I have to meet...Punchperm."

There was silence on the other side. Then there was a buzz and the door opened. I took a deep breath and walked into a modern den of thieves.

Everybody was laughing. The guys playing *hanafuda* in the corner, the two shirtless young toughs drinking beer by a Foosball table, a group of chubby older guys in suits reading *Speedboat Times* and *Beppin Schoolgirl,* the sour little Crewcut I'd met the other day—all of them were guffawing and looking at Punchperm. He wasn't laughing at first, but eventually he, too, chuckled like a good sport.

"Punchperm!" bellowed a huge fellow over by the weight bench. He looked over to me and gave me a thumbs-up sign. I didn't know what to do, so I gave him the dumbstruck *gaijin* smile.

The windowless cavern smelled of foreign cigarettes, stale sweat, and cut-rate alcohol. It wasn't like the swanky yakuza headquarters I'd visited before, the ones with designer furniture and original Warhol prints. Instead, there was an old poster of movie icon Takakura Ken, a *Sex Warrior Lesbian* calendar, and a faded picture of some *enka* songstress tacked to the gray walls. Even with the laughter, it was like some cheerless fraternity rec room. Maybe they kept it like this to remind themselves of prison, always just one slipup away.

The laughter died as spontaneously as it had erupted and suddenly the boys were playing Foosball, lifting weights, and reading comics as if nothing had happened.

I was happy when Punchperm got up and walked toward the door, Crewcut following. The Yamagama Gang Local 312 was just not my scene.

We weren't yet to the car when I felt the first blow to the back of my head.

"Lower!" Punchperm barked. I stumbled forward, trying to catch my balance by bracing myself against a car.

The second punch caught me on the neck, a little off center.

"Fuck," Crewcut muttered.

"Goddammit!" Punchperm said, shuffling over and pushing Crewcut out of the way.

"I did like you said—"

"Shut up," Punchperm grumbled.

I could have tried to fight back, but I didn't see the point. From the placement—or misplacement in Crewcut's case—of the blows, I knew they weren't really trying to hurt me, just make me lose consciousness for a while. It was crude, but that's just the way yaks think. Violence is the first solution.

I waited for the third blow. It had been a rough couple of days, and I could use the rest.

It wasn't long in coming.

My face was moist and there was a terrible smell. I awoke to see a giant mastiff licking my cheek while a roomful of yakuza laughed approvingly. The fetid breath of the creature was better than coffee for bringing me to my senses. I pushed the dog's slobbering muzzle away and ran my hand over the bump on the back of my head. My whole body ached.

"Good morning, journalist," a voice said, hissing the last word. The speaker's open robe revealed a torturous-looking tattoo that covered his sagging, swollen belly. The tattoo depicted a dragon standing atop the erupting Mount Uzen, its tongue a fiery orange flame licking a pale blue moon. Bubbling red lava flowed down the mountain. A giant carp was leaping from the lava stream, carrying a miniature rendition of the gangster himself on its back. The overwrought, confused symbolism of the tattoo had to be the product of a feverish megalomania.

It was Kwaidan in the flesh. And there was a lot of it. So there was truth to at least some of the rumors.

"I'd like to introduce you to Shinobi, champion fighting dog," he said. On command the dog bowed to me. I bowed back out of reflex to the delight of the gathered flunkies.

"Look at this crazy writer!" the boss bellowed. "He bows to a dog, and yet he shows us no respect." Their laughter took on a more menacing tone.

"Sorry," I said. "I guess I'm just a little dazed from being cracked on the back of my head." There were about nine of them, too many to fight while I was groggy. Besides, I didn't like the looks of the dog.

"I humbly beseech your forgiveness," Kwaidan said with florid sarcasm. "But it was viewed as a necessary precaution. You have proven yourself to be quite a slippery fish. And quite an insubordinate one as well. We don't like to be kept waiting." I tried to recall if I'd even been accused of being an insubordinate fish before.

"Seismograph!" Kwaidan barked, before I could decide.

Two of his henchmen scrambled out of the room. Kwaidan silently looked down at me while the dog scratched behind its ears. I looked around the room. It looked like some makeshift office in an abandoned warehouse. There were a few busted crates, a table with some chairs, and not much else. The high windows were blackened with paint. Odd digs for a living legend of organized crime.

"So you're the big-deal reporter, huh?" he said.

I shrugged.

"The voice of cool. The thinking teen's idol."

"Who told you that?" I asked.

He didn't answer, but continued to looked me over closely. Finally he just shook his head.

"I don't get it," he said. "Why would anyone look up to a guy like you? You dress like an eight ball. You're not rich. You've got the charisma of a . . ." He shot a look to the goons.

"A chunk of tofu!" shouted a goon.

"A chunk of tofu." Kwaidan nodded. "I don't get it. What do kids see in you?"

"Kids these days are weird." I shrugged. "Who knows what goes on in their minds?"

"All the same," he said, "I don't get it."

Two henchmen returned with a computer printout which Kwaidan unceremoniously snatched away. After a quick study, he tossed it aside.

"We are safe for now. Help this *gaijin* to his feet." At his command, Punchperm and Crewcut lifted me by the arms, and set me down in a chair by the rickety table. Another henchman pulled out a chair opposite me, which Kwaidan settled into with some difficulty. It seemed he wasn't used to being fat yet. The dog strolled over and slumped down at Kwaidan's feet.

"I hear you don't golf." He sighed.

I answered him with a blank look.

"Well, no matter. Some people don't appreciate life's pleasures. What can you do?" He threw his hands in the air.

I wondered what else they already knew about me, and more importantly how they found out.

"Quite a show you put on the other day in that little bar," Kwaidan resumed. "Shinpa Sam needed seven stitches in the hand."

"Sounds like a nursery rhyme," I said.

Shinpa Sam held up his stitched hand and scowled. I didn't recognize him or his hand.

"Is the girl a friend of yours?" Kwaidan continued.

"Never seen her before."

"But Sato Migusho was your friend?"

"He was." So my mind wasn't the only place where Sato and Orange Blossom were linked. Good to know my instincts hadn't gone completely haywire. Kwaidan nodded noncommittally, like something was troubling him. Then he suddenly leaned forward to speak.

"Was Migusho really that great at making movies?"

I was a little taken aback at the question. Typically, yakuza bosses weren't the type to solicit opinions. Kwaidan looked deadly serious.

"He had his ups and downs," I answered.

Kwaidan stared at the floor like he was trying to intimidate it. Then looked around to his troops. None of them let their faces betray any thought. Conformity has always been a stifling factor in Japanese society, and it was acutely felt in the yakuza world. I guess when mistakes meant losing a finger, people tripped over themselves not to say the wrong thing.

"You don't think he was a genius?"

The idea seemed to trouble him. I thought for a moment before answering. Not about Sato, but Kwaidan, and where the hell he was going with this.

"He might have been a few times," I said. "But it didn't stick."

"So he *wasn't* a genius?" He seemed to like the idea.

"It boils down to personal taste. Whether you liked his movies or not."

I was getting uneasy. There's something unsettling about discussing genius in an abandoned warehouse full of gangsters. Then again, if genius had to be discussed, maybe this was the ideal forum. Less room for pretentious crap.

Kwaidan rocked slowly back and forth in his chair, thinking. "I didn't like his movies much," he said finally.

All the troops nodded in agreement. The more they thought about it, the more they really didn't like Sato Migusho's movies at all. They started grumbling how terrible they were, how much they sucked, how maybe they were some of the worst movies ever made.

"Quiet," Kwaidan said calmly. They all tried to outsilence each other. Kwaidan smiled at the dog, and then at me. "It is decided. I don't like his movies. What do you say to that?"

I shrugged. "A lot of people didn't. A few did. Most couldn't care less. They're just movies."

He considered this for a while, too. They all did. I could practically see the thoughts going through their head.

Hmmm, just movies. Even the dog seemed to be thinking it.

"I didn't bring you here to talk about dead film directors," Kwaidan pronounced at length.

"I was starting to wonder."

He shot me a gangland stare. His previous uncertain look disappeared. He leaned forward, just to make sure the stare took.

"Her name is Orange Blossom. We want you to find her."

Sounded familiar.

"What's that got to do with Sato?" I said.

"She was with him. Just before he burned up."

I couldn't tell if I was surprised or not. Part of me suspected it all along. Another part of me figured Kwaidan was lying. A third part wondered why the yakuza cared.

"What gives you that idea?" I asked.

A flunky handed him a photograph. He looked at it disinterestedly, then pushed it across the table.

It was an eight-by-eleven of poor quality taken from a distance in bad weather. But there was no mistaking it. There they were—Orange Blossom and Sato Migusho, standing at the curb of some nameless urban street in the rain. They were both drenched, neither with an umbrella. Perhaps they were waiting for a cab after a movie, perhaps they had been at a love hotel . . . who knew? An ordinary scene from an extraordinary life.

"So she was with him when it happened," I said. "What of it?"

"Don't you find it interesting?"

"Sure. I find a lot of things interesting."

I was interested to know who was the primary subject of the photo and who just happened to be there. Same with the flame job on Sato's house. Could it be that they really wanted to kill Orange Blossom in the fire? Or had Sato been killed for some secret which they feared he'd passed on to the haunting geisha girl with the silly name? Or vice versa?

It occurred to me that I'd never actually just asked these guys what they wanted with her. The chances were slim I'd get a straight answer, but what the hell? Asking questions was part of my job.

I gave it a shot.

"That's not your concern." Kwaidan frowned. "You bring her here. I thought that was perfectly clear."

"None of this is perfectly clear."

"*Soba!*" he shouted. Again, two of the henchmen disappeared for a moment, reappearing with a bowl of steaming noodles. Kwaidan scooped them up greedily, waiting to respond until he'd had a mouthful. Looking at his expanding waistline, I recalled traditional Japanese thinking held that the body's *hara-gi*—the center of spiritual power—was in the abdomen. If it were true than Kwaidan had the makings of a spiritual Hercules.

"Get us Orange Blossom. What could be simpler?" he said, and went back to slurping his noodles.

Anything seemed simpler at this point. Kwaidan sensed my hesitation.

"Hasn't anybody told you about our terms?"

I shook my head. Kwaidan scowled at Punchperm, who looked like he'd just swallowed some bad puffer fish. He dug into his pocket and produced a crumpled piece of paper.

"Well? Speak up," Kwaidan barked.

"Um...two hundred fifty thousand dollars and...let's see here...a membership at the Asahi Golf Club." Punchperm smiled weakly, crumpled the paper up, and put it back in his pocket.

I couldn't help laughing.

"What's so funny?" Kwaidan growled.

"Nothing," I said, trying to regain control. "Is the Asahi golf course anything like the Joon Park course?"

"What do you care? You don't golf."

He had a point.

"You find these terms agreeable?" he continued. It wasn't really a question, but I nodded anyway. "Good. I expect to see her right here in front of me in one week's time."

My face went white. Or whiter, anyway.

"Don't worry. You just need to clear your head and focus on the job at hand," he said in a fatherly tone. "She's just some broad."

Right. I refrained from reminding him that if she was just some broad then they wouldn't need me. They could get any two-bit bounty hunter in Tokyo to track down just some broad.

"Mr. Chaka, let me illustrate my point. Shinobi here," he said, petting the huge drooling beast at his feet, "is a five-time champion, undefeated by all the fighting dogs of Japan. Do you know what makes this dog such a terror?"

"His breath."

"You are part right," he said humorlessly. "But what makes this dog invincible is the fact that he has been trained according to the classical samurai philosophy of Miyamoto Musashi, perhaps the greatest of all swordsmen. You are no doubt familiar with Musashi?"

I was, and the notion of a dog mastering the complexities of the *go-rin-no-sho* would surely have Musashi spinning in his grave like a cartoon Tasmanian Devil. Kwaidan might be crazier than I thought.

"One of Musashi's tenets is 'Do nothing which is unnecessary.' You should pay particular attention to this lesson." I glanced at the prize beast Shinobi. He was busy licking his own balls, no doubt necessarily.

I thought it over, and decided that Musashi was right but Kwaidan was an idiot. This only heightened my fear of him. There is nothing scarier than an idiot who can order a hit as impulsively as he demands a seismograph or a bowl of *soba* noodles. I'd stay on his good side as long as I could, but I wasn't going to hand over Orange Blossom. I wouldn't hand over a stray cat to these Yamagama-gumis.

"Boss," a goon said cautiously. He handed Kwaidan another computer printout. Kwaidan took one look at it.

"Helicopter!" he bellowed.

The goons all went for their cell phones.

Kwaidan smiled at me.

I forced myself to take a good look at this criminal, full of superficial notions of honor and courage he'd stolen from some of history's great warrior heroes and twisted into a self-serving code of violence for money's sake. And I smiled at him.

May the many faithful readers of *Youth in Asia* forgive me for this my moment of weakness.

Traveling over Tokyo by helicopter was something I'd always wanted to do. I'd fantasized about weaving through the towering monoliths of the Shinjuku district, the helicopter a tiny insect making its way through a dense forest of glass and steel. I'd fly around the famous buildings—the Tokyo Metropolitan Government offices, Tokyo Tower, the 1964 Olympic Stadium—maybe drop a paint-filled balloon on Tokyo Disney's Cinderella Castle.

And now, thanks to a fat psychotic gangster boss, I finally had the chance to fly above this great city. He even gave me a running commentary to accompany my aerial tour.

"I remember when I was a kid, this whole section was just a mountain of ashes. Thanks to you Americans. Hell, that's war for you. But just look at now."

That would have been swell. But my head had been covered by a black hood. I might as well have been traveling by bus through Cleveland. Kwaidan kept pointing things out, oblivious to my inability to see.

"From up here you'd never guess that this city has been almost completely wiped out twice. Not just in 1945, but earlier, in 1923—and that's just this century. Never mind the fires of 1657, the earthquake of 1703. Makes you wonder why people kept rebuilding it."

"Especially when Godzilla is gonna wreck it all again," I said inside my bag. I don't think he heard me. He grew silent for a moment, then continued.

"Did you know that there are approximately fifteen hundred earthquakes in Tokyo every single year? Most of them you can't even feel, but they happen just the same. An average of more than four per day, every day. It's just a matter of time before the Big One. And all these damn architects and politicians have been talking about earthquake-proof buildings since the sixties. 'We are fully prepared.' Blah, blah, blah. I knew it was all bullshit. Kobe proved me right."

Kwaidan quit talking. I could hear the whirring drone of the propeller. My nose itched, but my hands had been bound again, so I couldn't do much about it. I wondered what Miyamoto Musashi would have done in such a situation.

Probably never gotten into it in the first place.

When they took the sack off my head, I was back in Ikebukuro, outside the Yamagama Local 312. Punchperm halfheartedly apologized for the blows I'd received from Crewcut.

"He's still learning," Punchperm said with a shrug.

"I'm sure he'll do better next time." I mounted my stolen motorcycle.

"Confidentially, Mr. Chaka"—Punchperm beamed—"you are only the second foreigner ever to ride in Kwaidan's favorite helicopter."

He seemed to be congratulating himself rather than me, but I didn't mind as long as he was naive enough to use the word "confidentially" in front of a journalist.

"You know who the last guy was?" he said.

I didn't.

"I'll tell you," he said at length, a smile stuck on his face. "The last guy—he got dropped into Mount Dzogen volcano."

I still didn't know who the guy was, but I guess that wasn't the point. I was supposed to be feel lucky I didn't suffer such a fate myself, but gratitude didn't come naturally to me. I revved the *Velvet Fuck,* drowning out Punchperm's laughter. I wanted to get the hell away from there.

While I was busy beating up a teenage motorcycle gang and listening to a lecture on earthquakes, it seemed nothing much had happened. Back at the hotel the concierge gave me the same smile and handed me the same key to the same room. People were in the lobby doing what people do in hotel lobbies. I took the stairs and they went where they were supposed to go. The key fit in the lock and the door opened. Everything seductively normal, abnormally so.

The feeling didn't last. All I had to do was hit "play" on my answering machine to remind me that I'd left normal behind a long time ago.

The first message was from Nabiko. He took a deep breath then said he wouldn't be working on the tournament documentary anymore. Instead, I should meet him at Toko Studios tomorrow because he thought there were some things we should discuss and that he'd soon be in a very unique position and maybe something good came out of all this after all, for both of us and for the memory of Sato. He'd leave my name at the gate, and I could come see him—he was working with a bunch of pretty girls dressed as fish, quite a change.

See me tomorrow, gotta run, the man is on the megaphone, and that meant work.

I had no idea what he was talking about.

The next message was a full minute of silence. One minute and twenty-four seconds, actually. I listened to it seven times, before I was able to tear myself away.

It was Sarah. Her silence was as recognizable as her voice and it shared many of the same qualities. Intense, deep, and forlorn. Overseas and even on my cheap answering machine, it held a certain unfathomable power. Silence as something full, something real. Not a lack of sound but a presence. It had always been this way, even when she was practically a kid.

And when had she become an adult, anyway? I hadn't noticed. I was off being Billy Chaka—not a bad thing to be, but it took up a lot of room in a life. Now that Sarah was grown up, I wasn't sure she'd fit anymore in an existence so crammed with everything. She could sense that I felt this way, and she didn't know what to do. Neither did I.

I thought about it for an hour and decided things would go one way or they would go another. Lot of good thinking does.

Kwaidan had let me keep the photograph of Sato and Orange Blossom. It wasn't much to go on, but at least it established that they were acquainted. Plus, there were some old comrades in the geisha world I wanted to shop the photo around to, see if she rang any bells.

Back in my room at the hotel I gazed at the photograph for a long time, studying it for clues. But it was just a photograph, and not even a very good one.

It was raining. Sato had on a brimmed hat and the water was rolling off where it dipped in the middle, creating a small waterfall which neatly divided his face. His left hand was tucked inside while he pulled the front of his jacket across his body with the right, almost like he was trying to conceal something. Or maybe he was just trying to keep something dry, or maybe the zipper on his jacket had simply broken. There were all kinds of possibilities.

Orange Blossom stood just a little behind him, to the left. Her face was slightly blurred—she seemed always in motion—but still recognizable. She was pulling her coat over her head, clutching the lapels at either side of her face. It looked a little like she was peering out the flap of a miniature tent. The photograph was black-and-white, but I bet the jacket was red.

What else? There was a scraggly white line at the corner of the photograph that looked like a crack in the emulsion. Rain bouncing off the slick streets. Unreadable writing on a blank wall of a blank building. The street receding in the distance. It was daytime and even looked sunny despite the rain. Maybe that's why neither of them had any rain gear. Come to think of it, they did look a little surprised. Like, "What the hell is going on with this rain, anyway?"

And that was the photograph. Nothing much to go on. Still, I couldn't put it aside. I half expected it to come to life and transport me back to the moment of its creation, like in movies where a frozen image suddenly bursts into action.

Sato himself had used this device in his unfinished film *Singing Samurai,* a musical farce based on the legend of the forty-seven Ronin. The film was shelved when the producers decided that people wouldn't flock to see their historical heroes portrayed as a band of cavalier homosexuals who faked their famous mass suicide in order to move to the mountains, form a commune, and belt out ribald songs celebrating their forbidden love. I'm not sure the producers were entirely wrong.

I let my mind drift. Outside, it had begun to rain, just like in the photograph.

Shinto never showed up the next morning to take me to the tournament. I guess he figured being ditched outside McDonald's was the same as being served notice. That was all right with me, because I knew things were going to escalate, and I couldn't be constantly wavering in my trust of him. Maybe he knew something, maybe he didn't. I didn't have time anymore to find out.

Still, I wanted to end on good terms and actually give the guy some severance pay. I called his pager several times from the hotel, but no dice.

I decided it might not be a good idea to continue my travels on the stolen motorcycle, so I dropped it by a mechanic I'd once rescued from a severe ass-kicking several years ago in the Kabuki-cho. He was more than happy to fix it up and throw in a free tune-up, though he seemed a little confused as to why I wanted it delivered to the kid's house. But he was too smart to ask many questions. I wished my expense accountant back in Cleveland had those kind of smarts.

I hailed a cab. The driver was the talkative sort, so I had to resort to feigning sleep. An adult human being using the old possum con. Sometimes I wonder how far our species has really come.

My fake slumber was made difficult by a Tsuguri Society sound truck barking out their ridiculous slogans behind us. They probably had more trucks than the Japanese National Defense Force—a fact they'd probably use to point out the need to bolster Japan's autonomous armies and make the whole continent nervous.

While I played dead I tried to block out their noises and think about Kwaidan.

The encounter had been instructive. If anything, it reinforced the notion I'd always held that mob bosses are poor role models for young people and that I would do my part to end their glorification in the media. Recalling my own youthful fascination with these underworld figures made me cringe.

Beyond his oddball behavior, there was nothing terribly charismatic about Kwaidan. He was missing that off-kilter charm, the allure of killers you see in the movies. But there wasn't anything particularly coldblooded about him, either. He lacked the detached quality of the total misanthrope, that subhuman dead-eye look of predation and lethargic menace. Instead, he came off as just some old businessmen with a few paranoid eccentricities.

But I felt that Kwaidan was more complicated than he wanted you to believe. The trained dog, the tattoo, and the helicopters seemed part of a calculated affectation, a complex red herring. All the questions about Sato and genius seemed to have been a ploy to keep me off balance. It was as if Kwaidan was trying to play the eccentric type in order to hide the fact that he was actually the calculating type. If this was true, it made him especially dangerous.

Maybe I read too much into things sometimes. But what if I was wrong? Pretending to be crazy and actually being crazy aren't much different, really. Either way it makes you a dangerous guy. Just ask Hamlet.

. . .

Sitting in the tournament bleachers, a thought I'd been trying to avoid punched itself into my brain like Jake La Motta on a bender.

The tournament was already half-finished, and I still had no story. It's not that they weren't there. Any room full of world-class handicapped teen martial artists is bound to have its fair share of material. I could easily do a profile on just one of the gifted teenagers and the difficulties they had to overcome. Show how full of courage and determination they were, and wax about how these kids should be an inspiration to us all. Maybe this was true enough, but any reporter could write it. I had a higher standard.

And I had to admit, my heart just wasn't in it this year. Everything was different now. Sarah seemed to be going through more than just another routine tooth pull. I could hear it in her voice and in her silence. There was something else besides the narcotics going through her head.

Sato was dead. There was a geisha on the loose. Some unmentionable religious organization on my case. Yakuza imposing threats and deadlines. Maybe there were more important things than another handicapped teenage martial-arts championship.

I watched a couple of quarterfinal matches in the women's three-limb sparring competition with mild interest. It was hard to get very excited about the matches. I already knew who would be in the final. Yoko Torikata was a given and then there was the girl from Kyushu—the one I thought the legendary Master Yado may have been secretly coaching.

The Kyushu kid was a Korean from Japan named Young Sook Koo. That afternoon, I watched her make short work of a pretty little thing who'd lost a leg to a Khmer Rouge land mine, which was practically a childhood initiation rite in some unfortunate Cambodian villages. That display was all it took to make up my mind. Those movements—a swift, precise mix of power and delicacy—could only be taught by one man on this earth.

But the odds of meeting Master Yado this year were slim. It would take an ace reporter at the top of his game putting in overtime to pull it off. I was the best, but the situation I'd put myself in had gotten the better of me. I couldn't hang around watching teenagers fight and waiting for a glimpse of Yado. Not when Kwaidan wanted Orange Blossom in a week. Somehow, I got the feeling Kwaidan wouldn't be as forgiving as my editor back in Ohio.

It pained me to have to leave the tournament and all its glories. I was forced to really take an honest look at myself. In the past, I'd always been a functional geishaholic. I'd never let my personal appetites get in the way of a story. But now things were spinning out of control. I knew that in compromising my gift for writing, I was committing an unpardonable offense in the eyes of the reading public. But my thoughts just weren't on the mat this year.

As I walked from the tournament, I hoped that this would be the rock bottom addicts talk about hitting before they start twelve-stepping. But I knew it wasn't. Things would have to get much worse than this.

I was nearing the exit when I happened upon the NHK camera crew unloading equipment. I decided to use the opportunity to learn more about Nabiko's sudden new status, so I approached Tonda, the squatty director. He was scribbling on a clipboard and looked characteristically frustrated.

"Hello," I said, making it lot more pleasant than I felt.

He replied with a grunt.

"I'm a pal of Nabiko's. I was wondering where I might find him."

"Nabiko?" He didn't like the way the word tasted. "He's quit. Trying to push his own project through Toko, that idiot."

"Good for him."

"Yeah," he replied. "Real great for him. I don't know who he had to blow, but someone was impressed."

I wrinkled my brow like I didn't understand.

"Will I be able to get ahold of him there?"

"Listen, I've got shit to do."

"Thanks, anyway," I said.

One day Tonda was going to insult someone who wasn't as even-tempered as myself. Then he'd find out that a movie director's nose breaks the same as anybody else's.

Toko Studios was founded in the 1930s by the merging of several smaller studios, eighteen years after Japan's first studio was born. In the years since, the Japanese film industry in general and Toko in particular had undergone huge changes. During the war, they were forced to make propaganda films by the monarchy. After the war, they were told by the Occupation that they could no longer make *jidai-geki* (period dramas) because they were feudal and militaristic. Sato Migusho once told me, "It was like telling John Ford he couldn't make Westerns." The cinema was in disarray, as thousands of samurai costumes hung uselessly in wardrobe storage.

This all changed in 1950 with the release of *Rashomon*, acclaimed as one of the greatest films of the century and certainly the film responsible for bringing a world audience to Japanese cinema. Though set in feudal Japan, it focused not on heroic samurai but instead the subjectivity of truth, or more simply the fact that everyone is a liar. By allowing this film to be shown, the Americans unofficially relinquished their stranglehold over the indigenous cinema.

What followed was a remarkable period of creativity. For the first time in their history, Japanese directors were able to explore any range of themes in any number of ways. Kurosawa, Ozu, Mizoguchi, and other talented directors flourished. The four major studios were producing a huge number of movies, second only to the American studios of the twenties and thirties. This was also the period when a young filmmaker named Sato Migusho was rising through the ranks.

The excitement of the period was matched only by its brevity. The advent of television crippled the studios, forcing them to turn their back on art and embrace commerce. The cinema of subtlety became the cinema of monsters in rubber suits, pornimation, and formulaic yakuza flicks.

"Even now," Migusho had said in the final interview before his death, "we have yet to fully recover." Serious filmmakers either had to go abroad for their finances or find a way to translate their vision into the bizarre S&M cult cinema. While their Asian counterparts in China, Hong Kong, and even Vietnam had been gaining international critical recognition, the mainstream Japanese film directors contented themselves with cheapo soft-core flicks and derivative sword dramas.

With high real-estate prices and ticket losses, Toko was now less than one-quarter of its postwar size. When I arrived, a large black banner was strewn across the gates, mourning the loss of Sato Migusho. It might as well have been mourning Toko's last thirty years.

"I'm here to see Brando Nabiko," I told the guard at the gate. "The name's Chaka. Billy Chaka." The guard typed on a computer, and then paused to turn something over in his head.

"Forgive me," he said. "But your name sounds familiar. Are you an actor?"

"Nope," I replied. "I'm a writer."

"A screenwriter?"

"A journalist. There are still a few of us."

"Hmm. I wouldn't recognize the name of a journalist, yet I know yours." It seemed a great puzzle to him, apparently one he'd have to solve before he opened the gate. He contemplated it for a moment, muttering my name to himself. Then he burst out laughing.

"Oh, I get it," he bellowed. "Billy Chaka, *Tokyo Suckerpunch*. I can't wait to see it!" He laughed some more. My cabdriver didn't seem to like the sound of it, and he glanced back at me in the rearview mirror to let me know.

"That's good. *Billy Chaka*," the guard said. "And I'm Sansho the Bailiff. Who are you really?"

"I told you. I'm Billy Chaka."

"Yes, yes! Writer for *Youth in Asia*! I've read the screenplay." So much for Sato's "top secret" script. Even the damn security guards had gotten their hands on it. "I need to know your true identity before I let you pass."

My driver turned around and gave me the same look he'd bounced off the mirror. I dug for my passport and handed it through the window to the guard.

"That's a real passport. I'm the real Billy Chaka, and I have a real appointment to meet the real Brando Nabiko." I was a little more rude than I should have been, but I was anxious to see Nabiko. The security guard didn't even glance at the passport before beginning his defense.

"Look, I'm just trying to do my job. I may not be the head chair of the Tokyo University physics department, but I know the difference between a real person and a fictional character. I don't have time for your jokes. I'd be a damn poor security guard if I just let every comedian in here who claimed to be Billy Chaka."

"What's your name?"

"Mr. Yojimbo," he said. He pointing to his badge, nothing more than a grinning photo of him above the words MR. YOJIMBO.

"Mr. Yojimbo," I echoed, digging into my vanishing politeness reserve. "Tell me, does it or does it not say that Billy Chaka has security clearance and expected visitor status?"

He scanned his eyes over the computer monitor. "Well, yes . . . but—"

"And what name does that passport have on it?" He looked at the passport he'd been angrily shaking during the exchange.

"Billy . . . Chaka?"

"And whose picture does that look like to you?" I leaned out the window and gave him a big stupid grin like the one I had on my passport, taken years ago when smiles came a little easier.

He looked at me, then back to the picture. Then to the cabdriver, to the picture, and back to me again. And back to the picture. His face got redder every time he shifted focus.

"Mr. Chaka," he said. "Please accept my most humble apologies. In my ignorance, I did not believe there was a real Billy Chaka. I am but a foolish security guard, my unworldliness perhaps destining me to this humble station in life." The apology came out like dry heaves.

"Don't worry about it, buddy," I said.

He looked like he was choking. "Such a large mouth encases my loose tongue, a tongue governed poorly by a feeble mind—"

"Forget it. A simple misunderstanding."

"I performed terribly on my exams, as you might well guess when confronted with such a simpleton—"

"Please. Just open the gate."

"Even as a small child, I was always the stupid one—"

"Yojimbo! Open the gate!" I commanded. It seemed to be the only way to counter his spewing self-abasement. He stopped in midsentence, pushed a button, and the gate arm rose.

"Mr. Nabiko is on soundstage three, the second one on the left," Yojimbo said, waving us on.

"Mr. Yojimbo," I said, almost afraid to ask.

"Yes?"

"My passport."

His Adam's apple jumped and he handed me the passport. "Again I have made an insulting error. Thankfully, my impotence will assure that my stupidity cannot be passed on to future generations. It is a wonder that..."

We drove toward soundstage three, leaving Yojimbo to shout what a terrible person he was across the studio lot. I wasn't out of hearing range until I exited the car and made my way inside the giant soundstage.

I felt like I'd just walked into a Busby Berkeley film. There was a massive swimming pool with overblue water surrounded by fake seaside cliffs that extended some sixty feet toward the ceiling. Dozens of tiny women with tinier glittering swimsuits stood around smoking cigarettes and looking tantalizingly bored while they waited for the next shot to be set up. Their hair was slicked back with a thick silvery goo that shimmered under the hot lights. I wondered about the prudence of smoking when a single ember would set their heads aflame.

I spotted Nabiko sitting on a camera-mounted dolly. If the size of the camera was any indication, he was worlds away from NHK documentaries.

"Okay," a loud speaker boomed, "all carp in their places, let's go." The school of little women put out their cigarettes and began filing off toward a long flight of stairs that led to the top of the cliffs. They formed two single-file lines, and waited.

"Striking!" I heard over a megaphone, and turned around just in time to be blinded by two huge flood lamps. I staggered backward, covering my eyes even though it was too late. There was only dead white and an electric buzz.

"Speed!" someone shouted.

"Okay, we're rolling," the loudspeaker instructed.

The big pool. Someone jumps in. The sound of the water.

Then another splash, and another. My eyesight returned just in time to make out the silhouettes of aquatic acrobats twisting through the air. They tumbled in rapid succession from the cliffs above, suits flashing silver in the light as their lithe bodies plummeted toward the pool in front of me. For a moment, I thought I was having a flashback from the hallucinogenic algae I'd sampled years ago at a waterskiing tournament on the Mekong. After I'd eaten the stuff, everything turned into fishtrees, fishpeople, fishbuildings, mosquitofish. For three days, everything was aquavision. Thankfully, this time it was all over in less than seven seconds.

"Good work, carp," the bored loudspeaker voice said. "That's a print. Roll call in one hour."

I spotted the owner of the loudspeaker voice eating a "ChocoTasty" and glancing at a video monitor in front of him, more interested in his candy bar than the spectacle of a dozen or so flying synchro swimmers. One of those jaded artists.

"Billy Chaka!" Brando Nabiko called as he made his way toward me. A few heads swiveled at the sound of my name, followed by some suppressed giggles. I decided that if *Tokyo Suckerpunch* somehow made it to the big screen, I was going to have to change my name.

"I got your message," I said to Nabiko. "What's all this?"

"*Turbulent Waters.* It's about the troubles of a community of carp living in the bay off of Choshi," he said flatly.

"Smells a little fishy," I said. Mercifully, the bad pun didn't translate too well and Brando ignored it.

"It is about much more than fish. It deals with issues of loyalty, honesty, and brotherhood unifying the carp community during underwater hardships." Brando stopped and waited for my reaction. I wasn't sure I had one.

"Heavy on the subtext, huh?"

"If you ask me," Nabiko said, looking over his shoulder to see if there was anyone within hearing range, "it's heavy on the bullshit. Who wants to watch a bunch of people pretending to be troubled fish?"

"There's an audience for everything," I offered lamely.

"And the budget! Do you know how much it costs to film a costume drama underwater? Or how much you have to pay an actress to be submerged in water for up to eight hours a day?"

"A whale of a sum?"

"They were gonna have Yoko Torikata playing the fish who loses a fin to the boat propeller, but her agent wanted the studio to take out an insurance policy covering the possibility of Yoko's skin becoming permanently wrinkled from the water. This whole business is crazy," he said, shaking his head.

"That Tonda guy told me you were wheeling and dealing with the studio on one of your own projects."

Brando didn't say anything for a moment. A smile came across his face and left just as fast. It only lasted long enough for me to think there was something strange in it.

"What Tonda doesn't know can't hurt him. Otherwise he'd constantly be in terrible pain."

I had to unpack that thought, but Nabiko hardly gave me the chance.

"What did you think of the script?" he said.

At first I wondered what script he was talking about, then I figured it must be that monstrosity I was trying to forget.

"I haven't finished it yet."

"No?" Brando looked disappointed. I guess he had gone through a lot of trouble to get me a copy. I hoped he hadn't invited me to the studio to talk about the script. Hopefully, he just wanted some bowling tips.

"Did you get to the part where he—well, *you,* I guess—fights off the evil spirits at Nikko?"

"Not yet."

"There's a fight scene inside the mausoleum of Ieyasu. Of course, we'll never get a permit to shoot there, but we can build a replica. I think we're going to have a sizable budget."

Did he mean they were actually going to film this thing?

"There are still some things to be ironed out." He chuckled, obviously mistaking my alarm for excitement. "Always are when this kind of money is involved. But don't worry—once it gets momentum, this thing is gonna be unstoppable. We'll be in constant touch. The numbers are really starting to look good."

Numbers? Most cinematographers I knew weren't real interested in numbers. It was unsettling.

"I'm sure there are bound to be some legal complications, what with Sato's death and all," I said, feigning disinterest. I hoped it would never even get that far. If it did, I'd create some legal complications of my own.

"I wouldn't worry too much. It's all being worked out," Brando said. And there was that flash of a smile again.

I fished the photo out of my jacket and handed it to Nabiko. He looked at it for a moment. I watched his face for that smile but it didn't come back.

"Have you ever seen that woman before?" I asked.

"Not sure," he said, handing the photo back to me. "Speaking as a pro, I have to say it's not the greatest picture ever taken. Her face is kind of blurry."

"You ever see Sato with this woman?"

Brando thought it over. I couldn't tell if he was actually trying to remember or just trying to decide what to tell me. Complicated world. Finally, he shook his head.

"Maybe years ago. I can't remember. I only saw Sato with actresses, and no actress I know would be out in the sun without sunglasses. See how the sun was still shining, even though it's raining? Squinting gives you wrinkles. Wrinkles wreck careers."

That and burning to death.

"You can also tell that it was taken at eye level, with a telephoto lens. See how the wall behind them is indistinct? You can't read the writing? That's because longer lenses tend to have a very limited depth of field. Of course, that also depends on the aperture opening."

"Anything else?

"It's midday. You can tell by the way the light is relatively flat—the sun is directly overhead. Oh, and I'd guess they are in the mountains."

"The mountains?"

"It's just a hunch. They could be anywhere, really."

"But why the mountains?"

"Well, a few things. See how the sky is pretty dark? Normally, in this type of black-and-white picture, the sky appears a blank white—unless you use a filter to darken it."

"But you don't think they used a filter?"

"For this type of photo? Why bother. Surveillance photos are not meant to be aesthetically pleasing. More likely the sky is dark because they are at a high elevation. It has to do with atmospheric haze and the fact that black-and-white emulsions are more sensitive to blue light than the human eye—lots of boring technical stuff."

"That's damned impressive, Brando. But couldn't the sky have been altered somehow during the printing process?"

"Oh, sure. It could have been burned in. They could have done it digitally. But again, why bother? Another thing—see how the section toward the end of the street back here looks really flat, kind of hazy off into the distance? That can be caused by ultraviolet radiation, which is another feature of high-elevation photography. It can be corrected with filters, but some snoop wouldn't care about that."

"What's this little lightning-looking thing up in the corner?" I asked, pushing for more. "I guessed it was a crack in the emulsion."

"No, but you've hit on something pretty interesting."

"How so?"

"It actually is a lightning bolt, of sorts. Not in the sky, but in the camera. That all but confirms it was a high-elevation photograph. But that also means that this photographic print was taken from a motion-picture still."

"I don't get it."

"The camera was not properly grounded, and when filming at high elevations there is a lot of static electricity in the air. Add this to all those whirring gears in the camera and you get sparks that actually show up on the negative looking like a series of lightning bolts."

"Weird."

"Only if you consider scientific principles weird." Nabiko shrugged.

"I do."

"Well"—Nabiko chuckled—"fair enough. What's this all about, anyway? You still think Sato was murdered?"

"I know he was."

"You think the girl in the picture did it?"

I took a deep breath. I suppose it was possible. I hadn't even thought about that angle.

"I hope not." I sighed.

Someone announced something I didn't catch over a megaphone, and Brando looked over his shoulder nervously.

"Back to work?" I asked.

"This director is not only bad, he's a slave driver," Brando answered. "Too much chocolate. But you just wait, Billy. I'll be calling the shots before you know it." He turned and walked back on the set. But not before he gave me one more look at that weird new smile.

I was running out of leads and running out of time. I wanted to go to Kyoto tonight and show the picture to a well-connected aging matri-arch of a geisha house I knew, but I had a couple hours to kill before my train left.

Not knowing what else to do, I decided to stop by the Purple Dragnet to see if there had been any more trouble. It was one of only two places I'd ever seen this woman, and though I doubted she'd been back, I wasn't completely without hope.

In the taxi on the way over, I watched the small TV mounted in the backseat. Yoko Torikata had a new movie coming out where she played a schoolteacher at an academy for handicapped kids. The catch was, she was wanted by the mob because she was also the world's best gambler. In the preview, there were stupid shots of her playing a one-armed bandit with her one arm. The movie was actually called *One Armed Bandit*. It was supposed to be a comedy.

I got out of the cab and noticed a construction worker monkeying with the sign over the entrance of Bhuto's joint. For a moment, I feared Bhuto had been forced to close. The yaks can make it real hard to stay in business if they decide they don't like you. And if they didn't like Hiro, it would have been my fault. I walked inside and prepared for the worst.

"Welcome to the Purple Web." Bhuto beamed, flourishing his arms in a wide gesture of introduction. It was still the same dusty, lightless dive. Only now there were computers at three of the tables and one at the end of the bar.

"The Internet is the wave of the future! Surf the Web highway of information net while you inhale oxygen!" He gleamed. He was holding up a mask just like the one airline stewardesses are always demonstrating.

I shouldn't have even blinked when I saw the sign out front being changed. I'd seen the place as a jazz club called the Purple Note, a tiny disco called the Purple Beat, a vampire dive known as the Purple Coffin, and most inexplicably the fisherman's bar it had been only a few days ago. I guess this was only a matter of time for Bhuto, always vigilant to any trend to make a blip on the cultural radar screen. Never what you'd call an early adapter, he was always about three or four blips behind. But when he got an idea, he got it all the way.

"You still serve beer here or just air?"

"Air, beer, and information."

Everything a fella needs. I took a seat at the end of the bar and logged onto the terminal. Bhuto brought me a Kirin lager and told me about all of the software he'd loaded onto the machines, then suggested a few sites to visit.

"You should check out Yoko Torikata's homepage," he said. "Lots of tasty images!"

Instead, I logged onto my machine back at *Youth in Asia* headquarters. I had tons of e-mail, digital affection from the fans who had seen my address in the magazine. Downloading it all would probably crash Bhuto's machine, and I had some fact checking to do.

I'd long ago made it a habit to keep files on the people I found interesting. It made research a lot easier, and if my facts were ever questioned, I had the documents to prove it. Before I left, Sarah had been busy with the unenviable task of putting my wealth of scribbled notes and newspaper clippings into digital form to store on the server. The more I thought about the stuff I made her do, the more her little narcotic vacations seemed to make sense.

I pulled up Sato's file and began to read. There were a number of articles I'd clipped, mostly film reviews from esoteric cinematic journals. Then there was a whole section of compiled quotes called "Sato on Film." I decided to skip those and go directly to the brief biography I'd compiled.

Sato Migusho—birth date unknown. Father a semifamous *benshi* whose fans called him Big Ears, and his mother was a geisha-school dropout who became an actress specializing in playing foreigners.

Representative quote: "My childhood was spent watching my father narrate those old silents. I thought he must have been the smartest man in the world, because people would come every night to hear him speak. It didn't enter my head until sometime later that the movies had anything to do with it. I thought they just wanted to listen to Papa tell them stories, or explain about the Eiffel Tower or whatever else. Still sometimes when I watch a silent, I can hear his voice. "Chaprin gives the woman a flower. It appears to be a rose, a flower with romantic connotations in the Occident. The woman is grateful and shows it with a coquettish smile…""

Sato Migusho attends a private school that emphasizes the performing arts. In his final year in the program, he pens his first work, a play entitled *Seppuku in Ishikawa*.

Migusho later destroyed the work, as he was ashamed of its amateurish elements.

Representative quote: "It was just a rip-off of all those old Kabuki dramas, where the unhappy lovers end up falling on their swords. I tried to modernize it a little, so I had them shoot themselves in the head using Russian revolvers. That was my only formal innovation at that point. The play was never produced and I destroyed every copy I could find. It was that bad."

It was shortly after this that Migusho claims to have had his first romance. The woman's name was ????

Then he made a bunch of movies and got famous. I can't read these notes, Billy. Your handwriting is terrible. This is pointless. You're never gonna look at this stuff, anyway.

Sarah, Sarah, Sarah. Fifty-plus pages of notes on Sato Migusho, reduced to this. And she accused me of being passive-aggressive. I decided to print the "Sato on Film" section to read on the train to Kyoto. Unfortunately, Bhuto still had some bugs to work out, because the printer wasn't working. So I logged off the Big Daddy at *Youth in Asia* and downed the rest of my beer.

Bhuto apologized profusely for the printer problems, and cursed the top-of-the-line machine.

"You know what they say," I said.

"What?"

"If it works, it's already obsolete."

Hiro Bhuto just looked at me, and then he turned around and slapped the printer, telling it in no uncertain terms what would happen if it didn't clean up its act.

The printer just took it.

. . .

I tried Shinto's pager one more time on the way out of town, but my call was promptly unreturned. The guy sure knew how to hold a grudge. Maybe if I'd just let him stick around awhile he would have come out of his shell, but I guessed I'd never know.

A funny thing occurred to me, though, which seemed to justify my paranoia about the guy. I had no evidence whatsoever that he was really Sato's driver. I'd never heard of him or seen him with Sato. Whoever arranged to have Sato killed could have easily orchestrated it so that Shinto Hirohito picked me up just as Sato's house was filling with smoke. I remembered Shinto shouting and running breathlessly toward me as I stepped out of the Purple Dragnet. Sato would have been choking on his dying breath about then.

What an idiot I was. The key link to Sato's murder had driven me around Tokyo for days and all I could think about was his mustache. He'd doubtlessly learned more about me than I had about him. I got the feeling that I was the one who had been ditched, played for a fool.

I looked at the picture anew as I waited for the Bullet Train. I was concentrating on the photo so much I hardly even noticed the people around me. You know you're in trouble when you start paying more attention to pictures than to real people.

I had to ask myself how the yakuza had gotten hold of the photo. Possibly it was taken by a private detective or maybe a really confused paparazzo who thought Sato was still famous enough to make the tabloids. But if Brando Nabiko was right about it being a still from a 16mm motion-picture camera, that put a different spin on things. Since the advent of video, nobody in their right mind would use 16mm for surveillance or even to make home movies. The film was expensive, didn't capture sound, and required some expertise to get a coherent image. Aesthetes and film students champion 16mm for its superior image quality and the fact that one has greater control over the subtle elements of lighting, focus, frames per second, and the like. The kind of people who like to say things like, "Theater is life. Film is art. Television is furniture." In other words, not the kind of people likely to care much about practicality.

And so film snobs emerged as the prime suspects. But because of the obvious flaws in the picture, it would have to be a film snob who didn't really know what they were doing, or didn't really care about the quality of the image—image quality being the only reason to use 16mm in the first place.

Baffling, and maybe not worth worrying over. I didn't have to solve every mystery, after all. Finding the woman in the picture would be hard enough.

As I gazed at her image it occurred to me that she was becoming more and more unreal. Trying to track her down was like playing tag with a ghost. Lots of Zen koans came to mind, the ones about tasks which seemed simple but were impossible. But that kind of thinking was self-defeating folly. Mystery is just ordinary reality tied in a knot.

I knew only three things for certain. One, she was a geisha. Granted, that was cheating. It wasn't a fact, just a damn powerful hunch. Call it *hara gei,* the art of the stomach. Two, she knew the late Sato Migusho—I had the picture to prove it. Three, she was fleeing something, already desperately running when I'd first seen her at the Purple Dragnet. Probably from the yaks, but maybe from something more.

By calling on my favorite *okamisan* in Kyoto, I hoped to find out what that something was.

Sure, you'll find some damn good geisha in Tokyo. The physical beauty of Tokyo geisha has always floored me, and their hospitality is graciousness itself. But comparing the Tokyo geisha experience to that of Kyoto isn't really fair. It's like comparing riverboat gambling in Iowa to the Strip in Vegas.

Kyoto is to geisha what Paris is to intellectuals. It's what Los Angeles is to blondes, what New York is to Jewish comedians, and what Berlin is to leather pants.

To put it another way—Tokyo is Tokyo, but Kyoto is Japan.

By that I mean the Japan of legend, of palaces and shrines, samurai, and yes—geisha. It is said that Kyushu was the birthplace of Japanese culture, but Kyoto is where it really flourished, transforming the ideas imported from China into something uniquely Japanese. It served as the imperial capital of Japan for over one thousand years, as well as the cultural and religious center of the nation. Even Westerners recognized its importance to the world, lobbying to have it spared during the WWII bombings that destroyed much of urban Japan.

Kyotoites themselves seemed more ambivalent about the value of their city. Since the end of the war, they'd enlisted an army of bulldozers to wage war on old Kyoto under the guise of modernization—a goal apparently measured per mile of pavement. Luckily, the war to become another Tokyo was not yet won.

In a sense, Kyoto remained all that was left of traditional Japan, and so paradoxically is flooded with tourists almost year-round. As Sarah once put it, the mass impulse for experiencing authenticity is exactly what makes such an experience impossible. Once culture is preserved, it's no longer authentic.

Sarah said my geisha problem was related to this. My love of geisha was a manifestation of an impossible longing to experience a Japan that doesn't exist anymore. She said I would continually be frustrated in my quest for something culturally savage and pure in a world where culture is a domesticated mutt. I would keep falling into the arms of the lovely geisha, searching for an epiphany which would never come because I was after something forever lost.

Maybe she was right. But then again, maybe I wasn't completely deluded. I argued that it was the quality of the fantasy itself that attracted me. Geisha were never about reality, even when they flourished hundreds of years ago. Everything about them was exquisitely ornamental, not superficial, but not natural either. Instead they were, and a very few still are, living works of beauty. They are the embodiment of romance, as a concept and as an art—a reaction to the drudgery of rigid social hierarchies and arranged marriages that once ruled Japan. What they sold were dreams, and it was a product that required a lifetime of diligent training. It is a magic that perhaps can only be understood in a society where individual needs are invariably subjugated to that of the community. Geisha aren't just some tarts with *shamisen*—they are the very symbol of the ephemeral quality of youth, beauty, seasons—and life itself. Their existence is the product of a Zen tradition that recognizes the inherent sadness of knowing that these happy hours shall pass, this very life will pass—and experiencing a joy in this sadness.

And so I babble, until she finally shuts me up.

Maybe, Sarah said. But you are not Japanese, not even a Buddhist, so what's your excuse?

I don't know how to answer that and I don't particularly care to, anyway. It's a deeply personal matter, and if I were a psychologist perhaps I could come up with some theory she'd buy. She's a sucker for theories. As it is, I am a journalist. My trade is facts, and the fact is that I love geisha enough to wreck my life.

And if you are going to wreck your life over a geisha, the best place to do it is in Kyoto.

The jumbled network of tiny wooden houses that made up the particular area of the Gion district where I was headed gave me some idea of how urban Japan would have looked hundreds of years ago. People that kept score liked to point out that Kyoto had already burned down and been rebuilt twice before the Pilgrims plopped down at Plymouth.

Right now, though, I was stuck in a thoroughly twentieth-century traffic jam on Kawarimachi-dori.

"You British?" my cabbie asked.

"American," I said. "But I mean well."

"Hell. It doesn't matter to me. As long as you pay in yen, you're free to ride. You speak Japanese pretty good. I'm Korean myself, so don't think I hold any grudges."

I got the feeling that what he meant was "to hell with the Japanese if they don't like foreigners like us." He wasn't the first Korean I'd met with mixed feelings about Japan. Like most countries that had at one time or another been power hungry, Japan had a historical tendency to look down on other peoples as inferior. As the Koreans were the nearest inferiors, they bore the brunt of the blow.

I got the feeling the cabbie was trying to bait me into a conversation that I didn't want to have, so I just nodded and looked out the window. And what should pull up beside me but another goddamn sound truck from the Tsuguri Society. It was like they were following me.

There was that solemn face, plastered on the side of the truck only a few feet from my own. There were no chanting guys in hopi-coats this time, maybe because the weather looked iffy. Fanaticism is one thing but rain is another. The speakers were raging, though, blasting a message mostly lost in the wind. Whatever they were saying, I was certain I could live without it.

"You believe these guys?" the cabbie said, shaking his head.

"I'd hoped they were just a Tokyo phenomenon," I said. The truck blasted something about whiskey being more popular than sake, but I couldn't tell what they were getting at.

"They are everywhere now. I got a cousin in Kagoshima and they're there, too. It's because people are stupid. Not people so much, but *groups* of people. Yeah, groups of people are stupid and they will believe anything."

It was about as un-Japanese a sentiment as I had ever heard, but then this guy wasn't Japanese. I wondered if he felt comfortable speaking like this because I was a fellow outsider, or if he thought disdain for the masses was an American sentiment I would appreciate so far from my homeland.

"I mean, you get more than three people in a room and they are bound to do something stupid. They are going to start a political party, or an Internet company or a rock band or something. You know what I mean? You take every single thing in the world that requires more than three people— soccer teams, restaurants, motorcycle clubs, churches, karaoke clubs, ex-smoker groups—take all of those and I think, What's the point? Does the world really need another one of those? Another origami union, or squash team or cat lovers' group?"

He was gripping the steering wheel hard and his knuckles stood out like rolling mountains on a curving horizon. I could see this thing was really bugging him, or more likely something else was and this was how he got at it. People are generally mad about some other, hidden cause when they begin to pick on cat lovers' clubs. I didn't dare ask him if he thought the world needed another antisocial cabdriver.

"Yeah," I said. "Well, people are social animals. What can you do?"

"They're animals all right. If I knew how to change it, I'd start my own damn club and drive around in one of those trucks," he said, nodding to the Tsuguri-mobile that pulled away beside us. "I'd tell everybody in earshot it was time to quit getting together and doing useless things."

There was no appropriate response that I was aware of. The Tsuguri Society truck sped off ahead. I thought maybe as a professional driver my cabbie might know why the other lane is always faster but I didn't ask. He had plenty on his mind already.

In a few minutes I was happily out of the cab and wandering through the hidden labyrinth of wooden houses. The neon Western hotels and cheap tourist strips with mass-produced Buddhas and plastic samurai swords seemed worlds away, though in truth I was less than a block from the late-twentieth century.

The rain had just started and the streets were emptying fast. I tried to slow my pace to a leisurely stroll so I could enjoy the semisolitude. It was no use, though. I was too anxious to see Mama Mayumi.

She was the *okamisan* at the first geisha house I ever visited. As proprietress, she was the highest ranking of the nine women there, which included four geisha, three *maiko* (teenage virgin geishas-in-training), and two "eggs" (prepubescent maiko-in-waiting who begin their training at age six and a half and six days). I met her working on a story about teen singing idol Sam Torayuki. When he failed to show for the interview, I contacted his record company. They apologized profusely and I must have made a good impression because the A&R guy invited me to a geisha party to make up for Mr. Torayuki's gaffe. I accepted the invitation out of politeness. Truth was, I didn't really think geisha would be my thing.

I was wrong.

And now here I was standing once again in front of Mama Mayumi's. It didn't look any different than when I'd visited that first time or any of the years since. In fact, it really didn't look any different from the houses on either side of it, if you didn't know what to look for.

Normally, one does not just go knocking on the door of a geisha house without invitation. Strict protocol is observed as far as making arrangements to visit the *zashiki* beforehand, and it is typically done in groups of three or four. But I wanted to surprise Mama Mayumi, and at any rate it would be a few hours until her scheduled revelers arrived. Behind the door, the geisha would be painstakingly coloring their faces and carefully assembling the layers of elaborate dress that create such breathtaking entrances.

At least I had not made the mistake of showing up empty-handed. Coming here without invitation was excusable from a foreigner, since I didn't want to do anything but ask a couple of quick questions, maybe arrange to meet somewhere later for a drink. But had I shown up without a gift, I doubt Mayumi would even have taken a look at the picture.

I lightly rapped on the door and waited. After a few moments, I heard a shuffling inside and got that little jump I get in my stomach when waiting outside of strange doors. A small wooden partition slid open. Inside, a pair of dark eyes against a porcelain-white face stared back at me. The little jump quickened. I felt like Humbert Humbert at a junior-high gymnastics tournament.

Before I could say anything, the eyes suddenly disappeared. I stood there holding my present. Suddenly another face was in the tiny slot. It had the kind of large, dark eyes that take years off my life. But that face, too, was suddenly gone. I heard a commotion and a shrill-sounding woman bark out something with authority. Certainly this was Mama

Mayumi coming to see what all her girls were fussing about. I smiled to myself like an idiot, standing at the door in the rain.

"What you want?" the voice said. Even before I'd seen her eyes I'd begun a deep, reverential bow. I had my honorifics all prepared.

"Please forgive me for calling at this hour without invitation. I have violated the custom and I apologize for disturbing the household," I began, my eyes still facing the ground. I was sure Mayumi was getting a kick out of this.

"I have been away on travels and have not visited this district for a number of years and—"

"What number?" I heard a girlish voice cry out behind the door to a burst of giggles.

"Be quiet!" the *okamisan* scolded. They did. I went on.

"I have been traveling and I didn't know how else to reach the woman I seek. And so I come here, a place of business, to embarrass myself in seeking her and ask for your forgiveness. My intentions are honorable and I come on a matter of urgent business. My name is Billy Chaka and I seek Mama Mayumi."

I waited with my head bowed. The rain tickled the back of my neck.

"Tough luck," the voice responded. "She is no longer a geisha of this house."

I looked up suddenly. An old, unfamiliar pair of eyes greeted me. They were as empty as a Buddha's mind.

"She's not here?" I said.

"That's right. I'm the new *okamisan*—Mama Saikuku. I can't help you. Tough luck."

"I am honored to make your acquaintance," I said. I thought about handing her one of my cards through the slot, but I was worried I might poke her in the eyes. Then I remembered that I didn't have any cards anyway.

"Do you know where I might be able to find her? It's terribly important." Continuing this way was a mistake. In a world of jealousy and illicit liaisons, secrecy is as much a part of a geisha as the kimono. Who knows but that I might be some crazed ex-client who took Mayumi's attentions too seriously and had crossed the line and fallen in love and so we'd have to kill ourselves. If you've seen enough Kabuki, you would be certain this was the logical progression of events.

"I can't tell you that," she said with a hint of rebuke in her tone.

"Of course. Forgive me for disturbing you and please accept my gift to your house." The gift was six exquisite leather bound diaries that came with quill pens carved from artificial whalebone. I'm sure it would be a topic of discussion with my accountant back in Cleveland. We always have a lot to talk about.

"No thanks. Good day, Mr. Chaba." And with that mispronunciation, she slid the little portal shut with a dry click.

There was nothing to do but stand there in the rain like a heel, or walk away like a heel in the rain.

I wondered if I had gone to the wrong house, but the woman seemed to know who Mayumi was. Perhaps Mayumi had finally found a patron and was settling into the closest thing most geisha ever get to marriage. I felt a sudden panic. Maybe she was dead. She had died and the *okamisan* didn't want to upset me, or maybe there was a superstition about mentioning the dead through sliding portals to men standing in the rain.

I got angry, reproaching myself for always thinking the worst. Sarah would say that I do it because it is easier for my ego to conceive of someone's death than to imagine they have gone on to a life without me. But I can't help what I think any more than I can stop the rain from falling on my head. So then I started to rebuke myself for getting mad at myself for what I thought. The Möbius strip of uselessness that is the unenlightened mind.

"Mister...mister," I heard being called behind me in a tiny voice. It was as good as a knock to the head to bring me into the here and now. I turned around and saw a little girl running toward me, her tennis shoes splashing along the puddles of rain on the street. She was wearing aqua-blue sweatpants and a yellow T-shirt that said MOM'S LITTLE KISS.

"What is it, little sugar dumpling?" I said, nearly going down on one knee so that I might be eye level with her. Being called sugar dumpling made her laugh, or maybe it was just the sight of a silly man in the rain.

"I have a message for you," she said matter-of-factly. I knew by then that she must be one of the "eggs" from the house. She couldn't have been older than eight.

"Well, let me put on my good ears, then," I said, and did a pantomime I'd learned from a street magician in Jakarta whereby I reach into my pocket and put on my "new" set of ears. Usually kids love it, but this one just raised one of her eyebrows. Tough customer.

"Are you ready?" she asked.

"Go ahead."

"Okay." She took a deep breath and rolled her eyes skyward. "Rei told me to tell you that she remembered you and you were a gentleman and she was only a *maiko* then but now she is a geisha and you should visit her."

Rei...Rei. I remembered two *maikos* from my last visit and they were both stunning, precocious little devils who were all the more alluring because with *maiko*, it is strictly hands-off. There was one in particular who attracted me. She had a distracted quality about her, always glancing off into strange corners and gazing at nothing in particular. Some women look dopey when they do this, but with others it comes off as deeply mysterious. The makeup and the whole geisha getup helped. I wondered if this was Rei.

"Good," I said to the little girl. "Thank you."

"There's more, too."

"Okay."

"She said that the other lady, the one you wanted, she knew where she was, and then she wrote this and then said I should give it to you." The little girl handed me a neatly folded piece of paper. I tucked it into my pocket.

"Are you going read it?" the girl asked. She wrinkled her brow in concern.

"You bet I'm gonna read it," I said. "But first I want to give you something." I handed her the wrapped gift.

"What is it?"

"Do you know how to write?" I asked.

"I'm not a dummy." The little girl giggled.

"Well, good. Because there are some books in there that you can write in. You can write what you do every day, or you can make up stories, draw pictures, or whatever you want."

She looked at the box with mild interest; I got the feeling she was hoping it was an e-pet or a cell phone. "Okay," she said finally. "See ya later." She turned around and walked a zigzagging course back to the house. I watched her go, turning the box over in her hands to inspect it some more and then tucking it under her arm like a football.

Someday she would be a geisha and I would be an old man. In between, the future held a lot of uncertainties that probably didn't matter much, anyway.

The paper said,

Mayumi
Club Pineapple
in Pontocho

It was signed simply and elegantly "Rei."

I couldn't really believe that Mayumi had left the geisha world. I looked over the card again. Not much to look at, really. I decided the only way to find out was to go to Club Pineapple and hope she was there.

Amazingly, when I hailed a cab, I ended up with the same Korean guy who'd just dropped me off. More surprising still, he didn't even recognize me after half an hour. He asked me if I was British again, complimented my Japanese. This time, though, he skipped the antigroup rhetoric and instead tried to bait me into a conversation about the controversial decision to hold the 2002 World Cup in both Japan and South Korea. He said it demonstrated the West's ignorance of Asian affairs, as if to their minds one was the same as the other. Then he said that if they thought the World Cup was going to bring these countries together, well then, they had another thing coming. I kept my opinions to myself, thankful that it was a short ride. Shinto's silence looked more appealing with every mile on the meter.

After I got out, it took me only a few minutes to find Club Pineapple. It was one of those tiny places down some crooked little street, not unlike those in the Gion districts except for the abundance of neon. Even the pavement seemed electric as the lights shimmered in the pools of rain.

The place was a Hawaiian nightmare. A string of lit-up hula dancers hung across the bar like Christmas lights on Planet Kitsch. The five small tables were draped with shaggy faux-grass skirts, making them look like miniature weeping willows. There were only a few people here this early, and they sat huddled at a corner table, hardly speaking as they sipped drinks from mock-coconut shells.

I took a seat at the end of the bar. Ukulele music undulated quietly through the air, coming in small waves as if it had traveled from some distant, tropical paradise. A bar hostess approached casually, her hips swaying like palm fronds in a cool breeze. She wore a grass skirt and her floral bikini top was fighting a losing battle of containment. She couldn't have been older than twenty-two, max.

"What can I get for you?" she cooed. I thought about asking if she knew where a guy could get lei'd around here, and shuddered. I always hated that pun and it didn't translate, anyway.

"What are they drinking?" I asked instead, nodding to the group in the corner.

"Piña coladas," she said. She was leaning over the bar toward me, and I stole a glance at her breasts. I'd long since accepted that cleavage was inherently interesting. I didn't gawk and tried not to linger, but there was no way I could keep from looking. Biology.

"How do you make it?" I asked.

"However you like."

"I like it strong. Strong, but sweet."

"I know how you want it," she said, drawing out the words. "A squeeze of rum. A handful of juicy pineapple. A few delicious drops of coconut milk."

"Do you milk the coconuts by hand?"

"That's one way to do it," she said.

"It's a good start."

"Sure. But first, I have to crack the nut. I get an iron hammer and swing it down as hard as I can. Bam!"

"Ouch."

"The nut doesn't always crack the first time. I have to bash it with the hammer over and over. Bam! Bam! Bam!"

"Maybe I'll just have a beer."

"Whatever you like," she said with a sly smile. I watched her sashay over to the fridge behind the bar. When she opened the fridge door, a rush of cool vapor flowed over her upper body, and I could see the goose bumps start to form on her taut shoulders.

Sarah used to catch me ogling women from time to time, but even she quit reprimanding me after I started lecturing her about studies on chimpanzees that proved male sexuality was visually oriented and that's just the way it was. She finally just sighed and said, "If you want to be a gorilla, be a gorilla." Chimps weren't gorillas, but I guess that wasn't her point.

The bar hostess drew the beer, giving it plenty of head. Suddenly two hands clapped over my eyes. Just when I was really enjoying the view.

"Guess who? "

It was Mama Mayumi. I'd almost forgotten why I'd come.

"How you doin', Mama Mayumi," I said. She took her hands from my eyes as I swiveled around on my stool. I'd never seen Mayumi dressed in anything other than a kimono and the sight was a little jarring. She was older now, into her fifties, but she'd kept her looks and appeared every bit the modern woman in her modest summer dress.

"What are you doing here?" she asked, taking my hands in hers.

"I might ask you the same thing."

"I run this place. I have a patron now, nice old guy who made a fortune in video games."

"No kidding?"

"Sure. You ever play Alien Motorcycle Cop? Cyborg Samurai? Those are from his company. He got me out of the geisha world, set up this place for me to run. I see him maybe three or four times a month. He's a real sweetie." She seemed content, and I felt happy for her. The geisha world is often one of sorrow, filled with ephemeral loves and stoic tragedies. Fun from a dramatic standpoint but living through it could be a different story.

"Congratulations." I beamed. "I guess you're living the life now, here at Club Pineapple."

"It's a stupid name, I know. His idea."

"The Hawaiian thing, too?"

"Of course." She giggled. The beautiful young bar hostess handed me my beer inside a plastic coconut cup. I thanked her and she gave me a smile worth contemplating.

"Well," I said to Mayumi, "it definitely has its charms."

Mayumi laughed again, rolling her eyes at me. "You should have seen me when I was her age, Mr. Chaka."

"I think I would have enjoyed that," I replied.

"I know you would have," she said with a wink.

We settled into the only corner booth, just opposite a demure party of three who paid us little attention. By the looks of their table they'd been knocking back piña coladas for a better part of the afternoon, but it didn't seem to have loosened their tongues. They were a strange mix. One fairly pretty young lady in her early twenties—a college student probably—an older gentleman, and a guy around thirty. I don't know what would have brought them together, unless they were family. That would explain why they weren't saying much.

"Lively bunch over there," I said quietly to Mayumi.

"They are members of a local religious order. Some new group," she said with displeasure in her quiet voice. "They've all taken vows of silence."

"Looks like vows of cirrhosis, too. What's the group called?"

"I don't remember the name. Anyway, they're all the same. In this one, every Thursday is drinking night, but it is also the day of silence."

"The sutras must have been written by a real comedian," I said, sipping on my drink.

"They are good, paying customers. But they kind of give me the creeps sitting there like mutes all night, getting plowed. Sometimes, I wish they'd just get rowdy. It's not natural."

Like a good hostess, she quickly changed the subject to me, inquiring all about what I'd been up to since we last met and what I was doing in Japan. I told her about the tournament and left out pretty much everything else. I felt a pang of regret, knowing that even at this moment, teenage combatants were giving it their all, forgetting their handicaps, capitalizing on them even, to immerse themselves in the drama of their unfolding lives. And they were doing it without knowing or caring that I was in Kyoto on a wild-geisha chase. Why should they?

She told me about how she'd met the old video-game guy at a *ryotei* here in Kyoto thrown by his company, how he'd taken her away from the geisha life. She admitted that she missed aspects of it, but that everything was different now. The younger girls expected more out of life and didn't really

understand that geishadom was about sacrificing your immediate desires in service of others, about forgetting your dreams
in order to become one. The aesthetes who sincerely appreciated a skillful dance or *koto* tune and treated geisha not as
party favors but as living works of art were getting older and
dying. The younger guys, she complained, just wanted a dog-
and-pony show with drinks and a little grab-ass. She said the
world needed more people like me, who could really value
the geisha. Thinking of everything that had happened since I
ran into Orange Blossom, I wasn't sure I agreed.

I had another drink, one of the piña coladas this time. It
wasn't bad for one of those fruity deals. The bar hostess
made eyes at me when she served it. Not too much, just
enough to make me want to see more. It was working and so
were the drinks.

I decided it was time to get down to brass tacks with
Mayumi, so I took out the photograph of Orange Blossom
and pushed it across the table.

Mayumi glanced at it playfully. "I was wondering why
you came." She smirked.

"Not at all. Just happened to have this on me. Thought
it'd make a good conversation piece."

"Not the greatest picture, is it?"

"I wanted to ask you if you recognized the girl."

She leaned over a few inches and squinted hard at the
photograph. I pushed the pineapple-shaped table candle closer
to throw more light on the picture.

"It is tough to make out her face. Still, she looks familiar.
Now, how can that be?" Mayumi was transfixed by the photo,
gazing at it like it was one of those chaotic stereographic
images that suddenly go 3-D when you cross your eyes.

"Want a clue?"

"Sure," Mayumi said, not looking away from the picture.

"She's a geisha. Least I think so."

"Of course she is. What else?"

"How can you tell?"

Mayumi looked up at me and shook her head. "What else?"

"Her name is Orange Blossom."

"Ha!" Mayumi yelped, pounding the table. My drink hopped from the table's surface, the thick white liquid lapping over the edge of the glass. She even jarred a startled syllable from one of the three mutes in the corner.

"I knew it!" she hollered. Then, catching herself, she quieted down and leaned over the table and hissed, "I knew it was her. Where did you get this picture?"

"Can't tell you. You know her?"

"Sure I do. But it has been so many years since I have seen her. Wow, this is really strange. I can't believe this is her, but this is her. Who is the man?"

"Can't tell you," I said. I could have, but I wanted to see if she could come up with some kind of connection herself.

"Where was this photograph taken, anyway?" Her eyes darted across its surface for clues.

"I don't know."

"You don't know much, do you?"

"That's why I'm here. Tell me about her."

And she did. And things got that much stranger.

Mayumi met Orange Blossom when she herself was only a young *maiko*. Orange Blossom just showed up one day from out of nowhere at the geisha house looking for a place to ply her trade. This was unusual, unheard of actually, since geisha tend to stay with one house their whole life. Rare exceptions went and started their own place. Nobody went to other houses, it just didn't work that way. But there she was.

She had some tragic yarn or other about how her patron had abandoned her after she'd irreparably burned all bridges to her former house. Normally, the tough old *okamisan* that ran the place would have listened patiently and then shown Orange Blossom the door. She was used to tragic tales, they were just part of the life. And she would be naturally suspicious of any rogue geisha who had the nerve to breach protocol and try to switch houses.

But there was something in Orange Blossom that won the heart of the old matriarch. She listened to the story and took note of Orange Blossom's immaculate manners and stunning beauty. She would clearly be a great asset to the house, if she could be trusted. And somehow, through one of those nameless mercies of the heart, the *okamisan* decided that she'd give her a chance.

The other geisha were furious. They invented all sorts of sordid histories, all manner of unspeakable transgressions that could have brought such a woman to this fate. Certainly they were jealous of her charms, and fearful of competing with her for manly attentions. But they were more afraid of raising the ire of the *okamisan,* so they kept their protests silent.

And so Orange Blossom was adopted, as it were, into the house.

She was a most extraordinary woman, talented in every aspect of her profession. She played the best *shamisen,* knew more songs than all the other women combined, and had a voice that seemed even to the most jaded patrons somehow otherworldly. At the annual festival dances, she stunned everyone in the audience with the grace of her movements. Everyone wondered, Who is that girl? What house does she belong to?

When they found out, the house was booked solid. Two parties almost every night for months. The whirlwind of activity brought in more money than the *okamisan* had ever seen. Soon, even the *maiko* were outfitted in kimonos of the finest silk, so great were the bounties of the house.

But success came at a price. Reveling into the night day after day only to get up and do it all over again was taking its toll on the women. Their voices grew thin, scraped raw from nightly singing. Their eyes began to sag from lack of sleep and new lines crept into their faces almost overnight. Petty grievances were aggravated and the women began to plot against each other even more viciously than usual. The *okamisan* must have noticed, but she was too overwhelmed with the material successes to do anything about it.

As the women grew dazed and venomous they turned their animosity toward Orange Blossom. They knew she was the cause of their troubles, like some curse visited upon the house, and they constantly conspired to exact minor revenges.

But Orange Blossom was above their petty squabbles. She had only kind words for everyone and the nightly revelries did nothing to diminish her spirit. She was always cheerful in her rather distracted and isolated way. There was a dreaminess to her character, an almost preternatural solitude that would overcome her at times. There was something frightening in it, something humbling. The other women finally warmed to her, but only after she did the unspeakable.

After a particularly wearying week of parties, the girls were at their wits' end. They withered under the weight of the ceremonial apparel, and even the thick pancake makeup could not hide their fatigue. Things had reached a breaking point and any moment the house was bound to crumble from the strain.

It was then, amazingly, that Orange Blossom—the only one seemingly immune to the pressure and the girl at the bottom of the official hierarchy—chose to confront the *okamisan*.

When it became apparent what her intentions were, the other geisha could not believe their ears. One dropped an exquisite teacup, which shattered with a calamity all but unnoticed, so transfixed were the women at the confrontation.

Orange Blossom told the *okamisan* that the girls were overworked and needed a break. The matriarch was aghast, her face reddening as she listened to Orange Blossom's insolent plea. The other geisha practically cowered under furniture, fearing the tsunami that was sure to follow.

But it never came. Instead, as Orange Blossom went on, the mama's anger dissipated by degrees until it was no longer visible at all. No one even really heard what Orange Blossom was saying, for now she was talking in a whisper audible only to the *okamisan* herself. The women had never seen anything like what followed. They never would again. After Orange Blossom had finished her speech with a bow, the *okamisan* smiled. Not the reflexive smile she gave to patrons, but a joyous, deep smile like they had never witnessed.

They were given the following week off, the whole week, and it was all because of Orange Blossom's crazed impudence, her ridiculous courage. After this, none conspired against Orange Blossom anymore.

Yet none truly befriended her either. They were thankful, true, but they were also in awe. She wasn't the sort of woman given over to the easy confidences and little private jokes that make up friendships. Her aloofness was impenetrable, as if she were only there in body but her mind, and her spirit, were miles away.

The confrontation with the *okamisan* only reinforced the mystery of Orange Blossom. What could she have said that made the crusty old woman go soft? Why would she take such a chance? How could she know it would work?

The older, rural-born geisha talked of magic and supersti-

tion, telling tales of strange harpies that lived in the mountains. They spoke of ghosts and demons, archaic curses
chanted in the dead of night. The younger and more edu-
cated spoke of hypnotism, and the power of suggestion. But
neither group seemed satisfied with their hypotheses, and
Orange Blossom remained an unknowable, vaguely troubling
presence in the household.

And then a very strange thing happened. About a month
later, while hosting a party for the usual business higher-ups,
it came Orange Blossom's turn to perform on the *shamisen*.
This was one of her greatest talents, and a part of the evening
even her fellow geisha had come to look forward to.

The first plaintive notes rang out with a delicate clarity,
and already the geisha realized this was a song they had
never heard before. As all eyes fell upon her, she seemed to
be in a trance, as if somehow transporting herself into another
world. It was a powerful, frightening thing to watch. In such
moments, she became not another modern girl working as a
geisha to pay the bills, but someone ancient and mysterious,
conversing with some god the world had abandoned.

The song went on, building slowly, exploring the perimeter of the melody before settling into the chosen notes.
Even the space between the sounds seemed charged with an
unknown energy. And then she began singing.

It was not a voice any of the geisha had heard before. It
was the voice of a woman much older, filled with weariness
and a resolute sadness, but with such a beautiful, peaceful
quality that all in the room were soon brought to tears.

The melancholy ballad told of an old woman that had
outlived her family, seen the lovers of her youth grow old
and feeble and finally die. Now there was nothing left for her
but to sift through pale memories while awaiting a death that
seemed reluctant to claim her. No one in the room would

ever forget the last lines of this song, or the voice that articulated the terrible longing of the words.

> *"The flowers wither,*
> *Their color fades away,*
> *While endlessly*
> *I spend my days in this world*
> *As the long rains fall."*

When she had finished, all sat around crying quietly. The men wiped their tears on the sleeves of the women's kimonos like little boys seeking consolation from their mothers. Orange Blossom sat silent and unmoving, her eyes vacant and her white face still as marble.

Suddenly she looked around in confusion at everybody weeping silently, as if unaware what had caused them to sob, and hurriedly excused herself from the room.

After everyone had a good cry, the party went on. But it wasn't the same. The laughter was hollow, the flirtation perfunctory. After a short time, the *okamisan* went to inquire after Orange Blossom. She returned and informed the gathering that Orange Blossom had fallen ill, and would not be returning to the party.

In truth, she had not seen Orange Blossom at all. Orange Blossom had already gathered her meager belongings and vanished. They were never to see or hear from her again.

Two days later, a group of men came to the house in the daytime, inquiring about Orange Blossom. They were not clients of the house, and their questions had a formal air. Though they said they weren't policemen, they acted the part. The visit confirmed everybody's suspicions about Orange Blossom—that there was something wrong with her, that she was part of some great, insoluble mystery.

When word spread that Orange Blossom had gone, business dropped off to a more reasonable pace. Winter came and went and the cherry trees blossomed again. The women resumed their bickering and intrigues and all were secretly relieved that Orange Blossom was no longer among them. Her presence was something that had put them ill at ease, something they couldn't quite explain. Now that she had left, the house became itself again.

But no one was ever to forget her. On moonless summer nights, the geisha would tell fairy stories to the little ones. They would tell them how the wind through the trees was really the moaning of a forlorn woman punished by the gods for her beauty, forced forever to wail sad songs in the empty night. At such times, they would think of Orange Blossom.

"Quite a yarn," I said after a short silence.

"And every word is true," Mayumi added. She always knew the right buttons to push and was proud of her story-telling abilities.

"Sounds like one hell of a dame, whoever she was."

"What do you mean?"

"She wasn't Orange Blossom," I said, placing my glass on the table with an authoritative thump. "At least not the one I'm looking for."

"I will never forget her. That was her all right. Just like in the picture."

"You said Orange Blossom came to the house when you were eleven, right?"

"Yes."

"That would make her an old woman now. At least ten years older than you."

"I'd be careful with that old-woman language."

"But she isn't older than you. The woman I know as Orange Blossom, the woman in the picture, is no older than twenty-five."

"In the picture, certainly. It must be an old picture," Mayumi said confidently.

"It's not. This picture was taken a month ago. A year at most," I said with a shrug. Another lead had come to nothing.

"But how can you be sure the picture is new?"

"I have it on authority."

"Authorities often lie."

"I know the man in the picture. It's a contemporary photo, because that's how he looked before . . . well, he died recently." I felt like apologizing.

"I know that is the same woman."

"It's not a very good picture. I mean her face is—"

"If the picture is so bad, then how do you know it is the woman you're thinking of?" she countered. She had a point. If I insisted it was my Orange Blossom, she could be equally certain that it was her Orange Blossom.

"Maybe it's her daughter or something."

"Even mothers and daughters don't look that alike, Billy. Wake up. Somebody is toying with you. I don't know why, but somebody is trying to screw you up."

"They're doing a good job so far."

"I know this woman. I can never forget her. This picture is old, or a phony. You know the things they are capable of these days. Computer tricks, superimpositions, whatever. Ignore it. Get out of it altogether is my advice." She patted my hand, genuinely concerned.

"I can't." I watched the three acolytes settle their bill and amble out of the bar, drunk and silent. Now it was just the bar girl, Mayumi, and me.

"That's rotten eels. Don't sit there feeling sorry. There is always another choice to be made," she admonished with a patient, motherly tone. I must have looked how I felt. Pitiful.

And she was right. There were always choices. But choices just weren't my thing. Trouble and geisha were.

"Cheer up. Have another drink. Sleep with Yuriko or something," she said, nodding to the hostess I'd been eyeing all night. I couldn't help but smile at the thought.

"You're making me blush," I said.

"Ah, nonsense. She's yours. You want her?"

"I didn't realize it was that kind of place," I mumbled.

"Don't be stupid. I don't mean like that. Just that she likes you. I can tell. Take her out for a while. Go for a couple drinks. Go to a love hotel. I'll cover the bar, it's no problem. What do you say?"

I looked over at Yuriko. I looked at her for a long time. She caught me and smiled mischievously. What a dangerous kid.

"I gotta get back to Tokyo," I said quietly.

"Don't be stupid, Billy. Tokyo will still be there in the morning. Tokyo will still be there when you are eighty. Girls like Yuriko won't."

"Where's your percentage in this anyway?"

She just looked and me and sighed. "I don't care what you do. You look like you have too much on your mind, that's all. I don't like to see people like that. I like to see people having fun, enjoying life. It's my profession. But I suppose you think you know what's best for you."

I wasn't sure I did. But there was nothing that could happen between Yuriko and me in a few quiet hours in Kyoto that would alter the course of my life. Strange girls in strange towns were still enchanting and I wasn't through with those nights, but they'd ceased to offer the possibilities they once did. Maybe I was just getting old.

"Thanks for all your help, Mama Mayumi," I said after a time. "If I listened to more women like you, I'd probably be a much happier guy. Just because I'm stubborn doesn't mean I don't appreciate you looking out for me. But I really must return to Tokyo. When this thing is played out, I'll come back for some R and R."

"She might not wait for you," Mayumi said. "Young girls are fickle."

"That's okay. You'll still be here."

Mayumi laughed and clapped her hands together. She was one hell of a woman. She'd lived according to her own code, and I admired her for it. It took courage to face uncertainty the way she had, but it looked like things were working out for her. As for me...

I paid my bill and tipped Yuriko generously. Her lingering gaze nearly changed my mind, but like I said, I'm a stubborn guy.

Mayumi walked me to the door and I started to feel the full effect of the drinks. I thanked her again, congratulating her on her new life at Club Pineapple. She wished me luck with whatever this thing was.

"One more thing," I said, suddenly struck with a thought. "The girl you knew as Orange Blossom, did she do weird things with lipstick?"

Mayumi wrinkled her brow. I think she was imagining lipstick tricks of a racier nature. But then she snapped her fingers.

"Yes. She would always paint her mouth so that the color smeared just a little at the corner. Everyone thought it was kind of odd, but she refused to fix it. Ring a bell?"

Yeah. Like the seventy-four-ton bell at the Chionin temple across town. I nodded to Mayumi but said nothing more.

She waved good-bye and then I was alone in the Kyoto night, the dripping moon shining in pools at my feet. A poet probably could have made something out of it, but I just headed toward the trains.

I barely made my train back to Tokyo, and when I arrived it was raining there, too. I switched trains at Tokyo station and headed west, arriving in Shinjuku just as the nightly parade of drunken salarymen were stumbling onto the outbound trains, headed home to the suburbs after another evening of letting off steam.

I passed more of them on the streets, wobbling toward the station in groups of three or four, laughing and singing songs. Some tried vainly to keep themselves under umbrellas that seemed always too small, others just let the rain drench them, as if hoping to wash away the shame. Some groups called out greetings as they passed, others smiled, but mostly they just ignored me. I didn't work at their corporation, I wasn't a salaryman, I wasn't even Japanese. There was no animosity in our mutual indifference, no racial ugliness—we were just from different walks of life.

I must admit the sight of their camaraderie made me feel a little lonely. Here were men who knew exactly where they stood in *their* society. They were surrounded by others like themselves, immersed in the almost constant feeling of belonging, in the pleasure of sameness. Sure they were just people like everyone else in the world. But at times like these, it dawned on me that I didn't belong to anything but a small magazine from the other side of the globe and had no family waiting for me there or anywhere else.

I didn't envy the life of a salaryman—if it was so wonderful, why did they feel the need to get soused every night? And yeah, a lot of them had families and the kind of lives they led prevented them from seeing them much. And yes, Sarah was right that people who choose to be alone, people who push others away and reject those who claim to love them only to wallow in self-pity are the worst kind of hypocrites—spiritually bankrupt individuals who don't even deserve the small joys of loneliness.

Maybe that was going a bit far, and I had no romantic misconceptions about the life I'd chosen. I wasn't trying to live out some existential fantasy of me against an indifferent world. It's just the way things worked out. On this particular night I had some vague pangs of regret, but they would pass. In the morning I'd forget all about it.

When I finally reached my hotel room I was anxious to sleep. Everything would look clearer after some rest, I thought as I opened the door to my room. I was already feeling better.

But not for long.

She was standing in the corner of the room leaning against the wall next to the big window. The rain was coming down hard against the glass, throwing strange shadows across her face as she gazed outside. Smoke from her cigarette curled in a winding stream toward the ceiling. She wore a thin, wrinkled purple dress with a plunging neckline and a hem that rose to reveal the kind of legs women hated on other women.

"How did you get in here?" I said, closing the door behind me. If my voice sounded cool and detached, it was only a device to keep from fainting.

She didn't move a muscle, just kept looking outside.

"Secret," she said finally, exhaling a tendril of smoke from the corner of her mouth. A lock of dark hair fell across her face and over her eyes. She let it stay there.

"I imagine you're the kind of girl that has a lot of those," I said. It was then I noticed the graveyard of empty bottles littering the small table.

"You're the type of guy that probably imagines lots of things," she said flatly.

I stopped imagining long enough to cross the room and have a look inside the hotel mini-fridge. There wasn't anything left but a single kiwi-lime-strawberry-flavored wine cooler. I needed a drink, but not that bad. I hoped I never needed a drink that bad and closed the fridge.

She turned away from the window and caught me in her gaze. From the amount of bottles on the table she should have been floating, but her eyes were steady. She pulled on the cigarette again.

"You keep up with those things," I said, indicating the cigarette, "and they'll kill you."

"You're cute," she countered indifferently.

"You shoulda seen me when I was a kid."

"What's changed?"

I couldn't help but crack a smile. "You're one of those people who always gets the last word, right?"

She let out a perfunctory grunt, then dropped the cigarette and crushed it out with the bottom of her heel. It hissed as she ground it into the carpet. I noticed she must have done the same thing about a dozen times. It was a nice carpet, too, or used to be. A lush red, thick-woven fibers. Between the ruined floor and the liquor binge, she'd promoted my hotel bill to the level of conversation piece between me and Chuck back in Cleveland.

I walked a few paces and sat down in the chair. She was silhouetted against the window, her features half-hidden in the darkness of the room. It occurred to me to flip on the light, and then it occurred to me not to. Instead I sat there and listened to the rain drum its rhythm against the window.

"So did you just drop by to have a few beers?" I said finally, distantly wondering why sarcasm is always my first impulse.

"I'm going now," she said. But she didn't move, she just let the words hang in the air with the smoke.

"Don't be stupid."

I was talking to myself more than to her. I rose from the chair and crossed the room until I was standing only a few feet away from her. She stopped me with her eyes before I could get any closer. Not a red-light kind of look, just a yellow. Slow. Proceed with caution. Normally, I was the type of guy who gunned it through yellow lights.

"There are a lot of people after you, you know."

"Are you one of them, Mr. Chaka? Are you after me?"

"Yes."

"Well, here I am. I am here. What do you intend to do with me?" Her eyes shone a little, pulling me in.

"I was thinking"—I gulped—"a little conversation might be nice for starters."

"I bet you think that makes you an old-fashioned guy, right? I bet you think that makes you chivalrous." She half laughed, half hissed. She moved past me, brushing against me as she made her way toward the mini-fridge. As she bent at the waist to open the fridge I tried not to stare, and then thought, What the hell? I watched the bottom of her dress rise up the back of her thighs, my head full of chivalry.

"You sure you need that?" I said as she turned around and twisted off the lid of the wine cooler. A sickly-sweet, fruity scent filled the room.

"Don't worry about my needs," she said, walking toward me slowly. "Let's have this conversation. That's what you want, right? A conversation. Let's converse, Mr. Chaka."

"Call me Billy," I said.

"Okay, Billy. What shall we talk about? In our conversation. What shall we discuss?"

She moved a step closer. I could feel the heat from her body, smell the sugary liquor on her breath. I felt my whole body tense as I tried to clear my head, seeking out the one-mind.

"For starters, what happened to our friend Sato Migusho?" I blurted, my voice cracking a little.

Her face froze and she recoiled a few degrees. I had a talent for killing the mood.

"Sato is dead," she whispered. She produced another cigarette and put it between her lips. With a quick movement she flicked out a lighter and a flame shot upward, illuminating her face. I could just see the lipstick smudged at corner of her mouth as she put the cigarette into the flame.

"They killed him," she said. "Burned him. They killed him, burned him, and now he is dead."

"I know all that. Who did it?"

"The bad guys. Who else?"

I thought it over. "Bad guys" wasn't the most exclusive category in the world. She could have meant just about anybody, but chances are she meant the yakuza. I decided not to press it for now.

"You don't seem too broken up about it," I mused quietly, almost to myself.

That got her attention.

"Does it matter how I seem?" she began. "People come into the world, and they go. I learned long ago that tears never brought them back."

"That's beautiful. Is it from a Zeami play, or some song by Hibara Misora?"

A faint smile played on her lips. She put the wine-cooler bottle down on the table by the window and walked across the room. Her slow, graceful steps mimicked the stylized sloth of Noh actors. She sat down at the edge of the bed and crossed her legs like it was a big deal. Actually, from where I stood, it *was* a pretty big deal.

"A long, long time ago when I was little girl there was a little boy who lived a few houses down from me," she began, her eyes settling on an empty corner of the room. "Every day I would walk by his house. He'd be waiting there for me, watching for me from the window. When I went by, he'd come running out of his house like a madman. I would run away and he'd chase me, picking up rocks and throwing them at me. This went on and on, every day the same thing. He never caught me, though he could have if he had left the stones alone and concentrated on his pursuit. Just before I left the village, the day I was sold to a geisha house, he came running out as usual. At first I ran as always, but after a few meters I stopped. I turned around and waited. He was so confused he forgot all about the stones, and just stood there gaping. So I walked right up to him and said, 'Choyo-san, every day I walk by your house and every day you chase me and throw stones. But tomorrow I am leaving this village and I am never coming back.'

"Choyo-san just looked at me. His eyes filled with tears. And then he fell to his knees and started crying, right there in the middle of the road. Begging me not to go, saying he would never throw stones again, never chase me. 'But you see,' I said, 'I must go. It is already decided.' And so I did."

"Kid sounds like a dumb-ass," I mumbled.

"So they're after me again," she said, rising from the bed. "And you are after me. Chasing me. But I know that with you, it is different. I can see it in the way that you look at me. *Look at me.*"

I hadn't been doing anything but since I walked in the door. But now I gazed upon her unabashedly. It was no use doing anything else.

"Now you're looking at me," she whispered. "You're looking at me and you want me. You have always wanted me. But you must be mindful. You must not be reckless."

I didn't know what to say. I felt anything but mindful. The room seemed to be moving, slowly circling like a carousel gathering speed. Objects began losing their edges, softly blurring into shadow. The only sound was the rain coming down, tapping out its odd beat on the window. She stood before me, close enough that I could touch her.

"Why me?" I asked.

"Questions," she said, rolling the word out. "A woman comes to you and you give her only questions."

Throwing rocks, I thought.

Before I knew what was happening, her mouth was on me. I don't know who closed the distance—whether it was me or her or both of us simultaneously, pushed by unseen forces. I could feel nothing but her lips against mine. Then her body.

One of the last coherent thoughts to squeeze through my brain before instinct consumed everything in its path was that this was what they call *a bad idea.* The thought expressed itself not in words, but as a flickering, looping montage. A praying mantis ripping the head from its mate. A black widow spider moving with mechanical deliberation toward the anxious male vibrations in her web. And believe it or not, Barbara Stanwyck coming down the stairs toward Fred Mac-Murray in *Double Indemnity.* Too many movies can ruin you forever if you're not careful.

But these flickering images didn't have a chance against the onslaught of signals coming from every fiber of my being. My synapses ignited in a firestorm as my hand traveled across her back, down over her dress, down further until I felt the smooth curve of her legs and her cool skin. And now it moved with a purpose of its own, detached from any thoughts I might have of insects or old movies or Fred Mac-Murray. Around her legs, up her thigh, up farther still, close enough to sense the heat, to be warmed by it, to seek it out.

And then no thoughts at all, just colors. A bottomless crimson, moving rhythmically, pulsing. The color and movement of my own blood. I could feel her hand delicately trailing the contour of my neck, across the back at the base, as if tracing a pattern for the executioner, *Cut Here,* while her other hand tugged at my shirt, then slid beneath it.

Suddenly I felt myself reeling backward. I stumbled trying to regain my balance and reached out toward the edge of the table to steady myself as I toppled over. Several of the empty bottles crashed across the table, a clattering glass crescendo. In a daze, it took me a moment to figure out she'd shoved me. Now she stood halfway across the room, gazing down at me, her eyes blazing.

"*Now you are the one,*" she hissed.

Before I could do a thing, she whirled around and was out the door. I leapt to my feet and hauled ass across the room, smacking my shin against the edge of the bed frame.

The shooting pain in my leg helped me focus just enough to make it to the door without further mishap.

I lunged into the hallway and heard her laughter echoing through the corridor. There was nothing lighthearted about the reverberating noise, nothing you could call joyous. I hesitate to use words like eerie or harrowing, but that's how it sounded.

The laughter was all there was. The hall was totally empty.

I don't know if she took the stairs or the elevator or hopped out a window, but before I could say "criminal thoroughfare" I was racing down the concrete stairwell. The bottom of my wing tips rattled over the smooth stairs in an insane staccato descent as I plummeted scattershot like a tumbling can. Down, down, the dim light blurring, my lungs sucking the stale air.

I reached the bottom and yanked open the steel door with too much force, throwing myself off balance.

I lurched into the lobby a stumbling, gasping mess of dizzy panic. The room was huge, swimming with too many lights and too many people. I could hardly focus as I scanned the room looking for some sign of her.

Somebody grabbed my arm.

"You okay, fella?" I heard. I pulled free and took a few steps, the room a vertiginous swirl as I spun around, looking this way and that, ignoring the fact that everyone was staring, that I must have looked insane. That I might not have just *looked* insane.

"Easy, pal," I heard, and felt the hand on my shoulder once again. This time it wasn't gonna let go.

And then there was another hand, grabbing my other arm.

"Please come quietly."

A trap. The easiest trap they could have set and I had taken the bait, not even realizing I'd been fooled until it was pathetically, laughably late. A mouse with its neck shattered just getting around to wondering if the cheese tastes a little metallic.

I turned around prepared to face some yakuza scumbags. To face the men most likely sent to kill me.

The sense of relief I felt the next moment was almost enough to make me forget about Orange Blossom.

It was the cops. Just the goddamn Tokyo cops.

They came on soft. A laid-back approach. Politenesses exchanged. A casual query. Query returned. They refused to answer my questions, I refused to answer theirs, and reluctantly we drove down to the station—all of us unhappy. The classic progression.

Orange Blossom. So close I could touch her. So close I *did* touch her. Gone.

If I dwelt upon it much more I was going to throw a tantrum in the back of the cop car. I was in police custody now. I had to salvage what was left of my wits. It took all the strength I had to try to forget about her for a few moments.

I erected a protective barricade of mundane observations: it struck me that I'd spent more time in the backs of cars driving silently through Tokyo than I cared to recall. I'd kind of grown to like it in a strange way. Out the window the riot of light and noise and everyone going about their lives, and inside the *gaijin* alone with his thoughts—and his hostile escorts. It was relaxing in a way I can't describe. I decided I should start a company that offered silent tours through the city. A driver would show up, not speak a word. You'd get in the car, he'd drive you around for an hour or two, no set route, and then return. Maybe I could get Shinto to do the driving. He'd be a natural.

My second thought was that everyone always knew where to find me. Orange Blossom, the cops, whoever. Of course, I had been staying at the same hotel since my first visit to Japan all those years ago. I always ate at the same four places and drank in maybe six. If you knew I was a reporter from a teen mag, then you'd know I'd be at the tournament. Not a lot of distance to cover, even for an average cop. Funny, one day you notice you've become completely predictable.

I was whisked into a back room without ceremony. No signing anything, no fingerprinting, not a word as to what this was all about. My irritated chaperons took me into one of those archetypal interrogation rooms with windowless white walls and a few beat-up chairs surrounding a spartan table. There was even one of those single lightbulbs suspended above it. The room could have been a movie set. They told me to take a seat, then left without a word. The dull thud of the door closing behind them even echoed just like in the movies.

There's not much to do at the Tokyo Municipal Police Headquarters, so I busied myself with my new favorite hobby—trying not to think about the one thing I couldn't forget. I don't know how long I waited. I must have fallen asleep, because suddenly there were four men in the room looking at me like I didn't belong there. Somehow, I didn't think it meant they were gonna let me go.

"I am Chief Inspector Arajiro," the tallest cop said. He was a good-looking guy. Athletic build, fashionable haircut. A real alpha male. He didn't even bother to introduce the other three, whose main purpose was to glare at me. The two guys who'd brought me here were nowhere to be seen.

"Billy Chaka," I said, rising and bowing. His own bow was less than a nod. It told me a lot about where I stood.

"We know who you are " he said. "Sit down."

As if on cue, one of his silent goons handed him a file. Arajiro began reading it.

"It seems, Mr. Chaka, that this is not your first time in Japan. Nor, it appears, the first time you've had some trouble with the law." He looked at me over the top of the file. His eyes were at once searching and focused. It was a stare that would have made any detective proud.

"I can explain."

He held his hand up to silence me. Then he continued to read from the file, this time aloud.

"May 1985, arrested for participating in the Rock Cottage Riot..."

It wasn't a real riot. The police just weren't used to seeing slam-dancing, so they rounded everyone up. The band, Ginza Pitbull, was forced to apologize to the mayor for inciting the disturbance at the Rock Cottage Club.

"...Acquitted. January 1987," he continued. "Felony destruction of private property..."

I'd forgotten about that episode. It was at an auction house in Nara, where people were bidding on works by Japanese artists of the fifteenth century. There was a work by Kuwata, one of the period's most revered Buddhist nature painters. Of course, I knew the work was a fake because there was a turtle in it. Kuwata had a deep reverence for the many wonders of nature and a love for all sentient beings. Except turtles. Apparently, there was some trauma in his childhood that developed into a pathological hatred of the animal. Not only did he refuse to paint them, he often captured and tortured them for hours before killing them. This made him kind of an outcast among monks, but they kept him at the temple and tolerated his turtle torturing because of his artistic talent. Anyway—I got up from my seat, walked up to the painting as if to examine it, took out the giant red Magic Marker I always bring to art galleries, and circled the turtle. Then I made a giant slashing *X* over the canvas. Then I was tackled to the ground and arrested.

"...Dismissed."

Not only that, I was offered hundreds of thousands of yen by the would-be buyer for saving him several million. Of course, I declined. I don't believe in art criticism for profit.

"February 1989, assault and battery of a stand-up comic in Roppongi..."

I didn't want to recall that one. It was a very complicated affair, full of cultural misunderstandings and personal miscommunications. As it happens, I may not have been entirely in the right. Nevertheless...

"...Charges dropped," Arajiro continued, circling me as he spoke. Then he stopped and stood directly in front of me. "You seem to be a statistical oddity in our country, Mr. Chaka. Three previous arrests and no convictions. You must be a lucky man."

"I have a good lawyer," I said.

"You are going to need one," he countered. "Perhaps you would like to call him now, before the questioning begins."

"He's already here," I said with a smile.

"I see," said Arajiro, cracking his knuckles. "Then let us begin." He sat down opposite me, and placed a tiny Sony mini–disc recorder on the table between us.

"You are familiar with a man named Aki Rokahara?" he asked.

"I can't say that I am."

"You should be," he said. "A few days ago you broke his nose and stole his motorcycle." He scowled across the table at me, letting the accusation settle in.

That Aki Rockahara. I almost smiled with relief. I didn't know why I was brought in and had figured it was yakuza-related. Worse, I feared it might have something to do with the Man in the Hat. Still, what was I to say? That I had to requisition Aki's vehicle in order to elude my suspicious private driver so that I might meet in secret with the head of the Yamagama-gumi?

"So you know him?" Arajiro said.

"I wouldn't say I know him, exactly…"

"But you did assault him and steal his vehicle."

"Well… yeah, but…" My brain raced through a catalog of lies, but none seemed good enough.

"Is this normal behavior in America? Beating up strangers and robbing them?" Arajiro said, his voice thick with derision.

"I apologize. Usually I'm quite reserved, contented to be a chronicler of events for my humble publication, and a gracious guest in your wondrous—"

"Fuckin' spare me," Arajiro spat.

"I did return the motorcycle," I offered weakly.

"Oh, we know. We know all about it. Aki's idiot mother refused to press charges. She thinks you are an enlightened man. She thinks that thanks to your actions, her son has made a real turnaround. Swore he'd go back to school, stop running with the wrong crowd, all that jazz. But it won't last."

I couldn't help but grin this time. I made a mental note to call up the subscription department back in Cleveland and have them send the young man years' worth of magazines.

"So why am I here?"

"Because you are in trouble, Mr. Chaka."

"I didn't think I was here for karaoke. What kind of trouble?"

"Does he seem a little jumpy to you, Haruki?" Arajiro asked one of the silent cops. I don't know which one was Haruki, because all three of them nodded.

"It's official. You seem a little jumpy, Chaka. Why would you be jumpy? Something on your mind?"

"Always is. Right now it's sleep."

"Having trouble sleeping, huh? I don't doubt it," Arajiro said. "I've seen a lot of weird shit in my life, but even I'm having a little trouble sleeping. And Haruki? He vomited yesterday. A hard-boiled fifteen-year veteran of the force, puking like a tyke who had too much taffy before a ride on the Tilt-A-Whirl. So yeah, I bet you're having trouble sleeping."

"Look, you've obviously got a real talent for this song and dance," I said. "But it's been a long night, so could you just put it on the table?"

Arajiro blanched like he'd just been slapped. But he pulled it back together quickly enough.

"Hey, Haruki," he said, keeping his eyes locked on mine.

"Yes, sir?" I heard, turning my head too late to see who had spoken.

"He says we should put it on the table."

"That right?"

Arajiro paused. "It's official," he said. Then he pantomimed to the silent ones. I couldn't get a make on the gesture, but they seemed to be in the know, and out of the room they went.

I couldn't say I was sorry to see them go, but at the same time, I wasn't exactly thrilled to be left in the room with

Arajiro. He was a bruiser, and I got the feeling he wasn't one of my fans.

I waited for him to get down to business, but he never did. Neither did he engage me in small talk. He just cleared his throat a few times and wearily rubbed his eyes with the heels of his hands. He glanced my way once or twice and cracked his knuckles. That was the extent of our interaction. It seemed he wasn't interested in performing solo.

I thought about Orange Blossom. Then Punchperm. Then Kwaidan. Just as I began to picture the slobbering mastiff, I heard footsteps approaching. They stopped and the door swung open. The three silent cops entered in a single-file line, the one in the middle carrying a metal box.

He laid it in front of me on the table. The guy trailing him shut the door, and the guy in front produced a pair of surgical gloves. He snapped them over his hands ceremoniously. The words "cavity search" did an ugly dance through my mind.

Arajiro's disinterest turned to rapt attention. I suppose he'd choreographed this whole thing just for me. Somehow it still didn't make me feel very special.

One of the cops strolled over and lifted the lid of the box, like a waiter in some pretentious restaurant. The air was instantly filled with a fetid odor. The gloved guy glanced at me nervously, then reached into the box. Averting his face, he pulled the thing out.

I couldn't even tell what it was at first. He held the battered ball aloft by its thick tendrils of oily string, only inches from my face. As he turned it around slowly, I saw the sickly mauve flesh and the empty mouth, slack and gaping like a bludgeoned fish. And above its colorless swollen upper lip, I saw the mustache.

I had to fight back waves of nausea over the next couple of hours while I refused to answer question after question. Throughout the interrogation, Shinto's head rested in the metal box in front of me. Once in a while Arajiro would have them hoist it out of the box just to make certain I didn't recognize the guy.

They'd traced my calls from the hotel to his pager. The questioning led me to believe that's all they had on me. I wasn't going to let them get more.

I could have told them that the head in the box used to belong to my chauffeur, a guy I hired after Sato Migusho died. But that would only open the floodgates. It takes cops a lot of time to understand a situation like mine. They have to ask a lot of annoying questions, and that makes them annoyed. I knew I wasn't a suspect. And I knew that Shinto was no mere chauffeur. Something in their questions told me they knew it, too.

I told them I had dialed the wrong number by mistake. They asked me what number I was trying to dial. I said I didn't remember. They asked why I had dialed the same wrong number on two different occasions.

That was their mistake. I called Shinto at least six times since I'd ditched him. The only two they'd traced were the ones to the hotel. The others were from pay phones at the tournament, at the Purple Web, and places on the streets. They might be able to link me to those, but it would take some work.

So I told them I must have dialed it again because I'm the kind of guy who just doesn't learn. Not even a chuckle in response.

Instead, he asked again. And again. Then he backed up and asked me to name all the places I might have called since I got here. Then he asked me to name all the people I knew who had pagers. Then he asked why I had tried to call this man whose head was in the box. Then he asked me if I killed him. Then he asked me if I knew who killed him. Then he asked if I knew who the man in the box was. Then he asked me why I called his pager, over and over, trying to wear me down like water and air turn stone to dust. It was a real dull conversation.

Finally, I got bored and refused to speak Japanese. I'd just shake my head.

Arajiro didn't like that. He began berating me. "C'mon you son of a bitch! You can do better than that! Speakie Japanesie!"

But I couldn't. Instead, I broke into English, which really ruffled Arajiro's feathers. He'd curse at me for a while, then he'd get soft and apologetic. A one-man good cop/bad cop routine.

Eventually, though, he tired.

"Get him outta my face," he said, dismissing me with a wave of his hand. His boys stood me up and led me out of the room.

I looked back over my shoulder as we neared the door and caught a glimpse of the mangled object lying awkwardly on its side in the metal box.

Poor, dumb Shinto. Speechless forevermore.

. . .

The holding cell wasn't much different from any of the ones I'd been in before. Whether you're in Beijing, Battambang, Katmandu, or Cleveland, when it comes to incarceration the world is indeed a small place. The only real difference is how long you'll wait before trial, or if you'll get one at all. That and the food—but I didn't think I'd have much of an appetite for a while.

I knew they weren't going to charge me with anything, but that didn't mean they wouldn't hold me for the two weeks allowed by Japanese law. Good-bye tournament. Good-bye Orange Blossom. Hello yakuza retribution.

I could use a friend in the police department right about now. For all of my Japanese connections, I had never befriended a policeman. I knew tavern owners, arsonists, gangsters, handicapped martial-arts masters, film directors, and the odd bar hostess or five. I knew university professors, taxi drivers, an amputee actress, and even the former mayor of Osaka. But despite my past encounters with the law, I didn't know a single policeman.

As I was led to a holding cell, I thought about what an unfortunate oversight that had been.

Who could have done such a thing to Shinto Hirohito? I thought as I sat on my plastic cot. The only thing mildly offensive about him was that silly mustache. Other than that, he was just a regular guy. He might have been married with children for all I knew—we just never got around to talking about it. He was too quiet and he smoked too much—nothing to kill someone over.

Shinto Hirohito, as interesting in death as he was unremarkable in life. A pathetic epitaph.

I wondered things now that never would have crossed my mind when he was alive. Stupid things. What were his favorite songs? Did he love or hate Yoko Torikata? Did he play chess or Go or *hanafuda* or *pachinko* or what? Bet on the speedboats? Surely his life couldn't have consisted solely of driving other people to the places that made up the geography of their lives.

An elegy for Shinto sprang to mind.

> *I once was a regular guy,*
> *Driving people more important than I.*
> *When Billy Chaka fled,*
> *They cut off my head,*
> *And no one will ever know why.*

I slapped myself in the face. Shinto was dead and all I could think of was a bad limerick. I'd like to think it was shock rather than callousness, but who knows? Prison can do funny things to a guy.

I reminded myself that I'd felt all along Shinto wasn't the everyman he appeared to be. Had I actually believed he was Johnny GoNormal, I wouldn't have ditched him so hastily. He might still be alive, driving around with those ubiquitous white gloves and that unlit Mild Seven dangling between his lips. But the truth was, he'd given me the creeps. I left him outside McDonald's, and sometime later his head was ripped from his body. I knew there was no cause and effect in these events, and that there must have been a secret Shinto beneath the surface, but I still couldn't help feeling some oblique complicity in his death.

The odd thing was, I didn't really care why he was murdered. It was just another ugly event in what was easily my worst trip to Japan. I didn't even care anymore why Sato was killed. He was dead, and maybe it had taken Shinto's death to really underscore the cruel finality of it.

Yes, there were mysterious circumstances and I am a curious person by nature, and I like to see justice done as much as the next journalist. But no heroics would bring him back. And if more people were going to die just so I might satisfy some personal desire for truth—and worse yet, some horrid longing for the mystery geisha—well, at what point do you throw up your hands and be done with it? At what point do you unmask your obsessions, identify them for the demons they are, and cast them out?

I was there. When I got out of this prison, I resolved to get out of Japan, do a write-by-numbers article on the tournament just like everybody else, and forget the nightmare that began in a purple fisherman's bar. Maybe I'd lose a few fans, maybe even a few hundred, but nobody would be killed over it. Besides, teenagers need to be let down by their idols now and again. It gives them a taste of the disappointments waiting in adulthood.

Sarah and I would have a long talk, a series of talks, a summit if that's what it took, until we finally resolved what to do now that she had outgrown her role and everything had become complicated. I couldn't bear the thought of her getting another tooth removed every time I went to Japan until there were none left. Then what would she do? Start removing her fingers?

And Orange Blossom?

If I couldn't catch her, I was certain the yakuza wouldn't be able to, not with their pedestrian methods. I hadn't heard from the so-called religious order in the black suits since day one, so I doubted they'd miss me, whoever they were. She wanted to disappear, let her disappear. She was probably safer without me, and I was unquestionably safer without her.

Now you are the one, she'd said. Not anymore, toots. Not anymore.

I recalled the proverb *Ju yoku go o seisu*—win by yielding. It didn't fit. This was a retreat plain and simple, and I wasn't going to win anything. There was no way to dress this up as a courageous move, or even a tactical one. It was simply the only move left.

The uselessness of the cliché made me suddenly feel very much the foreigner I was. No matter how many *kanji* I could draw, I would always be a *gaijin*. In a way, investing myself so wholly in this foreign culture only underscored my alien status. Real Japanese men my age listened to Miles Davis and read Raymond Chandler. I was some unhip goofball weeping over *enka* ballads and taking Mishima far too seriously. They ate at Pizza Hut and drank Jim Beam while I was choking down sushi with sake.

I thought of Shinto in his ridiculous cowboy gear at the Yotayo Love Hotel. Granted, I didn't go around in a samurai outfit, but I was still culturally clothed in a nostalgic costume, pining for the way things never really were. Why couldn't I moon over bar hostesses, Ainu princesses, bubbleheaded actresses, or cute little schoolgirls like my Japanese contemporaries? Why this deadly, destructive love of geisha?

Maybe the why of it didn't matter for now. When an avalanche is coming down a mountain, you don't sit there wondering about the geophysical and atmospheric conditions that caused it, you just try to get the hell out of the way. One day they would probably discover a genetic predisposition for my affliction, but I couldn't wait around for science to catch up. I had to take action.

If it meant staying away from Japan, I would just have to live with it. There were plenty of stories waiting in China, Korea, Vietnam. Asia was a big place, and the magazine could always find people to work Japan.

Thus decided, I began to clear all thoughts of Orange Blossom from my mind. "Sorry, kid," I said to her mental image. "Just chalk it up to bad timing." Then I turned the the knob and let her walk out of the room in my mind.

The imaginary door was still open, though, and light was shining in from the hall. Mentally, I was still chasing her.

There was nothing to do but wait. I spent the time doing push-ups and sit-ups—it seemed the prison thing to do. As a way of trying to cheer myself up I thought about all the famous good guys who'd spent time in jail. Muhammad Ali, Gandhi, Dostoyevsky, Malcolm X. Even Paul McCartney had been in prison, right here in Japan as a matter of fact, for marijuana possession. He even wrote an unpublished manu-script detailing his detainment, called *Japanese Jailbird*. If the mop-top could emerge with his humor intact, I shouldn't have anything to worry about.

After who knows how long, I spotted a lone prison guard making his way down the hall. Inmates shouted out to him, but he paid no attention to them as he carried a single tray of food in my direction.

"Where's my fuckin' *yakatori*?" somebody yelled to applause and guffaws.

The guard continued with the same measured gait, slowly marching through the gauntlet of verbal abuse. He must have had some serious Zen detachment thing going on to take it as well as he did, or maybe he was just going deaf.

After what seemed like forever, he materialized in front of my cell. I looked up toward him and then back to the floor.

"It's time for your meal," he said quietly.

"Give it to someone else," I said.

"But this meal was meant for you," he replied, still stand-ing erect as a soldier.

"Look bull"—I sneered—"I ain't hungry."

"You need this food to survive," he said, nonplussed.

I gave him the once-over. He had a smooth, youthful face and dark, far-off-looking eyes. He would have been more at home in a monastery than a prison—though I suppose they're similar in ways.

"I don't want no special treatment. I eat when the other guys eat," I said.

"They've already eaten. This food is for you."

I wasn't gonna eat, but I wasn't gonna argue with him all day either. I got up off the floor and made my way to the prison bars. As I neared, he opened the door.

It was a stupid thing to do. A couple quick blows and I could have escaped. But to where? I just let him step inside the cell, unmolested. He stood directly across from me, a couple feet away, like he was waiting for something.

"What's the idea?" I said.

"Please take this tray of food," he said. I searched his face, but an expression was nowhere to be found. I reached out to take the tray.

His arm shot out and grabbed my own. Before I could even try to pull away, his other hand popped out and shot something into my forearm. I felt a tiny sting as the tray went clattering to the floor.

"What the..." I said, eyes darting up at him in confusion. His face was the same blank page. I readied to attack him using the Way of the Caged Bird, but then realized I wasn't going to be attacking anybody. I was just too damn dizzy.

He released my arm and I stumbled backward. My legs buckled and I fell uselessly to the floor, right on top of lunch. He turned slowly on his heel, stepped outside of my cell, then locked the door behind him.

That was the last thing I saw before everything went dead.

. . .

"That's him," I heard from somewhere far off. The world moved with a strange underwater cadence. Someone grabbed my arm and someone grabbed my other arm and I felt myself being hoisted.

"What'd you say that condition was again, Doc?"

"Get me some water."

"Only because I've never heard of it."

"You'll hear plenty about it in court if you don't help me get him out of here. *Now.*"

"You can't just walk out of here with him—"

"Chaka, can you hear me?"

I tried to speak but it came out a moan. My eyesight was returning and I could just barely make out the forms around the room. Three men in glowing white coats. Big blue guys on either side of me and a guy in a gray suit across from me.

"God have mercy. Tagemoro—phone the clinic and tell them to prepare the isometaphonic chamber and get twenty cc's of betadioloxcene on ice. Tell them we're on our way."

"You can't take him. He's a murder suspect—"

"He'll be a murder *victim* if we don't move. Fast."

"Well, he's . . . he's . . . we still need to question him. He's a potential witness."

"If I don't get him to the clinic within an hour, you are going to have a dead witness on your hands officer . . . Arajiro, wasn't it?"

"Goddammit."

I never figured yaks as the lethal injection types. They preferred the violent physics of baseball bats and bullets over subtle chemistry. It wasn't the way I'd choose to go, but it wasn't so bad. Better than getting your head cut off.

"Dr. Oyashi, you stay behind and take care of the paperwork. Fill out whatever releases are necessary on my authority and then hurry down to the clinic. We are going to need everybody."

"Why can't you just go to Tokyo Municipal?" Arajiro butted in.

"Because, you idiot, he would be dead before they got him in the building."

I was loaded onto a stretcher and whisked down a long hall at a speed that made my stomach churn. My eyesight was improving. I saw Arajiro looking down on me disdainfully, as if it were my fault I was dying. Maybe it was. I still couldn't see the doctor doing most of the talking, but I could hear him giving instructions in a hurried, controlled tone that seemed to inspire confidence in those around him. If I was dying, at least I was in good hands.

We burst through the doors and into the light. The last time I was outside, which could have been days or hours ago, it was raining. Now the rain had subsided and it was a beautiful autumn day. I felt the sun warm my skin and hoped it wouldn't be the last time.

I was lifted into the ambulance by the two doctors on either side of the stretcher. I heard Arajiro address the head doctor.

"I've arranged for an escort. One car is all I can do right now."

"It's not necessary," the doctor replied.

"I did it anyway," Arajiro snorted.

"I'll contact you as soon as he's stabilized."

"No you don't. I'm coming with you," Arajiro said. "It's official."

There was a short silence. I wondered if doctors and cops were always like this, or if I was a special case.

"Hop in," the doctor said.

Arajiro said nothing. He stepped up into the vehicle and we were off.

• • •

The ambulance wasn't like any I had been in before. There were no medical instruments lying around, no emergency charts on the wall. I didn't hear a siren. The floor was covered with a dull red carpet. Probably to disguise the bloodstains. It was better than my cell, though, and if I was dying I couldn't very well complain about the carpet.

Arajiro looked around uncomfortably.

"Where is this clinic again?" he asked. No one answered.

"Dr. Oyashi . . . The injection."

Dr. Oyashi produced a hypodermic from his black bag and filled it with a bottled solution. He held it up to the light and squirted out a tiny stream, which arched into the air like a leaping dolphin.

"I need to give our escort directions. Where are we going?" Arajiro demanded.

"Straight for now," the head doctor said. Arajiro's jaw clenched and I thought I could hear his teeth grinding.

"Roll up his sleeve," Dr. Oyashi ordered Arajiro. "Now!"

Arajiro knelt over me reluctantly and rolled it up. The whole time he was looking at me like maybe it wasn't worth the effort.

"Hold his arm down," the head doc said. There was no real need to, as I was strapped down to the gurney. But Arajiro did it anyway.

"What are you waiting for?" the head doc said from behind me. Other than a slight headache, I was feeling fine for a dying guy. I thought about protesting the injection—something just wasn't right. But there was nothing I could do.

Dr. Oyashi raised the needle in the air, hesitated, then plunged it into Arajiro's arm.

"I fucking knew it . . ." Arajiro spat as Dr. Oyashi and the head doctor wrestled him to the floor. "I fucking . . . it's official."

He only struggled for a moment before blacking out cold.

"Get him off that thing," the head doc said, nodding my way. Somehow I got the feeling they weren't really doctors.

"Dr. Oyashi" undid the restraints.

"What are my chances, Doc? Don't sugarcoat it."

The head doctor looked at me and I finally got a good look at his face. It was that weird guy from the tournament, the one in the glasses and fedora. The Man in the Hat. I assumed the other two were his buddies in the cheap black suits.

"You're not dying, Mr. Chaka," he said solemnly. "But Orange Blossom is."

The Man in the Hat and one of his assistants lifted Arajiro's silent body and strapped him onto the gurney I'd been lying in moments before.

"We were hoping we wouldn't have to do this, but he insisted on coming along," the Man in the Hat explained. "It was imperative that we rescue you. The situation has become desperate. We have no time for police interference."

"They're going to leave you alone now?"

Their idea of a rescue put me in more danger than ever. The squad car leading us couldn't have known that Chief Inspector Arajiro was unconscious and strapped down on the stretcher, but they were going to find out soon enough.

"You will have to go underground. We have already made arrangements, so you needn't worry."

Right. Said the spider to the fly...

"What is your name anyway?" I asked the guy.

"It's not important," he said, taking a tiny cell phone out of his doctor's jacket and dialing.

He handed the phone to the driver.

The driver said about three words into it, then handed back the phone with an expressionless nod. The Man in the

Hat put the phone in his pocket, then swiveled his head around to look out the front windshield.

"You may wish to witness this," he said.

I leaned over and looked out the window. As if on cue, our driver yanked the wheel hard to the left, throwing my head against the van interior. Just before my head hit the wall, I saw a white truck smash into the police car in front of us, sending it spinning in a hurricane of broken glass.

As we sped off in the other direction, motorists jumped from their cars and pedestrians rushed into the street to sort out the damage. No one seemed to have noticed us. We were already gone.

The Man in the Hat almost smiled.

"What the fuck is going on? Where the hell are you? Arajiro!" the radio walkie-talkie cackled. The Man in the Hat picked it up off the floor of the van, rolled down the window, and tossed it out with elegant casualness.

I watched it scuttle across the street and land right in front of some little kid no older than five. He squatted by the curb and regarded the object curiously, afraid to pick it up. He was probably learning all sorts of new words.

Minutes later, after more twists and turns than I could count, we wound up on a street that looked a little bit like every backstreet in Tokyo, but not like any I could name. The Man in the Hat ditched his medic getup and hopped out of the van. An assistant followed suit and grabbed my arm to make sure I came along. It wasn't necessary. I wasn't about to stick around and wait for Arajiro to regain consciousness.

The driver sped off with Arajiro still inside, unconscious and strapped to a gurney. Or maybe he was dead. I wondered what they were going to do with him, but didn't ask. It was abundantly clear who was in control here.

I looked around. I had no idea where the hell we were. It was Tokyo, but it was the anonymous Tokyo of movie sets and *manga* drawings, where everything is familiar but uncanny. The noise of Tokyo was missing and even the sky seemed slightly off-color. It was as if whoever penciled in reality had overlooked a few details.

My two escorts walked me to a faceless corporate highrise. It was the same concrete-and-glass labor camp that capitalism seemed to leave in its wake the world over. No one talked as we walked into the building. The receptionist glanced up but didn't pay us any further attention as we strolled over to the elevator. While we waited in silence, I recalled my discussion with Ihara regarding the whole stairs-vs. -elevators thing. I got a creepy feeling I had been right all along.

The elevator came and we stepped inside. The assistant produced a key and opened up the control panel. Then the Man in the Hat took out a different key and placed it inside a lock beneath all the floor buttons. He turned it and we started moving.

A Muzak version of "Silly Love Songs" lilted harmlessly through the air. Beneath it was the quiet hum of an efficient elevator. It was difficult to tell if we were going up or down and there was nothing to do but wait.

I gazed down at my shoes. They were in good shape, all things considered.

After a time the elevator stopped. Its doors whisked open and the assistant strode out wordlessly. I began to follow him but the Man in the Hat placed a hand on my shoulder, gently pulling me back in. It wasn't our stop.

We continued down, Paul McCartney and his band floating through the speakers. The elevator lights began flickering. Suddenly a painful grating sound came from all sides at once, like two ancient iron vessels colliding in surround sound. The elevator rattled sideways for a moment, nearly knocking me from my feet. My first thought was *earthquake.*

I flung a panicked look toward the Man in the Hat, but he just smiled and braced himself against the walls. Suddenly the floor seemed to fall out as the elevator shot downward. The grating sound became a rhythmic screech, like a locomotive with fingernails for wheels and a chalkboard for rails. "Silly Love Songs" was pretty much drowned out. It crossed my mind that it could be the last song I ever heard.

We stopped moving as suddenly as we'd started. For a few seconds, the rusty gears of the device beat out their tune. I looked over to the Man in the Hat. He was still as a stone Buddha. His lips moved through a single word but I couldn't hear what it was above the din of the cage. He smiled sardonically and said no more. Then everything fell silent. Everything, that is, except Paul McCartney. It would take more than a beat-up elevator to stop the mop-top.

The elevator opened into a utility tunnel of pipes, wires, and dust. A narrow concrete passageway lit only by the occasional soot-encrusted bare bulb. Either the abandoned industrial motif was the latest trend in office decor or we weren't in the executive suite anymore.

"So where's the Amontillado, Montrésor?" I quipped. The Man in the Hat didn't respond, only motioned me down the hall. Maybe he didn't read Poe. Maybe he just didn't like me.

Our footsteps echoed in the chamber as he turned left then right, right then left. I tried keeping track of our course but soon gave up. I had relinquished control of events long ago and it was time that I acknowledged it. Trying to chart our twists and turns wasn't going to have any bearing on what happened next. I didn't think anything I did would.

This actually cheered my spirits. If I was utterly helpless, well, so be it. It meant I could relax a little, instead of plotting what I would do next. I was floating down a dark, swift river. For me, the struggle was over.

The situation reminded me of a stupid joke I'd heard years ago while doing a story on a fifteen-year-old Bengalese python trainer. I figured the Man in the Hat could use a joke. I started to tell it and realized he was gone.

I nearly called out to him, but I didn't want to hear the sound of my own voice echoing through the empty corridors. I wasn't scared yet, but that might be all it took. I stopped walking and plopped down on the cold ground. Time to simply sit. Somewhere, Tokyo shop girls were smiling and young handicapped athletes were creating moments they'd remember for the rest of their lives and I was...where exactly? I guess it didn't really matter. "Silly Love Songs" was stuck in my head and I didn't even mind that so much. Every time I tried to take stock of my situation I'd hear Paul McCartney's sugary voice reply, *"So what's wrong with that? I'd like to know..."* Maybe he had a point.

Suddenly the ghostly white face of a little girl appeared out of the darkness. I blinked and ran a quick check on my system to make sure my major faculties were still intact. She smiled and suppressed a giggle. Her head turned and I followed her glance to another girl standing beside her. They were both attired in dark crimson kimonos and their fine black hair was perched on their heads in perfect little mounds. The twin apparitions looked at me like I was the silliest thing in the world and started to laugh. I broke into a coughing fit, and once I was breathing again, I began to laugh, too. They reached out their tiny hands in perfect synchronization and helped me to my feet with strength far beyond their diminutive bodies. I was convinced I was either hallucinating or dead as we three strolled off down the dark corridor, our laughter echoing through the maze of lifeless concrete.

The girls knew where they were going, and they kept me moving at a steady clip. I was enjoying the stroll, pretending we were in park on a sunny afternoon instead of stuck in a dreary underground catacomb. I concocted a whole scenario—I was their uncle and we were having a picnic during the spring blossoming of the cherry trees. We had packed a bunch of sandwiches, some crackers, a jar of cocktail olives, some strawberries, and, at the girls' insistence, some Oreo cookies. A real spread. I tried to imagine other things, like maybe they brought a kite or had a dog or something, but nothing else really came together. Besides, too many details would ruin it.

Finally we stopped at door near the end of one of the corridors. It was a stained wooden deal with that damn symbol painted on it and a brass doorknob right out of a corporate furnishings catalog. The everyday office door looked ridiculous set in the dusty cinderblock walls. One of the girls knocked on it lightly, her little hand curled into a tiny seashell of a fist.

"Enter," a booming voice said from the other side. One of the girls stretched as high as she could to get her hand on the doorknob and give it a turn. It took all of their effort to open the door as I just stood there dumbly trying to quit thinking about sandwiches. I had recovered just enough to start wondering what the hell was going on.

The door swung open to reveal a pleasant-looking fatman squatting on the floor of a spacious room. He looked like the *fukusuke* doll old shopkeepers displayed for good luck.

There was no furniture or anything else to help me ascertain whether it was an office, living quarters, or just an unfinished torture chamber. It was lit with fluorescent bulbs that threw a ghastly green tint over the bare white walls. Just that, and a vaguely familiar-looking grandfatherly guy sitting on a crimson carpet that matched the radiant kimonos of the strange little girls.

"You could use some of these in the hallway," I said, pointing at the ceiling bulbs.

"Ah! You've found him. Wonderful, wonderful!" he said to the girls, smiling effusively. The two girls laughed. Then one put her hands over her mouth and whispered something to the other. They laughed some more.

The old guy looked up at me conspiratorially, as if to say "Kids—aren't they wild?" Then he turned his attention back to the children.

"You've done a great job. Superfantastic. Now run along and play."

Why a kid would want to play in this dungeon I don't know, but they raced out the door with their musical giggles and slammed it shut behind them.

"Have I seen you somewhere before?" I asked the old man.

He laughed, rocking back and forth, barely managing not to topple over. It was the kind of answer you'd expect from someone who looked like a good-luck doll.

There were about ten thousand follow-up questions I wanted to ask, but the only one I could think of at the time was, "Who are the little girls?"

He stopped laughing.

"Them? They are my nieces." He seemed annoyed by the question, answering it with a dismissive wave of his hand.

"They live down here?"

"Of course not. They live near Osaka with my sister." He shook his head in disgust. Disgust not at them or Osaka or his sister, but at me for asking.

I thought of asking him why they were made up like exquisite *maikos*-in-waiting, or what the hell they were doing here. I'm no expert on child rearing, but it seemed a little uncouth. Still, I was his guest—even if by kidnapping. So I figured I'd hold my tongue and hear the old guy out.

"Is anything else troubling you?" he asked.

I shook my head.

"Then please," he said, looking much relieved, "have a seat."

I looked around and I noticed there wasn't a chair, as the song goes. So I just plopped down in the middle of the floor. It was probably the softest carpet I'd ever sat on in my life. It always surprises me what you find in the basements of giant sky-rises.

"So you are Mr. Billy Chaka," the old man said with a smile.

"Pleased to meet you, Mister..."

"My name is not important."

"I kinda figured it wouldn't be." Everybody in this damn group seemed to have something against names. Must make for strange company parties.

"My function here is to inform you of what will transpire over the next forty-eight hours and to tell you what we're all about. I'll be elucidating some of our general philosophies, telling you about the history of our organization, and getting you up to speed with our goals for the future."

It was like that part in job interviews where they try to tell you what a great outfit they are. It was a little late in the game to sell me on the group, but maybe I could get a few facts.

"Who are you—"

"Mr. Chaka, my name is not important," he said with the same smile.

"Not you. The organization. I've done some looking into this, and I can't even find out a name. So what are you guys called?"

The old man wrinkled his eyebrows. "Well," he began haltingly, "you've hit upon a matter of some embarrassment, I'm afraid. We don't really have a name as of yet. Let me correct myself. Our name has not been rediscovered, though I assure you we have put some of our best researchers on the task. They have even traced the loss of our name back to a clerical error in the Tokugawa period. It was here that, through a complete accident, the symbol which you are familiar with became completely divorced from its meaning. It was little more than a bureaucratic gaffe, but look what trouble it has caused us." He got a real chuckle out of it, his big face wrinkling as he laughed. Trying to figure out where I'd seen this guy before was giving me an itch.

"So what do you call yourselves?" I asked.

"We don't. Not until the name is unearthed. We wouldn't want to go around calling ourselves something incorrect just to have a name, would we? Our name is sacred. Can I get you anything to drink? Something to nibble on perhaps?"

I declined.

"Very well then. First of all, I'd like to congratulate you on being selected. Since Orange Blossom chose you, we've done a lot of research into your background and we think she made a fine choice. Frankly, she doesn't always."

Now you are the one, she'd said. I played ignorant. "She chose me?"

"When she approached you at that Purple whatsomacallit bar. That was the first sign. Consummation occurred at your hotel."

Pretty disappointing concept of consummation.

"All of this is confidential, of course. As you are a reporter, I know this goes against your nature. But you must never tell anyone that which I am about to tell you now. We are an organization that cherishes our privacy. Our survival is dependent on anonymity. Very few individuals even know of our existence, and we are willing to use violence to keep it so. In the preservation of Orange Blossom, there is no boundary we will not cross. Her life is sacred. Every life is, of course—that's the doctrine—but some more than others. You know a small part of what we are capable of, so I needn't elaborate. I say this not as a threat, but as an explanation. So there's the tough-guy part of the speech."

He smiled an insurance man's smile. Whatever it was I recognized about the old man was making me nuts. I knew I'd encountered him on this trip to Japan. But where? Not at the tournament. Not at the studio. Not in the hotel or the police station or the yakuza headquarters. Before I could check off the other places, he continued.

"Orange Blossom has an incredible history, more incredible I'm sure than anyone you will ever encounter in your life. Part of our duties involve continuous research into her past, one that is wide and varied and fantastic beyond the bounds of reality as most people experience it. Chronicling her history is a losing proposition, because even as we discovery new facts surrounding her, she is out there—living and creating new mysteries. We are always playing catch-up. After the Thirty Years' Dream, we are closer, but never quite there. However, we have great hope for the coming period. Since her last furlough there have been a number of technological advances."

I felt my eyelids dropping. I shook my head and straightened my shoulders. Bad time for a nap.

He continued. "Let us begin with the beginning, which is perhaps the vaguest period of Orange Blossom's life and the one furthest from our expertise. We are always working backward, starting with who she is at present and trying to trace the source. One of our chief metaphor technicians likened it to canoeing up an endless winding river trying to discover where it begins, always imagining it's one bend of the water away. Of course, we eliminated the metaphor department because, by their own admission, metaphors fail where Orange Blossom is concerned. She is not like anything, she just is, and trying to come up with some complicated linguistic trickery... well, we just decided it was dishonest."

His words were washing over me like the sound of a distant bell made of silk. A rustling, pulsing sound reverberating somewhere under the words. A dull buzzing, like an electric bumblebee—but soft, like a bunny. Like a bunny? I jerked my head upright. They were right to fire the metaphor department.

"So then—her origins. We know not when she was born, nor where. There is a raging debate among our scholars as to whether she was born in China and came to Japan or was Japanese by birth. Obviously, we'd like to think she was born here, but it's impossible to know. There are no written records of her existence until the seventh century, but since there was no written language in Japan until that time, it doesn't mean much. The early centuries are murky and filled with many conflicting legends. She is said to have lived near Osaka around the time of Jimmu Tenno's ascension of the chrysanthemum throne in 660 B.C. But a folk song from Nara suggests she dwelt there instead, where she performed the Seven Years' Dance before retreating to a secret cave guarded by the demons of the forest. It's all very sketchy. Even scholars talk only in centuries when dating these things. Our methods are not nearly as crude as the average academician's, but we still have our limits.

"In 712, we find two very coded references to her in the *Record of Ancient Matters,* and later, in 720, she is mentioned in the *Chronicle of Japan.* Don't bother yourself trying to check the sources, though, as our organization has systematically eradicated these passages over the centuries. Even if you were allowed access to the original documents, the references are horribly obscure and cannot be deciphered without a key. That said, as an experiment we sent Lafcadio Hearn—a writer just like you—the cipher in 1843. He damn near cracked it. But he was a genius, rather than a teen-rag hack." He paused and glanced up at me. "I'm only joking, of course. I've heard your stuff isn't half-bad."

Even the insult wasn't enough to snap me out of my stupor. All this time spent, all the answers I was searching for, and nothing he said made any sense. I'd been kidnapped from jail and taken beneath the earth to listen to the mangled, digressive history of an organization so screwed up they'd lost their own name. And now I was falling asleep. Maybe after all the drama my only psychic defense was to retreat into an unconscious state where the distinction between past and present, reality and fantasy, was a warm blur. My head bobbed as I struggled to follow the old man's tale.

"Starting in 847, the pattern fully emerges. It is during this time that our organization was formed. Now there are the Thirty Years' Blossom and the Thirty Years' Dream. Here, too, we find the first mention of the Reborn Youth and the first secret Temple of Golden Slumber is created in the mountains outside of Nara. It still stands, though, believe me, it looks much different today as it is no longer in use. We have had to seek out more secluded corners of the islands. These are big events for us, obviously. Significant milestones. However, the particulars of her day-to-day existence during this Period of Emergence, as we call it, are still quite obscure.

She could have been peddling potatoes for all we know—but of course, given her beauty and her temperament, surely this was not the case. Can you imagine Orange Blossom selling potatoes?"

He let the question hang in the air a moment and then burst out laughing.

The image of Orange Blossom and the word "potatoes" circled each other in my mind but never quite came together. I was slipping fast and decided I had to stand if I was going to stay conscious. I wasn't sure consciousness was worth the effort, but I stood anyway.

"Slow down, Chief," I muttered as I rose to my feet. The old man seemed surprised, either to suddenly see me standing above him or to hear me speak. His head jerked up in disbelief, like he'd never been interrupted before.

"Are you trying to tell me," I began, struggling with the absurdity of the idea, "that this woman, Orange Blossom, is immortal?"

"Well," the old man said as if relieved, "that remains to be seen. But she has lived off and on for thousands of years, so we take it as an article of faith that she is probably immortal. She is certainly a goddess of some sort."

"And your group was created to worship her?"

"Mainly to protect her and study her. But yes, I guess you could say we worship her, too. We don't pray to her or anything like that, though. There are a number of conflicting theological interpretations regarding exactly what sort of deity she is, or if she is a deity at all or simply a very strange woman who just so happens to live forever in thirty-year cycles of dreaming and wakefulness. Please have a seat, Mr. Chaka. You look a little ill."

I felt a little ill. Orange Blossom had bewildered and confused me, but compared to the number she'd pulled on these kooks, I was an unassailable fortress of logic. Unfortunately, I didn't know what a fortress of logic was supposed to do when stuck in a subterranean hideout with no chairs and only a familiar-looking lunatic to chat with. So I just sat back down.

"May I continue?" he said, perturbed with my interruptions. I shrugged. The warmth of the crimson carpet was suddenly very inviting. I felt like Dorothy stopping for a rest in the poppy field.

"Subsequent to the Period of Emergence, the life of Orange Blossom becomes only slightly less enigmatic. Again, our scholars have done a crack job of elucidating records secret even in their time, and it is a miracle of our faith that such accounts survived. Be that as it may, most of the narratives relating to Orange Blossom during this time remain anecdotal, and highly subject to the superstitions and—well, ignorance really—that characterized the era. There are goblins and demons and ghosts and all sorts of nonsense."

There was a soft hum beneath his voice. I closed my eyes, just for a moment, and listened to it.

"When you sift out all the myths and legends, you are left with only a handful of indisputable facts—indisputable, and yet often contradictory. She is two places at once, or she is awake when she was asleep. One story says she sleeps just before the first snow of the Thirtieth Year, one says just after. Since the last sleep of the Meiji era, it has been our custom to make sure she is in the Temple of Golden Slumber before the first snow. More than even a matter of belief or doctrine, it is a practical concern. Caution is the most bountiful of actions, as my own teacher liked to say. No point in having her out there while the Return to Innocence leaves her as helpless as a four-year-old, especially when so many of the old superstitions say she shall die if exposed to the snows of winter.

Superstitions perhaps, but violating them for the mere sake of curiosity—that would be an insane risk, given what we know, which, to bring me back to my original point, is really just a handful of indisputable but often contradictory facts."

Whatever he said next never made it to my brain. It had mercifully shut down my consciousness for a languid series of dreams and Orange Blossom was the star in every one. Lafcadio Hearn was there, Dorothy and Toto, too. We were eating sandwiches, drinking Amontillado, and listening to Paul McCartney. Compared to what was going on when I was awake, my dreams were perfectly intelligible, almost mundane.

And from what I dreamed, I believe this old man must have gone on talking to me for hours, even as I slept. Little phrases would pierce my sleep and linger in my dreams. *Consummation of the Choosing...Flight of Mortality...Return to Innocence...Deliverance unto Slumber.* They all sounded like epic heavy-metal songs.

And a funny thought came to me from somewhere while I slept. Wouldn't it be funny if everything this nutcase was telling me was true? Wouldn't that be just a lark.

I awoke to annoying electronic theme music endlessly repeating itself. With my eyes closed, I hoped against hope that it would end, but of course it didn't. I felt as if I'd been asleep for days. My face felt bloated and slack, threatening to slide off my skull with the slightest movement. The rest of my body felt so heavy that movement wasn't an option. Nothing to do but lie back and listen to the monotonous symphony of beeps and whistles.

"It is to be a glorious day," the old man suddenly chirped from behind me. His boisterous voice startled me into a more wakeful state than I desired. I had to keep myself from telling him what he could go do with his glorious day.

"How long did I sleep?"

"As long as necessary. That is one of the body's miracles. When it is tired, it sleeps."

Movement required another miracle. I got it over with all at once—sitting bolt upright like a zombie embalmed with espresso. The old man was engaged in a marathon bout of handheld video gaming. I wondered how long he'd been playing.

"You winning, Chief?" I asked. Their refusal to tell me their names gave me an opening for all sorts of insolent ways to vent my frustrations that the average Japanese citizen would never know. I was free to call the old guy anything I wanted, ignoring the rigid code of titles and their accompanying social complexities. It wasn't as satisfying as it ought to have been. I mean, what's the big deal about disrespecting your elders? It's practically a national pastime in the U.S.

He shook his head in answer to my question, then added flatly, "By design, there is no way of winning this game."

"Just what the world needs," I said. "Another game you can't win."

"Do you recall our conversation last night?" he asked, the facade of the circumlocuting insurance man going up again as he smiled far too enthusiastically for this time of the morning. If it was morning.

I shrugged and wondered at his definition of conversation. "I get the gist." I yawned. I wasn't trying to be insulting, I was just tired. For a moment, I worried that he'd launch into the whole mad spiel again, complete with the baffling digressions and offhand insults. But he didn't. He just tilted his head and smiled.

"Well, I guess that will have to do," he said. "We would like to give you a more complete education, of course, but we are under a deadline, as you journalists say. For now you'll have to content yourself with a scant overview of the history of Orange Blossom. One day, the theologians and researches will get tired of squabbling and finally produce some literature. That's really the next big step, after recovering our name, of course. Would you like me to send some to you?"

I nodded and told him to send it to the office in Cleveland.

"Excellent. I should warn you that it may take a while. I wouldn't be checking your mailbox until at very minimum the end of the upcoming Thirty Years' Dream. But anytime after that, within three or four years let's say, you can expect it."

"So around thirty-four years, huh?" He gave me a look of gleeful anticipation. "I'll keep my eye out for it."

"Wonderful." He clapped his hands together. "I have prepared some rice and miso soup to nourish you for this day. It is the traditional meal to begin the Day of Reclamation. We also have MuscleBars for extra energy. You may need them."

"Sounds great," I said, managing a smile. Trapped in the basement with a nutcase and his nieces. I wondered briefly where they were. Probably off rescuing men in the subterranean labyrinth. Perhaps there were hundreds like me down here, lured at the rate of one an hour, each guided to their very own room with their very own crazy old man to tell them stories and feed them soup for the rest of their lives, until they themselves became the crazy old men, and so on.

The Chief motioned me to a table set up in the corner of the room. From the looks of things, it was the only furnishing that had been done during my slumber. After he showed me the food, he headed off to the opposite corner to play the video game some more. I slurped down the soup in semiprivacy and finished off the rice in no time. It felt like I hadn't eaten in days, and even if the ambience was lacking, the food was pretty tasty.

When the Chief noticed I'd finished eating, he pointed out the MuscleBars. I politely declined. Several times. He seemed disappointed, but I don't think I broke any superstitions about Reclamation Day, or whatever it was called.

I still didn't have a plan. The yakuza were temporarily out of the picture. They had a talent for violently bursting back into it, but the guys I was with now seemed to have the jump on them. At the same time, this group definitely had a few loose pins in their *pachinko* machines. I wasn't planning on handing Orange Blossom over to them without trying to find out from her just what the hell was going on.

True, I knew why they wanted her now. If I believed the Chief, it was because she was some kind of goddess. Hence, they needed Orange Blossom because they were a secret society of raving loonies. Whereas the yakuza, who were an exclusive band of homicidal thugs, still hadn't let on why they needed her so badly.

I wanted to ask her myself. I wanted to ask her about Sato Migusho, about the photograph, and about a hundred other things.

But even if I managed to give these creeps the slip (and truth be told, aside from their idiotic beliefs, I somewhat liked these creeps so far) there were few places I could run. With the cops after me and no money or ID, the options were pretty limited. The kinds of places I could hide out under those circumstances would have all been tipped off by the yaks. They'd be on the lookout for a down-and-out *gaijin* who spoke Japanese well and dressed like shit.

I burped in loud appreciation of the splendid meal, something frowned upon a little nowadays but formerly the highest gastronomic compliment. When I did it around Sarah, she'd shrivel up her nose in mock disgust, launching me into a lecture about culture and table manners. She'd counter by accusing me of adapting only the elements of foreign cultures which allowed me to be a chauvinist, a pig, or ideally, both. Burping without her around just wasn't as fun.

At the end of my eruption, a bald, monkish-looking guy entered the room. The monkish effect was tempered by his denim button-down shirt and khaki pants, making him look more like a weekending salaryman than a man of the cloth. Maybe he wasn't monkish looking after all, and it was only an effect of his smooth skull, which glowed a sickly green under the pulsing fluorescent bulb.

The Chief stuck the video game into his pocket, then the two men tried to outbow each other for a while. The Chief motioned me over to the center of the room, right on the insignia without a name.

"What does he know?" the bald man asked the Chief.

"I gave him a broad overview, you know, best I could." The Chief was kind enough not to mention that I'd fallen asleep, or maybe he was protecting his own hide by the omission.

"Is he aware of the time frame?"

"Vaguely." The answer didn't seem to satisfy either one of them.

"But he understands the Return to Innocence, right?"

"Well," the Chief said, clearing his throat, "I think he could use a refresher on that part. If you think it is necessary. And if you have the time, you know..."

"Are *you* aware of the time frame?" he asked the Chief with respectful concern. The bald man wrinkled the part of his face where his eyebrows used to be.

"Yes. I have been given an update of her condition."

"Not that. The secondary directive."

"Oh yeah. How gather the northerly clouds?"

"Swiftly," the bald one practically spat. "Swiftly and with great foreboding." He delivered the line like a bad episode of

TV's *Warriors of Buddha* and then reached into his briefcase, producing a mass of computer printouts. He handed them to the Chief. The Chief studied them quickly, his face tightening with concern. He looked over first one page, then another, then another, and finally back to the first.

"Are these accurate?"

"I fear they are," the bald guy said. The Chief looked over the printouts again, as if searching for some minor error he couldn't find.

"Shit," the Chief blurted.

"My sentiments precisely."

After that, I was escorted by the bald guy out the same door I'd entered into the same cheerless maze of utility tunnels the Chief's nieces had guided me through who knows how long ago. I thought I could hear the echo of the little girls' laughter somewhere in the distance, but I couldn't be certain. Lately, uncertainty and I had been having a passionate affair.

A few twists and turns and we were back at the deathtrap elevator. The bald guy pushed the button. We waited. After a few moments, the cacophony began above us, like some sick screaming beast descending from the sky, growing louder as it neared until it was a deafening roar that blew away all other thoughts and sensations. It slammed to a percussive halt in front of us and the doors struggled open. The bald guy motioned me in. What I wouldn't give for a nice flight of stairs.

He stepped inside after me and the doors began to close. Just as they were about to slam shut, a tiny hand jutted inside the claustrophobic box.

"Wait!" a small voice pleaded. The bald guy pushed a button on the operating panel and the door began opening again.

It was the nieces. They had on the same smashing little red kimonos and were giggling as usual. Life sure is fun when you're a little girl. Looked like it, anyway.

"What is it, my little sugar dumplings?" the bald guy said.

"Uncle says that the funny man should take this with him," one little girl said. The other stretched out her tiny arm and handed him the video game. The bald man looked it over, and then a broad smile washed over his face.

"Brilliant," he said. "Thank you very much. Superfantastic!" The little girls laughed and darted off. The elevator door wheezed shut.

"You might be able to use this," the man said as he thrust the video game into my hands.

I looked it over to see if any modifications had been made to turn it into a stun gun, or an infrared device or something more substantial than a handheld video game, but could find no ulterior purpose.

"What's this thing for?" I asked.

The bald man frowned at me. "You don't know? I thought you were supposed to be hip and all that." There was a note of panic in his voice.

"It looks like a video game."

"Very good," he said with noticeable relief. "It's a Game Boy."

"What's it for?"

"Playing video games," he replied, worry creeping into his tone again. The elevator started up, and then there was only noise as we rocketed back toward the surface of the world.

I didn't get another good look at the guy until we were outside the building in that archetypal nameless section of Tokyo. How could I have missed it?

The man at my side was The Man in the Hat—minus his hair, his mustache, and even his eyebrows. We walked to his car, a Yotayo RZ-5, parked in a space that said RESERVED FOR _____. Fitting. I waited until we got in to say anything.

"You lose a bet or what?" I asked as he motioned me to fasten my seat belt. He didn't understand what I meant, or perhaps just chose to ignore me. I persisted.

"The hair. What happened?"

"It was necessary that I remove it."

"Eyebrows and everything, huh?"

"Yes."

We zipped down a couple of side streets and merged perilously into traffic. I remembered that back when he had hair, the Man in the Hat had also worn glasses, and I hoped that they had just been a prop, because he wasn't wearing them now.

"Where are we going?" I asked. I didn't really expect him to tell me.

"We must take you to a safe place. The police aren't likely to forget about you now. You've really made a mess of things." He shook his head.

I could have reminded him that they were the ones who busted me out of jail and kidnapped a cop. Or that the only reason I was there was because I was being questioned for a murder that they had likely committed. Still, he was right. I'd made a mess of things.

"What day is it?" I asked. I hadn't seen a newspaper or a TV in days.

"The twenty-third."

Today were the finals of the sparring competition for the Nineteen and Under Handicapped International Martial Arts Championships. I'd missed practically the whole tournament, and after today it would be over. For all I knew, the legendary Master Yado himself had shown up to present the kata trophy. Or maybe there was a scandal raging due to rumors that Yoko Torikata had slept with the judges. Who knew? The only story I'd have would be far from the tournament compound—one nobody would believe, one that didn't have an ending. And so far, it wasn't the uplifting stuff *Youth in Asia* usually went for.

I remembered that first day of the tournament. It seemed like another lifetime.

"Do you golf?" I asked, thinking of the terms he'd offered me way back when.

"Not much." He shrugged. "When I get a chance."

That was maybe the first straight answer I'd gotten from the guy. I decided not to push my luck with more questions. Instead, I thought about my meager possessions sitting in some box at the Tokyo Metropolitan Police Station. My wallet, with my Alien Registration Card and passport. My watch—a prototype a friend at Seiko had given me of a failed experiment they called the "Apocalypse Y2K"—replete with a mini-cell phone, global positioning system, Geiger counter, heart monitor, Tetris, and a bunch of other crap I never used. My trusted accordion folder, which contained some clippings for the unenlightened. My notebook of cryptic scrawlings to be worked into feature articles. And the picture of Sato and Orange Blossom. The cops would probably find that photograph pretty puzzling, but there was no one to question about it. The guy was dead and the woman had disappeared.

And then there was my pager. Meaning that anyone who'd tried to call me was going to be contacted by the cops, and have that whole hassle brought into their lives. I'd put Nabiko on that list for sure. Maybe Hiro Bhuto, possibly Mama Mayumi. Maybe my editor back in Cleveland and maybe even Sarah. They were probably shaking their heads and thinking, Here we go again.

I hoped they were, anyway. I hoped that was all that they were doing, just chalking it up to another misadventure for their resident trouble-loving, crack wordsmith and teen sympathizer. Because if they knew what I'd really gotten into this time, they might hit the panic button and deploy a hastily formed posse of reporters to "rescue" me. And that wouldn't help anybody.

I tried to picture various scenarios, but it was hard to imagine what was going on back at the home office. Cleveland never seemed so far away.

The Man in the Hat was one with the machine and the machine one with the road. Once we got onto the highway, the other cars seemed to be racing backward on a turbocharged conveyer belt as we ripped past them, darting first one way and then the other like a boxer weaving to avoid lethal blows. He seemed to know when a lane was going to slow about three seconds before it did, and then he moved seamlessly into a faster one. And then he was onto the next one, always gaining speed and never even turning his head. I was awestruck.

"Where did you learn to drive like this?" I asked, cars whizzing backward on both sides.

"Yotayo Academy of Defensive Driving." He smirked.

"Bullshit."

"Class of eighty-one," he said, and held up his left hand to show me a class ring. Before I could read the engraving, his hand was back on the gearshift. He put it through its paces and the car hurtled through traffic like a coked-up mouse scrambling through a laboratory maze. No cop in the world would be able chase him down and this car was pretty much a piece of crap. Made you wonder.

"You know, I saw our friend Orange Blossom at the Yotayo Love Hotel—"

"Nice try," he said, shaking his head. It stood out in relief against the blur of the world racing by.

"What do you mean?"

"*The Yotayo Love Hotel?*"

"I was there."

"Oh boy. I'm afraid, Mr. Chaka, that you have been bunnyelked," he said with a chuckle.

"Bunnyelked?"

"It's like this. I had a cousin who once went to America. He was at someplace in Wyoming eating breakfast and the people next to him start talking about this creature that's part rabbit and part deer. They go on about how beautiful it is, how smart, how fierce, how hard to hunt. So my cousin bought a picture postcard of the thing and brought it back to Japan. He showed it to everybody and talked about how these things were all over the West—in the prairies and some in the mountains. Well, we'd never been to America. He told some of the stories about them that he overheard at breakfast—the whole deal. He got kind of obsessed, really. He even tried to organize a hunting trip for the next year with a group of his buddies. They were going to go to America and kill a bunch of these things. Anyway, he carried this postcard around all the time, always showing it off. One day, he showed it to a visiting American, some kid not yet out of high school. Of course, the kid just laughed at him. He said it was a phony, the creature was made up. They just glued elk horns on a dead bunny and called it a bunnyelk. It was something they did to fool stupid Easterners, like my cousin. Obviously, the man was crushed. That's why I say you've been bunnyelked. Hate to be the one to tell you." By his smile I could tell he didn't hate it that much.

"First of all," I began, "it's not a bunnyelk. It's a jackalope. It's made from a jackrabbit and the horns of an antelope. Jack-a-lope. And B, it was made up to fool Easterners meaning Yankees, not Japanese. Greenhorns from the other side of the Mississippi. Third, the Yotayo Love Hotel is real. I was there."

"No way."

"It's true," I insisted. "We could go there now if you want."

He hesitated a moment. If he called my bluff, I'd be chasing Sean Penn billboards all day. And I was sure the sumo sheriff wouldn't be pleased to see me back so soon.

"Nah," the Man in the Hat said, to my relief. "No time to look for imaginary hotels."

"Suit yourself," I said. I was beginning to like this guy, whoever he was. He seemed a lot friendlier now that he had me by the balls. If there's one thing I learned, it's that people are apt to treat you decently only if you're completely in their power or they want something from you. For now, both were true with me, so maybe that's why the Man in the Hat was giving me the regular Joe patter. Just two guys in a car flying down the freeway.

"I'm hungry," I said, realizing I was. The food in the basement hadn't done a thing for me. Maybe I should have had the MuscleBar after all.

"You want to get something to eat?"

"If you think it's safe," I said, like I didn't care one way or the other.

"Depends on where we go," he said. Then he made a face like he was thinking about it real hard. I hope he thought as fast as he drove, because now that I'd mentioned it, food was all I could think of.

Suddenly we ripped across all four lanes of traffic and bolted down an exit ramp. The Man in the Hat downshifted with lightning speed, working the gear knob like a paddle in an invisible game of air hockey.

"You like Love Burger?" he said.

No self-respecting yakuza would be caught dead at Love Burger. Cops were another matter, but we had to take our chances. Fortunately for my stomach, the parking lot was deserted.

Inside was the most unpopulated Love Burger I'd ever been in, which was just fine with me. I got a milkshake, cheeseburger, and a small fry. The Man in the Hat was more ambitious, opting for a Hugburger, ChickenTickle Fingers, and a large Coke. Since my wallet was still at the Tokyo Metropolitan Pigpen, he paid. We took our food and sat at a corner table that seemed to be designed for midgets on intimate terms.

"So we just go and pick up Orange Blossom," I said, my mouth full of burger. "Is that it?"

"If it were only that simple," the Man in the Hat said. The chumminess of the car ride was now absent from his voice. "We saved you a lot of footwork, which is lucky because you seemed to be spinning your wheels."

"I was making progress in my own way." I'd made more tangible progress on the burger than on anything I'd done since I got to Japan, but no reason the Man in the Hat should know.

"Really?" The idea amused him. He wiped some of the Special Love sauce from the corner of his mouth. "Well then, tell me three things that you have learned about this woman?"

I could have told him twenty things just about the shape of her mouth. But he was after facts, so I decided to stick to them. There wasn't much to stick to.

"She's a geisha..."

"You knew that before. Doesn't count."

"Okay...How about this? She knew Sato Migusho and was probably with him just before he died."

The Man in the Hat raised an eyebrow curiously. Like I was trying to bunnyelk him.

"All right, it doesn't make sense to me either. All I really know is she's gotten herself into a heap of trouble. She's wanted by the yakuza."

"That's not much to go on." He was into his chicken fingers now. The guy ate like he drove—delicate grace masking raging intensity.

"The Yamagama-gumis. Kwaidan specifically." The name didn't impress him as much as I'd hoped. He just looked at me blankly, daintily shoving chicken strips into his mouth.

"Should I know him?" he mumbled.

"He's been one of the most powerful gangsters in the country for years. Unless you've been locked away in a monastery, you'd probably recognize the name."

"Well, that explains it, then," he said. It didn't explain anything to me. "So what about this Kwaidan guy?"

"Is this the first you've heard about all of this?"

"They only tell me what I need to know," he said. "I'm fairly busy with other things most of the time."

"Like what?"

"Monitoring Orange Blossom. That is my number-one priority. I was trained since birth for the moment swiftly approaching. The time when she must return. Could you pass me the ketchup?"

If he was joking he didn't show it. He smothered his fries in ketchup like it was a contest and went right on eating. I didn't get him, but I decided I'd play along. Who knew how long it would be until I found someone as talkative.

"If you are so highly trained, what do you need me for?" I asked.

"She knows who I am. She can sense me. I get anywhere near her, she bolts. That would be disastrous. Worse than you can imagine."

"Seems to me she's already bolted."

"We know where she is at this very moment. We've got a lock on her. Soon as I finish these ChickenTickles, we're gone. It's destiny." He resumed eating, a one-man school of piranha.

"The Chief said she was deteriorating..." I said, trying to remember exactly what the Chief had said before I dozed off.

"Who's the Chief?" he mumbled.

"The guy in the basement. Where you took me, remember?"

"That guy? I don't know him. Never seen him before today."

"You really have no idea what is going on at all, do you?"

He didn't say anything. He just started dipping a lone fry in ketchup over and over again. With each successive plunge my heart sank. I was in the hands of an idiot. He wouldn't be able to tell me anything because he knew only what they told him. Whoever "they" were. He was just like me, and our combined knowledge was as useless as a lone chopstick. The same dumb force that had pushed me along since I got here had been pulling his strings—ever since he was born, supposedly. He knew nothing about Shinto's death, nothing about the Chief, and nothing about Sato Migusho, about the yakuza, or even about me. I wondered if he even knew anything about Orange Blossom.

"I know Orange Blossom. That's my part in this," he said with a contented shrug, like he'd read my mind and wasn't impressed. His tone wasn't even defensive, considering how much I was glaring at him. I liked the guy. Really I did. But the whole situation was fucked and there was no one else to glare at.

"Fine," I said. I ate a few fries of my own, but the burger had filled my stomach and the conversation was killing my appetite. I should have known he was in the dark. The talkative ones always are.

"Then I suppose you can tell me about this 'Return to Innocence' thing?"

He shrugged. "You know. Regressing. Getting younger. It always happens. Just before the Thirty Years' Dream, Orange Blossom goes backward mentally."

He said it like it was an everyday kind of thing, like getting gray hair or growing a paunch. So now I had an immortal geisha who regresses mentally before the Thirty Years' Dream. Peachy. I wondered if these people went insane all at once or if it was an incremental process.

"Let me ask you something, seeing as how you are such an expert on this geisha," I said. "Does Orange Blossom have a favorite song?"

He looked at me like it was a stupid question, and maybe it was. He inhaled another fry.

"She does. You probably haven't heard of it," he said dismissively.

I wasn't going to let him get off that easily. "Why don't you sing a few bars of it?" I asked.

"Forget it."

"C'mon," I said, pushing an unused plastic knife across the table. "Pretend this is a karaoke mike and give me a show. I'm not leaving until you do."

"You'll leave with me when I finish these fries," he said.

"Right. 'It's destiny.' Problem is, there's just you and me now. No one else around to make me cooperate. And I'm pretty good with my hands and feet. You might end up coughing up some of those ChickenTickles."

"Yeah, right. Then someone calls the cops and you wind up back in jail. Gimme a break, Mr. Chaka. Finish your fries."

"I'm just trying to get you to sing! I tell you what—you sing, you can have the rest of my fries."

"You're not going to let this rest, are you?"

"I'm stubborn." I gloated. Our eyes locked. It was high noon.

"Fine," he blurted. "But just this once."

"You want the mike," I asked, holding up the plastic knife. He waved it off with a disgusted look. Then he looked around furtively to make sure no one was paying attention to us. No one was. He cleared his throat. He closed his eyes.

> *"The flowers wither,*
> *Their color fades away,*
> *While endlessly*
> *I spend my days in this world*
> *As the long rains fall."*

His voice rang with a high falsetto, and had I not been right across from him, I would have sworn it was a woman singing. A damn good singer of a woman, too. The very sound of his voice conveyed the wistful sorrow, the longing, the resignation of the words. Even if you didn't know a word of Japanese, you'd know what the song was about. I was flabbergasted. It was the best performance I had ever seen at a Love Burger.

"Wow," I mumbled. "You're good enough to be geisha."

"Give me your fries," he said. He was either annoyed or embarrassed or both—it was hard to tell. I pushed what was left of my fries across the table. He ate them silently.

The moment reminded me of a scene in Migusho's wartime epic *Glory of Tanzaki*. A bunch of soldiers are telling jokes and carrying on the night before they are about to mount a huge offensive that will certainly leave many of them dead. It is late in the night and their carousing and laughter have woken the general. He walks in the barracks just as the wiseass of the group is about to start another ribald story. When the wiseass sees the general, he freezes in fear, prostrates himself, and begins apologizing profusely. The general orders him to stand.

"Please continue with your joke," he says. "Only make sure it is a good one. It is the last many of these boys are likely to hear."

And of course the wiseass is powerless to go on. The general waits a moment and then strolls out of the barracks, leaving everyone to contemplate their life and death until the coming of the morning.

That's how it was in the Love Burger at that moment. The song had done something to both of us, made us suddenly recall we weren't just two guys free to goof around in restaurants. We were involved in something deadly serious, and no amount of bonhomie was going to get us out of it.

But when I thought about it, I didn't know if the general had done the right thing. Too much introspection kills morale. You don't want your soldiers thinking about death when they prepare to confront it.

I thought about lightening the mood by spraying ketchup and mustard all over myself and doing the old "I'm a Jackson Pollock" joke. But I didn't have any other clothes and the Man in the Hat didn't seem like the type who would get it anyway. That left me with nothing to do but sit there and watch him eat, which as far as watching people eating goes, wasn't unbearable. At least it was action-packed.

As he ate, I cataloged all the things that I imagined were going on in the normal world.

Chief Inspector Arajiro would be at his desk, pissed about another day of overtime, probably still doing paperwork

related to my escape while his troops scoured the streets
hoping to collar me and get a promotion.

Kwaidan probably had his guys on the lookout, too,
maybe posting a couple of them at the Purple Web or whatever purple manifestation Bhuto might have changed it to by
now.

The tournament would be coming to a close. Nabiko
would probably still be working on the set of the fish movie,
shooting into the wee hours of the night. Ihara would be
telling some poor jerk that his wife was cheating on him, or
his son was doing drugs, while Ihara's goons twiddled their
thumbs behind the false wall. The Scandinavian girls of the
Old West would be squeezing into their costumes for another
night at the Yotayo saloon. And somewhere Orange Blossom
would be regressing and being immortal and who knows
what else.

I felt strangely detached from it all, as if the city and
everything that happened there was all part of a dream I
barely remembered. I looked out the window toward east
Tokyo, the Low City. Not a great view but good enough for
the inside of a Love Burger.

It was a haiku moment. I tried to remember a poem that
nailed it. It took me a while, but finally it hit me.

> Distant lights
> There they live
> This autumn night

That was it. Buson, I think, or Basho, or one of those
guys. I thought about telling the poem to the Man in the Hat,
but didn't. He already thought I was weird enough. What
kind of guy tells old poems to another guy he hardly knows?
If Sarah were here, I would have told her. She'd shrug it off

and tell me that the only reason I pretended to like haiku was because they were the only poems short enough for me to memorize.

"You ready to go?" the Man in the Hat said, wiping his lips.

I nodded and tried to shake thoughts of the normal world from my head. The normal world had nothing to do with me anymore.

Back in the car, the Man in the Hat gave me the lowdown on what would happen next. He was going to drop me at Harajuku station near Takeshitadori, where they'd got a lock on Orange Blossom. He himself would have to leave the area, otherwise she might "sense" him. Then he tried to explain the regression thing again.

"When you confront her, you must understand that she will think and act like a teenager. It is very important that you don't come across as uncool." I hadn't been pressured to be cool since I was a teenager myself. "Mentally, she is probably around fifteen or sixteen right now, but she could be even younger. There is always a lot of guesswork involved, and her rate of regression depends on lots of variables—her diet, the number of people she's had sex with, pollution, the weather, even her general mood. If things are going a certain way, she could be a virtual ten-year-old by now. A ten-year-old with looks like hers is dangerous."

Anyone with looks like hers was dangerous.

Traffic was lighter now, but the Man in the Hat still insisted on driving at top speed. We ripped by an aqua-blue *takushi* just like the one Shinto used to drive. It's funny, but you never think a guy like that is going to get killed, and then when he does you can't stop thinking about it. He seemed such a peripheral figure in life that killing him was needlessly cruel. The kind of thing a guy like Kwaidan would probably get off on.

"You're an expert on teenagers, right?"

"Sure," I said. We'd find out soon enough.

"Are you going to use the Game Boy?"

"For what?"

"To lure her away. To, you know, bait her or whatever." The Man in the Hat waved his hand around in a gesture foreign to me.

What an idea. I was supposed to use a video game to win the confidence of the most beautiful woman I'd seen in my whole life. I'd never read that approach in any men's magazine—then again no reputable magazine would tell you how to pick up immortal women regressing to a teenage mentality.

"I think teenagers are a bit old for these things. They might still play them, but I don't think they see them as especially cool. Maybe if she were younger..." I said, considering.

"She might be. Take it just in case," declared the Man in the Hat as he came within inches of pulverizing a Subaru.

Within minutes we came upon Yoyogi Park and the Man in the Hat pulled over to the side of the busy street. He motioned me to get out of the car.

"Well," he said solemnly, "good luck. I must go now before she senses me. Others will be watching, so don't feel you are alone. Just relax, act natural. Remember, she is the one who chose you. In the very core of her being, she wants to come. You do your part and everything will be super-perfect."

He gave me a big smile that took up his whole cueball face, showed me the thumbs-up sign and winked at me, and then smiled some more just in case I didn't get it. Then he was off.

·   ·   ·

As usual, Takeshitadori was crawling with teenagers of every denomination sporting every hairdo under the sun and a few even the sun would have laughed at. It was funny to think that they'd all grow up to look basically the same. Most of them would lose the flamboyant hair, the leather jackets, or the high-priced sweatsuits and gold chains. The nose rings would go, the platform boots would disappear, the bare midriffs would be covered with corporate casual blouses. In a few years, most of them would be indistinguishable as they crowded onto commuter trains to their jobs in faceless multi-nationals or government bureaucracies.

If you told them, none of them would believe it. "Fast Life Forever" as one motorcycle jacket slogan put it. Most of them still secretly thought they would become rock stars, famous athletes, glamorous actors, or brilliant movie directors. Maybe a few figured even they'd become well-respected journalists. Even the more down-to-earth kids, the ones who had modest goals of becoming software designers, or just wanted to work in Dad's accounting firm, still har-bored painful illusions about the life ahead of them. To them, life was an ascension. Adulthood, if it came at all, would come in one swift moment like an epiphany—or a coronation.

You couldn't tell them that adulthood was really like a slow kick in the balls. They'd never believe that in just a few years things which seemed so important to them would appear as trivial as the price of walnuts in Austria. Or that their dizzying inner life, one epic emotional melodrama after another, would lose its luster and share priority with things like getting raises, finding a place in the suburbs, or switch-ing insurance plans. That, in a larger sense, growing up is about loss. They'd lose their friends, their health, their free-dom, their dreams. Some would even lose that most visible, radiant plumage of youth—their glorious hair. Loss would happen slowly, inexorably, to even the coolest of them.

There would be gains, of course. But the scales would always tip the other way. All those clichés adults invented, like *c'est la vie,* shit happens, or *que será será* would one day become pillars of deep philosophical truth. Then they'd find themselves saying things like "youth is wasted on the young" and shaking their heads as they dealt with the next generation of adolescents. And so on.

But until then, the maddening carnival of their adolescence would go on. And why shouldn't it? Only bitter ogres or guidance counselors would want to bring their dreams to a premature end. Life would take care of that soon enough.

Of course, I beat up a bunch of teenagers only days ago, so maybe I wasn't the champion of youth I imagined myself to be. And if I had to do it again to get Orange Blossom, I wouldn't hesitate.

I thought that even from a distance the curvaceous Orange Blossom would stand out like a steak in a salad bar, but as I surveyed the hordes of teens I began to doubt it. A number of the women, or girls, were well on their way to physical maturity. In their sculpted PORN STAR T-shirts and micro-skirts, they left just enough to the imagination to drive their male counterparts to into nympholeptic stupors. It was easy to see why many of the boys looked so vacant as they sat smoking or playing with their hair. The girls gave them so much to think about that any but the most rudimentary physical movements would overload their mental capacity. Catatonia was their only defense.

I walked around the area for a while, wading through the angst and trying to look inconspicuous. I probably looked like a narc or an off-duty truant officer. And from the curious looks some of the girls gave me while I marveled over the miracles of a modern diet, probably a pervert, too.

I spotted a girl with purple hair leafing disinterestedly through the latest issue of *Youth in Asia* while the girl next to her did her nails and chatted on a cell phone about the freshest gossip or the insane demands of her uncool parents. I wondered if the purple-headed girl had perused my article about a cult of modern-day cat burglars in Okinawa accused of stealing the world's third-largest collection of erotic origami foldings from the home of the seventies teen idol Kizan Matsumata. It was an interesting story, but seeing this girl, I suddenly wondered what the hell she would make of it. What relevance could a story like that have for a girl like her? I don't know. I was doing something right, I guess—I had bags of fan mail that said so. Somehow, though, it just didn't seem real to me. I was struck with that queer feeling I always get when I see someone reading the magazine. It's just never the way I picture it.

Next thing I knew, Orange Blossom strolled right in front of me. So close I could have touched her.

After all I'd been through, she should have shown like a beacon. She should have been surrounded by a brilliant aura of sunlight, iridescent and majestic. She should have glowed. I should have been blown away. My heart should have beat like the bass drum of a thrash metal band, my eyes popped like bottle rockets, and my jaw dropped like a broken elevator. I should have swooned. I should've fainted, got a concussion, had an aneurysm. By all rights, I should've had a seizure and hit the ground hard enough to break it.

As it happened, she just walked by sipping on diet Coke and looking characteristically bewitching but wholly terrestrial. She had donned the teenage rebel costume to perfection, right down to a navel ring. Her makeup was applied as if by a bricklayer, though she retained her customary smear at the corner of her mouth. She wore a simple black baby T remarkable only for its elasticity, and a purple vinyl mini-skirt shorter than haiku. Seeing her was like spotting some gorgeous girl I went to high school with but never really knew and didn't care about one way or the other. Well, there she is. Still looking good. Whaddaya know.

Looking back, I may have been in shock. My defense was not unlike the catatonia male teens use to counter the untouchable beauty of the nymphs that innocently persecute them. It's a possibility, anyway.

I followed Orange Blossom from a short distance as she glided through the crowd. My head was clear and my heart unburdened. Desire and adventure and this whole silly mess didn't seem to matter much anymore. She was within reach, and the bald truth was that soon we would be together. There was nothing that could stop it.

We were nearing the edge of the park when she suddenly stopped walking. She stood absolutely still for a moment, as if listening for something. Then she began jerking her head like a nervous bird, looking around in panic.

I didn't want to be seen, so I leapt sideways, hoping it wasn't too late.

I was so busy watching her I hadn't noticed the row of motorcycles.

The big chrome beast wavered for a moment, deciding whether or not to fall. I shot out a hand to steady it, but it was too late. The motorcycle toppled over sideways. And so did the next one. And the next one. I don't know how many there were—ten, maybe thirteen. It didn't matter. Even one would have been too many.

After they'd all fallen, there was a moment of silence. I tried to enjoy it.

"Goddamn," a voice behind me said. "You're like a walking B-movie gag, you know that?"

I turned around and saw the Jester shaking his head and showing me his best snarl. His lips were still a little swollen from the shot I'd given him the other day, enhancing his thuggish pose. The rest of the bunch was behind him, all doing variations on tough. Aki and his *Velvet Fuck* were gone, but they had a ringer to replace him—a rangy kid who looked like Sid Vicious after a few years' worth of barbells and protein shakes. Jester punched Enforcer in the arm, and pointed at me. Enforcer spit out a mouthful of cola. His girl moved away from him, eyeing me curiously. I stole a quick glance over my shoulder. No Orange Blossom in sight.

"You gotta find a new park, round-eye," Jester hissed. He had a point.

"Looks like your mouth is healing pretty well, snaggletooth. I'd hate to give you a relapse."

"It ain't gonna be so easy this time."

"I see you've got yourself some new talent."

"That's right," he spat. The big kid swaggered over and stood next to Jester. "This guy ain't a pussy like Aki."

Ringer sneered at me, showing me choppers the size of mah-jongg tiles. He might be tough one day, but right now he was just a big kid. Under the muscles and the attitude he was scared shitless. He had about as much chance of coming out intact as a piñata on Cinco de Mayo.

"You ever thought about becoming a cartoon character?" I asked the kid. "I think you'd make a good one."

"Fuck you."

"That's good. Now can you say it in a high, funny voice?"

He couldn't think of anything to say, so he flexed his muscles.

"I'll break him in half," I said casually to Jester. "And he knows it."

Jester glanced over at Ringer and sensed the same thing I did. For a dumb kid, he wasn't that dumb. He didn't know what to do and was trying like hell not to show it. I was winning, but he wasn't going to back down in front of his friends.

"I'll kill you," Ringer said, his voice cracking. No one paid him any attention.

"I don't think you'll be breaking anyone in half," Jester said to me. "Not with a cop right over there."

I looked off toward where he pointed. Sure enough, there was a cop. Standing there in his blue uniform, thinking cop thoughts.

"So what?" I said.

"Hey, it's cool. I hate cops. Never done me any favors. That's why I didn't talk when they came around asking about you the other day."

"That right?"

"That's right. Pigs said you were a fugitive from the law. Oinkin' you might be involved in some heavy shit. Said if I had any contact with you, I'd better report it or I could be considered an accomplice after the fact. Real exciting stuff."

"What did you tell them?"

"I didn't say a word. I couldn't open my mouth because if I did, 'go fuck yourself' might come flying out."

"Thanks."

"You got nothing to thank me for. I just hate cops."

"They're not all bad," I said. I couldn't help it. It was the adult in me coming out at the wrong time. Jester just raised an eyebrow, the way some people do if you tell them you like country music.

"So what the fuck is going on?" he said.

"Long story."

He just crossed his arms and nodded thoughtfully. I measured the air for tension, and couldn't decide if it was there or not.

"Sorry about the bikes," I said. "Anyway, thanks for being a sport. I gotta be going now."

"Not so fast. I want you to take another look at that cop."

I did.

"You see the girl standing next to him? The one with the red-and-black hair?"

I did.

"That's Karimi. Enforcer's girl."

Enforcer grinned proudly. I would have, too.

"So?"

"If I raise my right hand in the air, she takes two steps to her left, taps the cop on the shoulder. Tells him there is a fugitive in his midst named Billy Chaka."

"Now, why go and do that?" I asked. "I thought you hated cops."

"I don't exactly like you, either."

I glanced at the cop again. I would have a pretty good jump on him in a footrace. Problem was, the *bososuku* would be chasing me, too. And the cop might call in backup, with dogs and helicopters and the whole big mess. I'd have to flee the area, something I didn't want to do when I was finally so close to Orange Blossom.

There was a larger issue, too. Fact was, if word got out about Billy Chaka being chased through Harajuku by a gang of teens, my street cred would be shot. The popularity of my column might suffer. The magazine's circulation might even drop off. Orange Blossom was serious business, but my journalistic reputation was my life.

"What do you want from me, kid?" I sighed.

The whole bunch smiled all at once, like somebody was taking a picture of their gang for the yearbook. Jester looked especially gracious, glad to finally have an adult at his mercy.

"I think you're gonna like this," he said.

From the way he said it, I knew I wouldn't.

Everyone hopped on their machines and we made our way out of the park. I had to sit behind Enforcer on his bike and he wasn't real happy about it. Ringer the muscle baby didn't even have a bike, as it turned out. He had to squeeze into a tiny sidecar attached to another dude's machine. If it bothered him, he didn't show it.

I saw the cop giving us a sidelong glance as everyone made a ritual of revving their engines before we took off. The roar was deafening. None of these kids would be able to hear fifteen years from now. I don't know if the cop noticed the older *gaijin* or not, but apparently it didn't matter. He just turned around and stared off over the crowd, oblivious.

We drove off in formation down Ometesando, going slowly enough to annoy traffic without causing any major jams. I got a kick out of watching the nervous drivers roll up their windows and stare rigidly ahead. Some of the upscale shoppers on the sidewalks unconsciously tightened their grips on Luis Vitton handbags. Others covered their ears. I didn't blame them. Every time we stopped, the bikers had to gun their engines gratuitously and one of the guys had an annoying horn that blasted "Dixie." He sounded it about every thirty seconds, for no other reason than it was obnoxious.

After a few minutes of this, we turned down an alley just before a big intersection. Everyone revved it up real loud and then cut their engines dead simultaneously. We glided silently down the alley, teenage ghost riders of the street. I saw a cat in a windowsill eyeing us curiously and then scampering away in fear as we passed. The sense of power was tangible. You could hear it in the motor's roar, smell it in the gasoline, and feel it in the beast rumbling beneath you. Try telling these kids that getting into a good school is more important than this and they'll look at you like you just said John Tesh rocks.

No one said a word as we slowed to a halt. Jester got off his cycle before anyone else. Enforcer and I dismounted next, and then everyone else followed suit in order. It was nice to see that even motorcycle gangs observed Japan's tradition of strict hierarchies. When everyone was off their cycles, Jester laid down the law.

"Attention, fellow hammerheads," he said, as if addressing a formal assembly. "We have a fuckin' awesome event in store for you this fine afternoon, a true mindfuck spectacular. I—Yaz, king badass monkey of the motorcycle—shall be racing this man, the menacing asshole known as Billy Chaka, in a no-holds-barred contest of skill and courage!"

A cheer and some laughs went around. He crossed his arms over his chest, nodding smugly and rocking on his heels before continuing.

"We shall make one lap around the perimeter of the neighborhood. I shall be riding my own machine, the legendary *DreamShredder,* a motorcycle know halfway round Tokyo for its power, ferocity, and crazy horn!" He gave it a squeeze and "Dixie" burst forth to everyone's delight. So it was him.

"Mr. Chaka has no motorcycle, so he shall be allowed to use whichever of your machines he chooses. If anyone has a problem with that, they can take it up with Sven." The muscle kid flexed and flashed his big teeth. How he got a name like Sven I'll never know.

"Very well. Mr. Chaka, if you please..."

I knew I was going to take Enforcer's bike. As he was second in command, chances were it was the best outside of the *DreamShredder.* But just to enhance Jester's street theater scene, I pretended to look them over one by one. Each guy had his bike customized and airbrushed and kept in immaculate shape. One was called *Bitchstomp,* another *Bunny Killaz.* Most featured the usual iconography of skulls, flames, and flaming skulls. A few had cartoonish renderings of some of nature's more sinister creatures—scorpions, snakes, vultures, sharks, vicious-looking weasels. They should put these things in museums, I thought. Time capsules of urban youth transportation in the late-twentieth century. More likely they'd end up in chop shops in the Ohana-jaya suburbs, where motorcycle theft was considered a legitimate industry.

"Let's go, old man. I'm not getting any younger," Jester said, interrupting my reverie.

"I'll take this one," I said, pointing to the Enforcer's bike. Enforcer seemed a little dismayed I had chosen his machine, but he wasn't going to say anything. I got the feeling he had lost some of his power since Sven had joined the bunch. Someday Enforcer would get sick of being the number-two tough man and not being treated with enough respect. There would be a power struggle. He would lose and have to find another tribe to run with. He'd rise to the number-two man again, but never get any further. It was his destiny.

"Very well. Mr. Chaka has chosen Enforcer's machine, a beautiful piece of work you all know as the *Devirginator.* Excellent choice. Now let me explain the rules. *There are no rules!*"

The declaration was met with a hearty cheer. They were having one hell of a Sunday. School-sanctioned events just couldn't compete.

"The vanquished shall feel the wrath of the victor. Should I defeat Chaka, he is to be subjected to the sight of my bare, pimply ass!"

Everyone laughed. Everyone except Jester's girlfriend. She just rolled her eyes. Eventually, she'd get tired of his constant clowning and leave him. He'd get upset about it for a few days, then move on. That's how it worked.

"In the unlikely event that Chaka somehow wins, he shall punish me in the manner of his choosing. Mr. Chaka?"

All kinds of fun possibilities raced through my head. I could make the kid take flower-arranging classes. Have him write me a book report on the Baikan Takizawa's hefty *Nanso Satomi Hakkenden*. Make him see some Kabuki. In the end, I opted for personal gain rather than forced cultural enrichment.

"I want that stupid horn," I said.

"This one?" It gave him an excuse to play "Dixie" again. Not that he needed one.

"That one."

"Very well," he announced. "We'll be racing around Ino-kashira-dori and returning to this spot. Everyone is to take up positions on the course, in order to watch for pigs and to throw things at Chaka. When everyone is in position, Kato is to call my cell phone, which will be held by our starter, the lovely and talented Bazooka Sujata!"

Bazooka Sujata crouched against the wall, looking lovely, talented, and bored. She had gorgeous orange dreadlocks and a face like a pincushion. Rings and studs dangled from her ears, her nose, her lip, and her eyebrow. She looked disinterested in the whole charade, like she wanted to be off getting pierced somewhere. She'd never really understand these stupid male rituals. Men would never quite figure her out, either. Her life would be plagued with uncertainty.

"When the phone rings, the race begins. Enforcer and Sven will wait here, at the finish. Should Mr. Chaka win, he is to get off his motorcycle, receive his prize, and leave immediately. I beseech you to offer him no resistance. I am an honorable man and this is an honorable contest."

Enforcer and Sven nodded in grudging compliance.

"If he loses, I will show him Tokyo's ugliest ass. If, however, he tries to leave the course prematurely...we chase him down, beat him up, and turn him over to the cops. Any objections?"

"I'd like a helmet," I said.

Jester laughed and someone tossed me a helmet. I caught it just as it was about to smash my nose. It was metallic black with a black Metallica sticker on the back.

"You, too," I said.

"What?"

"You gotta wear a helmet, too."

"I don't need no brainbucket, Baka-guy." He smirked.

"You're wearing one today or the race is off," I said. It might get rough and I didn't want anything on my conscience.

He smiled to his followers in disbelief, holding his arms outstretched in a gesture of puzzlement that he followed with a shrug. Then a short, busty girl in a T-shirt that said FUNK tossed him a beat-up, cherry-red, sparkling seventies number. It must have been cool because it was so uncool. Not much protection, but better than nothing.

"Okay," he said. "Any last words?"

I shook my head.

"Take your positions!" Jester barked.

Suddenly the air was filled with blue exhaust and a sound like a hornet's nest through a stack of Marshalls cranked to eleven. They motored down the alley and turned out of sight. I could still hear them as they drove off in the distance.

Enforcer tossed me the keys to his motorcycle with a cautionary sneer and then went to sit on top of a Dumpster next to Sven. I strolled over to the machine and saddled up.

Jester looked at me with a nervous smile, some of his bravado gone with his companions. The world had shrunk to just the two of us.

After a few minutes, Jester waved Bazooka Sujata over. He gave her a smile she didn't return and handed her his cell phone. Then he suddenly kick-started his engine with enough sound to tear a hole in the universe. I took it as my cue to do the same. I gave it some gas and let it roar like an angry lion on steroids.

Bazooka stood between us now, about six feet in front. She held the cell phone aloft and kept one hand on her hip, a classic pose from a fifties juvenile-delinquent movie.

"Good luck, loser," Jester said over the sound of the engines.

"Be careful," I said with perhaps too much sincerity. It was like telling a barracuda not to swim in the deep end. Jester raised his eyebrows and then pulled his flight goggles down over his face. I slipped on some borrowed Ray·Bans made for a smaller head.

Then we both fixated on the phone held aloft like an Olympic torch in Bazooka's hand. It was everything I could do to keep my eyes off her orange dreadlocks and piercings.

Jester suddenly rocketed off in a haze of milky blue exhaust. Somewhere underneath that, I could barely make out the buzz of the cell phone. It was like a mosquito in a hurricane.

The race was on, and I was behind.

I let the clutch out and the bike bolted under me. The front wheel rose into the air like the nose of a jet taking off, and it took some strength to wrestle it down. As I turned blindly from the alley onto Ometesando, I was almost broadsided by a taxicab. The driver gave me the bird and expressed his anger six different ways as I jettisoned off in front of him with no time for apologies.

I could see Jester ahead of me in the distance as he weaved around a green Honda and accelerated with a loud whine. Despite his holeshot start, he was only about thirty-five yards in front of me.

The first intersection was a six-way hub that was hairy enough in everyday driving. Lots of ways to get hit if you weren't careful and a few even if you were. He swerved to the left and bolted past the car at the head of the intersection, ignoring my advice to be careful. I followed suit, passing the bewildered motorist before he'd reached the crossroads. In the corner of my eye I could see blurred pedestrians on the sidewalk. The crosswalks would be thick with people if we missed a green.

I followed Jester's line through traffic and more than once had to swerve suddenly as he cut someone off and forced them to jam on the brakes in front of me. I don't know if he was just being an ass or if it was part of his strategy, but unless I made a move, he was going to continue doing it. It was time to quit sandbagging.

I spotted my opening and accelerated through the turn, nearly causing a collision when one of the drivers panicked and slammed on his brakes. Horns blared on all sides. Just another day of Sunday driving.

Jester took a quick look over his shoulder to see if he'd lost me. He hadn't. I decided to make my move.

I pulled a double-dip shoulder swerve move called the Lurching Pig. I learned it covering the Malaysian Solar-Powered Motocross trials back in '82, when solar was big. The corkscrew torque rocketed me through the confluence of bewildered motorists, and I pulled up right next to Jester.

Less than a foot separated us.

I reached across the gap and gave his little horn a squeeze. As it sounded, he looked at me in utter shock. I waved at him, then tore away, veering right and opening the throttle.

My move was met with the squeal of tires and several horns rising in an ugly symphony of alarm. I glanced at the rearview mirror. Jester was struggling to keep the *DreamShredder* vertical as it bounced uncertainly down the pavement. It slowed almost to a halt, but he managed not to completely lose it. Still, I was glad I insisted he wear a helmet.

I knew Jester was too shaken to make the kind of ballsy move it would take to catch me now. It was in the bag as long as I didn't do anything stupid. I spotted a couple of the *boso-suku* on their bikes at the next intersection, and popped a wheelie for them. Maybe that qualified as stupid, but no daredevil race is complete without a little showboating.

As I went into autopilot, I found my mind drifting back to Sato Migusho's only true action picture, a piece called *Hit or Miss* (it missed, by the way). It was about a minor-league, over-the-hill pitcher who gets in trouble with yakuza because he refuses to throw the final game of his career. The climactic chase had him racing on a motorcycle while the yakuza pursued him, swinging baseball bats out the window of their car. I think the bat part was supposed to be symbolic or maybe ironic. At any rate, now I could tell that Sato had never been in a motorcycle chase himself, because it wasn't at all like his movie. It was much cooler.

The finish line was just past the next intersection. I rounded the last corner cautiously, keeping the bike as upright as I could and slowing more than necessary, taking my time.

It was lucky I did, because just then a car came careening around the corner. As its tires squealed in protest, I had to swerve hard to avoid a collision. If I had been going even a few miles an hour faster, concentrating just a fraction less, I would have been sailing through the air, sans motorcycle, awaiting a painful reunion with terra firma. I'd learned the hard way during the annual rickshaw relay in Hong Kong that the race is never over until it's over, and I was glad the lesson was paying off now.

I screamed some obscenities at the car as it sped off in the other direction. That's when I noticed that it was a Lincoln Continental and started to get a queasy feeling in my stomach. When I got a glimpse of the rearview mirror, the feeling got queasier.

I knew the Yamagamas would be heading east. This wasn't their turf, so I doubted they would be stopping around here for *pachinko*. They didn't have much of a head start on me, but if I didn't make some lucky guesses they'd be gone for good.

I shouldn't have let her go in the park, but it was too late now. In a way, I was proud of myself for taking up Jester's challenge. Whatever happened with Orange Blossom, I knew I wouldn't have been able to face myself if I had backed down in front of my audience.

Maybe the choice I'd made proved my geisha problem wasn't so bad after all. When push came to shove, professionalism had won out. But the visceral panic I felt told me I was kidding myself. There was no way the last image I had of her would be the back of her head in a Lincoln Continental.

Both Shuto Expressway 3 and Shuto Expressway 4 headed east. Even though only about three kilometers separated the two routes, I'd never find them if I went the wrong way, and it was probable I wouldn't see them even if I did. Paranoid yakuza with a kidnapped woman in the car weren't going to take the simple route. Yakuza are wary of being tailed even at the best of times, and with a bounty like this, there was no way they were going to lead me or anybody else to their hideout. More likely, they'd meander around back roads for the next three or four hours.

I doubted they would take her to Yamagama-gumi headquarters. They wouldn't risk her presence there in case there was some kind of perfunctory raid by the police or trouble with a rival gang. They'd take her to some nameless safe house, or lock her up in some sleazy love hotel where no one would ever find her.

I couldn't understand how they had grabbed her. The park wasn't the kind of place gangsters from across town would just be hanging out in on a Sunday afternoon. Perhaps I had led them right to her. But how? They'd have had to been tailing me for a very long time, since even before I was at the police station.

There was a much simpler explanation. Somebody had tipped them off.

Maybe that weird organization with the Chief and the Man in the Hat had been working with the yakuza all along. They were both after the girl and maybe they'd worked something out. Maybe they were trading golf memberships.

Despite the Man in the Hat's mumbo jumbo about being the chosen one, I never understood why they needed me. And I never understood why the yakuza wanted Orange Blossom at all, much less bad enough for me to meet with *oyabun* Kwaidan. Maybe I was just a fall guy, a patsy to distract the police while the others went about their sinister, mysterious business. What could I do, a *gaijin* with no connections and nowhere to hide? Maybe the police bust had even been part of their plan. The whole damn thing had been a setup, right down to the motorcycle race. Just wind him up, watch him go. Get the girl and leave him cold.

I shook my head, but I couldn't shake her out of it. Her lips her hair her face the way she stood the kiss that night in the hotel. The anger and frustration of having her so close only to suddenly disappear yet again were making me crazy, causing me to imagine massive conspiracies and forge connections that just weren't there. Maybe it was easier to imagine I'd had no chance than to think I'd just screwed up. Twice. Fact was, I could have had her. Instead I had to prove to some teenage kid that I could ride a motorcycle.

Now I had to choose either Expressway 3 or Expressway 4 and hope against hope that some highway miracle would let us cross paths again. I was stopped at a red light still trying to make up my mind—3 . . . 4 . . . 3 . . . 4—when the goddamn Tsuguri Society barkers in their big white sound truck pulled up next to me.

"Young ladies today know more about rock and roll than they do about *ikebana* and no one seems to think there is anything wrong with that!" the guy shouted, practically right in my ear. I tried to shut him out, my mind desperately squirming for some resolution.

"Young men are more interested in computer gadgetry than purifying their minds and perfecting their bodies. They are not warriors. They have been spiritually emasculated by microchips, cheeseburgers, and boxer shorts!"

I revved the engine to drown out this idiocy and glared at the guy inside. He looked over at me and I could see his lips moving frantically but couldn't hear what he was saying. The way it should be. But I couldn't gun the engine forever. Three or four, what difference did it make? She was gone.

". . . in Kyobashi. Near the intersection of Yaesu and Sotobori . . ."

She was gone and maybe the best thing I could do was drive this motorcycle straight to the American consulate and try to figure a way out this mess, out of this country, before I ended up in jail or with my head lopped off. There would be other geisha. Maybe not like this one, but I wouldn't have to go through this crap again. I could just get on the phone and arrange a party and the rest would take care of itself. I thought about the girl back in Kyoto, Rei, the one who remembered me.

Maybe it was time to give up geisha altogether. Live a life less complicated.

"...that's where you can find Orange Blossom."

I cut the engine. I looked up at the sound truck. The guy was looking right at me.

"Go to Yaesu and Sotobori-dori and wait. She will be there."

I looked around at the other cars. None of the drivers seemed to notice anything. Had I finally lost it altogether, right here in the middle of the street?

"Kids learn more about General MacArthur than they do about Ieyasu Tokugawa. You are the chosen one. Glorious Shintoism must now battle with the empty glamour of television for the soul of our people. Hurry, there is no time to waste," the truck boomed as the light changed and it made a left turn. The sound receded as that old man's grinning, *fukusuke* face went off into the distance.

The Chief's face, that is. The revelation was long in coming but there was no mistaking it. The old man in the subterranean room had looked familiar because his giant face had been plaguing me the entire trip. The guy painted on the truck and the Chief were one and the same.

The car behind me started honking. Soon, more horns joined in the protest. If I had been able to claim my prize, I would've honked along with them, adding "Dixie" to the noise. I had as much to protest about as anybody.

The day was winding down, so eastbound traffic into the city was light by Tokyo standards. Still, it took quite a while to drive all the way to Yaesu. Even though I had plenty to think about, my mind was a blank during the ride. Twice, I nearly rear-ended cars in front of me. I was coming down from the adrenaline high of the race and the sedative power of the Love Burger grease was kicking in.

When I got to Yaesu I parked the bike in a garage under one of the big department stores. The attendant warned me that the shops were only going to be opened for another half an hour. I smiled at him and took my parking slip.

Then I took a quick look around on the off chance that the yaks had parked their car here, too. They hadn't. No big surprise.

I took off the dark glasses that had been pinching my head and nose, but then thought better of it. Being on the lookout for cops was an old skill I'd have to reacquire fast. Seconds later, I walked right past one on Sotobori-dori. He was a young guy, probably right out of the academy. He smiled at me and I smiled back just like an ordinary tourist.

I didn't see the Continental anywhere. The Tsuguri barker said I'd find her near the intersection, which wasn't specific enough to do me much good. He also said to wait, so I figured maybe I'd try that.

There was a café across the street with a nice big window overlooking the intersection. I could definitely use the coffee. The problem was that I didn't have any money. I'd have to pull some kind of trick, just like old times. Any writer worth his salt has more than a few ways to con the odd coffee or beer, and I knew them all.

I'd learned all about loitering, too. If it was the kind of place run by a sympathetic girl working her way through dance school or art classes, then I had nothing to worry about.

I walked into the tiny shop, and sure enough, a budding young cappuccino bohemian was working the counter. She looked like a sucker for a good Picasso joke. The place was pretty deserted, which also worked in my favor since people are more likely to let you be if there's no business to be hurt by your presence. My only competition was a guy sitting by the window reading the paper. Unfortunately, the only other seat with a window view was right across from him. I strolled over and started to pull the chair out from the table.

"Mind if I have a seat?" I said. The man didn't look up from his paper.

"I'd rather you didn't."

"I won't be a bother," I assured him. "I'm the quiet type."

"There's plenty of other seats in here," he said gruffly.

The barista made her way toward me, but stopped suddenly, sensing trouble. I knew I was causing a minor scene, but I had no choice. It wasn't going to get me in her good graces, though. Especially when she learned I didn't plan on ordering anything.

"I apologize, sir. I mean no disrespect, but I simply must sit by the window."

"Sucks to be you," the guy said, ruffling his paper without putting it down. "I was here first and I'm not moving."

The waitress retreated into the back room, no doubt pretending to count coffee beans until it was settled. It gave me the opening I needed.

"Maybe you oughta take a look at this before you keep talking," I said. I didn't plan on showing him anything but my fist. As soon as he lowered the paper, I'd pop him right on the button. When the waitress came back, I'd just tell her the guy decided to grab forty winks.

He folded the paper over with a protesting groan and I readied to let one fly.

Then I got a look at his face.

He got a look at mine, too. We stood there gaping for a moment in mutual surprise. Then he started laughing.

"Well, why didn't you tell me it was you? Have a seat."

It was Ihara, the private dick from SpyLens.

"Last time you invited me to have a seat I got my nose bent outta shape," I said coolly. I sat down just the same.

"You caught me off guard. My client is very secretive and I have to protect their right to privacy. But I've been told we're on the same side now," he said.

"So you're working for them, huh?" As soon as I said it, I wasn't sure if we were talking about the Yamagama-gumi or the nameless religious cult.

"Guys pay well. Hell, I think they're crazy, to be honest. Doesn't surprise me you're mixed up with them." This gave him quite a chuckle.

"Where are your goons? Hiding in the bathroom?"

"You've got to quit being so sentimental. Exist in the present." He took off his Coke-bottle glasses and began wiping them down. I still hadn't ruled out popping him one.

"So where are they?" I asked.

"Don't worry, Billy. My associates are not with me today."

"I mean the people you're watching."

"Office building across the street. Third floor. Lawyer named Nikka, like the whiskey. Favors clients who like trouble and can afford to get out of it, if you know what I mean. They've been there for over two hours."

"That's impossible," I said. "I was just with her. She couldn't have been here that long."

"The girl? She got here fifteen minutes before you did. She's a real knockout, all right. Looks like trouble."

"And how," I grumbled. Then something occurred to me. "Are you telling me she isn't the one you're following?"

"Never seen her in my life until just now. If I had, I'd remember." Ihara looked distractedly out the window.

"Who the hell are you tailing, then?" I asked. He didn't answer right away, so I started to say something, but he held a hand up to silence me. Then an odd expression came over his face. He moved his head like a snake sensing something warm.

"That guy," he said.

Brando Nabiko strolled down the street with a hangdog expression, one hand in his pocket and another clutching a patent leather briefcase. He was dressed in a nice suit and wore sunglasses in a different tax bracket from the ones I had on. He looked worlds away from the harried workaholic on the crowded film set.

Ihara waited until he'd passed and then rose to leave. Just then, I saw Orange Blossom being escorted out with two yakuza at her side, good ol' Punchperm and Crewcut. It was like a regular reunion right there on the sidewalk. Ihara threw some coins on the table.

"See ya later..." he said. He started to put on his coat. It was a stupid looking private-dick trench coat. Anyone who'd seen an old movie would instantly make him as a gumshoe.

I studied Orange Blossom for signs of damage. From far away she looked all right. They seemed to be treating her like gentlemen, or at least a gangster's version. I had to pull myself away from the window and do some fast thinking.

I might be able to take out Punchperm and Crewcut. Hell, I knew I could. I'd just walk right up behind them and they'd be on the sidewalk before they even thought about hitting back. There was that cop standing around, but I could give him the slip without much worry. But then what?

The Nabiko angle was bothering me. His presence made everything strange. Yaks and religious weirdos were the kind of people I expected to be involved with Orange Blossom. But Nabiko was a citizen. Maybe a little obsessive about movies, but not crazy enough to be in bed with this bunch. But there he was, walking down the street humming a tune.

I followed Ihara until he got to his car, which was parked at the curbside.

"I'm coming with you," I said.

"Scram. You'll blow my cover," he said, one eye on Nabiko going down the street.

"I'll blow your cover big time if you don't let me in the car this second."

The threat was enough. Ihara unlocked the door. I got in.

"No funny business, Chaka. I'm a professional man doing professional surveillance. It's my job, and I can't have you messing with my livelihood. I know we've had our differences in the past, but if there is something you want to settle with me, let's do it some other time. I know you are an honorable man—"

"He just got into that Datsun, Ihara."

"Sure, maybe you're a bit of a bum. It's expected in your profession. But I know you respect the fact that some people have to earn a living. Maybe they ain't as smart as you, so they have to do whatever they can to put rice on the table—"

"For chrissake, Ihara. He's leaving!"

"I'm not paid to bow politely and be everyone's friend. I don't get invited to go golfing on Sundays or to someone's wedding. I make people nervous. Maybe its because I've seen too much. I know what people are really like when the shoji screen closes. Maybe it shows on my face. Maybe it's my glasses. They're so damn thick. I've been meaning to get contacts, but—"

"Let's go! He's gonna get away."

"Don't worry about him, Chaka. And don't tell me my business. I just want to make sure we're in complete agreement here, that we understand each other."

"I understand you, Ihara," I said. I had no idea what he was talking about. All I knew was that I was taking a big chance not grabbing Orange Blossom when I could, and now it seemed like Nabiko was getting away, too.

"All right then." Ihara sighed wearily. "Very well."

He pulled gingerly into the street like he was driving a cargo of eggshells filled with nitroglycerin. I hoped he had a good idea where we were headed because Nabiko was nowhere to be seen.

Hours later we were inside a dark room on the third floor of a modest hotel in a modest west Tokyo neighborhood, staring intently across the street at a window supposedly belonging to Brando Nabiko. The curtains had been drawn shut ever since we'd arrived.

Ihara had set up shop in the hotel. He had all his photographic equipment and even his three goons. They sat huddled together in a back corner of the room, munching on Ponriki chips and whispering to one another. Every few minutes one of them would burst out laughing and Ihara would shoot them a look and they'd turn to the floor in shame and start whispering and eating Ponrikis again. He must have needed companionship pretty badly to put up with these clowns.

For a long time I sat in an uncomfortable chair next to Ihara, gazing across the street at that little square of light set in concrete. After a while I got bored and started fiddling with the Game Boy the monk had given me. I'd never played one before and it wasn't bad. There was this little guy who ran around, jumping over rocks and turtles and climbing trees and stuff like that. Every once in a while, a big rock would land on the guy's head, and he'd look up at me in cartoon pain and then fall to the ground. I know how it is, little man, I'd think to myself.

While I played I entertained second, third, and fourth thoughts about not grabbing Orange Blossom when I could. I tried to persuade myself I was doing the smart thing—if I figured out just what was going on, I could settle this affair once and for all. But it was a tough sell. Missing a chance at her went against my instincts. Maybe my instincts weren't anything special, though.

While we sat in the dreary hotel, Ihara gave me the rundown. He'd been observing Nabiko for some time, though he wouldn't say how long. The guy pretty much stuck to everyday activities. Rise at four A.M., commute to the studios at five, on the set from six A.M. until four P.M. Of course that was just a guess, because Ihara had no way of knowing exactly what went on behind studio gates. Nabiko usually stayed on the lot until around six or seven, and by then most of the other folks had gone home. Typically, Nabiko would grab a bite to eat after work at some cheap noodle shop, or occasionally go drinking with some studio guys at a small club in Roppongi—usually either Bitch's Brew or a more upscale place that catered to the film crowd called Parallax Pete's. Ihara had seen Yoko Torikata in Brando's company more than once, but I cut him off before he could share his sordid speculations.

That was the day-to-day stuff, and the only variations were on Sundays, when he'd twice seen Nabiko at Nikka the lawyer's office in Kyobashi. The first time they stayed for about an hour, and then there was today's meeting, which lasted over two hours. This, he reassured me, was the first time he'd seen Orange Blossom.

When I asked if Brando Nabiko had ever given him the slip, he admitted that he had, but only once. He said Brando had behaved strangely on that day, first going to the studio and then emerging wearing a trench coat, hat, and dark glasses. Even a fake mustache. He'd then hopped on a train. Ihara followed suit, but lost him at the massive Shinjuku station.

I chuckled.

"What's so funny?" Ihara said.

"Nothing," I replied. I was remembering how silly Brando looked in that Philip Marlowe/Fu Manchu getup when he gave me the atrocious script for *Tokyo Suckerpunch.* I never would've guessed then that he would be a player in this sinister plot.

That was about it as far as the day-to-day affairs of Brando Nabiko were concerned. "I think those guys are way off the mark having me tail this chump," Ihara said. They'd kept Ihara in the dark about Orange Blossom and I figured they had their reasons. I wasn't going to spill, but I was curious what justification they'd given for tailing Nabiko.

"Nothing," he said. "They never gave me a reason. Normally, I'd have told them to take a hike, but they offered me five times my regular fee. Their only condition was that I refuse to give out any information. Well, that's the standard practice anyway. So I did it. But I'm anxious to get off this one, to tell you the truth."

On the Game Boy, the little guy fell into a sewer pipe. It turned out well. There was a whole underground chamber filled with stars. I'm not sure what the stars did, but the game made a nice cheerful beep every time he ran over one.

"Don't like working for cults, huh?" I said.

"Hell, no," he replied, shaking his head violently. "Stay the hell away from religious groups, that's my policy. Especially those guys. There are certain people I will not work for."

"Ihara, the fact is you'd work for anyone if they paid you enough. You'd spy on your own parents. Take pictures. You can't help it. You like money. Most people do. Come to terms with it."

I looked up at him. He was glaring like he wanted to set the Ponriki chompers on me. But as disagreeable as I was being, he couldn't bring himself to contradict me. I went back to the game. The little guy scampered up the sewer drain, back into the LED sunshine. Ihara finally spoke.

"This job is different."

"How?"

"This guy I'm tailing. Nabiko. Something bugs me about him."

"What's so weird about a guy going to work and back every day?"

"On the surface, maybe nothing. But I've been doing this for a long time, and I get the feeling there's something strange going on. Everyone is being too damn careful. He knows I'm watching him. He can feel it."

"How can you tell?"

"For one thing, he's too regimented. Everyone is a creature of habit, but there is something forced about the humdrum of his existence. I can't put it into words. But I'll tell the most obvious sign, the one that really tipped me off."

"What's that?"

"He never picks his nose."

"Really?"

"He never picks his nose or scratches himself or does any of the things people do when they are alone. He did the first couple days, then he abruptly stopped. He's self-conscious now when he used to be at ease. I don't know what tipped him off, but that's always been the surest sign that somebody knows they are being watched. Once they stop picking their noses, I know I've been fingered."

I let the insinuation slide.

"Be careful," I told him. "If he knows you're following him, he might be trying to draw you into a trap."

"Really? How'd you come up with that?" Ihara shook his head. "I been in this business since before cable television, Mr. Chaka. I'll be damned if I'm going to let some cult bait me."

"Might not be the cult. Might be the yakuza."

"Fuck the yakuza."

The goons in the corner sneered and laughed thuggishly. They weren't unlike yakuza themselves, minus the street smarts. That didn't leave them with much. Wherever Ihara found these gorillas, they weren't going to be much protection if someone like Kwaidan decided Ihara had become a nuisance. They'd all end up little pieces in garbage bags. How Ihara could be paranoid enough to have security cameras installed in the office elevators yet complacent enough to think he was safe from yakuza was puzzling. Either he had a serious blind spot, or he'd worked out a protection plan with some gangsters. I decided I didn't want to know.

"Well, what next?" I said.

"We wait. We observe," he said, ripping into a bag of Gummi Bears. "Welcome to the glamorous, exciting world of private detection."

Ihara hadn't learned much watching Nabiko and I doubted I would either. I couldn't sit around all night waiting for something to happen, wondering about the fate of Orange Blossom. The time for finesse had long since passed. Maybe it was all right for Ihara to sit around. That was his job. But I was in this thing much deeper. I quit the Game Boy and put it in my pocket. The little guy wasn't making much progress, anyway.

I stood up and made my way toward the door.

"What are you doing?" Ihara said with his mouth full of candy.

"I'm going to pay our friend a visit," I said.

"Don't be a cowboy, Billy." Ihara's goons rose from the corner bed in unison and blocked my way to the door. The short one rubbed his nose and grinned. The other two cracked their knuckles like castanets. It was a regular talent show.

"Call off your dogs before I make them play dead," I said. "I'm going over there."

"I can't let you do that. You'll blow my cover," he said.

"This isn't about you, Ihara. This is about saving a woman's life."

Ihara sighed like I was a big pain in the ass. He wiped his glasses and pouted.

"Can't it wait until the morning?"

"It could, but I can't. I'm going now." I stepped toward the door and the short guy stepped up and bumped into me while the other two readied themselves for combat. That old dance never seemed to go out of style.

"Let him go," Ihara said. "He's going to blow our operation one way or another. You know, I should have turned you in, Chaka. It never hurts a guy like me to be in good with the cops."

"Yeah," I said. "You should have," and walked out.

I strolled across the street, aware that Ihara was watching me from above and cursing. Right before I rang the apartment buzzer, I turned around to face the hotel and nonchalantly dug my finger into my nose. That probably made Ihara curse even more.

Then I rang the buzzer for Apartment 312, home of one B. Nabiko. I was greeted with a blast of static from the intercom speaker and a voice that sounded miles away.

"It's Chaka," I said, trying to simulate the urgent desperation of a fugitive on the lam in a foreign country. It wasn't much of a stretch. "Billy Chaka."

There was a long pause and crackling static filled the peaceful night air. It was the moment upon which everything hinged, and maybe it wasn't much of a plan but it was the only one I had left. If he didn't let me in, I might as well go back to Cleveland and seek therapy. I was thinking about Sarah when Nabiko finally buzzed me up. She had a lot of forgiveness in her, but she'd never forgive me if I got myself killed over another woman. Everyone has their limits.

I took the stairs up to Nabiko's third-floor apartment. The stairwell was the stuff Ihara's paranoia was made of. It was narrower than Basho's road to the deep north, and not nearly as pretty. The dingy passage was lit by the few unbusted bulbs remaining and the cold iron handrail was covered with dust. As my footsteps echoed dully up the stairs, I noticed a whole generation of dead flies huddled on a windowsill housing a glass pane too small to even look out of. The mass insect grave filled me with an unaccountable sense of dread. It was still better than any elevator.

With a palpable sense of relief I reached the third floor and opened the door into the apartment hallway. It was like walking into another world. A nautical-blue carpet covered the floor and the walls were done up with tasteful frescoes of intersecting lines and multicolored whorls with the odd seahorse and starfish thrown in. Jacques Cousteau's idea of a child's bedroom.

Before I could knock, Nabiko yanked the door open and motioned me inside. As I stepped in, he poked his head into the hall as if to make sure I wasn't being followed and closed the door behind us.

"Are you all right?" he asked.

"Never better," I said, letting my voice tremble a little so he'd have his doubts. "I had nowhere else to turn."

"You were right to come here. Please." He motioned me into a tiny dining room, which consisted of a kitchen table and two chairs. "Let me get you something to drink." He walked all of eight feet into the kitchen to open the fridge.

The walls of the apartment were cluttered with movie memorabilia. There was a picture of Nabiko standing next to Yoko Torikata on a set. She was laughing and pulling up her shirt to expose one of her famous breasts for the camera. There was also a picture of Nabiko posing reverently next to a life-size model of Darth Vader at some tourist place. From the rapturous look on Nabiko's face, you'd think he was next to a holy relic.

"Here you go," he said, handing me a Scotch and water.

"Thanks," I said. I raised the glass to my lips and let my hand quiver just a little. I took a good slug and set the glass on the table. This was pretty much where the script ended.

"The police came by a few days ago looking for you," he said. "They wouldn't tell me what it was about. They wanted to know if I'd seen you in a while. "

"Yeah? What did you say?"

"I told them that you visited me at the studio a while back but that I hadn't heard from you since. They weren't real friendly," he said with a chuckle. I think it was meant to warm my spirits. I took another drink of the whiskey and water. It didn't warm me much, either.

"They think I cut off a guy's head," I said calmly.

"Your driver, right?" Nabiko replied with feigned confusion. It was a mistake. The police would never have said why they wanted me, much less that I was suspected of killing Shinto Hirohito.

"Yeah," I said. "Do you think I did it?"

"Of course not. Why would you!" Nabiko punctuated this with a nervous laugh. He glanced back over his shoulder toward the bedroom, which also served as a living room. From what I could see of it, there was all kinds of movie stuff lying around in there, too, including a movie projector facing a large blank wall. Beyond that was a window with the shades drawn. Ihara would be staring at it from across the street.

"How's the deal coming?" I said casually.

"What deal? I don't know what you're talking about." His eyes darted away when they shouldn't have.

"The movie. *Tokyo Suckerpunch.*"

"Oh." He chuckled. "Of course. It's moving along. It takes a while, you know. I think, though, that soon everything will be in place."

"By tomorrow, you think?" I downed the rest of my drink and stared at him.

"Tomorrow? Oh, well, perhaps. Actually, no. I doubt that soon. You know how it is. Would you like another drink?"

"If you need it."

Nabiko looked at me for a moment, then figured he'd misheard. He picked up my glass and now his hands were a little shaky. He got to the kitchen and poured two drinks this time, one for each of us. I watched him to make sure he didn't add any extra ingredients. He saw me watching and smiled weakly. Then he finished the drinks and brought them over.

"I guess you heard that Yoko Torikata won the woman's three-limb amputee sparring competition again this year," Nabiko said. "It was the best match of the tournament."

"So I hear," I said. Actually, it was news to me. The tournament was light-years in the past.

"Then you must have heard there was a confirmed sighting of Master Yado. They got pictures of him watching a match. Ran them through computers and everything. It's him, no doubt about it. He showed up the day of the finals and then disappeared before anybody cornered him. How do you like that?"

I didn't. It was a damn sorry piece of luck. Another time it would have crushed me to know I'd missed a chance to interview one of the greatest martial-arts figures to ever walk earth. And, to be honest, it still hurt a little even the now. I felt myself getting mad, but brushed it off. The past was the past, and at least no one had scooped me.

"You know," I said, "Sato Migusho and I had a bet that Yado would return to the tournament someday. If it was an even year, I won. If it was an odd year, he won."

"That right?" Nabiko said. His eyes did something funny at the mention of Sato's name.

"I guess he finally won after all," I said. Nabiko just nodded and glanced over his shoulder again toward the darkened back room and the window. I got a sick feeling in my stomach. I looked at the projector.

"What's the feature tonight?" I said. He looked at me blankly. "On the projector. What's showing?"

"Oh, that," he said. "It's just an old demo reel of mine. Stuff I shot a long time ago. Nothing terribly interesting."

"Don't be modest. I bet there's some very interesting footage on that reel."

"No," he said. "I hardly knew how to operate a camera then. I like to watch it every once in a while to remind myself how far I have come."

"Funny," I said. "Sato was your favorite director, yet you don't have a single Migusho poster among all this crap. Why is that?"

"Well..." he stammered. "I used to have all of them. Just got tired of looking at them for all these years. Thought I could use a change of scenery, you know."

"Especially lately, huh?"

"What do you mean?"

"Nothing. Let's have a look at that demo reel."

"No, it's terribly embarrassing, I hardly..."

I rose and walked toward the bedroom. He grabbed my arm. I looked at him coldly. His eyes flashed with animal panic. I shook him off and made my way toward the projector with long, angry strides. He hopped along behind me, wringing his hands, but he didn't try to stop me.

The 16mm projector was the one every kid in public elementary school had gotten a chance to run at one time or another. Back before video. I flicked the switch and the wall lit up with a square of white light. The projector whirred with that familiar noise and I watched Nabiko's dejected face as the leader counted down.

10...9...8...7...6...5...4...3...2...1

There was Orange Blossom walking hand in hand with Sato down a deserted street.

Cut.

Orange Blossom and Sato throwing snowballs at each other at the Winter Carnival in Sapporo, framed by a massive palace carved in ice.

Cut.

Orange Blossom making goofy faces at the camera and laughing as Sato looked on, smiling in his shades.

Cut.

Orange Blossom and Sato, taken from a distance, with those static lightning effects tearing through the upper corner of the frame, just like the picture I'd been given by the yaks.

Cut.

Orange Blossom and Sato, standing on some nameless street as the rain comes down—Sato in his brimmed hat, his left hand still concealing whatever it was he held in his jacket, Orange Blossom hiding under the lapels of her coat. It was red after all.

Cut.

Sato in a thick winter coat, his old body moving in a gross pantomime of a golf swing.

Cut.

Long shot of Orange Blossom. She walks up a snowy trail, into the trees. The camera loses her. There's only a forest.

Cut.

Long shot of Sato relaxing in a folding chair in the snow, smiling and looking off in the distance at who knows what. Suddenly he turns around awkwardly, the bulk of his winter clothing hampering his movement. He strains toward the camera for a moment. Then he turns back around slowly and settles back into the chair. Even from far away, he doesn't look quite as relaxed as before. The camera holds on him for a long time.

Fade-out.

The end.

The last of the film snaked its way through the projector and wound around the take-up reel. The tail flapped over and over as the reel spun around and around. Nabiko had his head half-buried in his hands. I flicked on the light.

"Not bad. Ending sucked, though," I said. "Who's the girl?"

"I don't remember. Some girlfriend of his. I shot that footage in Hokkaidō when I accompanied Sato on a location scouting trip, that's all. Just goofing around."

"Yeah," I said. "Funny you didn't mention that when I showed you the photograph. Then again, you didn't mention stalking, either. Anything else slip your mind?"

"Billy..."

"I bet you thought you were really clever, giving me that whole spiel at Toko. Atmospheric haze and all that other—"

"I can explain this. I can tell you how they got the film—"

"I don't care about that, Nabiko. I don't care that you've known who Orange Blossom was all along, or even that you had a meeting with her only this afternoon. I only want you to explain one thing."

He looked up at me, holding his breath.

"You told me Sato Migusho was your favorite filmmaker, your mentor, almost like a father to you. Isn't that right?"

Nabiko nodded.

"So why did you kill him?"

He looked up at me blankly, frozen in his
chair. For a moment, neither of us moved. The
only sound was the tail of the film whipping against
the projector and the hum of the lamp-cooling fan. Nabiko
rose slowly, his eyes searching mine. He stepped near me
and I felt my body tense. Then he reached out and shut off
the projector. The tail of the film rolled around the take-up
reel a few times then slowed to a stop.

Nabiko eased back into his chair by the nighttable. He let
out a long sigh, like he was ready to talk. Instead, he pulled
open the nightstand drawer. His hand shot into the drawer
and emerged with a Beretta 9mm semiautomatic. It looked
like he knew how to hold it.

He pointed it at me and smiled the first genuine smile I'd
seen from him all day. Then he stood up and motioned me
toward the kitchen. I walked the four steps and sat down in a
chair. He pulled out a chair opposite me, careful to place
some distance between us. He watched me, trying to gauge
my reaction. I was all out of reactions.

"There's a lot of things no one knows about Sato Migusho,"
he said earnestly. He mulled the fact over in his mind before
continuing. "I think it is safe to say there are things about him
that no one in the world knows. No one but me."

"Like how he really died."

Nabiko grinned the way people do at bad jokes. "Everyone knows how he died. Smoke inhalation. I'm talking about older things. The whole history of his character, his back story if you will," he said. He paused and sniffed a little.

His tone was one I hadn't expected. I was waiting for the arrogance of the villain elucidating his master crime while he holds the hero at gunpoint. But he wasn't smug, just sad. He was having trouble getting the words out.

"There is a way of thinking, an argument, that truly great people, in any field, but especially the arts, are beyond ordinary morality. In order to achieve greatness, they may do things that others find repugnant." He stuttered to a stop. He couldn't look me in the eye.

"The jury will never buy it," I said. "Juries hate artists."

"I'm not talking about me," he said angrily. "I'm talking about him. The person *he* was. He did things and people just dismissed them. 'Artistic temperament,' they'd say. Well, that's fine and good. Fine and good."

"Nabiko," I said quietly, "what the hell are you talking about?"

He started crying, trying to speak several times before the words finally poured out in a wet bubbling mess.

"What about me? *Artistic temperament.* A whole life of dodging responsibility. All along, refusing to help, denying me even at the very end. *You've got it all wrong.* Calling me crazy. Me! He knew. He knew. And what does he do? The script needs more work! This character is flat, that story is implausible. Acting like he's twenty. Running around with that bitch. When me...my whole life. I've worked hard. I *work* hard and I get denial. Rejection and denial. I'll confront him, I thought. Speak to him plainly, without formality. Things need to be said. He needs to realize. I'll mention my mother. But then *she's* there..."

He stopped talking and started sobbing. It came fast and hard, overtook him. The gun lay cradled in his lap as he rocked slowly back and forth. I easily could have made a play for the gun, but I didn't think it was necessary. Nabiko was too into his catharsis to be much of a threat. After a few moments, he regained some measure of control. He wiped his face with his sleeve and looked up at me through reddened eyes.

"So now you know," he resumed quietly. "Sato Migusho was my father."

Dawn was fast approaching, the deep blue sky glowing with hints of orange. I let him cry for a long time. He needed it. I'd get the details later, when he was in a more lucid state of mind. Nothing he'd said made much sense to me. All I got was that Sato was his father and wouldn't admit it. That and maybe Sato didn't so much like the script for *Tokyo Suckerpunch*. I don't know how much time passed, but I figured it was enough. I had to know one more thing.

"What about Orange Blossom?"

"Orange Blossom," he huffed. "You're just like him. Always interested in some stupid *megumi no ko*."

He let out a big sigh and rubbed his eyes.

"She was there," he said after a time. "At the Garden. Sato and I were talking. He sent her out of the room while we went over the script. He was giving me all kinds of crap. For some reason, I thought maybe he would feel different about all of this if I just said what we were both thinking. All these years had gone by, and he'd never once acknowledged our secret bond. I know he knows, I thought. He knows I know. Let's just say it. So I said it. And he laughed. My own fucking father, laughing at me, acting like it's a big joke. I just wanted to hit him. Just once, you know? After what he did, I had every right. So I hit him. Once. But then, I don't know. I just couldn't stop. I saw him laughing and I couldn't stop. I didn't stop until she came down the stairs."

He looked up at me now, seeking out understanding, maybe pity. The best I could offer was silence.

"That slut," he said. "Always in the way. But where was she when she really could have helped him? Why didn't she stop me? She saw what had happened and she took off before I could catch her."

"Then you torched the place?"

He didn't answer.

Anger seemed to bring him back to his senses. He grabbed the gun and leveled it at me, considering. Then he stood up out of his chair. He glanced at the Disney clock across the hall. Mickey's hands said it was six forty-five.

"I'd like to tell you all about it, Chaka. But I have a meeting at court in Roppongi. After this, it will all be over. I guess I should tie you up or something. Maybe just shoot you. What do you think?"

Nabiko was running on inertia. He'd obviously been sick and scared ever since he killed Sato. Probably long before that. He no more wanted to kill me than I wanted to kill him. But once you start down that path, things get out of control. What is one more death, after all? Be that as it may, I wasn't about to get killed by proxy.

"I wonder if I have any rope..." he muttered absentmindedly. When he glanced around, I sprang out of my chair and made my way into the tiny bedroom.

"Stop!" he said.

I kept going.

"I will fucking shoot you!" he yelled.

But he didn't shoot.

I threw open the curtains and the burning light of sunrise exploded into the room. Nabiko held one hand in front of his face while his other arm held the pistol extended in my direction.

"See that window across the street?" I pointed to Ihara's roost, the only window without the shades drawn. Nabiko squinted and gazed through the window. "Those are cops. Homicide. They're the ones who've been following you. I never escaped from jail. I have been working with them ever since Sato's death."

It confirmed his worst fears, even if it was a lie.

"Everything you've said has been recorded." I pulled out the Game Boy. "This device is actually a transmitter that has been broadcasting every word to the remote recording facility across the street."

He stared at the Game Boy in disbelief.

"Whether you kill me or not . . ." I shrugged. I was banking on his guilty paranoia, but I was also counting on the fact that he was not a hardened criminal. Nabiko's blood ran hot, and there may have been other factors I wasn't aware of, but I knew his was basically a crime of passion. A cold case would have killed me without thinking.

Things hung in the balance for a couple of seconds. I felt a curious detachment from it all, like I was simply watching a movie. The scene that came to mind was the one in Migusho's *Strangers in Osaka,* when the killer finds out his wife—who he's just saved in a harrowing, grisly sword battle with the local toughs—is planning on leaving him. He finds out she's been cheating on him all along with one of the thugs he's just disemboweled. So there he is, cuckolded and covered in blood, staring at the gruesome remains and trying to make sense of a world that didn't. It was a good movie, until the half-baked döppelgangers subplot took over.

Nabiko shrugged and slumped onto his bed. He chuckled weakly and tossed me the gun. He looked almost relieved that the whole thing was coming to a close.

"Property of Toko Studios," he said. "That was the same gun that killed Tsujiro Kurata in *Fighting Without Honor.* Not much good for anything else, I guess."

I looked it over and then set it next to the projector on the stand. Nabiko sprawled out on the futon, leaning back and taking a deep breath. We just looked at each other for a few seconds, two guys in an apartment.

"What now?" he said. "Cops come bursting through the door for the big climax?"

"No," I said. "Not yet. Not until I give them the signal." He nodded thoughtfully while I tried to figure out what to do. "But I'm not going to."

"I don't see why not," he said.

"I've got an appointment to keep with Kwaidan. What time were you supposed to be there?"

He grimaced and a flicker of dull suspicion passed over his features. If he'd had his wits about him, he would have known I'd been bluffing all along. But if he'd had his wits about him, I'd never have fed him the cop story. I had the advantage. I hadn't killed anyone.

"Courthouse on Hansei-dori. Eight o'clock sharp," he said with a low groan.

"Give me your car keys, " I said. His face fell slack again and he dug into his pockets and tossed me the keys.

"I'm going to stand in for you. Meanwhile, you are going to sit at that typewriter and write a full confession. As soon as you finish, you just pick this up"—I indicated the Game Boy—"and say 'lights, camera, action.' This is the cue for them to come over and arrest you. Take your time and make it good. There's no hurry."

He glanced over at the typewriter then closed his eyes. The idea didn't fill him with enthusiasm. "What if I just decide to make a run for it?" he asked.

"They'll get you before you even make it out of the building."

He considered it for a while, staring at the ceiling. Then he started laughing. It was a defeated sound, anemic and hollow.

"You know, Billy," he said. "I wrote the script, not Sato. It's mine. The movie of your life. If I go to jail, they'll never be able to make *Tokyo Suckerpunch*."

"I know," I said, with as much false sympathy as I could muster. Then I turned around and walked out of the apartment, leaving Nabiko to chronicle his unraveling. I figured in a few hours I'd call the cops, the real cops, and drop an anonymous tip that a murderer was waiting in his apartment, confession in hand.

But first I had to find Orange Blossom while she was still alive.

I found Nabiko's car, hopped inside, and revved it up. I could feel Ihara's eyes watching me from above as I sped away down the street. He probably wondered what the hell was going on, but then again, probably didn't care one way or the other. He was paid to be a professional bystander, a terminally disinterested third party.

Sarah would say that for all my hot air, that's all a journalist is, too. Someone paid to watch. A cultural voyeur who differs only in that he can't keep his peeping a secret—he has to tell the whole world what he saw. Maybe, but at least I didn't have to hang around all day in darkened rooms with a trio of Ponriki-munching idiots.

I was fishing through Nabiko's tape collection when it suddenly hit me that I was driving a murderer's car. Well, it wasn't the first time. Just to see what this one listened to, I flipped on the stereo and popped in a cassette tape. It was Paul McCartney and company singing "Band on the Run."

Hardly a soundtrack suitable to the oedipal nightmare Nabiko had been living through. Come to think of it, the last murderer had a Manhattan Transfer tape in the car. Maybe adult contemporary tunes really did drive people to violence. At any rate, I couldn't seem to shake Paul McCartney.

I ejected the tape and turned on the radio. News and weather. If the northerly clouds were gathering swiftly and with great foreboding, they didn't say anything about it.

I could see the sun in the mirror, creeping up behind me as it rose over the Low City. Western Tokyo lay ahead, shrouded in its special blend of ancient mist and industrial smog. Traffic was starting to get heavy as people dragged themselves out of bed for another Monday. Overhead the helicopters circled, keeping commuters up-to-date on which freeways were already jammed. Maybe even Kwaidan was up there, worrying about earthquakes, Orange Blossom, and whatever else a gangster has to worry about. Maybe he was even worrying about me. If he wasn't, he should have been.

Twenty minutes later, I spotted the courtroom. Ugliest building I'd seen in a while, but justice can be an ugly business. I parked Nabiko's car down a side street and hopped out. There was nothing to do now but wait, and waiting wasn't my specialty. It made me wish I hadn't left the Game Boy at Nabiko's.

I tried to imagine him at that very moment, hunched over his typewriter saying "lights, camera, action" into the Game Boy and listening for the steps down the hall. No one coming. He waits awhile and says it again, louder, carefully enunciating every word. Still no one comes to arrest him. He begins screaming into the little thing. He hurls it against the wall. Then maybe he rips the curtains open and begins a wild series of gesticulations to Ihara. "Arrest me, arrest me, arrest me, goddammit!"

Something like that.

Even now, it was hard for me to imagine Nabiko as a killer. For a guy that murdered his father, he was pretty easygoing. I liked him that first day at the tournament, and even though he started getting a little weird later on (understandably, I guess), I still thought he was a decent guy.

And now?

I'd have to reevaluate my opinion. For that matter, my esteem for Sato might be up for review. I was pretty openminded about these things, but I knew that if people like me ran the world there would be anarchy. It was close enough already.

I watched as all the people who made a living protecting us from anarchy filed into the building. They looked neither happy nor unhappy. I walked around the building to make sure there wasn't a back entrance where Kwaidan and Orange Blossom could slip inside unseen. Everything was closing in now, and I'd already blown enough last chances.

Of course, there was a back entrance. So now I was faced with a choice. Front or back? I didn't have a coin to flip, and I had a feeling no Tsuguri truck was going to drive by roaring out the answer. I chose the front without further hesitation. First thought, best thought.

I have no idea how long I waited there by the steps of the court. I started to wonder if I'd made the wrong decision and had to fight the urge to run around to the back of the building. Sooner or later you have to make a choice and stick with it, I figured.

Suddenly a huge black limo came rolling down the street. It moved with slow menace, like a shark lazily prowling the water. The massive chrome grillwork on the front of the vehicle violently reflected the rising sun in a dazzling, blinding light. It crawled to a stop so gradually that it took me a moment to realize the car wasn't moving anymore. The engine growled with a threatening, subdued intensity. That the car could belong to anybody but Kwaidan was unthinkable.

Punchperm got out first. He held the door open, and Crewcut emerged. Their movements were groggy, like maybe they'd been out carousing all night, but as usual they were dressed to let everyone know that crime pays. As they walked around the car, one of the passenger windows went down. Crewcut walked toward the window while Punchperm stood at the curb, hands in his pockets, looking at his shoes.

Crewcut stood at attention, nodding several times as someone inside the limo spoke to him. Then he bowed deeply as the automatic window went back up. Turning around, he joined Punchperm again.

The limo pulled away before I could decide whether to approach or not. One less decision to regret, anyway. I watched it make its lazy way down the street, wondering if Orange Blossom was inside.

Slowly, Punchperm and Crewcut ambled down the sidewalk and up the stairs of the courthouse. The usual yakuza swagger had been replaced with a dull shuffle that made them look like a two-man funeral procession. Punchperm's curly head drooped like a dead sunflower. He put a hand on Crewcut's shoulder for support. Crewcut held his head stiffly aloft and took halting steps, a toy robot running out of batteries. They were about twenty feet away from me now, and as I saw their expressions more clearly, it was safe to say that neither of them looked ready to put up much of a fight.

I started to make my move, then stopped.

Detective Arajiro had beaten me to it.

My eyes darted around, looking for hiding places and escape routes. The detective was flanked with two burly-looking plainclothes cops who seemed to take the plainclothes part literally. I spotted a row of bushes within leaping distance. The landing wouldn't be pretty, but neither would jail.

But I didn't jump, not yet. I just stood in the shadows and let Arajiro and his guys walk past me like I wasn't even there, right up to Punchperm and Crewcut at the top of the stairs.

Punchperm and Crewcut stopped. They glanced at each other. Then a very curious thing happened—they bowed to the cops. Funnier still, the cops bowed back.

Each nodded in turn as introductions were made. Another round of bows. Arajiro said something and Crewcut bobbed his shorn head. Punchperm gave Crewcut a pat on the back. One of the plainclothes guys said something to Arajiro, and Arajiro shrugged. I kept waiting for someone to pull a gun, take a swing, or at least spit. But it wasn't gonna happen. These cops and robbers were playing a more sophisticated game.

I wanted to move closer to hear what was being said, but I didn't think my presence would be welcome. I was lucky Arajiro hadn't spotted me, and I wasn't going to push my luck just to be the center of attention.

After a few more awkward stabs at conversation, they seemed to reach some kind of decision. Everyone stood around uncomfortably, crossing their arms, looking at the ground. The plainclothes guys looked like tired elephants in their gray suits. Punchperm and Crewcut looked utterly lost.

Suddenly Punchperm grabbed Crewcut and pulled him close. He threw his big arms around him and squeezed. I couldn't see the look on Punchperm's face, but Crewcut's went white. He didn't look embarassed so much as shaken.

The cops all averted their eyes from the embrace, looking around in every direction. If the hug went on much longer, the cops would see me by simple process of elimination. I found myself thinking back to my studies with the Black Spider Ninja Sect in Nara, wishing I'd concentrated on the ninjutsu art of invisibility instead of mastering the blowgun. Blowguns are pretty much useless in a lot of situations.

Thankfully, the hug didn't last long. As they parted, I got a glimpse of Punchperm's face. He was doing everything to look aloof, but his watery eyes and flushed cheeks worked against him. He made a show of dusting off his suit. He puffed out his chest and rubbed the top of Crewcut's bristled little head, more a shove than a caress. He punched Crewcut in the arm. He punched him in the other arm, harder. Then he playfully slapped Crewcut a couple times in the face. He seemed to be trying to reestablish his masculinity with every blow.

Nothing he did fazed Crewcut. Crewcut was a pile of ashes.

After the flurry of affection, Punchperm spun on his heel. Crewcut and the cops watched him make his way down the steps. You could tell from his overly rigid posture that Punchperm was determined to walk away without looking back. The cops turned to Crewcut. He nodded grimly. They took him by the arm and led him away.

Once Arajiro and his new friend were safely out of sight, I hurried down the steps to catch Punchperm. It wasn't tough. He was moving so slowly that he could have been working for the government. I had to concentrate in order not to overtake him too soon.

He stumbled down the sidewalk in a daze. Passersby gave him a wide berth, and kept their eyes averted as they rushed passed him. People were trying to avoid him so much they were causing mini–pedestrian jams on the sidewalk.

At the end of the street, he took a left. I followed about five seconds behind. He took another left into a parking garage. The attendant looked ready to say something, but then he caught the look on Punchperm's face and swallowed his comment. He turned around as Punchperm passed, pretending to be busy in the booth.

I walked right by, unnoticed.

Punchperm hit a button and stepped into the elevator.

I didn't know how high the building was. Maybe ten, maybe fifteen stories. If it was ninety, there was still no way I was getting into an elevator car with a distraught yakuza. Which meant I might as well kiss him good-bye.

As the doors whisked shut, I got a reprieve. I spotted a sign by the call buttons. ELEVATOR IN OPERATION TO FIFTH FLOOR ONLY. MUCH APOLOGIES. It was my first geniune piece of luck in a while, but I didn't stand around being thankful.

I bolted up the stairs, taking them two at a time. The sound of my ascent reverberated in the airless corridor. When I reached the fourth-floor landing, I heard the stairwell door open above me. I stopped moving.

Punchperm shuffled into the stairwell, mumbling. He started up the stairs with the same sluggish gait. I tiptoed, slowing my pace to match his, hiding my own sounds in the pattern of his steps just like the waifish Bangkok pickpockets taught me back in '89.

On the eight floor, he suddenly stopped.

I didn't. I'd been lulled by the hypnotic, laggardly pace. The extra footstep rang out like a gunshot. I could hear him turn on his heel in alarm, directly above me.

"Who's down there?"

I balled my fists and held my breath. I could practically hear his ears straining.

There was a rustling sound I couldn't identify. Then I heard a sound you never forget. The sound of an ammunition cartridge being snapped into place.

He waited on the floor above me. He sniffled a couple of times, but he didn't move.

After almost a full minute, he cautiously resumed his ascent. He tried another quick stop on the eleventh floor, but this time I was ready. When he stopped again on the thirteenth, I figured he was just getting tired. More mumbles and sniffles and then back up he went.

At the fifteenth floor, he started screaming.

"Goddamn son-a-fucking mother bitch!"

He pounded the metal exit door.

"Fuck Fuck Fuck!"

A shot rang out. Without even thinking, I hit the floor.

I heard the bullet bounce around, zipping into one concrete wall after another, ricocheting down the stairwell like a lethal *pachinko* ball.

Punchperm suddenly stopped yelling. I wondered for a moment if the bullet had hit him, but then I heard him clear his throat.

"Okay, okay," he repeated quietly to himself. "Okay, okay, okay."

He exhaled a slow, long breath and opened the exit door.

As it slammed shut, I darted up the stairs and peeked out the small window in the door. We were on the top of the parking garage, the roof level, totally empty save for one giant limo. I wondered how the hell the guy was able to maneuver all those tight turns on the way up. Not a bad view of Tokyo from up here, and it was shaping up to be a beautiful day.

Punchperm was moving a lot faster now, walking like a normal thug. You could see the swagger return a little with every step.

I pushed through the exit.

• • •

While on a recon mission with a secret group of South Korean paramilitary ops in the mountains outside of Pyongyang, I learned an interesting stalking technique that allows you hide not only from your victim, but from third-party observers. Basically, it's about perspective, and knowing how to shrink your movements so they are shielded. They called the technique "Walking in the Panther's Shadow."

I wasn't very good at it.

But since no shots rang out, no alarm call went up, I guess I wasn't as bad as I thought. Maybe the yakuza just weren't paying attention as I followed behind Punchperm, curling my body and mimicking his movements. Maybe they just didn't care.

When he finally neared the limo, a driver got out and opened the door. As he held it for Punchperm, the driver spotted me. He glanced inside the car. Then he gave me a second look, troubled by some dim recognition.

The alarm never got sounded. I shoved Punchperm out of the way, and dove through the open door.

Jumping into a limo full of yakuza is about as smart as bellyflopping into a piranha tank. The curses started flying. The fists weren't far behind. I put my hands up in the praying-mantis position, ducking and weaving as best I could in the cramped confines. Blows glanced off my neck, my chest, my shoulders. I saw nothing but knuckles, flashes of gaudy rings, and Cartier watches. I wondered if the Yotayo Defensive Driving School taught some kind of course in car interior combat.

"Stop this nonsense!" Kwaidan shouted.

The nonsense stopped, but not before one of the yakuza caught a cuff link on my nostril. There was a thin tearing sound, and my eyes filled with water. It stung like hell but I tried not to show it.

"Stings, doesn't it?" Kwaidan chuckled dully.

Punchperm slid into the seat next to me. The driver gave me a look like he was unimpressed with my antics and slammed the door shut. It cut off all sound from the outside world. Now it was just me and the yaks.

The inside of the limo was all done up in black leather and the one-way windows blocked out most of the light, making it feel like some well-upholstered cave. The front section of the limo was separated from the rear, with only a sliding panel to allow communication with the driver. I could just make out Kwaidan's lumpy form as he sat facing me from the opposite seat. He was wearing a white *yukata,* as if he'd just emerged from a hot-springs bath. Next to him was a guy in a suit that looked like it was made out of tinfoil. He seemed more interested in his handheld computer than anything going on inside the limo. There were three other gangsters inside, bringing the grand total to six.

"You're a mess," Kwaidan said. Punchperm nodded, thinking Kwaidan was talking to him. He might have been. My eyes hadn't adjusted to the darkness and my vision was blurred with tears, but I could see that Punchperm was a mess. His face was blotchy and his jaw kept quivering.

Kwaidan tossed a hankerchief to me. It was made of a fine silk, dyed the color of blood. Good for occupational hazards. I held it to my nose.

"Where is he?" Kwaidan asked Punchperm.

Punchperm shrugged.

"You didn't wait for him?"

"He knows where to find us."

Kwaidan grumbled his displeasure.

"Where's Orange Blossom?" I blurted.

Kwaidan's features crumpled in irritation. He glanced at Shinpa Sam, sitting to my right. Sam sent a sharp elbow to my ribs. It almost took my mind off my torn nostril.

"I'll get to you in a minute," Kwaidan said to me.

A minute passed.

"Do you have children, Mr. Chaka?"

"None that I know of."

"I'd rather be a boss than a father any day. In business, if people fuck up, you cut off their finger. They fuck up again, you kill them. People learn responsibility fast this way. They learn that real life isn't like in the movies."

I didn't know where he was going, but I wondered just how much he knew about the whole Migusho and Brando Nabiko affair.

He turned to Punchperm.

"What would you have done, Imanishi?"

Punchperm didn't know either.

Kwaidan sighed wearily, and looked at his watch.

"Where is he?" he muttered.

Then Punchperm erupted, filling the whole car with his sobs. Kwaidan looked at the floor. The other gangsters shifted in their seats uncomfortably. Punchperm began rocking back and forth, his hands to his face, wailing.

"Enough," Kwaidan said quietly. When Punchperm didn't stop, Kwaidan gave Shinpa Sam the look. Shinpa reached across behind me and smacked Punchperm's curly head.

"It'll be easy for him in there," Kwaidan said. "He'll make out better than we do."

"I know," Punchperm said.

"A few years. It's nothing. He'll grow up fast, learn a lot."

"You're right."

"Of course I am," Kwaidan said. "So what are you crying for?"

"I don't know."

"Well, don't. Show some goddamn guts."

Punchperm just nodded.

Kwaidan regarded him for a moment, shaking his head. Then he looked at me.

"I suppose you've come for your reward." His mood seemed to be getting worse. "Fair is fair. You held up your end of the bargain."

Kwaidan motioned to the yakuza next to him in the silver suit. The guy put down the handheld computer he was fiddling with. He knocked on the sliding panel. It slid open, and someone pushed a briefcase through. The silver suit handed it to me. It felt heavy enough.

"Take your money. Our business together is done."

"Where is Orange Blossom?"

Kwaidan rolled his eyes. He huffed and puffed and put on a show all about how incredibly annoyed he was.

"She's in the front seat," he finally said.

"I'd like to see her."

Kwaidan's mood worsened. He'd been surrounded by idiots all his life, but apparently he still wasn't used to it. He gave me a blank look and slid open the portal. From where I was sitting, it didn't reveal anything but the front windshield.

"Well?" Kwaidan said. "See for yourself."

I moved forward, but still couldn't see anything. I had to take a step and crouch over, practically leaning on the colossal gangster in order to put my face up to the portal.

I noticed the smell just in time.

Shinobi's teeth snapped shut as I jerked my head back. The dog thrust his head through the opening, snarling and slobbering and filling the air with his noxious breath. I went backward, scrambling into my seat.

The yaks were whooping it up. Everyone was laughing except for Punchperm. And me, of course. I was watching the dog as he made a big production out of trying to break through the divider to get at my face. When he figured out it wasn't gonna happen, he started barking. It was an ugly, stupid sound—one that lent credence to the theory that dogs eventually resemble their masters.

"Quiet!" Kwaidan barked.

The dog quieted to a low growl. The yaks stopped laughing.

Kwaidan lowered his head in concentration. He held up a hand and the dog slumped into the front seat, out of my view. Kwaidan shut the portal. Something was still bothering him.

"Listen."

Everyone listened.

"Can you hear it?"

His voice was trembling slightly. The tin man punched a few buttons on his handheld computer. He looked at Kwaidan and shook his head. Kwaidan angrily slapped the device out of his hands.

Then I heard it. A low rumble in the distance.

Kwaidan's eyes went wide.

"Helicopter!"

The Yamagamas all whipped out their cell phones, racing to dial. Kwaidan fidgeted in his seat, his eyes still lowered as he concentrated on the rumbling sound. It seemed to be getting closer.

"Out of the way!"

He shoved the silver-suit guy next to him. All the yaks scrambled to open the door, but Kwaidan pushed them out of the way. His hand clattered uselessly against the door latch, like an insect battering a windowpane.

"Open the goddamn door!"

Punchperm reached across and flipped the lever. Kwaidan tumbled out of the car. It was right out of the circus, but no one noticed. They weren't listening to the rumbling sound anymore—they were feeling it.

Kwaidan stood outside, his legs spread, crouched low to the ground. He held his hands out with his palms flattened, like a mime stuck in the invisible box.

He looked ridiculuous hunkered down in his bathrobe. Big laugh material, but no one was laughing. The car was rattling too hard.

I didn't know much about earthquakes, but I was pretty sure you were supposed to avoid being in a car full of yakuza when the Big One hit. I shot out the open door.

Someone grabbed my shirt from behind as I surged forward. I pulled away, landing on the pavement. The ground was trembling. I could hear the whine of a helicopter already on its way.

I stood up, and made for the stairs. Then I stopped. You can't outrun an earthquake.

Besides, I had to know.

I turned and lunged for the front door of the limo. The front seat was easily big enough to fit a chauffeur, a dog, and a beautiful geisha. So my reasoning went. I yanked the door opened.

I didn't even see her really, just the rumpled purple fabric of her dress.

Then the dog got loose.

He leapt at my throat, and this time there was no divider to stop him.

I hit the floor.

Teeth, claws, and all went sailing right over me.

I hopped up and circled around to face his next attack, but it never came. The dog was barking at the sky. More specifically, at the descending helicopter just overhead.

"Fuck!" the driver said. He darted from the car and started chasing the dog.

The other yakuza followed suit until all six of them were bumbling around after the dog like Keystone Kops as the helicopter hovered above, unable to land with all the commotion going on.

Kwaidan was still frozen to the spot, but the chaos finally got his attention. He whirled around, quick for a big guy. He was yelling at his henchmen, at the dog, at everybody. I couldn't understand a word he said.

Suddenly Orange Blossom vaulted from the car.

I swung around fast but she was a purple blur rocketing across the pavement toward the big white truck coming up the ramp at the far end of the parking garage. I watched her move and recognized the truck and forgot about the angry gangster boss behind me.

Kwaidan caught me with a suckerpunch to the jaw. A good one, right on the KO button. My knees buckled.

On the way down, I got one last look at him. His eyes were ablaze and sweat was pouring out all over his quivering fat body, drenching his silly *yakuta*. The dog barked, the yaks yelled, the helicopter hovered, the dull low boom exploded, and there was nothing Kwaidan could do about it. If this was the Big One, he'd have to ride it out on land, just like the rest of us. I felt a dim sense of satisfaction, a warm glow spilling from my brain and spreading throughout my body.

Then I hit the ground, hard.

I watched the purple blades soundlessly going round and round.

"He's opened his eyes," I heard someone say. The voice sounded like James Earl Jones underwater. I kept watching the ceiling fan.

"That's a good sign," someone else answered in a cartoon soprano. The fan kept time to the swimming sound in my ears. My mouth felt thick and dry, like it had sealed itself into a solid block of wood.

"Can you hear me, Billy?"

I tried to open my mouth and felt a dull pain roll into the front of my head. I blinked my eyes and groaned affirmatively, wishing whoever was speaking would move into my field of vision.

"What do you think, Uncle?" a voice said. It was beginning to sound normal by degrees.

"He'll be fine," the other voice said flatly. "Or he'll be totally brain-damaged for life. No way to tell without a CAT scan and an MRI. Even then it's fifty-fifty. I sure wish you'd let me take him with me. There's only so much I can do in this closet."

"We gotta wait. Six hours, she'll be here."

"Well," the other voice said, "it's your decision. I wouldn't wait too long, though."

"I know. But she's on her way."

"It's your decision."

There was a protracted silence during which I weighed the pros and cons of sitting up. Then the first voice resumed. I'd heard it before but couldn't figure out where. Between that and thinking about getting up, I was keeping my brain pretty busy. It didn't feel damaged to me.

"I owe you, Dr. Uncle Naoya," the voice said reverently.

"Forget it," Naoya replied. "I don't know what you've gotten into, but I'd be more careful in the future. Stuff like this is for the police."

"But the license..."

"I know, I know."

A pause.

"Yes, Uncle. You're right."

"Of course I'm right. I must go. Call me when you decide what to do."

"Thank you once more, Uncle."

A door opened and closed. And then the guy finally stepped up where I could see him.

"You remember me, Chaka-sama?"

It was Hiro Bhuto. I should have known by the purple blades of the ceiling fan that we were in the back room of his bar. His face had its old familiar smile.

"Hggrrl Bvvuotos," I mumbled. My mouth wouldn't open. Bhuto laughed and shook his head.

"Didn't understand a word, Billy. Your mouth is wired shut. Busted jaw. You probably can't even feel it with all the painkillers."

Well, that would explain it. I'd started to wonder about that brain-damage thing. Good to see the injury was physical rather than mental. Then again, maybe I'd get along better if my brain wasn't so active.

"When I told the people of your magazine that your mouth was wired shut, they loved it. They couldn't wait to see a silent Billy Chaka!" he roared. Despite his effort to cheer me up, he was actually cheering me up.

Sooner or later I was going to have to sit up, so I just did it. It wasn't as bad as I thought. Just a headache. Not much worse than some hangovers I'd had.

"Suu vwhet hepphuln wu hei?" I said.

"That's Vietnamese to me, pal. I assume you're wondering how you got here. Truth is, I don't really know. Two bald guys in white outfits dragged you in. Said I'd better not call the police unless I wanted to get you in serious trouble. Same for taking you to the hospital. You really got involved in a mess this time." He shook his head.

"Hvvlin hvvaben ber?" I said.

"You're gonna have to write it, Billy."

He handed me a pen and paper. I'm a writer, and I guess it was time to get back to writing. *How long have I been here?* I wrote. Not exactly poetry, but you gotta start somewhere.

"Two days," Hiro said. "You were out cold but my uncle the doctor was against forcefully reviving you. I've been here the whole time. My wife is pissed. I told her I'm looking after a sick friend, and of course she doesn't believe me. Oldest one in the book, right? So finally I just said, come down and see him, you don't believe me. So she did. Now she's mad because she thinks it was a setup to make her look stupid!" He flung his hands in the air in halfhearted exasperation.

Who else knows I'm here? I wrote.

"My wife. Her brother the doctor. The two guys who brought you. That's about it. Oh, and the people from your magazine."

Oh no. Please, oh please let it not be Sarah. I couldn't stand to have her see me like this. Looking down on me:

"Well—you've done it again." The whole shameful process of reproach and forgiveness. And of course, she'd forgive me. She'd nod patiently when I said it was a huge mistake, a fluke, it would never happen again. When I tried to explain how things got horribly out of hand, and how it really wasn't about a geisha this time, she'd act like she understood. And her kindness made my idiocy and selfishness all the more glaring, all the more unbearable. I liked it more when she'd just let loose and harangue me. Goddamn, she knew how to curse. But somehow, she had this mistaken notion I wanted to be understood.

What people exactly?

"When I called today, they were very relieved. I spoke to several people. They told me a woman named Sarah and two other people were headed to Tokyo on the next available flight. They didn't seem too surprised. Does this happen often?"

My head throbbed. A whole rescue committee, the funds for which would most likely be coming out of my salary. I realize I'm their most important writer, but they're far too protective and always too late.

I need a drink, I wrote, and handed it to Hiro Bhuto.

"I don't know. My uncle said . . ."

I NEED A DRINK, I scribbled emphatically, and shoved it at Bhuto.

He shrugged. "Well, all right. What the hell."

He went toward the door, presumably to fetch my drink and bring it back to me. I stood up and followed him. The little room was making me claustrophobic, and besides, I'd been missing from the world for two whole days. It was time to reestablish myself in ordinary reality. Bhuto seemed surprised at my sudden mobility, but he didn't protest. I followed him into the bar and took a seat.

The computers and all the techno trappings were gone. As I looked around, I could see none of the clutter signifying the latest lamebrain theme Bhuto had hastily adapted. It was still mostly purple, but otherwise looked like an ordinary bar. As Bhuto served me a pint of Sapporo, I pointed my finger around and did my best Marcel Marceau shrug.

"Oh yeah. It's just Purple now. Theme bars have kind of fallen by the wayside the last few days. New thing is anonymity. Couldn't give up the purple, though. Wouldn't be right."

I had to suck my Sapporo through a straw, but that didn't diminish the pleasurable effect. Empty stomach, residual painkillers, and beer. A prescription for recovery. I intended to get good and drunk before I met Sarah and the rest of the *Youth in Asia* rescue committee. At least if I was stinko my incoherent ramblings about the geisha and the nameless cult that worshiped her, the yakuza, the oedipal drama of Sato Migusho and Brando Nabiko could be written off to another confused tale inspired by old John Barleycorn. They'd shake their heads sadly, and wonder in amazement that a headcase like me was capable of writing some of the most captivating stories ever to grace adolescent journalism. I'd wake up over the ocean, halfway to Cleveland and sick as a dog, demanding more drink and babbling through wired jaws about the enigma of Orange Blossom.

More than anything, I wished I could forget her. I wished my crash with the pavement would have given me selective amnesia that erased the last weeks of my life, like in the soap operas.

But I couldn't forget. And even Kwaidan's right hook didn't knock the questions from my head. I didn't really understand the aftermath of Sato's death, or what Kwaidan had to do with Orange Blossom. I didn't really get what the cult was all about.

And Shinto Hirohito's death never made any sense. These thoughts were there, but they no longer really troubled me.

What bothered me was thinking of Orange Blossom.

"Let me buy you another drink," a voice said from behind me. I turned around slowly to assuage my body's various aching protests. If this was a preview of old age, maybe Sato was lucky to be dead.

In front of me stood a man with dyed blond hair and a thin black mustache. He was dressed like an aging, not-so-hipster whose fashion sense peaked with *Miami Vice*. The Man in the Hat again, in perhaps his worst disguise yet. He was virtually beaming.

Beer, I wrote. Then I crossed it out and wrote, *WHISKEY.* He motioned to Bhuto, who looked at me reproachfully, then poured the drink anyway.

Nice rug, I wrote to the Man in the Hat, and pointed at his hair. It was a pretty lame jab, but I was convalescing after all.

He just smiled and patted me on the back.

"I wanted to stop by to tell you a few things, Billy. I know how all of this must seem to you right now."

Funny, 'cause I wasn't at all sure how it all seemed, or maybe that's what he meant. I just nodded.

"First, I want to congratulate you on a job well done. Some of the old-timers in the group are saying it was the best Reclamation they've ever heard of, given the circumstances and all. A few now admit they had crises of faith, and doubted whether we would be able to preserve her. But you really helped us save the day. You'll be happy to know that she's ensconced in her chamber in a Hokkaidō forest at this very moment. Mentally, she has already regressed to the age of four. Within a few days, she shall begin the Thirty Years' Dream. Got her there before the first snow of the season, too. You gotta like that."

He smiled and patted me on the back. I sucked my drink through the straw so hard my cheeks puckered. I got the feeling it was going to be one of those days when no matter how much I drank I wouldn't get drunk. I'd just wind up sick and disoriented. You can't even rely on alcohol sometimes.

"Secondly, I want to give you this."

He handed me an envelope. Inside was a postcard with a pornographic picture of a well-endowed blond woman in a nurse's outfit, nude from the waist down. She was spreading her legs and using a stethoscope in ways they don't teach in med school. The only thought I had was that the metal end of the instrument must have felt damn cold. On the back was written *Get Well Soon!* It wasn't signed.

"Sorry things got a little rough at the end. You delayed them just long enough for us to reclaim her. We had to get you out of there in kind of a hurry, and you were dropped a few times in the rush. No hard feelings, I hope."

I shook my head. I couldn't remember anything after Kwaidan popped me, so there wasn't much to feel hard about. Thinking of Kwaidan made me wonder something, though. I wrote on a napkin and pushed it to him.

Earthquake?

"Nope. Earthquake simulation. High-decibel. Low-frequency cycles blasted through the sound-truck speakers. The truck was vibrating so much in the parking garage I was afraid I was gonna chip a tooth. We wanted to frighten Kwaidan, distract him. We worried he might renege on our agreement. Especially once he found out about what happened to so-called Brando Nabiko."

He shook his head as if the world was one hell of an confusing place. From where I was sitting, it was.

"We didn't know what to do with you afterward. Once Kwaidan found out what happened, he'd have his guys looking for you. At the same time, we couldn't take you with us. We didn't want you causing any problems during the remainder of the Reclamation. You seem to have grown quite attached to Orange Blossom."

I thought I detected a note of lasciviousness in his comment, but I let it slide.

"We had to bring you here. Your friend guaranteed us you would be safe, and we plan to compensate him for taking care of you. In fact, I brought something for him."

I waived Bhuto toward the bar and he came reluctantly, but picked up the pace a little when he looked at my glass and saw I wasn't ready to order another round. The Man in the Hat introduced himself, and of course I missed the name. Then he delivered a small speech of gratitude. In the meantime, I worked on my drink.

When he finished, he handed Bhuto the money order. From the depth of Bhuto's bow it must have had its fair share of zeros. Bhuto thanked him, bowed again, thanked him again. I made him bring me another drink before he tried licking the guy's shoes.

"Any other questions?" the Man in the Hat said. "I assume you've figured it all out by now."

I just nodded. I had enough questions to use up the bar's whole supply of napkins. I didn't even know where to start.

"I'll say this for the Yamagama-gumi," he mused. "They certainly know how to instill loyalty. Of course, the kid is young, doesn't have a record—they'll probably go easy on him. His lawyers will argue he was doing society a favor, getting rid of that guy."

Maybe Migusho's last films weren't so hot, but I doubted the lawyer could make a case that they justified murder. Of course, lawyers these days are pretty innovative. I was too confused to let it slide.

Rid of that guy Sato? I wrote on a napkin.

He shook his head, almost laughing.

"Not Sato. *The Lobster.*" The Man in the Hat snapped his index finger and thumb together like a lobster claw.

The name meant nothing to me. Maybe I did have amnesia.

"You didn't even know, did you?" He chuckled. "That chauffeur of yours was one of the most feared killers in the Tokyo underworld. They called him the Lobster on account of he only had two fingers on his right hand. Bosses cut off the others for killing out of turn."

I nearly choked on my straw. Shinto "The Lobster" Hirohito. No wonder he never took his white driver's gloves off. I wondered if they made him grow the mustache as some kind of punishment, too.

"Kwaidan had it worked out pretty neat. That kid with the buzz cut, Hideo Tamashi, takes a fall for killing the Lobster. He testifies that it was retribution for burning up Sato Migusho."

Lobster didn't do it, I wrote.

"Of course not. But with his reputation, they'll buy it. He's too dead to defend himself, and Orange Blossom was the only witness. With her out of the picture, they can fill it in any way they want."

I worked through it for a moment, but it still didn't make sense. Even if Kwaidan was a little nuts, I still didn't see what he had to gain by framing one of his own men. Something else was bothering me.

Brando Nabiko? I wrote.

The Man in the Hat looked at the question and played with his fake mustache for a moment. Then he was looking at me like I wasn't all there.

"He hung himself," he said quietly. "About two hours after you left his apartment."

So he'd had some rope after all. Terrible thing to think, but it was the first thing that popped into my head. I waited for something else to pop in and take its place, but nothing did.

The Man in the Hat cocked his toupeed head.

"Now I have a question. How did you know the Game Boy was equipped with a listening device?"

My drink stuck halfway down my throat.

"That private dick caught it all, right down to Brando saying 'lights, camera, action.' By the time we got there, he was dead. He left this."

He handed me a folded up piece of paper. It was a note. One sentence right in the center of a pristine white page.

Sato Migusho was my father.

Some note.

"Whacked-out as he was, I can't help but feel a little sorry for the guy," the Man in the Hat said.

I couldn't help feeling sorry for everybody. We were all whacked-out, every goddamn one of us.

"It would be tough being Kwaidan's kid. I'd probably concoct some crazy fantasy, too."

I'd been nodding in agreement for about two seconds, thinking about how whacked-out we all were, before I realized what he'd said. The drinks were starting to work on me, slowing me down. Maybe it was just taking in all this exposition in one sitting. But when it hit me, it hit me hard.

Not Sato's kid.

Kwaidan's kid.

I grabbed a pen and scribbled. A long scribble, with lots of commas. It took five napkins to get it all down, but it felt good to be writing again, to be thinking with a pen.

I handed the stack of napkins to the Man in the Hat. He read through them.

It was all in there. How Brando wasn't cut out to be a gangster, because he was arty and sensitive. How it frustrated Kwaidan that he couldn't just cut off the kid's fingers, but had to deal with the fact that his own damn flesh and blood worshiped some washed up film director. How the studio hadn't financed a Sato movie for a long time, but kept him on the lot out of gratitude for the early years. How Kwaidan convinced Migusho to take the kid under his wing, to encourage him. How the Yamagamas, in turn, financed bomb after bomb. How Brando never knew. How he thought Sato picked him because he saw talent. How the confrontation over the horrible *Tokyo Suckerpunch* script finally caused Migusho to admit the truth—a truth Brando couldn't accept. How he flipped out and killed Migusho.

The Man in the Hat read through the napkins, nodding from time to time. When he finished, a smile spread across his face.

"You got it all right. Even some stuff we didn't know. I was surprised you missed the name though. *Nabiko.*"

Even with the clue, it took me a moment. Once I figured it out, I wondered how I'd spaced it. "Nabiko" was the name of the hero in Sato's teensploitation masterpiece, *Cruel Twilight of Youth.* The Nabiko character gets killed in a knife fight while defending a retarded orphan from bullies. That Kwaidan's son identified with the character enough to take his name must have said something, but I wasn't sure what.

The Man in the Hat waved the napkins around. "Mind if I keep these? For the *Chronicles.*"

I shrugged. He tucked the napkins neatly into his jacket pocket.

"Needless to say, Kwaidan is not taking it well. Even if he hated his kid on one level, the kid was still his son. This may finally make Kwaidan lose his mind altogether. It won't be pretty."

I nodded in agreement. Loopy gangsters make for bloodbaths. There would be an orgy of paranoid, unnecessary violence. Eventually, the Yamagama-gumis would turn on their leader. His reign would likely end with a single bullet to the back of the head. For some reason, I hoped Punchperm was holding the gun.

I smiled to myself, or tried to, despite my immobile jaw. I was thinking of the movie Sato had made in his heyday about a yakuza with "senile dementia" who wreaks havoc in the underworld as he loses touch with reality. It was a great movie. Funny as hell, even touching in a way. It was one Sato could be proud of. Couldn't remember the name of it, though.

"I've got to be going, Billy. No more business to discuss. I'm retired now. The organization has rewarded me with a generous pension and I plan to begin enjoying it immediately. I nearly forgot..."

He dug into his briefcase and emerged with a large, colorful folder, which he tossed onto the bar. On the front was a panoramic picture of a lush green fairway lined by massive oak trees with leaves dancing in a gentle summer breeze. *Joon Park Golf Club* was written in a tasteful, understated font across the top. Inside, there was a membership certificate made out to one Billy Chaka.

"It's in Korea," he said. "I trust your travels must take you there occasionally. Besides, it's better than these tiny courses here in Japan."

I looked the folder over disinterestedly. I didn't want to insult anybody, but I just can't get excited about a picture of a golf course and a piece of paper with my name on it. Temperament I guess.

"If that doesn't do it, maybe this will." He reached into his bag again and extracted a pile of large bills. He did this a few times, placing one pile beside the next. When he was finished, a pyramid of cash sat motionless on the bar. It was more money than I'd ever seen. You could buy a lot of golf balls with it.

"Two hundred and seventy-three thousand four hundred and four dollars, just as we agreed, plus a little extra thrown in for all the trouble. No need to thank me, I'm just the delivery boy." He smiled.

Something about the way he said it made me think.

This time I didn't bother writing it all down, but I got it just the same.

He'd been the guy calling the shots all along. He'd disguised himself as a messenger, a doctor, a Reclamation specialist, and now a delivery boy, but it had all been to obscure the fact that he was the man pulling the strings. The Chief and the whole Tsuguri Society was a front. I even bet it was him dressed as the Indian with Orange Blossom at the Yotayo Love Hotel.

The Man in the Hat. Head of the cult with no name.

I didn't thank him, but I nodded courteously. The slight movement of my head was enough to make me realize that I was getting drunk after all. At least the booze wasn't going to pull a fast one on me.

I sat there looking at the lifeless pile of money. What a weird thing money is, I mused, but refused to take the train of thought any further. I decided to send the money to Chuck back in Cleveland. Let him worry about it.

"I'm off, but before I go, there's one thing I must say," the Man in the Hat said. "Don't be so down in the mouth. I know this was confusing, but it's a really good thing you've done. You will be celebrated in the *Chronicles.* Long after we're all dead, you'll be revered. You helped save a woman's life, and not just any woman, no matter what you believe. You think we're all crazy? Come back in thirty years. See if you don't bump into her again. Who knows?"

Who indeed. Maybe I would be back. I didn't even know what I'd be doing tomorrow much less thirty years down the line, but one thing was certain. I wasn't going to forget about Orange Blossom. Not in thirty years, not in sixty. Not as long as I was still breathing.

I raised my glass in a silent toast.

He bowed slightly, causing the cheap toupee to shift on his head. He finished his drink in a single swallow, then turned and walked out of the Purple bar. Just like that. I never did catch his name.

There was nothing left to do but wait and think, and I didn't feel like thinking, so I motioned Bhuto to flip on the TV. Bhuto turned it on and then brought me a bowl of fish crackers, even though I couldn't open my mouth to eat them. He meant well, I'm sure. He was probably just distracted at suddenly being rich, already planning to put a purple swimming pool or some such thing in the bar.

I thought about Sarah.

I'd done lots of things I was ashamed of in my life, but this just wasn't one of them. I wasn't convinced I'd done a heroic thing, as the Man in the Hat would have me believe, but neither had I done anything I couldn't live with.

Sure, I'd missed the U-19 Handicapped International Martial Arts Championship. I'd missed all the breathtaking katas, the furious sparring matches. I missed whatever controversy Yoko Torikata was sure to have caused this year. I'd even missed the return of Master Yado.

But in the process I'd come away the kind of story only I could get. A story bigger than the tournament, bigger even than my geisha fixation. I'd kept my head and come out alive. That was more than I could say for Sato. And Nabiko. And Shinto, poor dumb Shinto Hirohito the Lobster.

On the television, an attractive young woman in a red blazer chatted amiably with her coanchor. I couldn't hear what they were saying, but they cut to a shot of another woman reporter bundled in a puffy blue coat and pink earmuffs. On the screen, it said LIVE FROM SAPPORO, and behind the glow of the city lights, you could barely make out the dark mountains looming in the distance. Somewhere up there, Orange Blossom might be in a sleep chamber, slipping softly into the Thirty Years' Dream. I let myself believe it for now. After everything I'd been through, I deserved to believe something, even if it made me crazy along with everyone else.

The story was about Japan's first snow of the new winter. They cut to a shot of giant, dazzling flakes drifting lazily through the air, slowly descending on the mountains, dusting the pine trees a glittering white.

Even on TV it was beautiful.